"You'll never view a country roadside in the same way . . . Chizmar knows where both stories of terror and stories of the heart lurk—and best of all, he understands that they're found in the same places. Buckle up for a haunting ride."
—MICHAEL KORYTA

"Scary as hell, and it'll redline your fear meter. But it's also as much an ode to that time in our lives where we're no longer children yet not quite adults, when the road ahead of us was just beginning to clarify. Chizmar's writing has the power to take you back to that point in your own life and hold you there awhile, spellbound."
—NICK CUTTER

"Chizmar wows in an immersive and über-creepy novel that pays subtle homage to horror classics ranging from the works of H. P. Lovecraft to *The Blair Witch Project* . . . pulls no punches on the way to a thoroughly satisfying finale . . . It's a tour de force."
—PUBLISHERS WEEKLY (STARRED REVIEW)

"Destined to be a horror classic—this is broad-shouldered, bighearted horror written by someone with a distinct mastery of the form. It reaches a grim, unholy crescendo that can't be beat. Chizmar nails it."
—CHUCK WENDIG

"Such a unique idea and so wonderfully, insidiously creepy. Brilliant storytelling and fantastic small-town horror infused with real heart. I'll never look at a roadside tribute in the same way again!"
—C. J. TUDOR

ADDITIONAL PRAISE FOR
MEMORIALS

"You'll never view a country roadside in the same way once you've finished *Memorials*. Chizmar knows where both stories of terror and stories of the heart lurk—and best of all, he understands that they're found in the same places. Buckle up for a haunting ride."

—Michael Koryta

"Taut with tension and an increasing sense of doom, *Memorials* will leave you gasping for breath by the time you reach the final few pages. A pure horrific delight."

—Ronald Malfi

"*Memorials* is such a unique idea and so wonderfully, insidiously creepy. Brilliant storytelling and fantastic small-town horror infused with real heart. I'll never look at a roadside tribute in the same way again!"

—C. J. Tudor

"Richard Chizmar's *Memorials* is, on the one hand, a showcase for his ability to create warm, insightful characterizations and, on the other, a funhouse ride that grows more and more sinister. It's an all-around terrific piece of storytelling by an author who really knows how to entertain."

—Owen King

ACCLAIM FOR
BECOMING THE BOOGEYMAN

"A worthy and frightening sequel to Chizmar's *Chasing the Boogeyman*. Terrific storytelling. You won't be disappointed."

—Stephen King

"Compulsive, utterly immersive . . . masterfully blends reality and imagination to deliver something wholly original and totally gripping from start to finish."

—Lisa Unger

"At times almost unbearably suspenseful and at times incredibly poignant. Richard Chizmar delves deep into our worst fears and touches the darkness that lives there. An amazing book."

—S. A. Cosby

"A deliciously chilling follow-up to *Chasing the Boogeyman*—suspenseful, unsettling, and absolutely compelling. I couldn't put it down."

—Meg Gardiner

"Richard Chizmar knows his way around a frightening story . . . deeply unsettling . . . [he] blends reality and fantasy in a way that can only be described as intoxicating: heightening your emotions, blunting your skepticism, and luring you into trouble."

—*Vanity Fair*

"Sinuous and twisting and utterly unputdownable . . . slices deep from the start and twists the knife until the very end . . . A tour de force."

—Catriona Ward

RAVE REVIEWS FOR
CHASING THE BOOGEYMAN

"Genuinely chilling and something brand new and exciting. Compulsive reading and scary."

—Stephen King

"Unforgettable and scary-ass."

—Harlen Coben

"Hammer in hand, Richard Chizmar's come to shatter the idea that everything's already been done. An absolutely chilling mash-up of styles, media, biography, and legend. Elastic, unsettling, brilliant. And here you thought you knew the names of every genre."

—Josh Malerman

"Riveting. Chilling. *Chasing the Boogeyman* is an unflinching look at a real-life monster and the ordinary heroes obsessed with stopping him."

—Riley Sager

"A meticulously remembered, beautifully crafted hometown nightmare that reminds readers that nostalgia cuts both ways; sure, it can keep our past alive, but it can also be the shadow man standing at the foot of your bed. . . . For true crime and horror fans, this one's essential."

—*Library Journal* (starred review)

"If Ray Bradbury had written *In Cold Blood*, it would probably look a lot like Richard Chizmar's masterful *Chasing the Boogeyman*, a perfectly written and unnervingly suspenseful thriller about a series of murders that tear apart the fabric of a picturesque Maryland town and the writer who puts everything on the line to solve them. This is a mind-bendingly engaging book. Be prepared for the hairs on the back of your neck to be standing at attention as you devour every rich page."

—David Bell

"Perfect for fans of true crime, meticulously orchestrated, and clever beyond measure, *Chasing the Boogeyman* will leave you guessing long after you've read the last page."

—Alma Katsu

"We're all chasing the boogeyman, aren't we? The boogeyman's the past, the truth, our fragile memories that knit the two together. What Richard Chizmar's done for us in *Chasing the Boogeyman* is give that narrative a taut dramatic line he balances on, never quite tipping one way or the other, just stepping sure-footed all the way to the end—showing us that this is a walk we can all take, if we have the nerve."

—Stephen Graham Jones

"Chizmar's *Chasing the Boogeyman* has been written upon missing person flyers and published on telephone poles. HAVE YOU READ THIS STORY? For your own safety, you should . . . The Boogeyman will soon enter the pantheon of suburban legends that fill our backyards like summer fireflies, his name whispered into ears all over. Pray you keep yours."

—Clay McLeod Chapman

"Chizmar takes creepy to a whole new level. . . . A solid true crime facsimile, mixing background detail with action, suspense, and a compelling pace. As metafiction, the book excels: the proximity to reality adds an unshakable level of unease, and it is injected with just the right amount of self-reflection to forge an ironically honest, emotional connection with the reader. The result is strikingly original, a story that will thrill fans of intimately investigated nonfiction like Michelle McNamara's *I'll Be Gone in the Dark* and self-aware, psychological suspense like Oyinkan Braithwaite's *My Sister, the Serial Killer*."

—*Booklist*

Also available from
RICHARD CHIZMAR

NOVELS
Becoming the Boogeyman
Chasing the Boogeyman
Gwendy's Final Task (co-written with Stephen King)
Widow's Point: The Complete Haunting (co-written with W.H. Chizmar)

NOVELLAS
The Girl on the Porch
Gwendy's Button Box (co-written with Stephen King)
Gwendy's Magic Feather
Brothers (co-written with Ed Gorman)
Darkness Whispers (co-written with Brain James Freeman)
Dirty Coppers

SHORT STORY COLLECTIONS
A Long December
The Long Way Home
Midnight Promises
Monsters and Other Stories
The Vault

MEMORIALS

A Novel

RICHARD CHIZMAR

G
GALLERY BOOKS
NEW YORK   AMSTERDAM/ANTWERP   LONDON
TORONTO   SYDNEY/MELBOURNE   NEW DELHI

Gallery Books
An Imprint of Simon & Schuster, LLC
1230 Avenue of the Americas
New York, NY 10020

For more than 100 years, Simon & Schuster has championed authors and the stories they create. By respecting the copyright of an author's intellectual property, you enable Simon & Schuster and the author to continue publishing exceptional books for years to come. We thank you for supporting the author's copyright by purchasing an authorized edition of this book.

No amount of this book may be reproduced or stored in any format, nor may it be uploaded to any website, database, language-learning model, or other repository, retrieval, or artificial intelligence system without express permission. All rights reserved. Inquiries may be directed to Simon & Schuster, 1230 Avenue of the Americas, New York, NY 10020 or permissions@simonandschuster.com.

This book is a work of fiction. Any references to historical events, real people, or real places are used fictitiously. Other names, characters, places, and events are products of the author's imagination, and any resemblance to actual events or places or persons, living or dead, is entirely coincidental.

Copyright © 2024 by Richard Chizmar

All rights reserved, including the right to reproduce this book or portions thereof in any form whatsoever. For information, address Gallery Books Subsidiary Rights Department, 1230 Avenue of the Americas, New York, NY 10020.

First Gallery Books trade paperback edition August 2025

GALLERY BOOKS and colophon are registered trademarks of Simon & Schuster, LLC

Simon & Schuster strongly believes in freedom of expression and stands against censorship in all its forms. For more information, visit BooksBelong.com.

For information about special discounts for bulk purchases, please contact Simon & Schuster Special Sales at 1-866-506-1949 or business@simonandschuster.com.

The Simon & Schuster Speakers Bureau can bring authors to your live event. For more information or to book an event, contact the Simon & Schuster Speakers Bureau at 1-866-248-3049 or visit our website at www.simonspeakers.com.

Interior design by Erika R. Genova

Manufactured in the United States of America

10　9　8　7　6　5　4　3　2　1

Library of Congress Cataloging-in-Publication Data is available.

ISBN 978-1-6680-0919-2
ISBN 978-1-6680-0920-8 (pbk)
ISBN 978-1-6680-0921-5 (ebook)

For Richard Gallagher,
with gratitude and admiration

And what rough beast, its hour come round at last,
Slouches towards Bethlehem to be born?

—William Butler Yeats
"The Second Coming"

PROJECT PROPOSAL

Date: April 18, 1983
Class: American Studies 301
Instructor: Professor Tyree
Group Members: William Anderson, Troy Carpenter, Melody Wise

Roadside Memorials: A Study of Grief and Remembrance

We've all seen them. On our way to the grocery store or the post office or a faraway vacation destination. Keeping a lonely vigil on the side of the road. Stark white crosses, surrounded by candles and photographs; stuffed animals and flowers; ceramic angels and red or yellow ribbons. We slow down to take a look, shake our heads in regret, and then continue on our way—and they're forgotten.

Roadside memorials not only honor the accidental death of a loved one, but they also play an important role in the grieving process for surviving family members and friends. They often form a connective thread of remembrance and help survivors to maintain an emotional bond with the departed.

Roadside memorials originated in the early 1800s, most prominently in the American Southwest, especially in what is now Arizona, New Mexico, and Texas. Many Latin Americans placed such memorials to mark the location where their loved ones died. The first documented memorial to appear on the East Coast was in Connecticut in 1812.

Now, in 1983, there are thousands of such memorials scattered around the nation's bustling highways, suburban streets, and remote backroads. So many, in fact, that there is talk of legislation and regulation in some states/towns/counties. Even outright bans. But for now, these emotionally charged shrines remain a relatively new and increasingly controversial development.

And behind each of them is a *story*.

Our group proposes to travel by automobile throughout central and northwestern Pennsylvania on a five-day road trip. Utilizing a variety of visual mediums (still photography, film, and video), we plan to create a sixty-to-seventy-five-minute documentary entitled "Roadside Memorials: A Study of Grief and Remembrance." This visual presentation will be supplemented by dramatic commentary, as well as personal interviews with family members and close friends of the accident victims.

We will begin our journey on the campus of York College and then travel north via I-83 and a network of backroads, following the shoreline of the Susquehanna River. On our first night, we will stop in Sudbury, Pennsylvania, the hometown of group member Billy Anderson, where a very personal roadside memorial dedicated to his late mother and father still stands.

From there, we will navigate a winding path to the northwest, venturing deep into the heart of Pennsylvania's Appalachian region. We will drive without a preplanned route, wandering with a purpose, searching for roadside memorials and attempting to discover the heart-wrenching stories behind them.

VIDEO FOOTAGE
(8:43 a.m., Friday, May 6, 1983)

The sound of muffled voices over a dark screen.

After a moment, the lens cap is removed and we are greeted by blue sky and bright sunshine. The camera angle shifts and we see an orange Volkswagen van with black side panels parked at the curb. The rear double doors are standing open. Off to the side, on the nearby sidewalk, is a jumbled heap of what appears to be camping gear: knapsacks, a fishing pole, a rolled-up tent, a pair of lanterns, and folded-up lawn chairs. There are also two large Coleman coolers and a half-dozen brown paper grocery bags filled with packaged food.

A young woman—olive skin, dark eyes, long brown hair tied back in a ponytail, wearing a yellow sundress and white high-top Chuck Taylor All Star sneakers—emerges from the back of the van. She appears out of breath. A sheen of perspiration glistens on her bare arms. The camera zooms close. She sees it—and sticks out her tongue.

"Camera equipment's all loaded," she says. "What do you think? Food next, then the gear?"

"I think Billy should put down the camera and help pack the van," an off-screen voice says. "We're already behind schedule."

A young man carrying two grocery bags appears in frame. Brown-skinned and diminutive, he's dressed in tan khaki shorts and a matching button-down shirt. A red bandanna is tied loosely around his neck. He's wearing thick-framed glasses and his hair is styled in a large Afro.

From behind the camera, a cheerful male voice announces: "Meet Troy Carpenter, ladies and gents! Say something, Carp!"

Troy places the bags in the back of the van and glances over his shoulder. Adjusting his eyeglasses, he frowns and says, "Something."

The man holding the camera groans and slowly pans to the roadside where their female companion is leaning over to pick up a grocery bag. "Your turn, Mel. Introduce yourself to our adoring audience."

She spins around, her face lighting up into a million-dollar smile. Her teeth are very white and perfectly straight. We see a scattering of freckles across her nose and cheeks as she gives the camera a flirty wave.

"Hello, adoring audience! My name's Melody Wise. I'm here in York, Pennsylvania, on this beautiful Friday morning with the grumpy 'Boy Wonder' Troy Carpenter . . ." She gestures at the camera. ". . . as well as 'Billy the Kid' Anderson, our esteemed camera operator. As soon as we finish loading up the van, we're hitting the road in search of life's—and death's—eternal truths." Her smile fades and she shrugs. "That's all I got. I'm still half-asleep."

"You did great," Billy replies, and we see his blurry thumbs-up surface in front of the lens.

And then the screen goes dark and silent.

DAY ONE
FRIDAY | MAY 6

1

Later, when the trip went bad, I would remember the bleeding man on the bicycle and wonder if he was a sign of things to come.

2

The van—a Volkswagen Westfalia pop-top camper that, from the moment I first laid eyes on it, reminded me of the Mystery Machine from *Scooby Doo*—belonged to Melody's sister.

Tamara Wise was six years older than Melody and more of a mother figure than a sibling. She'd bought the van used from an old stoner who manned the ticket booth at a drive-in movie theater in Richmond, Virginia, where Tamara worked as a secretary in a real estate office. It was the first vehicle she'd ever owned and she was very proud of it. Once she managed to accumulate enough vacation days, she and her boyfriend planned to hit the road and explore the coastline of New England, something she'd dreamed about doing ever since she was little.

After a lengthy and at times rocky negotiation, Tamara agreed to rent the van to us for the princely sum of $300. I'd bitched and moaned about unfair price gouging, but after Troy pointed out how much money we'd be saving by not having to pay for nightly hotel rooms, the numbers didn't look so bad. In the end, we each agreed to chip in a hundred bucks and share the cost of gas.

To add insult to injury, Tamara's rental agreement came with a handwritten list of rules and regulations:

> No smoking cigarettes or weed inside the van (*Tamara was, of course, allergic*);
>
> No eating food of any kind inside the van (*can you see me rolling my eyes?*);
>
> The van must be returned within seven days with the exterior washed and the interior vacuumed (*reasonable enough*);

Photocopies of both my and Troy's driver's licenses must accompany cash payment of the rental fee *(just in case the entire trip was an elaborate ruse to kidnap and murder Melody)*;

And last but certainly not least, Melody Wise—and *only* Melody Wise—was authorized to drive the van *(no sweat off my back; I had no desire to drive that toaster on wheels)*.

At the bottom of the lined sheet of notebook paper upon which the rules were listed, Tamara had scribbled her name. Directly below, she'd neatly printed each of our names and drawn lines next to them. Melody and Troy had dutifully complied with their signatures. I had not. In a gesture of silent protest, I'd scrawled *William Shatner* in chicken scratch. For as long as I could remember, *Star Trek* had been my father's favorite television show. Either no one noticed what I'd done or they decided not to say anything. Not that it really mattered.

Unbeknownst to the other group members, our photocopy of the rental agreement was currently crumpled into a ball roughly the size of a half-dollar and crammed inside the van's back seat ashtray.

3

"I think we should take the Brookshire Road exit," Troy said from the passenger seat, a Pennsylvania state road map spread out across his lap. He squinted at it and traced a zigzagging route with the tip of his finger. "I like our odds better on the backroads."

"Quality over quantity?" Melody signaled to change lanes and sped past a pickup truck hauling an open trailer loaded down with lawn equipment. The driver—beard, sunglasses, faded green John Deere baseball cap—gave the van a double take, no doubt wondering how it came to be that such a pretty young woman was chauffeuring around a Black teenager. *Probably thinks it's a kidnapping in progress*, I thought. *Watch the idiot pull over at the next rest stop and call the cops.*

"Precisely," Troy said. Oblivious to the truck driver's stare, he began refolding the map. "The interstate's too much of a crapshoot. Half the accidents on 83 involve out-of-state victims. No way are we tracking down those families—not in a week, anyway."

Melody glanced at the rearview mirror. "Exit's coming up. You okay with Brookshire, Billy?"

"Fine by me," I said, trying to disguise the fact that my mouth was full of Hot Fries. "Backroads are a lot more camera-friendly, anyway."

Camera-friendly. Now that was an odd way to put it.

Not for the first time, I wondered if what we were doing might be an exercise in poor taste. No matter how we framed it—and no matter how well intentioned we might be—I had to admit the whole thing *was* a bit morbid. Maybe my Aunt Helen was right, and it was better to just leave the dead alone. After all, didn't they deserve their peace? As with the other times doubts had surfaced inside my head, I kept my mouth shut and didn't say a peep. The documentary had been my idea in the first place, and besides, it was too late to turn back now.

Stealing a peek at the mirror to make sure Melody wasn't watching, I snuck another handful of Hot Fries into my mouth and began chewing as quietly as possible. The bootleg Van Halen T-shirt I'd bought last summer from an Ocean City boardwalk vendor was covered in a bib of bright orange crumbs. I leaned over and casually brushed them onto the floor, getting rid of the evidence.

Earlier this morning, standing outside Melody's apartment, she'd flipped a quarter to determine which one of us got to ride shotgun. Troy called heads for the win, and although I'd initially been disappointed, I now believed I'd gotten the better end of the deal. Even with all the gear squeezed into the rear of the van, there was still plenty of legroom to spread out and, best of all, tons of snacks within easy reach. Not to mention, from my vantage point in the back, I didn't have to serve as copilot and take charge of giving directions.

"For chrissakes!"

As if reading my thoughts, Troy flung the wrinkled mess he'd made of the road map onto the dashboard. "Fifteen-eighty on the SATs and I can't even fold a fucking—" The wind grabbed at the map and tried to suck it out the open window. "Son of a—" Troy snatched it in midair, crumpled it against his chest like an accordion, and hurled it onto the floorboard, where he pinned it with the heel of his shoe. Before I could manage to get out a word, he spun around and wagged a finger in my face. "I don't want to hear it, Billy!"

Melody smirked at the rearview mirror and steered off the exit, leaving behind two lanes of northbound traffic on I-83. I leaned forward in my seat, ready to have some fun at Troy's expense, but at the last moment decided against it. It was too early in the trip to start poking the hornet's nest. There would be plenty of time for that later. Instead, I replied, "Not saying a word, my friend." And then I sat back and closed my eyes.

4

At eighteen years old, Troy Carpenter was the youngest of the group—last spring, he'd graduated high school a year early—and also the smartest one in the room. While technically still a freshman at York College, he was already pursuing a double major in accounting and English, and on pace to earn a degree in just three years. If he didn't end up in the hospital with a bleeding ulcer first. To say that Troy Carpenter was wound up tight was a little like saying the summit of Mount Everest offered a fairly decent view of the surrounding countryside.

I'd once watched Troy practically suffer a nervous breakdown because of a five-dollar parking ticket left on the handlebars of his moped. On another occasion, I'd talked him out of sending his Literature and Sexuality professor a rage-filled, borderline threatening letter because the man had had the audacity to give Troy an 88 on his midterm essay. And I know that being twenty points shy of a perfect SAT score absolutely gnawed at his soul. He drank Mylanta like it was water and chewed antacids as if they were breath mints. He rarely got more than four or five hours of sleep at night. And sometimes, he went all day without bothering to eat.

I genuinely worried about the guy—and yet I had to admit he made an easy target for my hijinks. It was virtually impossible to spend an extended period of time in Troy Carpenter's company and not be amused and entertained by his idiosyncrasies. He went through more mood swings than a pregnant housewife carrying twins. His bad taste in music (country and western, for God's sake, the twangier the better) was only rivaled by his horrible fashion sense. He was a die-hard conspiracy theorist, not to mention a passionate believer in both Bigfoot and the Loch Ness Monster, and had little patience for those who weren't. The most recent rabbit hole he'd disappeared into involved the rumored existence of a sophisticated network of underground tunnels running all the way from Baltimore City to Washington, DC. Troy insisted that government officials were using these hidden tunnels for nefarious purposes involving the urban drug trade. He'd left numerous messages for reporters at the *Baltimore Sun* and *Washington Post* newspapers but had yet to hear back from anyone.

Despite all of this, Troy and I had grown closer as the spring semester progressed. I found myself teasing him less and less, and actually feeling protective of him. Almost like a big brother. He may have been a tornado of anxiety-ridden, hormonal adolescence, but he was also the most authentic and nicest guy I'd ever met. There was no hidden agenda with Troy Carpenter. For better or worse, he was just *Troy*. And once he finally let me in and I *really* got to know him, it wasn't difficult to understand why he acted the way he did.

5

"How long . . . the Appalachians?"

"Depends," Melody said. ". . . tomorrow night . . . don't stay too long in Sudbury."

". . . the mountains?"

". . . grounded in truth . . . those folks *can* be odd . . ."

As I dozed in the warm wash of sunlight slanting through the van window, I overheard snippets of broken conversation. Like listening to a radio station with a weak signal.

"... not dangerous?"

"... talked about that ... be fine ..."

"... seen a Black person."

As usual, Troy was worried. After reading a handful of articles discussing the backwoods stereotypes of the Appalachian people, he'd developed an intense dread regarding how we'd be accepted by the locals. *"Just look at us,"* he'd quipped, staring at our reflection in the grocery store window as we'd stocked up on supplies for the trip. *"Toss in a blonde chick, and we'd look like a Benetton ad."* It also hadn't helped that we'd recently rented the movie *Southern Comfort*, in which a group of Army Reserve weekend warriors conducting maneuvers deep in a Louisiana swamp are stalked and killed by rifle-toting Cajuns with bad teeth.

"... just in case."

"... of those are rumors ..."

"That doesn't ... me feel better ..."

6

Although he would freely admit to being terrified of snakes, cockroaches, rats, ghosts, and any other number of potential dangers, there existed two great fears in Troy Carpenter's life. The first was losing his scholarship. As a high school student, he'd attended the prestigious Calvert Hall School thanks to a pair of academic grants provided by the Maryland State Board of Education and an independent alumni council. How else could a third-generation Cherry Hill kid graduate in the top 5 percent of his class from a private Catholic institution with a five-figure annual tuition?

Now, at York College, he was once again riding the scholarship train. Despite only needing to maintain a 3.0 GPA to keep his full ride—and never once coming within spitting distance of dropping below a 3.85—he shuffled his way around campus enveloped within a brewing storm of impending doom. Either he succeeded and made something of himself or it was back to the mean streets of Baltimore, where half the guys he'd grown up with were either dead or in prison. The daily pressure of such thoughts was enough to paralyze even the most emotionally balanced of students—something my friend clearly was not.

His second great fear was disappointing his parents. Troy's father, Raymond, a decorated Vietnam vet and former assembly-line worker out on long-term disability after losing most of his right foot in a factory accident, was the one who'd taught Troy the wonders of literature. Their Hanover Street row house may have been filled with secondhand furniture purchased at parking lot flea markets and the local Goodwill, but the numerous bookshelves lining the walls overflowed with literary treasures—stacks of hardcovers and paperbacks, most of them picked up at various library sales. There was everything from Hemingway to Bradbury, Faulkner to Haley, Joyce to DuBois. The complete works of Langston Hughes and James Baldwin and those from Toni Morrison thus far held special places of honor. A narrow shelf in the second-floor hallway was dedicated to the works of the world's great poets. Keats and Cummings, Shakespeare and Poe, Whitman and Frost. There was even a crate of old comic books—or "picture books" as Mrs. Carpenter called them—tucked away in the bottom of Troy's bedroom closet. *Star Wars* and *X-Men*; *The Incredible Hulk* and *Classics Illustrated*; *Tales of the Unexpected* and Troy's all-time favorite, *The Fantastic Four*. Most of them were missing their covers, but Troy didn't care. For him, it was the words that mattered the most.

Troy's mother, Claudia, worked in the cafeteria at nearby Union Memorial Hospital. She was the disciplinarian of the family. All about strict rules and consistent boundaries and tough love—but always with an emphasis on the love. According to Troy, she gave the world's best hugs. The kind that made you feel safe and strong and like you could fly. Regardless of how old you were. The summer before he'd left for college—while his father was busy playing his weekly game of hearts with friends from the neighborhood—Troy and his mom spent nearly every Saturday evening camped out on the sofa, watching whatever movies happened to be on television. If they were in the middle of a game, they took turns on the Scrabble board during the commercials. In preparation for those nights, they'd stockpile candy from the corner store—M&M's and strawberry Laffy Taffy for Troy, Hershey's Kisses and SweeTarts for his mother—and pop a bag of an amazing new snack invention: popcorn nuked in the microwave. Sometimes, if the movie was a long one, one bag wouldn't be enough, and they'd spoil themselves with a second. Heavy on the butter. Troy didn't talk about home very often, but when he did, you could really tell how much he missed those Saturday nights with his mom.

Unlike most young men in their late teens, Troy wore his love and devotion for his parents unabashedly on his sleeve. As a result, he took his fair share of mostly good-natured ribbing. At one point, his roommate, Brent—an alligator-shirt-collar-turned-up preppy from Washington, DC—had started calling him "Mama's Boy," but that came to an abrupt halt once Troy began tutoring him in math. Every Sunday night like clockwork, Troy called his folks collect from the pay phone in his dormitory lobby, and at least twice a week, he mailed home postcards with handwritten notes (usually updating them on his class grades and what he'd eaten for dinner that day). So, the mere thought of doing something that might cause them shame or disappointment sent Troy plummeting into an emotional tailspin. It wasn't until recently, when Troy allowed me to read a journal entry he'd written for his creative writing class, that I finally understood why.

> *The road was a maze of bloody footprints. It looked like red paint. He'd been running away when the bullets struck. Once in the back of the head, and again in the shoulder. When the police arrived, they covered him with a dirty blanket and wouldn't let me near him. They shoved me back onto the sidewalk with everyone else. They didn't care that I was his brother. They didn't care.*

In August 1975, Troy's eight-year-old brother, Morgan, was the victim of a drug-related drive-by shooting. He had been playing stickball in the street along with a group of friends in front of the Carpenters' home. These pickup games were a regular occurrence in Cherry Hill, and they often drew an audience. That day, a man named Tyrone Chester—"Big Head" to most everyone in the neighborhood—sat on a nearby stoop to watch while eating his lunch. Chester was a notorious heroin dealer and the intended target of the shooting. Troy was supposed to be there—in fact, whiffle ball had been his idea earlier that morning as he and his brother shared a Slurpee on their walk home from the 7-Eleven—but he'd dozed off on the living room floor while watching TV. The sound of gunshots woke him a short time later. The incident made the front page of the *Sun* and all four local television news channels, but the shooter was never identified.

In life, the two brothers couldn't have been more different. Troy was the bookworm, the showman and goofball, comfortable in his own skin. Morgan was quieter, more of an introvert, and the best damn athlete in the entire school. His death had almost broken Mr. and Mrs. Carpenter. In hindsight, if it hadn't been for Troy, I really believe it would have. During the years following the shooting, he almost single-handedly lifted them up and gave them hope. He stayed clear of trouble in the neighborhood. He volunteered at the humane society and a nearby nursing home. At school, Bs and B-pluses turned into As across the board. He won academic awards and was offered scholarships. Slowly but surely, the sense of doom lifted and the three Carpenters began to feel like a family again.

Troy told us all of this one night at Melody's apartment, after a breaking news story about a drive-by shooting in downtown Philadelphia interrupted the episode of *Magnum, P.I.* we were watching. When he was finished talking, there wasn't a dry eye in the room. After hearing what had happened to his brother, and especially after reading his journal entry, I realized that all Troy had to do to save his family was place the weight of the world upon his skinny shoulders—at a time in his life when he wasn't even old enough to vote or buy a six-pack of beer. The pressure he felt on a daily basis had to be staggering.

I'd tried my best on more than one occasion to get him to loosen up. There was an Eddie Murphy concert in Philly, a handful of late nights at the local college bars (try finding a fake ID for a guy who looked like the cartoon owl in the Tootsie Pops commercial), a hike at Codorus State Park, and even a rowdy frat party featuring a pair of live bands. All resulted in rather limited success—the low point coming when Troy vomited all over my brand-new Nikes after downing a single shot of tequila.

A month or so ago, I decided to give him a nickname. A timeless fraternity tradition even though neither of us belonged to one—good-natured in mindset, and maybe I thought it would help him feel more like one of the guys. Initially, I was tempted to call him "Owl"—which was the first thing that came to mind due to his obvious intelligence and the way his glasses magnified his already perpetually wide eyes—but I knew that wouldn't be well received. Then, I thought possibly "Oscar"—after the New York Yankees outfielder Oscar Gamble, the proud owner of the biggest Afro in Major League Baseball. But when I brought it up, Troy looked at me like I had two heads and said, *"Don't be ridiculous. I'm a Baltimore boy. I want nothing to do with the damn Yankees."* Finally, I ended up settling on "Carp." A genius move, I thought, a short and simple play on his last name. So far, though, it hadn't really taken. Not even a little bit. Like I said earlier, what you saw was what you got. Troy was just . . . *Troy*.

7

I wasn't exactly sure how long I'd been dozing.

I opened my eyes to blinding sunlight streaming through the van window, blinked a couple of times, and then remembered where I was. Groaning, I squeezed my eyes shut again.

Day One. Morning. Or maybe even early afternoon by now. Either way, it was going to be a long-ass week cooped up inside this van. After a while, I forced my eyes open again. Squinted out the window at rolling green hills. A farm pond glistening in the distance. A copse of faraway trees surrounded by cows. David Bowie's "Let's Dance" was playing too loudly on the radio. I felt the itch of a headache coming on.

"Do you think he'd been in an accident?"

"Probably," Melody was saying. "Although he was heading in the opposite direction of the hospital."

MEMORIALS

"His bike seemed fine. I didn't see any damage."

"I'm just glad I didn't hit him. Can you imagine if . . ."

They were talking about the man on the bicycle from earlier this morning. Once we'd finished loading the equipment, Melody went inside to say goodbye to her roommate—a very nice older woman named Rosalita—while Troy and I waited by the van. A few minutes later, she returned carrying a casserole of homemade empanadas. Even covered with Saran Wrap, they smelled delicious. With my stomach grumbling, I took the still-warm-from-the-oven dish from Melody and stowed it inside one of the coolers. And off we went.

I remembered what happened next with the slow-motion clarity of a waking dream:

As we pulled up to the stop sign, Troy swiveled in his seat and looked at me. I could tell he was nervous. His eyes, behind his glasses, were enormous. "Did I ever mention that sometimes I have pretty bad nightmares?"

Melody inched the nose of the van into the intersection. With the radio turned down, I could hear the rhythmic *tic-tic, tic-tic, tic-tic* of the turn signal. She leaned forward, glanced both ways, and began to make a left onto Margrove Street.

As she did, I answered Troy. "Great, you and me in the same tent. Maybe I should—"

Melody slammed on the brakes—

—as a man on a ten-speed bike zipped right in front of us, missing the van's front fender by no more than six or eight inches.

Even though he was speeding along, I could make out his details crystal clear. The stranger with the death wish appeared to be in his thirties, maybe early forties. Tall and slender. Receding hairline. Skinny legs covered in coarse, dark hair. He was wearing navy-blue athletic shorts and a plain gray T-shirt. Dark rivulets of what I first believed was muddy perspiration streamed down his neck and chest, soaking the front of his shirt.

But it wasn't sweat.

It looked like blood.

His face a mask of crimson.

Even his teeth were stained red.

The man was smiling, a macabre full-tooth grin.

And then in a blink—he was gone, swallowed up by the morning traffic.

"WHAT IN THE HELL WAS THAT?!" Melody had practically crawled onto Troy's lap in an effort to get a better look at the stranger.

"I-I have no idea," he stammered. "I don't think . . . I want to know."

"Should we go after him?" Melody asked.

"And do what?" I said, still staring out the window.

"I don't know . . . maybe try to help him?"

"Yeah, that's a big fat *no* from me." Troy actually crossed his arms over his chest and shuddered. "That dude looked like the devil himself."

Melody raised her eyebrows. "The devil on a ten-speed bike?"

Before Troy could respond, the driver behind us laid on his horn.

Melody frowned at the rearview mirror. "Yeah, yeah, hold your goddamn horses!"

She checked both ways for cars—and lunatics on bikes—and made a left onto Margrove Street, driving in the direction from which the man had come. Leaning across the seat, I searched the road for a blood trail or signs of an accident but didn't see anything. Two blocks later, still nothing, and then Melody had to turn right on Logan and merge into a steady stream of northbound traffic. The bloody cyclist still a mystery, we were finally on our way.

8

The three of us had met five months earlier in Professor Tyree's American Studies class.

AMST301—as it was listed in the spring 1983 course catalog—was one of York College's most popular electives. Professor Marcus Tyree, who'd recently celebrated his thirty-second year with the faculty, was highly regarded as both a charismatic and innovative educator, someone who went out of his way to connect with his pupils. His classes invariably attracted the brightest young minds on campus. Melody Wise and Troy Carpenter were exemplary students with sterling track records. They belonged in his classroom. Me, though—Billy Anderson: unheralded sophomore, recovering degenerate, and angst-filled orphan—not so much. The fact that I was enrolled in AMST301 to begin with was nothing short of a miracle.

This was how it happened:

Following a less-than-inspired freshman year—a polite way of saying I'd bombed most of my classes and landed on academic probation—I'd spent the summer of '82 hauling concrete at a local construction site and taking a couple of night classes to hopefully boost my GPA. When I wasn't working or going to school, I kept to myself and rarely left my studio apartment overlooking the river. I watched a lot of television that summer. I did newspaper crossword puzzles. I taught myself to play the guitar. Every once in a while, when a restless mood struck, I ventured into the city proper and caught a Phillies game from the cheap seats in left field.

Mostly, I did my best to stay away from the bars. Even at the recklessly young age of eighteen—with a fake ID purchased for forty bucks tucked away inside my wallet—I'd recognized that my drinking was becoming a problem.

By the time Fourth of July weekend rolled around, the construction gig had given me a perpetually sunburned neck and thick calluses on my palms. I had some difficulty playing guitar, and my medium T-shirts no longer fit. The hard work was good for me, though, and not just because of the newly added muscle. It was good for my soul. In a way, it felt like I was sweating out my demons for eight or nine hours a day. Some of them, at least.

At the end of each week, while the full-timers peeled out of the parking lot in their pickups with paychecks burning holes in their jeans, I was too worn out to follow them into town and get myself into trouble. Weekends were spent sleeping until noon and catching up on laundry. Every

Monday afternoon, during my lunch break, I walked across the street to the First National Bank and deposited my check. I didn't need the money—the insurance payout from my parents' accident was earning interest in my savings account—but I was proud of myself, nonetheless.

I rarely felt lonely or homesick. I actually preferred being alone. It was just easier that way. Most of my old friends from Sudbury had returned from college early that summer. They'd unpacked their suitcases and settled into their old bedrooms and picked up right where they'd left off. Working part-time jobs at the mall or the swimming pool. Hanging out nights at the Scoop and Serve or the drive-in movie theater. Cruising the backroads with six-packs of beer and the radio cranked up or floating downriver on inner tubes. Fishing. Tossing the ball around. Rekindling summer flings.

Just the idea of all that felt like too much work to me. I'd moved away and moved on. I had no interest in looking back or going back—or even trying to stay in touch. Everyone in town had treated me differently after the accident. Overnight, it felt like I'd become a stranger to them. Someone whom folks had a hard time looking in the eye. When I walked into a room, there were stealthy glances and whispers. God, I hated it. I hadn't even bothered to hook up the phone line when I moved into the new apartment. Who needed it, anyway.

As the summer wore on, my Aunt Helen paid me a number of surprise visits, usually with a back seat full of groceries to restock my pantry. It was good to see her, and a part of me was always sad when it came time to say goodbye. But another part of me—and it would've deeply hurt her had she known I felt this way—was filled with relief when I watched her drive away. As much as I loved her, my aunt was a remnant of my other life. A fucking *reminder*.

Late at night, after her visits, I often found myself unable to sleep, staring at the ceiling, my head ravaged by a tsunami of dark thoughts and bittersweet memories. Those nights felt endless and lost and even a little bit scary, and when I finally did fall asleep, long after the witching hour had come and gone, I almost always dreamed of my parents.

Still, for a while during that summer, it felt like my efforts were paying off. I managed an A- and a B in my night classes, and by the time students arrived back on campus for the fall semester, my confidence was on the upswing. At registration, I signed up for a full class load of eighteen credits. I was no longer working construction, so I had plenty of time to study. I was steadfast in steering clear of the bars. I signed up for intramural basketball. I even went to visit my Aunt Helen for a long weekend in early October. When midterm grades were posted a short time later, I was shocked to discover that I'd earned four As and a pair of Bs. I must have checked the list at least a half-dozen times to make sure it wasn't some kind of mistake, and nope, it wasn't.

Not long after, I ran into Mr. Skelley, my econ instructor, in the cafeteria and he suggested that I might be interested in Professor Tyree's American Studies class that next semester. Early registration was beginning in a week, he explained with a mouth full of turkey sandwich, and he and Tyree were longtime colleagues and racquetball partners. The class was very popular and usually filled up immediately, but he'd be more than happy to put in a good word for me. Flattered, I thanked him for his generosity, and walked away not really anticipating anything would come of it. I signed up for American Studies 301 early the next week—and to my surprise was promptly accepted.

I still hadn't made even a semblance of peace with what had happened to my parents—many days I woke up angry and sad and confused—but I no longer felt completely adrift in my life. For the first time since before the accident, I had some sort of direction and focus. I was no longer drinking and was doing a lot better at pushing away the itch. I was sleeping and eating better. Getting a little exercise. There was even a girl in my English class that I kind of liked. I actually began to feel hopeful about what the future might hold.

And then the holidays arrived—and everything went to shit.

9

VIDEO FOOTAGE
(1:49 p.m., Monday, May 2, 1983)

The classroom is empty.

"Testing . . . one . . . two . . . three . . . four . . . five . . ."

As the camera swings around in a slow circle, we see a dozen rows of desks and chairs stretching from the front of the room to the rear. Five or six in each row. It's a narrow room. The walls covered with maps and charts and indexes. A large metal desk sits center stage at the front. Behind it, a length of chalkboard covered in messy handwriting. An exit sign hangs above the only door, which is closed.

". . . six . . . seven . . . eight . . . nine . . . ten."

The image blurs and then quickly sharpens again as the camera operator zooms in on the blackboard. ROANOKE and CROATOAN and 1590 swim in and out of view—

—and then we hear a door bang open off-screen.

And a loud, boisterous voice. "Billy! I am so sorry to interrupt!"

The camera abruptly shifts to the left—and a grizzly bear of a man comes into focus. Professor Marcus Tyree is wearing a huge smile above his unmanageable beard and carrying a stack of books in his arms. He walks to the large desk at the front of the room and puts them down with a thud.

"No problem, Professor. Just giving the camera a test run. This thing's pretty amazing."

"The A/V department to the rescue." He sits down behind the desk—and we hear the chair groan beneath his weight. "Glad it worked out for you."

"Thanks to your help."

"Happy to put in the good word . . . although I admit I'm still a bit worried about the three of you going on the road by yourselves."

"Don't be. It'll be fun." As Billy walks closer, we get a shaky glimpse of the professor's tattoo-covered forearms. "Melody'll watch over me, and I'll watch over Troy."

"And who'll watch over Melody?"

"That girl can take care of herself, believe me."

And then they're both laughing.

10

At York College, the last day of exams before Christmas break was Tuesday, December 21. I had an 11 a.m. British Lit final—and that was it. Semester officially over. I finished my blue book essay on Emily Brontë in just under an hour and walked outside to a winter wonderland. A steady, wet snow was falling from a slate-gray sky. The ground was already covered, and the mostly abandoned campus resembled a New England postcard. As I walked to my car, I listened to distant laughter and cries of joy coming from a handful of sledders on the hill in front of the library and a gang of grade-school kids waging a snowball fight across the pond. Another week or two of this frigid weather, and they would be ice-skating and playing hockey. When I pulled out of the parking lot with "Silent Night" playing on the radio, it felt like I was driving inside of a snow globe. Thrilled to be finished with my exams, I spent the rest of the afternoon Christmas shopping. Later that evening, I went out for pizza and beers with the guys from my intramural basketball team. It was the first time all season that I'd accepted an invitation to join them. When the waitress asked for my drink order, I told her a pitcher of Sprite. No one at the table said a word about it.

When I got back to my apartment later that night, I wrapped the only two gifts I'd purchased. A silver necklace and a set of carving knifes. Both for my Aunt Helen. I wasn't sure if she'd like what I'd picked out, but I figured she could wear the necklace to church if she wanted to and use the knives to cut up the vegetables she grew in her garden. I'd agreed to spend Christmas week at her house in Sudbury and was actually looking forward to it.

I left the wrapped presents on the kitchen counter beside my keys, poured myself a glass of water from the tap, and got ready for bed. Once I was settled beneath the covers, I turned on the television. *White Christmas* was playing on cable. I immediately felt a lump form in the back of my throat. This was my mother's favorite movie. Growing up, we'd watched it as a family at least a dozen times. Probably more. She always made hot chocolate with tiny marshmallows and turned off the lights so it felt like we were at the movie theater.

On the TV, in my dark bedroom, Bing Crosby and Danny Kaye, both dressed in makeshift hula skirts, began dancing across the screen, crooning about devoted sisters . . .

. . . and for just a moment—as clear and present as if she were sitting right next to me—I heard my mother's voice singing along with them.

It should have made me happy.

It should have made me remember.

And smile.

But it didn't.

Instead, my heart broke into a million pieces.

All over again.

And then it was as if all the hope and goodwill and progress that had been stored up inside me those past few months bled out of my body in one great arterial gush.

Leaving behind nothing at all.

Except for tears.

I lowered my head and let them come.

Before long I was sobbing—and couldn't stop.

And still I didn't change the channel.

I couldn't do it.

The next few days, I left the bed only to use the bathroom.

I didn't sleep.

I didn't eat.

I drank only from the glass of water on my nightstand—until it was gone.

And then I stopped drinking.

And stopped getting up to use the restroom.

I just laid there in bed, curled onto my side, staring blankly at the wall, my face a mess of tears and snot, piss-stained blankets in a tangled heap at my feet, television on the floor, screen shattered into dozens of jagged pieces, just like my heart, listening for my mother's voice to come again . . .

Until finally my landlord used his master key to let a frantic Aunt Helen into the apartment—and she got me cleaned up and whisked me away.

11

"Nope," Troy said, staring ahead at the hitchhiker. "Don't even think about it."

We'd crossed a one-lane bridge spanning a dry creek bed, then rounded a long, winding curve in the road—and there he was. Leaning against a 35 mph speed limit sign. Dirty blond hair hanging down to his shoulders. Cigarette dangling from his lips. James Dean cool. When he saw us coming, he snapped to attention and stuck out his thumb.

"Why not?" Melody asked, pressing the brakes. "He looks harmless enough."

I knew she was kidding. Troy did not.

"He looks like he escaped from an insane asylum."

Melody threw back her head and laughed, a high, cheerful sound that made my heart flutter. "You really are such a scaredy-cat." She gave the man on the side of the road an apologetic wave as we cruised slowly past. He shrugged and grinned at her.

"It's not about being scared," Troy insisted. "It's about being safe. Who wears corduroys and a long sleeve T-shirt in this weather? He's probably hiding a hunting knife . . . or maybe even an axe."

"I think you've rented too many scary movies," she said.

"And you see how baggy his pants were? No telling what he's got in there."

She glanced at the mirror. "Whoa! Hear that, Billy? Troy's talking about the hitchhiker's package." Her eyes twinkled with mischief. "He *was* kinda cute."

"His *what*? No! Oh my God!"

"I'm not judging you," she said, struggling not to smile. "Whatever floats your boat."

"That's not what I meant and you know it! I was going to say he could have a machete or even a sword stuffed down his pants for all we know."

"Oooo, a sword, huh? A really big one?"

"Melody, come on!"

She laughed. "Maybe I should start calling you Zorro."

Did I mention that this was going to be a long trip?

12

Marcus Tyree didn't look like a typical college professor.

At six-four and upward of 230 pounds—sporting an unruly nest of dark, curly hair atop his head, a full beard and mustache without a hint of gray, and massive forearms covered in tattoos (my personal favorite being an ultrarealistic portrait of Bob Marley)—he more closely resembled a starting offensive lineman on the Pittsburgh Steelers, or perhaps even a lumberjack. In a word, the guy was *intimidating* . . . until, that is, he opened his mouth and began to speak. Tyree's soft, reasoned voice stood in stark contrast to the rest of him and immediately put his students at ease. As the semester began, I witnessed firsthand the reason why he was so popular on campus. Pacing back and forth in front of his cluttered desk, a toothpick jutting from the corner of his mouth, Tyree spoke with an energy and enthusiasm that was contagious. Unlike so many other by-the-book professors, he never spoke *at* you; he always spoke *to* you. His class didn't feel like a boring lecture; it felt like an intimate conversation—between two dozen people. In no time at all, I found myself looking forward to those Monday/Wednesday/Friday 10 a.m. meetings, often arriving early with the hopes of having some one-on-one time with the professor. No matter the topic, he had a way of communicating that made you feel as if you were the most important person in the world at that moment. I could definitely think of worse ways to start my day.

In that regard, Professor Tyree was a lot like the new therapist I'd started seeing on Friday afternoons. Her name was Kathy Mirarchi, and I not only liked her right away but also trusted her. So far, we'd only met at her downtown office a handful of times, but it felt like I'd known her for years. Going to see a counselor had been my Aunt Helen's idea. She'd first suggested it shortly after the accident in June, but I wouldn't even consider it back then. In my mind, I didn't need an expensive shrink to help me feel better. I'd read all about the five stages of grief in a pamphlet I'd picked up at the funeral home. I was going to be okay. I just needed more time.

But after what had happened in the days leading up to Christmas, I now knew better. I needed all the help I could get. Following my breakdown, Aunt Helen tried to convince me to skip the spring semester and remain at home with her in Sudbury. "*You need to take your time getting back on your feet,*" she'd pleaded. "*You need to focus on rest and recuperation.*" But the more I'd thought about it, the more that idea terrified me. Even then, somewhere inside my addled brain, I knew that if I didn't drag my ass out of bed, and soon, I might never find the wherewithal to do it—whether for classes or anything else.

So when the third week of January rolled around, I shaved the uneven patches of whiskers off my chin, stuffed some extra clothes into a backpack, and returned to my quiet apartment by the river. My aunt had hired a local service to come in and clean, so the place was spotless. It even smelled good. She'd also surprised me with a brand-new television for Christmas to replace the one I'd broken. I spent most of that first evening setting it up in the corner of my bedroom and figuring out how to connect it to the cable box and VCR.

Two days later, at 9:30 a.m., I shrugged on my coat, scraped the ice off my windshield, and drove the mile and a half to campus. I parked my car behind a mound of dirty snow in Lot C. When I got out and locked the door, my heart was beating so hard it felt like it was going to break free of my chest.

From the back row of room 114, I watched the other students arrive for the first day of Professor Tyree's American Studies class. I wasn't the only one. Like me, the short Black guy with the thick eyeglasses showed up bright and early. Unlike me, he sat smack-dab in the middle of the front row and placed what looked like a brand-new spiral notebook on top of his desk. I immediately thought that whoever sat behind him was going to have a hell of a time seeing the blackboard over that magnificent Afro of his. A few minutes later, Raquel Welch walked into the room. Okay, not really, but that was my first impression of her. A dark-complexioned waif of a girl dressed in jeans with butterfly patches on the knees and a baggy dark green sweater with matching holes for elbows, she glided down the aisle and found an empty chair along the wall. When she smiled at the guy sitting next to her and started chatting in a friendly voice, I immediately felt a stab of irrational jealousy. With multiple strings of colored beads intertwined in her long dark hair and a refreshing lack of makeup, she looked like one of those carefree hippies I'd seen in old photographs of Woodstock and Haight-Ashbury. When Professor Tyree called out her name during attendance roll call, I somehow wasn't surprised by what I heard. *Melody Wise.* Even her name was pretty; it sounded like a song title.

Two weeks later, we were assigned our project groups for the semester. When I heard Melody's name announced alongside mine and two others I didn't recognize, I covered my smile with my hand and pretended I had to cough. Once Professor Tyree finished going down the rest of the list, he instructed the students to get up from their desks and gather in their individual groups. Standing, I spotted Melody sitting beside a girl with red hair at the front of the classroom. I hurried down the aisle and was about to slip into the empty chair next to Melody when the Black guy with the giant Afro stepped in front of me and plopped down in it. Somehow I resisted the urge to push him and sat on his other side. We scooted our chairs into a circle and began introducing ourselves.

By the end of that ninety-minute class period, I'd learned that Melody Wise was from Fairfax, Virginia; a senior and computer science major; and set to graduate after the completion of a four-credit summer course. A job with IBM was waiting for her in September. By the time I'd walked her to the bus stop after class, I'd discovered that she was a proud third-generation Puerto Rican; worked evenings at Giovanni's, a popular local restaurant; lived in an off-campus apartment with a roommate; and was contently single after a tumultuous breakup a year earlier.

She was also twenty-three—almost four years older than me.

And *completely* out of my league.

Once I came to terms with that somber reality, we quickly became friends.

An actual friend. Someone I could talk to. A first for me after nearly two years of college.

Not that I had anyone to blame for that but myself.

I'd seen girls in the hallway crying as they said farewell to their roommates for winter break. Overheard guys in my freshman dorm drunkenly promise to include each other in their weddings one day. Others sat in the cafeteria and planned summer vacations together or visits to each other's hometowns. College had a way of doing that: creating closer than normal bonds in a remarkably short amount of time. As far as I could tell, it was the combination of sudden freedom and overwhelming vulnerability that was responsible for this pattern of behavior. It all happened so fast. On drop-off day, your parents and siblings drove you to campus, and spent the morning and afternoon unloading the car and helping you set up your room. They met your roommate and exchanged pleasantries with your roommate's parents. Maybe, if there was enough time, you grabbed one last family dinner together at a nearby restaurant, and then they hugged you goodbye at the curb in front of your building and headed back home with a mournful *toot-toot-toot* of the horn—leaving you all alone for the first time in your life. As you stood on the sidewalk, waving and blinking back tears, watching their car disappear in the distance, the world suddenly felt very big and the silence in your head was deafening. You slowly turned and stared at your reflection in the glass door entrance to your dormitory and thought: *Now what?* Panic tightened your chest. Your head began to spin. You glanced over your shoulder, fighting back the urge to take off running in the direction your parents' car had driven. Until, finally, you looked around and realized you weren't really alone after all. There were others all around you wearing the same lost expression on their faces, experiencing the same roller coaster of emotions you were feeling. Others who—just like you—were about to spend the next several weeks trying their best not to lock themselves out of their dorm rooms and oversleep and be late for class and do their laundry and homework and figure out how their meal cards worked and what to do with their fleeting moments of free time. And then before long, after sharing all of these terrifying, new experiences with people who were once complete and total strangers, if you were lucky, you took another look around—and realized that you were part of a different kind of family now.

Which is exactly what happened with Melody and Troy and me—thanks to a better-late-than-never assist from Professor Tyree.

I mentioned earlier that Professor Tyree initially announced four members of our project group.

The fourth was the girl with red hair, Charlotte Livingston. She was painfully quiet—it always sounded like she was mumbling—and had a distressing case of acne. She told us that she was a townie who'd grown up on a dead-end street just south of campus, and she was studying to become a teacher.

A couple of days after the four of us got together for dinner at Giovanni's—a gathering that Melody had organized so we could all get to know each other better—Charlotte dropped the class without a word of warning to any of us. We never saw her again after that.

None of us took it personally.

Melody had been waiting tables at Giovanni's since mid-November, the shortest tenure of any of the half-dozen part-time waitresses who worked there—and because of this, she was often the recipient of last-minute schedule changes. As a result, she ended up being a no-show at two of the

MEMORIALS

group's first three meetings at the library. Although she felt terrible about her absence and apologized profusely, I didn't really mind. It not only allowed Troy and me to get to know each other better but also presented us with the opportunity to speak freely about our beautiful new friend.

By this time, the third week of February, I had already worked through most of my schoolboy crush on Melody. Of course, somewhere deep inside, I still held on to a sliver of hope that a romantic spark might one day be kindled—but I think, even then, I knew better. It was the way she looked at and spoke to me. Like she was the adult and I was the teenager (which, at twenty-three and nineteen, I *guess* we were, even if it didn't feel like it most of the time). I always expected her to pat me on the head when we said goodbye after class. Or tell me she was proud of me for raising my hand and giving the correct answer. Not exactly fuel for late-night fantasies. Still, I told myself, it was okay to admire from afar what I couldn't have.

Troy, on the other hand, had surprisingly little to say when it came to Melody's God-given physical attributes. When I pressed him on the subject, he agreed that she was attractive, but insisted it was her spirited and kind personality that made her so. Not one mention of her smoldering brown eyes . . . hourglass figure . . . or the way she walked in jeans. At first, I thought Troy might be gay—not that it mattered even a lick to me—but it soon became apparent that he was simply a lot more mature than I was. Something I would never admit out loud. Even now.

It's fair to say that after spending one-on-one time with Troy in the library, I felt an immediate attachment to him. He was different from anyone else I'd ever met before. Sure, the guy was smart as a whip and laser focused on his studies—you couldn't help but notice that right away—but it was more than that. He was odd and interesting and, most of all, immensely likable. He showed up for our first meeting wearing a puke-green cardigan sweater and carrying a scuffed-up briefcase, both of which he later told me he'd bought from a thrift store. After taking a seat, he opened the briefcase on his lap and pulled out a stack of spiral notebooks and a pair of individually wrapped Hostess Twinkies. He handed one of the cream-filled snacks across the table to me, and then pulled out a sheaf of papers and began going over the notes he'd taken earlier that morning in class. He'd even made copies for me and Melody. In so many ways, Troy Carpenter was eighteen years old going on forty.

But then some kind of internal switch would be thrown, and his eyes would swell up behind those thick glasses of his, and off he'd go on a tangent, rambling with childlike glee about UFOs and Stonehenge, Superman and Mark Twain, baseball and astrology—you name it, and Troy could speak extensively on the subject.

Not to mention the barrage of questions he carried around with him—the guy was curious about *everything*.

"*What was it like growing up in the suburbs? Did you ever have a tropical fish aquarium? Who taught you how to drive? Did you have a vegetable garden in your yard? Do you believe in ghosts?*"

It was as if all the vast knowledge and experience he kept stored inside his brain had come from words printed inside books, and no matter how wise and vibrant those words might prove to be, he was starving for the one thing they couldn't provide: basic human interaction.

It took a while—as it usually does with me—but I eventually realized that the hunger he was experiencing was something we both had in common. And it drew us together, like moths to a flame, in those frigid days of February.

As the semester went on, Melody and Troy and I began spending more and more time together—and not just while working on our American Studies project. Soon, Troy and I began stopping by Giovanni's on slow nights to keep Melody company. We helped her assemble a pair of bookshelves she'd purchased from a mail-order catalog. Melody taught us how to make *pollo guisado*, a spicy chicken stew, from an old family recipe. They both came to watch me play intramural basketball. We began doing homework together and took turns hosting game and movie nights. Most of the time, it was all three of us—at some point, Melody began referring to us as the Three Musketeers—but every once in a while, Troy was busy writing a paper or meeting with a professor, and it was just me and Melody.

On one such night, she talked about the future and the life she hoped to live. The plan was to work her way up the ladder at IBM until she was promoted to a management position. Then she'd get married and have children. Buy a big house somewhere near the beach. She never said much about her ex-boyfriend Mateo. Only that it had ended badly. Unsurprisingly, I was equally reticent about my own love life—or should I say, my complete and total lack of one. After significant probing, I finally admitted that I'd once had a high school sweetheart named Naomi, but we'd gone our separate ways shortly after my parents' accident. And there hadn't been anyone else since. It was a part of my past that my therapist and I were diligently working through.

On a rainy evening in early March, while I was walking her home from work, Melody told me the story of how she'd lost her mother to an accidental drug overdose. Only sixteen at the time, Melody returned from school to discover her mother's body sprawled on the floor of their upstairs bathroom. Her face had turned blue and there was a needle poking out of her arm. Shaking and in tears, Melody had immediately called 911 and then phoned her sister, Tamara, at work. Melody's father had long been out of the picture by then, and there were no relatives living nearby. Faced with the choice of moving closer to family in Puerto Rico or remaining in Virginia on their own, Melody and Tamara had been taking care of each other ever since.

Sharing such a painful chapter of her life story brought us even closer together. She'd known about my parents by then, so I guess she'd felt that I would understand—and know what to say and what not to say. As more time passed and the departure date for our trip approached, our relationship continued to evolve. A mutual respect and trust had been earned. Melody became the wiser older sister I'd never had, and I became the knucklehead younger brother she'd always wanted.

What happened to us later—during the trip—was the biggest regret of my life.

13

"Anyone else have to pee?"

"Uh, no." I looked up from the notebook I was scribbling in. "I used the bathroom when we stopped for gas . . ." I checked my watch. ". . . an hour and a half ago."

"Well, so did I." Troy peered down his nose at me. "And now I have to go again."

Melody sheepishly raised her hand from the steering wheel. "Me too."

Troy flashed me a smug look before swiveling around in his seat.

"At this rate, we might make it to Sudbury by . . ." I made a show of studying my watch again so it could be seen in the rearview mirror. ". . . oh, I don't know . . . Sunday or Monday."

Sudbury, Pennsylvania. My hometown. And the first overnight stop of our journey.

"Oh, hush," Melody said, laughing. "We'll be quick about it."

The plan was to set up camp in Liberty Hollow Park just north of town. We'd grab a late dinner, go over whatever footage we'd managed to assemble today, and discuss the following day's route. The only problem was, at this point, we didn't have a single frame of video to look at.

The day had gotten off to a rough start. It was almost four thirty, and so far, we'd only run across a pair of roadside memorials, neither of which proved suitable for filming. The first one had been located at a rural four-way intersection in the town of Rockville. A huge wooden cross—at least six feet tall—surrounded by a scattering of empty whiskey bottles, burned-down candle nubs, and a water-logged leather jacket covered in patches. A dozen or so photographs had been haphazardly stapled to the cross, their contents long ago stolen by sun and rain. In the biggest of the photos, I could just make out the ghostly image of a large bald man astride a Harley-Davidson motorcycle. He was wearing a black T-shirt with the sleeves cut off. His muscular arms were covered in tattoos. Someone had printed *RIP J.D.* across the bottom of the photo in permanent black marker.

Right as we were leaving, Troy had accidentally nudged one of the whiskey bottles with his shoe, upsetting a nest of ground wasps that had made their home in the nearby weeds. As he spun around in circles, arms flailing, legs kicking, squealing in terror, he was stung twice—on the hand and neck. You would've thought the guy had been shot, the way he carried on.

We stumbled across the second memorial on a curvy backroad just outside of Hancock. A shallow, weed-choked drainage ditch ran parallel to the shoulder. Just beyond it, a grassy knoll separated the ditch from a stretch of nearby woods. Sometime ago, a child had died there. There was no cross, so perhaps the family hadn't believed in a higher power. Instead, staked upon a single wooden post, leaning perilously to one side, was a poster-sized photograph of a young boy with short dark hair and big brown eyes. He was standing beside a stream, fishing pole in one hand, fat brown trout in the other. He was wearing a Pittsburgh Pirates baseball cap and a big happy grin on his freckled face. The boy's two front teeth were missing. Below the laminated poster with its curling and discolored edges was a mound of stuffed animals—giraffes and bears, unicorns and horses. All of them filthy and rotting, the stuffing leaking out from their rain-swollen bellies. A pair of glass vases, nearly hidden in the tall grass, held bouquets of bare stems. Whatever flowers had once bloomed there were now long gone—just like the boy in the photograph.

I stood there for a long time, staring at the boy's face on the opposite side of the ditch, wondering what his name was and if he'd played Little League baseball and whether he had any brothers or sisters. I listened to the birds singing in the trees and felt the warmth of the dappled sunlight on my face and wondered what had happened to the boy's family. Clearly no one had been here for a while, so why had they stopped coming? Had they moved away? Or simply moved on? And what about the Harley guy with the tattoos? His memorial had appeared even longer neglected—maybe even forgotten. What had become of his family and friends? Why did they no longer visit?

Before we left each of the memorials, I snapped a handful of photos with the 35mm and Polaroid cameras. I figured I could find a spot somewhere in the documentary to include them. Melody could even record a short voice-over once we got back to campus. Maybe the man on the motorcycle and the boy with the missing front teeth didn't have to be forgotten after all.

14

While Melody and Troy used the Sunoco station's restroom, I stretched my legs in the parking lot, sipping a Pepsi I'd taken from the cooler.

The place wasn't much to look at. The narrow slab of asphalt where Melody had parked was scarred with potholes, and the plate glass window out front was swathed in a spiderweb of cracks, most of them patched with fraying gray duct tape. There was only one working pump—the other three adorned with OUT OF ORDER signs handwritten on crudely cut pieces of oil-stained cardboard. A phone booth stood lonely and forlorn at the corner of the lot. You didn't have to work for Ma Bell to know that—just like the trio of defunct gas pumps—the telephone inside had long ago ceased to be operational. Scrawls of graffiti decorated what was left of the booth's filthy glass enclosure. One particularly witty soul had written CARLY JEAN TUCKER DIGS MY BIG PECKER in bright red permanent marker. Directly below that was a clumsily drawn penis and balls next to an upside-down cross.

Still feeling the funk from the little boy with the missing front teeth, I wandered aimlessly around the parking lot, my shuffling feet sending up plumes of road dust. A plane soared high overhead, its vapor trail slicing open the sky behind it. I watched as it disappeared into the clouds. Kicking at some stray rocks, I sent them skittering into the weeds—where at least one of them struck something metal with a distinctively loud *tink*.

Empty beer can? I wondered, walking closer to investigate. What else did I have to do? My traveling partners were taking forever, and I had a sneaking suspicion that one or both of them were doing a whole lot more than just peeing. Most likely, the empanadas we'd scarfed down earlier had come back to haunt them. Trying not to think too much about that, I walked back and forth, nudging the tall grass with the toe of my shoe. But I didn't find anything, metal or otherwise. A mosquito buzzed in my ear and settled on the back of my neck. I swatted it away. Spinning around in case it was circling for a renewed attack, I glimpsed a flash of bright yellow among the green and brown foliage alongside the road. At first, I thought it was a sign someone had posted. NO HUNTING or maybe PRIVATE PROPERTY—KEEP OUT. Then I realized it was a portion of yellow ribbon draped around the trunk of a tree. Walking closer, squinting now, I spotted what appeared to be the tip of a cross not far from the ribbon.

Bingo.

Draining the rest of my soda in a single gulp, I hurried along the gently sloping shoulder of the roadway. Ahead of me, two squirrels played a noisy game of chase in the branches of a towering oak. Butterflies danced in the late afternoon sunshine. Somewhere in the distance, there was the deep-throated *thrum* of a tractor working a field.

And then it was right in front of me.

A painted cross, so white it was almost blinding against the backdrop of trees. A name had been written on the horizontal plank: CHASE HARPER. On each side of it, a pair of painted red hearts. Bundles of cut flowers rested at the base of the cross, too many to count, none of them in vases, but most of them still relatively fresh. Someone had left a horseshoe next to a small American flag. Someone else, a baseball. Off to the side, a small hand-painted sign read: "AND THE DUST RETURNS TO THE EARTH AS IT WAS, AND THE SPIRIT RETURNS TO GOD WHO GAVE IT." ECCLESIASTES 12:7. A child's crayon drawing—three stick figures, two grown-ups and a child, standing in front of a house with crooked windows and a peaked roof, *I MISS YOU DADDY* printed over a cluster of puffy blue clouds—had been enclosed in a Ziploc bag to protect it from the weather and pinned to the base of the tree. A little higher up, just below the strand of yellow ribbon, the bark of the tree was deeply gouged and scarred.

That's when I looked down and noticed the tire tracks in the grass at my feet. Glancing over my shoulder at the road behind me, I spotted the remnants of a messy smear of skid marks.

All of a sudden, it was very clear what had happened here.

Despite the somber display surrounding me, I felt my heart begin to race with excitement.

This was exactly what we were looking for.

15

As Melody readied herself to appear on camera—brushing her hair, adding some color to her cheeks (whatever the hell that meant), and changing her earrings to something a little less dangly—I began photographing the memorial. Beginning with wide-angle shots to lend it some perspective in relation to the surrounding countryside, I worked my way in from various angles, trying to bring life to the subject. I finally concluded with a series of close-ups of each of the items that'd been left at the base of the cross. My ultimate goal was for the audience to be able to *see* and *feel* what I was seeing and feeling. The smudge of dirt on the baseball. The rough-hewn grooves along the bottom of the horseshoe. The perfect imperfections of the painted red hearts. I wanted viewers to feel like they could reach out and touch those things.

Only a handful of cars drove past us, each of them slowing down to take a closer look at what we were doing. An older gentleman in a Ford pickup came to a full stop and slowly rolled down his window. But when Troy approached him, the man reconsidered whatever it was he'd been planning to say and quickly sped away. Troy, who had minutes earlier donned a two-sizes-too-big bright orange safety vest as if he were a member of an actual road crew, gave us a shrug and returned to the shoulder of the road.

The gas station attendant—the name tag on his chest read Henry, but I would've bet every last dollar in my wallet that he went by "Hank"—studied us from a distance. If the man wasn't yet seventy, he was a birthday candle or two away. His tan face was a maze of deep wrinkles, his long-fingered hands speckled in liver spots. His slicked-back hair was littered with dandruff, and when I'd spoken with him earlier, I'd noticed a scattering of crumbs in his untrimmed mustache—and yet the baby blue Sunoco overalls he was wearing were perfectly pressed and spotless. Even his boots were shined to a shimmering gleam. All of which almost certainly meant that Henry had a doting wife waiting for him back at home. As he watched us with a sour expression on his face, he began pacing back and forth, crossing and uncrossing his arms, looking every bit like a man who believed he was witnessing a law or two being broken.

A short time later, I returned to the van, and gave the old man a polite nod as I walked past him. He pretended not to notice and quickly looked away in the opposite direction. I wasn't surprised. Earlier, when I'd asked if we could leave our van parked in the gas station lot while we filmed the memorial, he'd merely grunted and walked away.

After returning the 35mm and Polaroid cameras to their respective cases, with a tidal wave of absolute glee surging through me—picture a six-year-old boy rushing downstairs to open his gifts on Christmas morning—I carefully removed our secret weapon from the back of the van. A boxy silver hard-shell case with gray protective foam interior, it looked like something out of a James Bond movie. I clicked the double latches and slowly opened the lid. Inside, a state-of-the-art JVC VHS video camera with all the bells and whistles. Thanks to Professor Tyree's letter of recommendation, the camera was officially on loan to us from York College's award-winning A/V department. The deal came with only three stipulations. One: we make a quality film. Two: we give the A/V department its proper due in the closing credits. Three: we return the camera in perfect working condition upon the completion of our trip. Go figure. The techno geeks had turned out to be a whole lot more trusting than Ms. Tamara Wise—not to mention much cheaper.

The camera was a dream. Compact and lightweight, it could be used on a tripod or as a handheld. The gimmick was that it utilized a special cassette that was inserted right into the back of the camera. Footage was then recorded onto the cassette, which could later be played on a standard VHS-format VCR. You could also use a newly designed A/V cord to plug it into your television set for immediate playback without any additional equipment. But those weren't even our secret weapon's most exciting features. In addition to having 6x power zoom, freeze-frame capabilities, and a kickass fast lens for shooting in low light, the camera offered instant replay directly through the eyepiece—which meant I could double-check my work as I went. It also meant no nasty surprises later on in the editing process.

After making sure there was a blank cassette already loaded, I popped in a fully charged battery and ran a quick systems check. Both video and audio appeared to be in perfect operating condition, so I locked up the van and made my way back to the others. This time I didn't even bother glancing at the old man.

As I approached the memorial, Melody looked up from the makeshift script she was studying.

"Ready to go?" I asked.

She gave me a nervous smile. "Ready as I'll ever be."

"Just take your time and try not to talk too fast." I led her to the shoulder of the road, maybe seven or eight feet wide of the memorial. "You'll start here, and as you begin speaking, make your way, slowly, to this mark."

Using blue chalk, Troy had drawn a small *X* on the asphalt. I would be sure to rub it away with my shoe when we were finished. It was important that we left this place exactly as we'd found it.

"We'll open with an introductory take on roadside memorials in general, and then we'll go again and focus on what we know about Chase Parker and his family." We'd already been able to gather a handful of pertinent details from the numerous keepsakes left at the scene.

"What if I screw up?" Melody asked, brushing her hair back over her shoulder.

"Then we start over," I said. "No big deal. We can do as many takes as you need."

She nodded and took a deep breath.

I looked at Troy. "Keep an eye out for traffic. But if we're rolling, don't say anything out loud unless it's absolutely necessary." I started to turn around, but stopped. "Oh, and if you see Bigfoot stomping out of the woods, ignore everything I just said and give us a holler."

He lifted both hands in front of him and slowly extended his middle fingers.

"I guess I deserve that," I said, laughing.

"Can we please do this?" Melody said. "Before I lose my nerve."

"Yes, ma'am, let's do it." I lifted the camera and peered through the viewfinder. Backing up a couple of steps, I readjusted the focus. Melody appeared in crisp detail at the center of the frame, fading sunlight slanting down through the trees behind her. Bathed in golden rays, she looked like an angel. "Ready when you are," I said and pressed the record button.

Another deep breath from Melody. Then:

"*We've all seen them. Whether we're out running our daily errands or traveling to a faraway destination.*" She began walking. I carefully sidestepped to my left, once, twice, three times, smoothly mirroring her progress. "*Roadside memorials . . . much like this one behind me . . . found in the small rural town of Exeter, Pennsylvania. Once rare, these sacred displays of grief and remembrance now dot the nation's landscape . . .*"

16

VIDEO FOOTAGE
(5:32 p.m., Friday, May 6, 1983)

"Modern-day roadside memorials serve a variety of both spiritual and practical purposes."

Melody's voice is strong and measured. She stares into the camera with a confident yet relaxed intensity. She's not lecturing the viewer. She's sitting across the dinner table telling them a story.

"They publicly honor a recently deceased loved one and, similar to a headstone in a cemetery, represent an expression of love and remembrance. Many memorials also serve as a cautionary message for other drivers, and at times, even a warning of potential danger.

"But these public displays are not without their detractors. A number of people, private citizens and government officials alike, claim that roadside memorials limit sightlines and act as distractions for rubbernecking drivers. In addition, some concerned opponents insist that over time, the memorials often become eyesores and, in some specific instances, environmental hazards.

"With a marked increase in the number of roadside memorials and a wave of mounting complaints, numerous restrictions have been put in place by many legislators. Oversized signage, wreaths, and balloons are no longer allowed in more than a dozen states. Offensive photos and messages, as well as burning candles, are also prohibited. And in certain areas, religious symbols are strictly forbidden, citing the clear constitutional separation of church and state.

"Although state and local laws often forbid the assembly of roadside memorials on public land, these bans are rarely enforced . . ."

17

Not bad for our first shoot, I thought, checking the display window on the camera. *Three takes for a total of eighteen minutes of unedited footage. And even as nervous as she was, Melody knocked it out of the park.*

I knelt down in the grass in front of the memorial and placed the video camera on a towel Troy had laid out for me. Off to the side was an extra battery and a small leather pouch containing various filters. Despite the ridiculous-looking safety vest, Troy had done a fine job of making sure I had everything I needed and collaborating with Mel on her commentary. Glancing over my shoulder, I saw them both talking to the dinosaur of a gas station attendant by the van. *Better them than me.*

I did a quick count to make certain we didn't leave behind any filters, and then I zipped up the pouch—and felt a sudden chill wash over me. Gooseflesh rose on my forearms. The tiny hairs on the back of my neck began tingling, like when I was a kid and I'd wandered too close to one of those big electrical substations down by the river.

And then I felt a whisper of ice-cold breath on the back of my neck.

There's someone standing right behind me.

But before I could turn around to look, my throat swelled and suddenly

I couldn't breathe. Invisible smoke filled my eyes and clogged my nostrils. I began to cough and wheeze. Panicking, I jumped to my feet and spun around—but no one was there.

What the hell . . . ?

And then just like that . . . the feeling was gone.

My throat felt fine. I could breathe again.

The spring air all around me warm and clear and still.

Not even a breeze rustled the treetops.

I glanced down the road, my heart jackhammering inside my chest. Troy was walking toward me, maybe twenty yards away. "You okay?" he asked, a curious look on his face. Behind him, I could see Melody still talking to the attendant.

I waved a hand in front of my face. "Eh, couple of pissed-off hornets. One of them almost flew down my shirt."

He rolled his eyes, assuming I was being a smart-ass—but didn't come any closer just in case. Rubbing the bump on his neck where he'd been stung earlier, he said, "I think I'll just wait right here, then . . ."

I knelt down again and began rearranging the camera equipment. On the shoulder of the road, Troy was still talking—but I couldn't hear a word.

All I could think was:

What in the hell just happened?

18

As it turned out, our not-so-friendly gas station attendant ended up being a huge help.

While Troy and I packed up and loaded the van, Melody worked her magic. First, she offered the old guy a cold drink from the cooler, and then while he sipped his Diet Coke, she explained in great detail what it was that we were doing. At one point, their voices dropped to a whisper and the two of them strolled away from the van with their heads huddled close together. I was pretty sure she was telling him about the loss of my parents and how their memorial in Sudbury had served as the original inspiration for our project. Whatever she said, it worked. After a few minutes, they returned to the van, which Troy and I had just finished loading.

"My name's Henry Whitaker," the station attendant told us, rubbing at the whiskers on his chin. *Ah,* not *Hank,* I briefly thought. I was losing my touch. "Chase Harper was a friend of mine. We went to the same church. My wife did some sewing for his missus." He stared off in the distance.

"Chase worked in electronics of some kind. Was on his way home from a business meeting in Baltimore when the accident happened. Fell asleep at the wheel is what most folks around here think." The old man shook his head. "Not more than ten minutes from his own driveway."

Shuffling his feet, Troy said, "I recently read an article that claimed over fifty percent of all accidents occur within a mile of the victim's home . . ."

The old man stared at Troy, who was still dressed in his bright orange vest, as if the teenager had three eyes instead of two and a big green booger dangling out of his nose.

Troy's eyes went huge behind his glasses and he quickly looked away.

"Anyway, I was saying . . . Chase had a wife and son. Jennifer's a math teacher over at the middle school. Off for the summer, of course." He glanced back and forth at Melody and me. "If you'd like, I guess I could telephone her and see if she's willing to speak to you all for your movie."

"That would be—"

"Lovely," Melody said, cutting me off in midsentence. "We'd be ever so grateful if you would give her a call." And then she took Mr. Whitaker by the arm and escorted him across the parking lot.

Just before they disappeared inside, the old man lifted his head and let loose with a loud, raspy cackle. It was a dry, sickly sound—like someone had tossed a strip of sandpaper into a blender and turned it on.

"Damn," Troy said as soon as the gas station door banged shut. "She's good."

"Better than you and me, that's for sure."

Five minutes later, they were back and smiling.

"She's willing to sit down with you for half an hour after supper," he said. "She's going to ask a neighbor to watch her boy." He gazed fondly at Melody. "I gave the girl here the address. Should be easy enough to find."

"We really appreciate it, Mr. Whitaker." Without thinking, I reached out my hand. "Thank you again for all of your help."

He took my hand and gave it a surprisingly firm shake—as he did, I once again found myself thinking about sandpaper—and then he added with a crooked-tooth grin, "You can call me Hank, son. Everyone around here does."

19

VIDEO FOOTAGE
(7:10 p.m., Friday, May 6, 1983)

```
"The sad thing is we moved out here to be safe."
    Jennifer Harper sits in a lawn chair in the shade
of a weeping willow tree. A tire swing hangs from one
of the lower branches. She's pretty in an unadorned
fashion. Little makeup. No jewelry. Shoulder-length
chestnut hair. But she looks and sounds tired.
    "We really wanted to raise Lucas in a small town.
Somewhere he could play outside after dark and walk to
his friends' houses." She laughs without humor. "He loves
it here . . . but I'm not sure we'll be able to stay."
    The video blurs as it's fast-forwarded—and then
abruptly stops.
    "What was my husband like?"
    She repeats the question in almost a whisper. The
camera slowly creeps closer on her face. The wrinkles
around her eyes deepen as she stares at something
off-screen we can't see.
```

"He was funny and sweet . . . clumsy and forgetful . . . . He loved to give us gifts. Everyone, really." The hint of a smile. "We'd be in bed at night reading and some ridiculous commercial would come on television. He'd grab his wallet from the nightstand and start calling the 800 number on the TV. I'd look at him like he was crazy and he'd laugh and say, 'Hey, my sister needs a knife that cuts through tin cans.' Or 'What could possibly be cooler than a fishing rod that folds up and fits inside your pocket? Lucas will love it.' And you know what? He was usually right."

She clears her throat. "Chase was a wonderful father. These last few years, he traveled a lot. And even when he was home, he'd often get phone calls from the office. Sometimes, that can be difficult . . . finding a balance between work and family life." A shake of her head. "But he never had that problem. He'd get up early to work or stay up late if he needed to. Whatever it took to have enough time with Lucas. Chase coached his Little League team and—"

A blur as the video once again fast-forwards.

". . . will sound weird, but I feel him sometimes. His spirit . . . or maybe his presence would be a better word for it. It'll be a muggy and still afternoon, like today, and suddenly there'll be a cool breeze on my face where there shouldn't have been one. There and gone, like a quick kiss on the cheek. Other times, I'll feel a touch at the small of my back, right where he always used to put his hand when we were walking in a crowd. One morning, when I was getting out of the shower, I could've sworn I heard him whisper my name . . ."

The screen blurs for several seconds, then stops.

"He'd been having trouble sleeping before the accident. I asked him several times if there was anything bothering him . . ." She looks away as a train whistle sounds in the distance. It's a forlorn sound that matches the expression on her face. "It was . . . odd. Usually, he slept like a baby. I tried to talk him into getting a hotel room that night, but he wouldn't listen. He wanted to get home to—"

Another blur. Longer this time. And then it finally halts.

"Chase's sister, Nancy, started the memorial. The morning of the funeral—it was six weeks ago yesterday, as a matter of fact—she stopped on her way to the church and tied a ribbon on the tree. Later that afternoon, a neighbor from down the street made the cross in his garage workshop. A lot of people brought flowers. They still do. Every day, there are fresh ones. I go there a lot. Usually while Lucas is at a friend's house or during his swimming lessons at the Y. I feel closer to my husband there . . ."

20

Sudbury hadn't changed much since I'd left for college.

It honestly never did. And why would it? If you looked up "small-town America" in the encyclopedia, I'm pretty sure you'd find an aerial photograph of my hometown. And this is what you'd see: A shop-lined Main Street where the Fourth of July parade was held every summer. Red-white-and-blue bunting draped over light poles and telephone lines and front porch railings. Across the street, a wandering stone pathway threading its way through a park with a grassy slope for picnics and flying kites, a covered bandstand and a playground, and the requisite statue of a not-so-famous Civil War general. Bordering the park, a series of ball fields, numbered one through five on painted wooden signs hanging from chain-link backstops. Just beyond the outfield of Field Five, a lake where children sailed homemade boats made of balsa wood and fished alongside retirees for sunnies and yellow perch and catfish. Running parallel to the business district—if you could even call it that—were several blocks of single homes, most of them built around the time of the Second World War. The houses and lawns were neat and well tended. The cars and trucks in the driveways American-made. To the north and the east, farm fields and barns and grazing cows as far as the eye could see. To the west, the river and the railroad tracks and a single dead-end street lined with derelict buildings and shanties where trash can fires burned day and night and where the locals knew better than to linger after sundown.

It was 8:43 p.m. by the time we crossed over the town limits. The streetlights were just beginning to turn on. A stray dog padded down the sidewalk in front of the Western Auto. At the corner of Alden and Rayburn, a young couple pushing a baby carriage waited to cross the street. In the Scoop and Serve parking lot, teenage boys rode bicycles and skateboards, trying to impress their girlfriends. The homemade ice cream shop had been one of my favorite hangouts when I'd lived here. The sight of all those kids made me think of what Jennifer Harper had told us earlier—about her and her husband wanting their boy to grow up in a town where he could play outside after dark.

Following my back seat directions, Melody drove us past Sudbury High School and across the old stone bridge before looping around and making a left onto Broadway, where my Aunt Helen lived. When I was eight years old, my Uncle Frank died from liver cancer. Barely four months from diagnosis to funeral, it ate him alive. I could still remember what he smelled like at the end. Like spoiled meat. I'd spent the next year of my life terrifyingly certain that any day now I was going to lose either my mother or my father to the Big C. I even checked out a book about cancer from the school library. As it turned out, fate had other, more perverse plans in mind for my parents, and they didn't involve a life-threatening illness of any kind.

After Uncle Frank passed away, everyone expected Helen, a year younger than him and a notorious life of the party, to move on to someplace faster and more exciting. Philly or Baltimore, maybe even the Big Apple. Instead, she surprised us all by sticking around and taking on a full-time job at the local library. With Uncle Frank gone, I think she couldn't bear to leave my mom. For as long as I could remember, they were more than just sisters; they were best friends.

Aunt Helen's house on Broadway—the same one in which she'd lived all those years with my uncle—was located atop a gently sloping hill that was a stone's toss away from the exact center point of town. My father once showed me a map of Sudbury upon which he'd drawn a circle around the property where Aunt Helen's house stood. It looked like the bull's-eye on a dartboard.

A hundred-and-sixty-year-old two-story farmhouse with a wide wrap-around porch and a white picket fence out front, it was the kind of majestic home you saw featured in antique-shop watercolor paintings. The porch and fence were the only modern additions. For the past decade, my Aunt Helen's constant companion had been an ill-mannered poodle named Tucker. When I was growing up, I'd spent countless summer afternoons chasing that irascible mutt around the several-acre expanse of swampy woodland that bordered the old firehouse down the street. More often than not, I came back covered in ticks and mud and thorn thistle, a filthy and stinking Tucker squirming in my arms, licking the sweat from my face. After nearly a decade of such wanderings, and several close calls with speeding cars, Aunt Helen finally hired someone to put up the fence.

After my parents' accident, I moved in with my aunt for the remainder of the summer—by then, she'd been widowed going on nine years—and remained there throughout my final year of high school. I often woke in the morning with Tucker curled at my feet at the bottom of the bed. Aunt Helen claimed that he could tell I was sad and was watching over me. Before long, I began to believe her. Wherever I went in the house, that old dog followed. If I took a shower, he would be waiting outside the bathroom door when I was finished. If I did my homework at the dining room table, he'd fall asleep at my feet. Sometimes, right on *top* of my feet. If I was watching a movie, he'd hop up on the sofa and lie down a few feet away from me, then slowly inch his way closer, and closer, until finally his head was resting in my lap. After a while, I began taking him to the park to chase birds and swim in the pond. Sometimes, we'd hop in the car and go for long drives with no destination. Windows down. Radio up. His little head poking out the driver's-side window, those floppy ears of his catching the wind and taking flight like furry little kites.

Last April, I'd received a two-page letter in my dorm mailbox from Aunt Helen letting me know that Tucker had died in his sleep. She'd buried him in the backyard underneath his favorite shade tree. She'd thought I would want to know, since the two of us had gotten so close. After I finished reading it, I'd slid the letter back into the envelope, stashed it in the top drawer of my desk, and walked to the local bars and got blackout drunk. Back then, it was the only thing that helped.

It was a few minutes past nine when we drove by her house. The porch light and the windows were dark. Not even the flickering glow of the television from my aunt's second-floor bedroom at the end of the hallway. I closed my eyes and pictured her there, alone in the dark, dressed in gym shorts and one of her old T-shirts, curled up beneath a blanket, dreaming about Uncle Frank and old Tucker. I'd spoken with her on the phone yesterday afternoon, and she was expecting the three of us for breakfast in the morning. It hadn't been that long since the last time I'd seen her, but I was looking forward to catching up.

I thought about asking Melody to cruise past my ex-girlfriend's house on Cedar Lane and my parents' old split-level on Bayberry—the house in which I'd grown up—but decided that could wait until tomorrow. Maybe it wouldn't be quite so depressing in the daylight.

21

"I think it looks pretty damn good," Troy said, standing back to admire our handiwork.

When we'd first pulled into the campground, Troy's apprehension was immediate and palpable. He'd exited the van, taken a good, long look at the surrounding woods, and promptly announced, "*All this* nothing *makes me nervous as hell.*"

I'd laughed and called him a city slicker and opened the back of the van to retrieve the tent. As usual, Melody was a bit more thoughtful. She'd put her arm around him and patiently explained that there were dozens of other campsites just like ours, spread out in the dark all around us. We were far from alone. From the look on Troy's face, I couldn't tell if that made him feel better or worse.

The van was parked in a cleared-out section of trees deep in the heart of the campground. A small wooden sign reading SITE #14 guarded the narrow entrance. The side door of the van had been slid wide open and the tent had been set up perpendicular to the opening. The tent's nylon ceiling was attached to the roof of the van with a series of padded metal clamps so that it joined together to form a single enclosed T-shaped structure. We'd learned about the setup from an outdoor lifestyle magazine article.

"I don't know," I said, prodding the side of the tent with my hand. "A good stiff breeze or passing rainstorm, and the whole thing's likely to come down on our heads."

Melody walked by carrying a lantern and swatted my shoulder. "Stop teasing him." She smiled at Troy. "You'll be just fine."

"I hope so," Troy said. He walked over to the stone-ringed firepit and sat down on one of a half-dozen tree stumps that had been arranged in a wide circle. He picked up a twig and began poking at the glowing embers. The flames quickly grew, casting flickering shadows on the nearby trees. Behind him, resting on a blanket of pine needles a safe distance away from the fire, a pair of Coleman coolers sat side by side.

The plan was for Melody to sleep solo in the van. With most of the gear unloaded, the back seats folded down into a reasonably comfortable bunk. Troy and I would crash in sleeping bags inside the tent. It all promised to be quite an adventure. I hadn't been camping since I was a kid, and Troy had confided in us earlier that he'd only seen tents and campfires on television and in Patterson Park, where great numbers of Baltimore's homeless population congregated.

Melody skirted past us again on her way back to the van, where she began rearranging the bags of groceries. After all the driving she'd done today, I was impressed by her high energy and cheerful mood. She was even humming. A tune I didn't recognize. I watched her work for a moment longer and then went over and grabbed a couple of beers from the cooler. I tossed one to Troy and sat down on the stump next to him.

"Writing your folks?"

He looked up from the missive he was scribbling on. "I thought I'd get a postcard from each of the campgrounds we stay at. That way they can track our progress."

"That's a great idea," I said, cracking open my beer. "They'll like that."

Now that I was feeling better, I was no longer wary of enjoying the occasional adult beverage. I was still steering clear of the bar scene and hadn't stopped in at the corner liquor store near my apartment in months, but that was due more to my renewed social life with Melody and Troy than any real fear of a relapse. Dr. Mirarchi had assured me that the occasional beer or two wasn't going to cause any harm. Even on top of the daily antidepressant I'd started taking back in February. I wasn't sure if the meds were helping me or not, but after what'd happened at Christmas—my aunt now referred to it as "the incident"—I was more than willing to give it a try.

"You know I was just yanking your chain earlier. Our setup's good to go." I took a sip and gazed up at the stars through a break in the trees. "Clear skies overhead and no sign of Bigfoot anywhere."

Troy didn't even crack a smile. "I was afraid we'd be all alone out here." Capering reflections from the flames of the fire painted the lenses of his glasses orange and yellow and transformed his Afro into a dark halo. "I'll be perfectly honest . . . I'm really glad we're not." He sounded much younger than his eighteen years.

"Pretty far out of your comfort zone?"

"I can't even *see* my comfort zone from here."

"Take a deep breath," I said, echoing my counselor's frequent advice. "Think of it like this . . . a few months ago, the three of us were complete strangers." I gestured all around us. "Now we're the Three Musketeers, sitting around a blazing campfire in the middle of nowhere, far, far away from school, breathing clean air and drinking beer under the stars. I'd say we've got it pretty good."

He didn't say anything for a while. Just stared straight ahead into the fire.

Finally, he spoke in a quiet voice: "I don't have many friends."

I looked at him. "I know that. I don't either . . . not anymore."

"Do you ever miss them?"

I picked up a pine cone from the ground and tossed it into the flames. "Not as much as I thought I would."

"Why do you think that is?"

"After the accident . . . everything was different. *Everyone* was different. After a while, I realized *I* was too. It was almost like, I don't know . . . we became strangers overnight."

"That's . . . sad."

"That's life," I said with a shrug.

He gazed up at the stars. "You know who would love it out here?"

"Who?"

"My mom. She's always complaining about how noisy the city is."

"Well, then you should take her camping this summer." I gave his shoulder a nudge. "All you need is a tent."

"Would you come with us?"

I smiled in the darkness. "As long as she brings some of those homemade peanut butter cookies she sends you."

"You know what? You're right," he said, sitting up straight and nodding his head. "We do. Have it pretty good, I mean." He raised his beer. "Thanks for reminding me of that."

We clinked cans and took a drink.

"Now will you tell me where you got that cute little safari outfit you're wearing?"

A sigh. "Eat shit, Billy."

"Does the bandanna make you feel like a pirate?"

"Go fuck yourself."

Giggling, I drank what was left of my beer.

22

"I wonder who invented s'mores."

Troy paused in midbite and looked over at Melody. "I'd imagine some eight-year-old in his backyard." He shoved what was left of the graham cracker into his mouth and licked a glob of melted marshmallow off his fingers. His chin and cheeks were smeared with the sticky mess. From where I was sitting, it looked like he was wearing a fake beard.

It was late, nearly midnight, and the fire was dying. A chill had crept into the air. All three of us were exhausted. Whereas earlier in the night had been filled with spirited conversation—the highlight being when Melody and Troy got into an argument involving quantum physics that somehow evolved into a discussion of alien life-forms—no one had spoken for at least the last ten or fifteen minutes. I was pretty sure I'd been dozing off when Melody asked about s'mores.

"Well, whoever it was," she said, "I'd sure like to thank them."

Troy yawned. "Tent be damned, I'm going to sleep like a log tonight."

The yawn proved contagious, and Melody let loose with one of her own. When she was finished, she said, "Hey, question. What did you start to say earlier this morning . . . about having nightmares?"

Troy took a moment to answer. "It started . . . I don't know, when I was a kid." A look of embarrassment flashed across his face. "I thought I'd finally outgrown it when I got to college, away from home and everything, but then my roommate told me I'd been crying out in my sleep."

"Do you remember the dreams?" I asked.

"Yes," he said, "and no."

"What does that mean?"

"I remember . . . you know, parts of them." No one said anything, so he continued. "It's always the same thing. I'm being chased in the dark. Sometimes, I'm inside a house. A basement, I think, with no windows. Other times, I'm outside, in a park or maybe just some woods. I can see buildings off in the distance, but they're too far to run to." He lifted his beer to his mouth, but the can was empty. He placed it on the ground at his feet. "I never see who's chasing me, but I can hear their footsteps and hear them breathing. I try to hide, but they always find me. I hear this awful laughter, and then I see hands reaching for me out of the darkness. And that's when I wake up."

"And these are recurring dreams?" Melody asked. She looked horrified.

"Yes."

"For how long?"

"Ever since I was little."

"That's insane," she murmured.

"Has anything like that ever really happened to you?" I asked.

"God no!" he said loud enough to hurt my ears. "Don't even say that. You'll jinx me."

Melody scooted closer and put a hand on his knee. "How often do you have them?"

He thought about it. "Maybe . . . once a month. It used to be much more often."

"You poor thing. That's just awful."

"I've done all the research," he said. "They're probably just stress dreams, to be honest . . . a manifestation of all the pressure I put on myself . . . but, God, they feel so real."

"Just so you know," I said with a smirk, "if you wake up screaming, I'm liable to piss my pants and—"

Troy jerked his head around and stared off into the trees behind us. "Did you hear that?"

I followed his gaze. Melody did the same. The woods beyond the firelight were pitch-dark—and silent. "Hear what?" she asked.

"It sounded like . . . branches breaking . . . like someone walking around."

I tilted my head and listened. "I don't hear anything."

"I don't either," he said after a moment. "Not anymore."

"Probably just an animal." Melody stood up and stretched her arms above her head. "A deer, maybe, or a rabbit."

Troy didn't look convinced. "Would have to be one big-ass rabbit."

"On that note . . ." I got to my feet and brushed the dirt from my jeans. "I'm going to use the bathroom and turn in for the night." I headed for a stand of overgrown brush not far from the van.

"Not without me, you're not," Troy said, hurrying to catch up.

23

"I'm telling you what I heard."

"I was right there, and I didn't hear anything."

"It was when I was waiting for you to finish. I'm not crazy."

"No one whispered your name, Troy."

"I heard it clear as day."

"It was your imagination."

"I didn't imagine it, Billy. I *heard* it."

"Maybe it was an owl."

"Smart fucking owl."

"Maybe you're related."

Fighting back a smile, he said, "You're such an asshole."

"And clean the marshmallow off your face. You look like Soul Train Santa Claus."

24

"I don't see it," Melody said, sliding the grocery bags out of the way. With the rear seat folded down, the storage area in the back of the van had been reduced by at least half. It was a mess, everything stacked on top of each other. "Are you sure you didn't move it somewhere else?"

I rolled my eyes at her. "Yes, I'm sure." I pushed aside a camera case and checked behind it. "It's fine. I'll find it in the morning. I can just sleep in my underwear."

"Troy?" she said, her voice raised. "Can you hear me?"

Muffled from inside the tent: "What's up?"

"Is Billy's knapsack in there?"

A brief pause, then: "Sure is. Right behind the lantern."

She turned and looked at me with a smug expression on her face.

I put my hands up. "I did not put it there."

"Troy?" she called out again.

"Yes?"

"Did you move Billy's knapsack?"

"Never touched it. Is something wrong?"

"Not a thing," she said, grinning now. "Sorry to bother you."

Mumbling, I started walking away.

"Hey, Billy."

I stopped and turned around, expecting more foolishness. But her smile had vanished.

"You going to be okay tomorrow?"

I thought about it. "Yeah . . . I think so."

"As far as I'm concerned, tomorrow's all about you and your mom and dad. You call the shots, okay?"

"Thanks," I said, my head—and heart—suddenly feeling very heavy. "Good night, Mel."

25

Leave it to Troy to cheer me up.

By the time I joined him inside the tent a few minutes later, he'd scrubbed the marshmallow off his face, changed clothes, and zipped himself into his sleeping bag. He was lying on his stomach, reading a textbook by the glow of the lantern.

"Really?" I said. "You're such a Boy Scout."

He didn't bother looking up. "Final exams in two weeks and this trip is wreaking havoc on my study schedule." He wet his finger with his tongue and turned the page. And began whistling. I recognized the tune immediately. The theme to *Star Wars*, his favorite movie. I could almost guarantee he had Luke Skywalker pajamas tucked away inside a drawer in his bedroom back at home.

"Umm . . . I wouldn't do that if I were you."

Now he looked up at me. "Do what?"

"Whistle."

"What are you talking about?"

"Appalachian folklore. If you whistle at night, it conjures up whatever spirits might be lurking nearby."

"You're lying."

"Swear. My Uncle Frank told me when I was a kid."

"Oh."

"It's only supposed to work if you're in the Appalachians . . . which I guess we kinda are? Close enough anyway."

He didn't say anything, but I could see the cogs turning inside that big brain of his. Finally, he pushed away the textbook and reached over to switch off the lantern. In the sudden darkness, I heard him roll onto his back.

"Nite, Troy."

"Good night."

I waited for about thirty or forty seconds—and then I began to whistle.

A sharp intake of breath from the other side of the tent.

I whistled a little louder.

And abruptly stopped.

A whisper in the dark: "Have I mentioned that you're really and truly an asshole, Billy?"

"Pretty sure you have."

"Okay, good. Just making sure."

26

Despite my exhaustion, sleep eluded me.

I lay on my back and stared at the ceiling of the tent, listening to Troy's snoring. It had an almost melodic tone to it, like someone softly humming in the dark. On any other night, I might have found it comforting. But not tonight. I was too creeped out.

Twice now, I'd heard what sounded like branches breaking somewhere close by. The second time I was almost certain I heard footsteps. Slow and stealthy, like someone skulking around our campsite. And then I'd seen the ripple of a shadow on the side of the tent. There and gone in a matter of seconds. I was tempted to call out or switch on the lantern so whoever it was knew I was awake, but I didn't want to rouse the others. Especially if I was imagining the whole damn thing.

Thanks, Troy. First, you spooked yourself. And now you've got me spooked. It wasn't like me to let that kind of nonsense get inside my head. Hell, I liked being scared. Stephen King books. Horror movies. *Creature Double Feature* on TV. I ate that stuff up.

Or maybe it was my fault—and I shouldn't have teased Troy about whistling. I'd been telling the truth, as far as I knew it—Uncle Frank really had told me that story when I was little—but it was still kind of mean. Especially on our first night in the middle of nowhere.

Appalachian folklore was full of bizarre superstitions like that. If you pricked your finger on the night of a full moon, someone you loved would soon die. An uneven number of eggs in the henhouse foreshadowed imminent danger. A broom falling for no reason was bad luck. As was a rabbit crossing your path before sunrise. And my all-time favorite: if a pregnant woman saw a falling star on her birthday, the baby would be born evil. None of it grounded in reality, of course—I mean, come on.

As sleep continued to evade me, I found myself blaming it on the little boy with the missing front teeth. No matter how hard I tried, I couldn't get his dirt-smudged face out of my mind. Like he was haunting me.

And there was something else too.

I hadn't said anything to the others about the bizarre incident that had taken place at Chase Harper's memorial—but it had been nibbling away at the edges of my brain all evening. At first, I'd tried to pass it off as nothing more than an overreaction on my part. I'd been alone when it happened. Mentally exhausted from taking photographs and filming. The stretch of road where the memorial was located had been as quiet as a graveyard. Something buried deep inside my subconscious had reached up and goosed me when I least expected it.

Later, I'd blamed it on an allergic reaction of some kind. I remembered my father used to get shots twice a month for grass pollen and mold spores and something else I couldn't remember. Growing up, I'd always been fine, but maybe some type of allergies were catching up with me? I guess it was possible.

But then we'd driven to Jennifer Harper's house and recorded our interview in the backyard—and something she'd said about her dead husband had struck a nerve.

I feel him sometimes. His spirit . . . or maybe his presence would be a better word for it. It'll be a muggy and still afternoon, like today, and suddenly there'll be a cool breeze on my face where there shouldn't have been one. There and gone, like a quick kiss on the cheek. Other times, I'll feel a touch at the small of my back, right where he always used to put his hand when we were walking in a crowd.

I'd sat there on the edge of the picnic table, holding the camera steady, and remembered the ice-cold breath I'd felt on the back of my neck—and the feeling of absolute certainty that someone had been standing right behind me.

A presence.

DAY TWO
SATURDAY | MAY 7

1

We were five minutes early for breakfast.

Aunt Helen, dressed in baggy gym shorts and a flannel shirt with the sleeves rolled up, greeted us at the door. It didn't matter one bit that this was her first time meeting Melody and Troy. They each got big hugs. I also got kisses on both of my cheeks and forehead. Then, not wasting another minute and already apologizing for the messy condition of her house, she ushered us into the dining room. I stopped in the doorway, staring in disbelief. She had prepared a feast. Scrambled eggs and hotcakes. Bacon and sausage and thick slabs of country ham. Wheat toast and croissants smeared with butter. Fresh strawberries topped with homemade whipped cream.

"You know it's just the three of us, right?" I said, laughing. "We didn't bring along the entire class."

Smiling, she shushed me and told us to take our seats at the table. Once we did, she bowed her head and gave a quick blessing—and then it was time to eat. The mouthwatering aroma and taste of the food along with the steady hum of lively conversation brought back a flood of pleasant memories from my childhood. I found myself grinning and watching the others as I ate.

Growing up, back when my parents and Uncle Frank were still alive, we'd often shared Sunday brunch here at the house after church services at St. Ignatius let out. My mom and her sister took turns doing the cooking. If the weather was warm enough, we usually ate outside in the yard. Dad and Uncle Frank would talk baseball and fishing. Mom and Aunt Helen would trade good-natured gossip. Neighbors often stopped by and joined in on the fun. There was always more than enough food to go around. Father Paul from Saint Iggy, as the kids around here had jokingly called it since time out of mind, was a regular attendee at these family gatherings, something for which my mother seemed particularly proud. She'd been considerably less enamored with the long-standing weekly poker game in which Father Paul and Uncle Frank both participated. Short and round and bearing a striking resemblance to Friar Tuck of Sherwood Forest—especially while wearing his robe during mass—the jovial priest once scarfed down eleven of Aunt Helen's pancakes in a single sitting. Not because he was starving or being a glutton, but because Uncle Frank had bet him he couldn't.

"I wish you all had spent the night here with me," my aunt said, passing a platter of bacon, "instead of some nasty old tent."

"It's a brand-new tent," I said, "and thanks, but camping out is an important part of the project."

"I vote for staying here if there's a next time," Troy said, shoveling another forkful of eggs into his mouth. He was wearing the same matching khaki shorts and button-down shirt from yesterday. The red bandanna was once again looped around his neck. He looked ridiculous.

"I still don't know why you want to traipse around the countryside looking for those things." She reached over and gave my arm a squeeze. "I mean, of course, I understand, honey. I get what you're doing and everything, and why it's important to you. But it's just so . . . depressing. I think you should be looking for things that make you happy instead."

We'd had this conversation many times before. I knew that she was worried about me. "Getting an A on this project would make me pretty darn happy." *And hopefully balance out the B- I'm most likely getting in statistics*—but I didn't say that part out loud.

She rolled her eyes at me. "What about you two?" And looked across the table at Melody and Troy. "You on board with all this?"

Melody nodded. "Yes, ma'am. I believe it's important to bring increased awareness to these roadside memorials, especially now that some local administrations are trying to do away with them."

"Our intentions go above and beyond earning a good class grade," Troy said, giving me a snooty look. "If our collective vision is properly realized, the documentary will serve as an important reminder that grief is universal. If we're lucky, the powers that be at school will submit it to film festivals all around the country. Maybe even the world."

Aunt Helen considered that for a moment. "And how do you plan to get your background information about the people who died? To tell their stories, I mean. As much as we may wish otherwise, the dead tell no tales."

Much like the town of Sudbury, my Aunt Helen never changed. She was as crudely practical as ever. She'd lost more than anyone—a husband, a sister, and a brother-in-law, not to mention old Tucker—and all within the span of a decade. But she was a tough cookie, and believed the hard truth of it was this: there wasn't a single thing you could do to change the past. Unlike in books and movies, time machines and alternate realities didn't exist in the real world. Eventually, you just had to swallow your misery, accept what had happened, and let go of the past. Like grains of sand sifting through your fingers at the beach.

All of which—at least for me—was a whole lot easier said than done.

"We're mostly traveling backroads," I told her, "so picture small towns like Sudbury where everyone knows each other." I thought of our favorite gas station attendant from the night before. "And if we can't find a bystander to talk to us, we'll pay a visit to the local newspaper office or police station."

"Or even the library," Melody added.

My aunt looked at Melody in surprise. "Ohhhh, of *course*. I should've thought of that. Our microfiche files for the *Sudbury Sun* contain exactly the type of information you'd be looking for."

"All it takes is finding that one person who knows the story," Troy said, his magnified eyes sparkling with excitement. "Whether we uncover it in a newspaper article or by talking to someone we just met at a grocery store or one of the officers who worked the accident scene . . ."

"It's almost as if you're on a scavenger hunt," Aunt Helen said, beginning to grasp the bigger picture. "A scavenger hunt for memories."

"That's a pretty cool way to describe it," I said.

"Still . . . I worry about the three of you being on the road by yourselves. You're heading into the heart of Appalachia. Some of those folks aren't exactly the friendliest. And they're not real keen on outsiders."

"I tried to tell him that," Troy said. "So did Professor Tyree." He shook his head. "But you know Billy . . ."

"Boy do I," she said, laughing.

"Don't listen to him, Aunt Helen. We watched *Deliverance* last week, and he's been a nervous wreck ever since."

Troy nodded. "I hear a banjo twanging and I'm outta there."

2

On my way to the bathroom after breakfast, I stopped in the family room to look at my aunt's collection of Hummel figurines. I wasn't entirely sure, but it appeared that she'd added a couple more pieces since my last visit. In the front row, there was one I didn't recognize—a young boy pushing a wheelbarrow. There had to be at least thirty or forty of the miniature porcelain statues arranged on the glass shelves of the curio cabinet—including my aunt's longtime favorite, a pair of pink-cheeked girls in pigtails huddled beneath a mushroom-shaped umbrella. My mom had given it to her one year for Christmas.

For as long as I could remember, Aunt Helen had been obsessed with the German-made figurines. She had an I ♥ HUMMEL magnet on her refrigerator door and even belonged to a collector's club that sent out a quarterly magazine. My Uncle Frank used to tease Helen about her unusual hobby, claiming it was barely a step up from playing with dolls. That was one of the few times I'd disagreed with him—although I never said so out loud. Especially after the "doll" comment. When I was a kid, I'd been fascinated by the idea that the statues were made halfway around the world. It wasn't like walking into town and buying a pack of baseball cards from Plaza Drugs. It was so much more *exotic* than that. Each time a new figure arrived in the mail, I begged my aunt to tell me everything about it. *What year was it made? How much did it cost? Where did you order it from?* And, of course, the million-dollar question for any curious eight-year-old boy: *Can I hold it?*

Grinning at the memories, I made my way around the sofa and headed for the hallway that led to the first-floor bathroom. Halfway there, a photograph hanging on the wall above the end table caught my attention. It was a ten-by-twelve black-and-white print of my Uncle Frank's high school basketball team. I walked over and stopped in front of it. A teenage Frank was standing on the second row of the bleachers—sandwiched in between two giants, each of them at least five or six inches taller than him—wearing a number ten sleeveless jersey. Back in January, on New Year's Day, I'd helped my aunt hang it, switching out a photo with a broken frame of Uncle Frank standing over a glazed-eyed four-point buck. She'd never liked that one very much.

Something about the old basketball photo had intrigued me from the first time I'd laid eyes on it—and I once again found myself studying it with an almost feverish intensity. *Is it Uncle Frank's face filled with such youthful innocence? The ill-fitting uniforms and funny-looking sneakers? The downright tragic haircuts?* I honestly had no idea. All I knew was that there was something about the picture that made my brain itch. Maybe my aunt could help me put my finger on it. I would have to remember to ask her later.

Then again, maybe that itch was just a sugar high from the four glasses of orange juice I'd drank at breakfast, also working overtime on my bladder. I gave up trying to solve the mystery and made a beeline for the bathroom.

3

When I came back from washing my hands, Melody was standing in the middle of the family room, staring up at the photographs on the wall. I tried to slip quietly past her, but she was too quick.

"I didn't know you were such a big shot." She nodded at the array of photos of me in my football and basketball uniforms.

"It's a pretty big stretch to say I was a big shot."

She pointed at a framed newspaper clipping on the opposite wall. "That one says you were All-County cornerback. Three years in a row."

I shrugged. "It's a small county."

"Since when did you become so modest?"

"Since never. I'm just being honest. I wasn't *that* good."

Gesturing to a wedding picture in the corner, she said, "So I guess that's your Uncle Frank?"

"Actually . . . that's my parents."

"Oh, wow," she said. "Your mom and aunt could be twins."

"People used to say that all the time." I pointed at a pair of smaller photographs centered above the end table. "*That's* Uncle Frank on the boat holding the fish." I moved over and tapped the glass protecting the second photo. "This is his high school basketball team. They won regionals that year. He's the one with the big ears in the second row." Once again, my gaze lingered on the photo. Dammit. It felt like the reason for my fascination was hiding just out of view.

"Look at those teeny-tiny shorts," Melody said, leaning closer for a better look. "And big ears or not, your uncle was a cutie."

"My uncle was a piece of work."

"Just like his nephew." She looked around to make sure we were still alone. "How's it feel to be home again?"

"Weird," I said. "It feels weird." She and Troy knew nothing about "the incident" that had occurred during Christmas break and the couple of weeks I'd spent here afterward. I still wasn't entirely sure why I hadn't told them. Most likely, it was shame.

"Your Aunt Helen's pretty amazing." She patted her swollen belly. "That breakfast was incredible."

"She's the best."

Melody's gaze returned to the photos on the wall. Lowering her voice, she asked, "She never had any kids?"

"They tried . . . but there were problems. Eventually, they gave up."

My aunt's laughter rang out from the other room.

"*Wait, wait*," Troy said, practically screaming. "*This one's even better!*"

"Oh, shit," Melody said. "I think he's telling jokes."

"*A lawyer, a pelican, and a jazz musician walk into a bar . . .*"

"C'mon," I said, already heading for the dining room. "We need to save her."

4

Placing the dirty dishes into the sink, I took a closer look at my Aunt Helen.

A few more wrinkles on her face, and maybe an additional streak or two of gray in her hair, but I thought she looked great. Her eyes still carried that familiar spark of youthful sassiness, and her morning walks and long stints in the garden had kept her in fine shape for a woman in her mid-fifties.

When I'd lived here at the house, I used to daydream—actually, daydreaming sounds like such a pleasant activity, which this most definitely was not; it was more like having a waking nightmare—that Aunt Helen was dying from some insipid disease. Her hair falling out and her organs slowly decaying as I watched helplessly from her bedside. Fortunately, those tortured thoughts had gone away once I'd left for college. They'd eventually made an encore appearance after I received my aunt's letter telling me that Tucker had died, but only for a short time. I hadn't even thought about those visions in months.

I circled back to the dining room to retrieve more dishes, and when I returned to the kitchen a few minutes later—this time cradling four empty juice glasses and an antique butter tray—a sudden burst of sunshine flashed through the window above the sink, illuminating my aunt's face like a priceless painting hanging in a museum.

Mouth agape, nearly dropping the glasses, I stopped in my tracks and stared.

Melody was right.

In the spear of golden sunlight, Aunt Helen looked exactly like my mother.

5

As I stood in the doorway to my old bedroom, I could hear the others talking outside in the backyard. The windows were open, a cool morning breeze rustling the curtains. At some point during the past few months, my aunt had hung up new ones. The old curtains had been thick and heavy and functionally plain, primarily designed to keep the sunlight out. These were nearly transparent and decorated in an intricate floral pattern.

I scanned the room for other changes.

Single bed tucked in the corner. Desk centered beneath one of the two windows. Narrow dresser. Bookshelf (more trophies on the shelves than books). Clothes hamper. Trash can. On the wall above the bed, posters of Pittsburgh Steelers wide receiver Lynn Swann and the 76ers Julius Erving. Hanging slightly crooked between the windows, a framed *Animal House* movie poster.

Reminding myself to breathe, I stepped inside. From the day of the accident until my final night of summer break before leaving for college, I'd slept here. I'd done my homework at the desk and daily sit-ups and push-ups on the hardwood floor. I'd dreamed of my dead mother and father while tossing and turning in the queen-sized bed.

I picked up a football from on top of the dresser—SUDBURY 34, EVANSVILLE 14 printed across its pebbled surface—and realized something. Melody had called this place my home, but it no longer felt that way. Most everything *looked* familiar, but none of it actually *felt* that way. Not anymore. Instead, it was like trespassing. It had only been four months since I'd last slept here, but in that relatively brief amount of time, I'd become a stranger to the most recent place in the world I'd considered my home. The realization didn't make me feel sad or angry or lost. A little numb, maybe, but that was all.

Laughter erupted in the backyard. I walked to the window and looked outside. Aunt Helen was giving Melody and Troy a tour of her vegetable garden. Earlier at breakfast, she'd taken an instant—and inexplicable—liking to Troy. First, she'd complimented his Afro (which was actually understandable; it *was* pretty glorious). But then she'd gone completely off the rails—peppering him with wide-eyed question after question about what it was like growing up in the city, heaping praise on his ridiculous outfit (and scolding me when I'd insisted that he looked like the Man with the Yellow Hat from *Curious George*), and even giggling like a schoolgirl at his selection of lame jokes. If I hadn't known better, I would've sworn she had a crush on the little cartoon owl.

MEMORIALS

The final straw came when she'd invited Troy to join her in the library to see her prized collection of rare Mark Twain books. Not even a mention of me or Melody coming along. Troy had flashed me that tight-lipped look of satisfaction I knew so well and said, "Why, I would love to." And then he'd stood and offered Aunt Helen his arm. "Shall we?" Melody had kicked me under the table and made a gagging gesture as we watched them disappear into the next room.

In the backyard, my Aunt Helen squealed with laughter. When she finally quieted, I heard Troy's high-pitched voice followed by more giggling. Frowning, I turned away from the window without even bothering to investigate what it was they'd found so damn funny.

I walked to the desk, slid the chair out of the way—its gray cloth padding still stained purple from a late-night grape soda spill several years earlier—and pulled open the top drawer. Inside was a jumble of pens and pencils, most of the latter in desperate need of sharpening, as well as a tangled mess of staples, rubber bands, and paper clips. In one corner, a small metal box housing my Uncle Frank's red, white, and blue plastic poker chips. There was also a single sheet of paper. A pop quiz from senior-year chemistry. Mr. Holland's class. A *72* was written at the top in red ink. I had no memory of why I'd held on to it.

I pushed the drawer shut and opened the one right beneath it. Empty. Not even a stray thumbtack or dust devil hiding in the corner. I closed it and absently slid open the bottom drawer. Resting inside was a piece of my childhood—the first 35mm camera I'd ever owned. A starter-kit Pentax my parents had given me as a birthday present the year I turned twelve. My father had patiently shown me how to work the manual focus and how to read the light. He'd taught me about shutter speed and filters and taken me on field trips to the park and the river so I could practice. Dad was the reason I'd fallen in love with photography all those years ago.

After the accident, I'd put away my cameras—by then I was using a Nikon I'd saved up for with my lawn-cutting profits—and did my best to forget they'd ever existed. It was just too painful of a reminder. The black-and-white prints I'd hung on my bedroom walls went out with the trash. The second-place plaque I'd won in the *Sudbury Sun*'s annual Fourth of July photo contest went right along with them. If it wasn't for Dr. Mirarchi, I probably never would've picked up a camera again. I most definitely wouldn't be shooting a documentary. But in one of our early sessions, when I'd broken down about it all, she'd suggested that I give it another try. *"Just go at your own pace and see how it feels,"* she told me in that soothing voice of hers. *"It may prove therapeutic. Heck, it may even be fun. Don't lose that part of yourself that gave you happiness, no matter how it makes you feel in the moment. You just may surprise yourself."* And I'll be damned if she hadn't been right. I think that's the moment I really began to trust her.

Movement outside the window caught my eye. Leaning across the desk, I nudged aside the curtains. The side yard of my aunt's next-door neighbor's house appeared much smaller than I remembered. There had once been a birdbath there, surrounded by a bed of flowers, but now they were gone. Grass had been planted, and a wooden bench and flagpole had taken the birdbath's place. A few yards away, on the sidewalk at the end of the neighbor's driveway, a little girl rode by on a bright pink bicycle with tassels dangling from the handlebars. I watched as she pedaled away and disappeared down the street. Not far behind her, a long-haired man dressed all in black hurried along the sidewalk. *The little girl's father trying to catch up? The lead singer from Journey on his way to a gig at the Scoop and Serve? Stranger danger?*

Before I could give it any more thought, Melody called my name from downstairs. I turned away from the window and started toward the hallway—

And stopped in midstride.

Backtracking to the closet, I pulled open the double doors and dropped to a knee. There were a half-dozen or so shoeboxes stacked along the floor. Remembering, I carefully slid out a dark blue box with the Converse logo stamped on the side of it.

I opened the lid.

And my breath caught in my throat.

Moving slowly, as if in a dream, I took the object from inside the box and slipped it into the front pocket of my jeans.

Then I carefully returned the shoebox to its original position and went downstairs to join the others.

6

VIDEO FOOTAGE
(10:32 a.m., Saturday, May 7, 1983)

```
"The day it happened . . . that horrible accident . . .
I was sick in bed with a summer cold."
   Helen Abbott, midfifties, dressed in jeans and a
chambray shirt, brown hair streaked with random strands
of gray, sits inside a screened-in porch. Her legs are
crossed, as are her arms. She looks uncomfortable.
That's the first thing you notice about her. The second:
her blue eyes are sparkling pools of liquid. She's on
the verge of tears.
   "That's why I didn't hear the phone ring or the
police knocking at my door. The cough medicine I'd
taken had knocked me out. That's why they tracked you
down—even though you were a minor—and told you the
news first, instead of me."
   A muffled male voice from off-screen.
   "I'm sorry. I keep forgetting."
   The picture blurs as it fast-forwards—then stops
in midconversation.
   ". . . but then it kept growing. As more and more
people heard about what happened, they started show-
ing up at the accident site. Almost like they were
```

holding a vigil. Many of them brought flowers or candles or balloons . . . or some other sort of memento. Then someone put up that big sign and left a message on it, and everyone else started writing down their condolences too. Your parents . . . sorry, I did it again . . . Thomas and Lori Anderson . . . were very popular in the community. There was an overwhelming outpouring of love and sympathy."

"And the surviving family members . . ." Melody's voice off-camera. "Were they also frequent visitors at the memorial?"

"Well, there's only me and Billy. Locally, I mean." She wipes a stray tear from her cheek. "Tom's folks came for the funeral, of course. Along with his sister and a bunch of cousins. But it was pretty much just me from Lori's side of the family. We have an aunt and uncle out west in Oregon, but they're older and in poor health and weren't able to make the trip. They sent flowers instead."

She pulls a Kleenex from the pocket of her jeans and dabs her eyes. "At first, I found myself stopping at the memorial quite often. Usually on my way to the mall or a friend's house . . ." She looks down at her lap. ". . . but that didn't last very long. Too many times, other folks would see me there and stop and want to talk—and that was the last thing I wanted most days. After that, I started visiting the cemetery instead. It was much more peaceful there.

"But Billy was a different story." She pauses. And when she starts speaking again, she's no longer looking at the camera. "He went to the memorial . . . a lot. Sometimes two or three times in the same day. And often late at night. People would call and tell me they saw him. Or they'd stop me on the street. After the accident, it felt like half the town was in our business. Eventually, I said something to him. I told him . . . I didn't think it was healthy to spend so much time there. Especially not alone. And that his parents wouldn't want him to. I tried to get him to come along with me to the cemetery . . . but he wasn't interested. He said he felt closer to his mom and dad there by the woods . . . where they had passed . . ."

She chokes up and begins coughing into her hand. When she's finished, her face is bright red and she's staring directly into the camera. "I think we should stop now, Billy. I don't think I can—"

The screen goes dark.

7

"Now *that's* a spiffy-looking vehicle."

Aunt Helen and I stood in the shade of the front porch, staring at the van parked along the curb. It was still early, but the sun, just now peeking its head above the trees across the street, was already swelteringly hot. It felt like July instead of May. A few minutes earlier, Melody and Troy had excused themselves and walked down the hill to "reorganize the equipment"—which, I later realized, was actually Melody's not-so-subtle way of giving us some privacy. My aunt's eyes were still swollen and red from her emotional outburst during our interview earlier. After cutting it short, she'd disappeared upstairs for fifteen or twenty minutes while the rest of us stood around in the family room in mute dismay. There hadn't been much to say at that point. We'd all felt awful about what had happened, but no one more than me. Talking to my aunt on camera had been my idea—and I should've known better.

"Yes, sirree, she's a real beaut," Aunt Helen continued, giving a whistle and starting down the driveway.

I couldn't tell if she was being serious or a smart-ass—so I just nodded and followed after her.

"You guys won't stand out in hill country . . . at all."

Okey dokey, smart-ass it was.

"But hey, at least the hunters will see you coming."

"We weren't so concerned about appearance. We just wanted something reliable." I realized I sounded like Troy, but didn't care. I was just glad to have the old Aunt Helen back.

She stopped on the sidewalk and waited for me to catch up. "Weren't so concerned about appearance, huh?" She arched her eyebrows. "I guess that explains how you ended up with a giant pumpkin on wheels."

"Are you done?" I asked, doing my best to keep a straight face.

"Not quite," she said. "It looks like Charlie Brown's sweater."

So much for keeping a straight face.

"I hope it was cheap at least."

I let out a deep breath. "You don't even want to know."

"Here," she said, stepping forward and handing Troy a pair of brown paper bags. "I made you all some sandwiches for the road. There's also chocolate chip cookies and oatmeal cookies."

"You didn't have to do that, ma'am," Troy said, smiling. "But I'm sure glad you did." He peeked inside one of the bags, pulled out a cookie, and headed for the rear of the van. "I'm going to stash the sandwiches in the cooler for later. Thanks again!"

"Why'd you give it to *him*?" I asked, only half-joking. "My hands are empty."

"Oh, shush," she said. "He's skinnier than you." She opened her arms to me. "Now come here and give your favorite aunt a hug goodbye."

I squeezed her tight, and for just a fleeting moment it felt like I'd traveled back in time. It was the way she smelled. Familiar. Safe. That comforting blend of Aunt Helen's drugstore perfume, the laundry detergent she used to wash her clothes, and good old human sweat. I closed my eyes and breathed it in. Maybe this was what home really was. Maybe there actually was a time machine you could step into to journey back to happier days. You just had to remember how to find it. And hold on to it. I felt tears swell in my eyes.

"I'm sorry about before," she said, her face pressed against my shoulder. "I made a mess of—"

"Stop, please. You have absolutely nothing to be sorry about." I looked at her. "It was my fault. I never should've asked you to sit for an interview."

"I still think about them every day."

"Me too."

"I'm so proud of you, Billy."

Between my schoolwork and Dr. Mirarchi and the meds I was taking, things were finally heading in the right direction. "One day at a time, right?"

She stepped back and wiped her eyes. "Okay, enough of that." When she was finished, she looked up at me. "So, there's something else I want to tell you before you go."

Bracing myself for bad news—because ever since the accident, that's what I always did—I asked, "What is it?"

"I've . . ."

She began rubbing the cuff of her shirtsleeve with her fingertips. Growing up, I'd seen her do the exact same thing hundreds of times, usually while we were watching a particularly tense scene in a movie or when she was sitting in the bleachers at one of my ball games.

"I wanted to tell you during the holidays . . . but . . ."

"It's okay," I said. "Tell me now."

She let out a deep breath. "I've started seeing someone."

It took me a few seconds to figure out what she meant. By the time I did, she was off and rambling.

"I didn't mean for it to happen. Neither of us did. We started out as just friends for the longest time. I'd bump into him at the store or around town. We'd see each other at bingo at the fire hall, and we'd chat and swap stories, and that was it. Then a couple months ago . . . something changed. I'm still not entirely sure how it happened."

"That's . . . awesome!" I said. And I meant it. I could feel my smile growing. "Who is he? Do I know him?"

"I don't think so." There was relief in her eyes. Relief that she had finally told me, and relief that I had taken the news so well. And why wouldn't I? I loved Uncle Frank as much as anyone—as I knew my aunt always would—but he'd been gone for years now and she was still here. She deserved to be happy. "He works for the sheriff's department."

"You're dating a cop!"

"Well . . . yes," she said, looking around to see if any of the neighbors had heard. "I guess you could say that."

"Do I get to meet him next time I'm around?"

My fifty-three-year-old aunt blushed a deep scarlet—and it made me want to hug her all over again. "He actually asked to come to breakfast today, but I wouldn't let him."

"Why not?"

"Are you kidding? Too darn nervous."

"You silly, sweet woman."

"So you're not upset . . . or disappointed?"

I shook my head. "Not even a little bit. Why would I be?"

"I don't know . . ." She was still blushing. "It feels sort of scandalous. You know how small towns are. People stare and talk. I'm still not sure Father Paul approves."

"Oh, who cares what he or anyone else thinks?"

"That's exactly what Jason says."

"That's his name?"

She nodded. "Come back soon and I'll introduce you." Her smile faded. "Please, Billy, don't be a stranger. I miss you."

"I miss you too." And it was true. I really did. I reached into my pocket, pulled out a folded piece of notebook paper and handed it to my aunt.

"What's this?"

"I know you're gonna worry no matter what, so I made a list of probable stops along our route. It's not definitive . . . we're mostly just following the road where it takes us . . . but I'm guessing we'll hit most of these towns at one time or another."

The smile on her face went right to my heart. It was just like my mother's. "That might be the sweetest thing you've ever done for me."

"Walking that old mutt of yours has to be pretty high on the list."

She laughed, and then reached up and touched my cheek. "Do me a favor?"

"Name it."

"Remember what you said your therapist told you. That it's important you take some time to relax and have *fun*. I'm so glad you're making photos again and working on this project . . . but maybe go fishing like you used to. Call your old friends. Catch a ball game." She glanced at Melody as she came around the back of the van, Troy trailing right behind her. "Get yourself a girlfriend, for goodness' sake."

"I'll try," I said. "My fishing pole's in the van. The plan is to catch dinner one of these nights."

"Well, that's a start, I guess."

She then took turns hugging the three of us goodbye—this time we all got kisses on the cheek—and, for the third or fourth time that morning, told us to be careful on the road. "I'd tell you to mind your own business, but that's not what this trip is all about. I just hope you'll use the common sense the good Lord gave you."

Smiling, I climbed into the passenger seat and closed the door. Earlier this morning, back at the campground, I'd called tails and won the coin toss for riding shotgun. Aunt Helen approached the driver's-side window. "You have my phone number, pretty lady. If he starts misbehaving, give me a call."

"In that case, you'll probably hear from me later this afternoon," Melody said with a grin. "If not sooner." She started the engine. "It was really great meeting you, Helen."

"Thanks again for the cookies," Troy said from the back seat, crumbs spilling from his mouth. If Tamara could see us now, she'd throw a fit.

Before we pulled away, I noticed a folded sheet of paper on the van's windshield. I leaned out the window and yanked it from underneath the wiper blade. Holding it up so my Aunt Helen could see, I said, "Hey, when did Fortunato's Pizza start advertising on windshields?"

She shrugged. "You know Sudbury. Always changing with the times."

I laughed as Melody pulled away from the curb.

And didn't think about the long-haired man dressed in black, who'd been hurrying along the sidewalk with a purpose, until much later.

8

VIDEO FOOTAGE
(12:04 p.m., Saturday, May 7, 1983)

```
A tree-lined street of suburban houses. Grassy lawns.
Cars parked in driveways. The occasional pedestrian
walking along the sidewalk.
    The footage is bumpy. Swimming in and out of focus.
After a moment, it becomes clear that the camera is
protruding out the open window of a leisurely moving
vehicle.
    And then the vehicle slows even more and finally
brakes to a gentle stop.
    The old-fashioned split-level home that's captured
in the center of the screen is neat and orderly. The
lawn is well tended. A covered porch runs along the
length of the house, a waist-high row of shrubbery
providing it with a measure of privacy. A child's bi-
cycle lies on its side in front of the bushes. A bas-
ketball hoop is attached to the garage.
    "It's a nice house, Billy." A woman's soft voice.
    The camera angle shifts slightly, drawing close on
```

one of the second-floor windows. It holds there for a moment, and then slowly pulls back and tilts lower again.

"Oh, shit." Billy's startled voice from off-screen.

And we soon see the reason—there's a man standing on the front porch, staring directly at the camera and its operator. He doesn't look pleased. The man steps into the lawn, striding toward the camera.

"Go! Drive!"

The video abruptly ends.

9

Church Street ran roughly parallel to the Susquehanna River for almost the entire length of town. Despite its meandering route and sporadic cliffside views of the swiftly flowing water below, it was rarely touted as a particularly scenic route. This was because the majority of the roadway was surrounded by nearly eight hundred acres of thick rock-strewn woodland and a network of government-owned industrial warehouse complexes that hadn't seen prosperous days since the end of the Second World War. The vast majority of these sprawling soot-covered buildings were surrounded by rusty lengths of chain-link fence topped with gleaming razor wire. Even with staff running at below 40 percent, there were still armed uniformed soldiers posted at each of the three main gates. Oftentimes, this level of protective measures served as a kind of magnet for a small town's younger population, tempting hordes of bored teenagers in the mood for making mischief. But not in Sudbury. There was plenty of other trouble to get into around here, and most of it didn't involve having your arms and legs sliced to bloody ribbons or being chased around by trained guard dogs.

At the road's southernmost tip, where Church Street took over the reins from Rural Route 155, a Burger King, Western Auto, and Rutter's did moderate business along its narrow shoulder. Some sixteen miles to the north, just beyond a stretch of road where stands of white pines and red oaks crowded close enough to the cracked asphalt to turn day into dusk—HEADLIGHTS MUST BE ON AT ALL TIMES, the signs read—Church Street made an abrupt ninety-degree turn to the west before crossing over the Susquehanna by way of the Albert Linden Bridge.

It was there, not far from the mouth of the bridge, along that shadowed length of roadway—created by a tunnel of trees, no more than three-quarters of a mile in length—that local legend claimed Church Street was cursed.

Most everyone in town knew the stories. They were as woven into the fabric of Sudbury's history as the river and the railroad tracks and Maury Templeton's horse farm, where not one, but two Belmont Stakes winners had been sired.

In the summer of 1863, a regiment of weary Union soldiers making a hurried march toward Richmond attempted a river crossing on a series of barges. A sudden, unexpected storm caused the river to turn violent. Several of the barges slammed into underwater boulders and capsized. Forty-six soldiers were swept away and drowned. Only a handful of survivors made it to shore. This all happened within view of where the Albert Linden Bridge stands today.

Shortly after the Second World War, a trucking accident involving explosive munitions occurred within sight of the newly constructed Albert Linden Bridge. A convoy consisting of eleven Diamond Ts blew up, one after the other, like a string of giant firecrackers. Seventeen men perished, and twice that number were injured, many of them missing limbs. Folks in town claimed they felt the ground shake when the munitions went off. House windows shattered. Floorboards splintered. Vases and knickknacks tumbled from shelves. The surrounding woods caught fire, and it took nearly a dozen fire departments almost thirty-six hours to put out the blaze. You can still see remnants of the stunted landscape even today. The resulting investigation revealed that a number of high-level military officers failed to follow proper safety precautions. There were even rumors of sabotage. Eighteen months after the accident, a local hunter discovered the decayed remains of a male adult's severed right leg suspended in a tree more than fifteen feet off the ground. The leg was still clothed in charred tatters of Army green.

A few years later, in August 1948, a train hauling timber to New York and Boston derailed in the same vicinity. Eight railroad workers lost their lives. Puzzled police officials claimed that three of the deceased had been decapitated, but there was no sign anywhere of the missing heads. Another corpse was found clutching a pistol in his hand and missing both of his ears. The cause of the accident was never identified.

In the decades that followed, tragedies in the area continued with alarming frequency. During the '60s and '70s, nearly a dozen local hunters disappeared in the woods east of Church Street. Most of them were never found. The sole matter of disagreement among longtime residents regarding the actual number of missing centered around a local barber named Louis Barksdale, whose wife was such a notorious nag that many of Barksdale's friends believed he carefully staged his own disappearance in January 1968 and instead simply ran away.

In the winter of 1974, a search party discovered the frozen remains of three local men more than thirty feet above the forest floor. In an apparent attempt to flee from impending danger, the men had climbed a tree and remained there throughout a raging blizzard. Evidently, whatever had been chasing them had posed even more of a threat than freezing to death. One of the men had used a pocketknife to carve what looked like two giant eyes into the bark of the tree in which he'd been hiding.

A number of factors—including mountain lions, wolves, black bears, and quicksand—were blamed for the numerous disappearances, but not a shred of evidence was ever provided.

And then, of course, there were the automobile accidents.

In 1962, the mayor of Sudbury's eldest son, seventeen-year-old Gary Wellington, who was headed to Yale that fall, burned to death in an overturned Plymouth Fury. He'd been drag racing with a friend and had lost control of his car just beyond the finish line. Witnesses claimed that Wellington's vehicle swerved without reason before violently rolling over approximately a half-dozen times. They could hear the teenager's screams as the fuel tank ignited and the resulting blaze overtook the Plymouth.

A decade later, four starting members of the Sudbury High School state championship basketball team died when the pickup truck in which they were traveling left the road at a high rate of speed and crashed into a mature pine tree, its ancient trunk shearing the truck into two near-perfect halves.

In 1976, a pair of local fishermen were struck down by a woman driving a convertible as they walked along the shoulder of north Church Street. The men were on their way to meet friends who were parked not far from the bridge. Both pedestrians and the driver suffered severe internal injuries. All three died within a week of the accident.

At some point, in the midst of all this pervasive tragedy, the locals began to refer to the northernmost section of Church Street as Dead Man's Road. And not just the town's fickle youth either. In January 1979, the *Sudbury Times* published a front-page article claiming that more than forty drivers had lost their lives due to accidents on that particular stretch of roadway. The banner headline read: DEAD MAN'S ROAD CLAIMS DOZENS OF VICTIMS.

As a result of the public outcry generated by the article, the speed limit—which had already been lowered many years earlier from fifty to forty—was dropped even further to thirty-five. Streetlights were added to a 170-yard section of the road's shoulder. An increased police presence was announced.

None of it made any difference.

The accidents—and deaths—continued.

On June 20, 1980, at 3:57 p.m., longtime Sudbury residents Tom and Lori Anderson, on their way home from Winfield—where they'd just had lunch with one of Tom's oldest friends—crossed the Albert Linden Bridge under clear and sunny skies. Tom, who was driving, braked to negotiate the hairpin turn onto north Church Street without a hint of trouble. Approximately eighty-five yards later, the Andersons' 1979 Subaru hatchback crossed the midline and crashed into the woods on the opposite side of the road. The police claimed the car was traveling at more than sixty-five miles per hour when it left the roadway. No trace of skid marks were found. Tom Anderson, his chest obliterated by the steering column, was pronounced dead at the scene. Lori Anderson, who was not wearing a seat belt, was thrown through the windshield. She died two hours later from blunt-force head injuries at Sudbury Medical Center.

Dead Man's Road had struck again.

10

VIDEO FOOTAGE
(1:07 p.m., Saturday, May 7, 1983)

```
The memorial is tucked in close to the trees, and we immediately understand why. The shoulder of the road is no more than eight or ten inches wide. Beyond that, there's a narrow stretch of mossy earth. And then the woods.

    It's dark here. Even in the daytime. Even with the portable light stands we see Troy setting up alongside the road. Shadows flicker in and out of focus. Like restless spirits on the move.

    As the camera steadies, we see a wreath of artificial flowers attached to one of the tree trunks. Below it, a large square of poster board covered in writing. Some of the messages are illegible, the ink smeared or faded or running down the board in dripping letters. Others are more recent and perfectly clear.

    The camera slowly pulls back, and a small wooden
```

apple crate—flipped upside down—is revealed at the base of the tree. Its surface is covered with various-sized candle nubs, none of them currently burning. All around the box are bundles of flowers, a handful still relatively fresh. To the immediate left of this display, a four-foot wooden cross has been staked into the ground. The white paint beginning to flake and peel. At some point, a visitor had tied a balloon to one of the arms of the cross. A thin string hangs limply to the ground, the balloon itself long deflated and hidden by shadow in the weeds.

A young man appears on-screen. "I think we're good on photos," he says. "Plus I have a ton of old newspaper clippings in the van."

He leans close to the poster, reading. When he's finished, he turns around and we get a better look at him. Not quite a man, but not a boy either. Tall. Athletic looking. A little too thin, maybe. Curly dark hair. A small scar on his left cheek. It makes his boyish face look a tad more masculine.

"You guys ready? We're gonna run through my introduction." He's talking a little too fast and a little too loud. "I can do the voice-over later on."

"I'll follow your lead," a woman's voice says from off-screen. Melody. "Should I—"

"Just keep it rolling," he says. "I can fix whatever needs fixing later on in post."

The view whirls into a kaleidoscope of browns and greens as the camera is lowered and readjusted—and then the picture is back and refocused.

"You sure about this, Billy?" Melody asks. "I can change clothes and do it if you want."

He shakes his head emphatically. "No. It's gotta be me. My aunt's tough as nails, but you saw her once the camera turned on. She was a mess. If her interview taught me anything, it's that I have to be willing to put myself in the story." He gazes up and down the desolate road. "This part of the film is my story. I have to own that. I can't expect other people to share what they've experienced if I'm not willing to do it myself. I owe them that, at the very least."

"I think we're just surprised you changed your mind," Troy says, appearing at Billy's side. "You were pretty adamant that you didn't want to be on camera."

"Well, you can thank Aunt Helen for that." He gives Troy a nudge on the shoulder. "And besides, it's only this one time. The other intros are all you and Mel."

The picture goes abruptly dark.

When it returns, Billy is standing directly in front of the memorial, blocking much of the view. He begins speaking, and this time, his voice is strong and measured.

"On a sunny June afternoon in 1980, Mr. and Mrs. Thomas and Lori Anderson, on their way home from lunch at a nearby restaurant, were involved in a single-car accident on a lonely stretch of road in Sudbury, Pennsylvania. Thomas Anderson died at the scene. Lori Anderson passed away a short time later in the emergency room at Sudbury Medical Center. I was holding her hand." Billy steps aside to allow the audience a clear look at the memorial. "Mr. and Mrs. Anderson were my parents. I was sixteen years old at the time of the accident."

> The camera zooms closer on his face. His brown eyes are somber but steady. He clears his throat and continues. "I'm actually not sure who started my parents' memorial. All I know is that by the time I drove by the accident site, it was the night before the funeral, and the memorial was already here . . ."

11

Troy switched off the light, folded up the retractable legs, and placed the portable light stand on the ground next to his knapsack. With no artificial illumination, the road and surrounding woods were blanketed in darkness. It was still early in the afternoon, but it might as well have been midnight.

"Can we hurry it up?" Troy asked, pulling out a flashlight from the pocket of his orange safety vest. He switched it on. "This place is giving me the creeps." He glanced in my direction. "No offense, Billy."

"None taken," I said, kneeling down and returning the video camera to its shiny silver case. "Gives me the creeps too. Always has."

"What's the use of having streetlights," Troy said, looking around, "if you're not going to keep them operational?"

"You're not alone with that complaint. Someone writes a bitchy letter to the editor of the *Sun* pretty much every month." I glanced at the nearest light pole, the glass globe sitting atop it as dark as the wall of trees looming over us. "The county keeps blaming it on faulty wiring."

"It's too damn quiet," he said. "I thought there'd be a lot more traffic than this."

"There used to be when I was a kid . . . but then they extended Route 405 and put up the new two-lane bridge. Most people use that now."

"Do you believe the road is cursed?" Melody asked.

"I don't know what I believe," I said. "*Something* has to account for all the shitty things that have happened around here." I latched the lid on the camera case and looked around. The forest was dead silent. No birds. No insects. No animals rustling in the brush. "The energy here has always felt so . . . *off*."

Troy bobbed his head in agreement. "You feel it too? The air's so heavy it's difficult to breathe. And the handful of cars that have driven past . . . you can't even hear them coming until they're right on top of us. It's like the trees are swallowing up the sound of their engines." He hugged himself, waving the beam of his flashlight up and down the road. "And I swear it feels like someone's watching us."

"Now you're just being paranoid," Melody said. "Billy . . . do the locals have any theories about this area?"

"Oh, they've got plenty." I stood and brushed off the knees of my jeans. "Everything from aliens to witchcraft to government experiments gone wrong. My Uncle Frank got drunk one Fourth of July and told me and a bunch of friends a story about a group of Shawnee women and children who were ambushed and massacred by drunken fur trappers. This supposedly happened back in the 1800s right down there by the river." I pointed to the opposite side of the road. "The women and children were bathing when they were attacked. Apparently, several of the women were raped before they were murdered. The children were tortured. Uncle Frank said that the woods around here were haunted by their vengeful spirits."

"Great," Troy said, looking over his shoulder into the woods. "Just what we need. A bunch of pissed-off Indians."

"You should've seen Aunt Helen's face when she heard what he was telling us. We were like seven at the time, so of course we believed every word. I'd never seen her that angry. Grabbed him by the *ear* right there in front of us like he was a little kid and dragged him inside the house. They didn't even stick around for the fireworks." I bent over and picked up the camera case. "And then it all got even worse when some of the boys who were there started to have nightmares, and their parents called my aunt to complain. Poor Uncle Frank . . . he was stuck in the doghouse for weeks." I started walking toward the van. "Now what do you say we get out of here, before Troy starts seeing things."

"Too late," he said, picking up his knapsack and following right behind us.

12

We'd only made it about fifty yards when a sleek white Cadillac rounded the hairpin turn—its high beams transforming the tunnel of trees into a spiderweb of shadows—and stopped on the road beside us. The driver rolled down the window. And smiled. With his round face and rosy cheeks, the man looked like a cherub in a Michelangelo painting. "Are my eyes deceiving me or is that the prodigal son returned?"

"Father Paul!" I said, matching his wide grin as I put down the equipment I was carrying. "I was just talking about you this morning."

He lumbered out of the driver's seat and we shook hands.

"Ahh . . . so that's why my ears were burning."

I gestured to the others. "Father, these are my friends from school. Melody Wise. And Troy Carpenter."

He stepped forward to greet them.

"It's nice to meet you, Father," Melody said.

"And you as well, young lady."

"I'm a Baptist," Troy blurted out in typical Troy fashion.

A dumbfounded Father Paul stared at him for a moment, and then tossed back his head and laughed. "And proud of it, I see!"

"You have to excuse Troy," I said. "He's a bit of a social misfit."

"Aren't we all, Billy?" His cheeks no longer merely rosy, the priest's chubby face resembled the summer tomatoes in my aunt's garden.

"He's also got a major case of the willies."

Father Paul's smile faded as he looked around at the woods, his gaze lingering on my parents' memorial. "This place has a tendency to do that to people."

"We just came from Aunt Helen's," I said, eager to change the subject. "She insisted on serving us breakfast before we hit the road."

He patted his ample belly. "Well, I'm sorry I missed it."

"I'll be sure to invite you the next time I'm in town."

"I'll hold you to that." He glanced at the piles of gear resting at our feet. "So, what's all this about?"

I told him.

13

VIDEO FOOTAGE
(1:49 p.m., Saturday, May 7, 1983)

The man standing in front of the memorial appears to be in his late fifties or early sixties. Short and rotund, wearing wire-framed glasses beneath a mop of dark hair, he looks like someone's favorite uncle or perhaps an insurance salesman. If not for the black clergy shirt and the starched white collar, you might never guess he was a priest.

"Whenever you're ready," the camera operator says.

"Where I'm standing is okay?"

"You're good." The frame widens as the cameraman takes a step back. "And don't be afraid to move around. I'll follow you."

The man takes a deep breath and starts talking.

"Tom and Lori Anderson were not only faithful members of my congregation. They were dear friends and I miss them terribly."

And just like that, it's easy to picture this man standing upon the pulpit on Sunday mornings, administering wisdom and comfort to his parishioners. His voice is clear and confident. His posture relaxed. His eyes focused.

"On the day of the accident, I was out of town attending a seminar. The moment I heard the tragic news, I left the conference, got into my car, and drove straight home. By the time I reached the family at the hospital, it was clear to see that although their hearts were broken, their faith remained steadfast."

He turns and gazes at the memorial, the cross directly in front of him.

"And then overnight, right here on Church Street, this astonishing memorial was born."

The camera lingers on the wide shot for a beat longer and then slowly closes in on his face.

"The Andersons' son, Billy, who's as fine of a young man as you'll find anywhere, recently told me that he doesn't know who started the memorial."

The priest stares directly into the camera.

"And I told him it doesn't matter. It wasn't just one person. It was dozens, perhaps hundreds, of loving hearts and hands that planted that cross into the ground. That lit the candles. And placed the gifts of tribute. Tom and Lori Anderson were special people. They made the world around them a better place. Tom and Lori believed in the eternal life that their Lord and Savior promised, and they lived their lives with . . ."

14

"'I'm a Baptist'?"

"Bite me. I was nervous."

"I thought it was kinda cute," Melody said.

I rolled my eyes. "You would think that."

"We were in there for so long, I forgot it was daytime," Troy said, squinting over his shoulder at the tunnel of trees. From out here on the road, it looked like the mouth of an enormous dark cave.

MEMORIALS

By the time we said goodbye to Father Paul and lugged the cameras, tripods, and lights to the van, we were all dripping with sweat. Hair Metal Harry, 98 Rock's resident weather guru—picture a modern-day Viking minus the helmet—had announced earlier this morning that the entire mid-Atlantic region was in the grip of a rare May heat wave with temperatures the rest of the week expected to climb into the low-to-mid-nineties. It felt like we'd already broken a hundred this afternoon. All I wanted to do was crawl inside the van, turn the air conditioner on high, and change into some dry clothes. After I sucked down about ten glasses of water.

We'd parked in a dirt pull-off not far from the bridge. Local fishermen used it all the time, but most often in the early mornings and late evenings when the smallmouth were biting. At nearly two in the afternoon, on a blisteringly hot day, we were the only vehicle in sight.

I slid the silver camera case into the back of the van and wiped my face with my shirtsleeve. Not that it mattered. I was drenched from head to toe. I was also mentally fried and in desperate need of something to eat.

But more than anything, I was ready for Troy to stop talking for a little while. He got like this when he was nervous—he wouldn't shut up.

"... and there's even been scientific experiments on the subject," he was saying. "Most of them focused on places where violent crimes had been committed. They even did a series of investigations at Auschwitz and one of the other, lesser-known death camps."

He unshouldered his backpack and tossed it into the van.

"The reports indicated that in those areas of extreme negative energy, visitors often felt a tightness in their chests, difficulty breathing, and even sudden spikes of depression. Their skin felt funny. They became paranoid. Some subjects even ..."

Melody looked at me, her face flushed. "Ready for lunch?"

"I thought you'd never ask."

"Even more unsettling," Troy continued, as if Melody and I had never spoken, "is what investigators began to refer to as 'stickiness,' a term they felt accurately described how certain negative energies existed in a specific location for an extended period of time, and to a larger extent how those energies would oftentimes get attached to visitors and remain stuck to them long after they'd left the infected area."

"Real quick," I said, gesturing for Melody to follow me. "I want to show you something before we go."

We walked to the edge of the pull-off.

Behind us, oblivious to our departure, Troy began loading the tripods and lights into the van. "Several of those same investigators went on to conduct experiments involving residual hauntings using infrasound technology and a kind of . . ."

His voice faded as we followed a narrow, weed-choked trail up a steep ridge. When we reached the summit, Melody gasped, lifting a hand to her mouth. "Oh . . . it's . . . *beautiful*."

In the distance, off to our left, we could see the hairpin turn that Church Street made in preparation to cross the bridge. Directly in front of us, far beyond a dizzying drop, was the Susquehanna River. Swiftly flowing and hundreds of yards wide. Strewn with half-sunken rocks and boulders. The sun was shining high in the sky, pinpricks of bright light reflecting off the river, as if a bucket of diamonds had been scattered across the water's sparkling surface. Looming on the horizon, the Appalachian mountain range shrouded in mist.

"Troy says those mountains were here before the dinosaurs," I said. "And that they're older than the trees, whatever the hell that means."

"The river . . . I've seen it before . . . so many times . . . but never like *this*."

"I used to come here when I was a kid."

"I can see why." After a moment, she turned and looked at me. "Are you okay, Billy?"

I shrugged. "I think so."

"Was it hard running into Father Paul like that? It sounds like he was close to your family."

"He was." I tried to remember the last time I'd seen him before today, but I couldn't. It'd been that long ago. "He was one of Uncle Frank's best friends. My parents really liked him too. Especially my mom."

"He seems like a lovely man." She touched my arm. "I'm sure he was a great comfort after what happened."

"He tried," I said, staring out at the river.

"Today's been . . ." She searched for the right words. ". . . a *lot*."

"It's been different than I thought it would be."

"How so?"

"I'm not really sure . . . I thought it would *feel* different." Far below us, a deer approached the water's edge and began to drink. "But I just feel kind of numb."

"I'm pretty sure that's normal. Maybe even a good thing. It might mean your brain is tired of feeling sad all the time."

Something nudged my heart. "You think I'm always sad?"

"Not always . . . but a lot." She softened her voice. "You hide it well."

I'm still not sure what happened next. I looked at her, and all of a sudden it took every ounce of strength I had to not lean over and kiss her. At that moment, I was completely certain she was the most beautiful woman I'd ever seen—and the realization absolutely terrified me. I opened my mouth but no words came out.

"I'm . . . sorry if that was the wrong thing to say," she said, lowering her eyes. "But it's the truth."

Oh God, I wasn't going to be able to stop myself. I was mute, and I was foolish. I was also weak. I was going to kiss her and make a complete—

"BILLY! MELODY!"

Back at the van, Troy had finally discovered our absence.

"WHERE ARE YOU?!"

He sounded on the verge of hysteria.

"We better go," Melody said.

"THIS ISN'T FUNNY, YOU GUYS!"

And just like that, the moment was over.

15

Troy was still bitching and moaning twenty minutes later when we pulled up in front of the diner.

"All the horrible things that'd happened around there," he said. "What was I supposed to think? Maybe you'd been kidnapped and dragged away into the woods."

"Lemme guess," I said. "By a family of Bigfoot."

"Wouldn't that make them Bigfoots?" Melody asked.

"Or Bigfeet."

Behind those thick lenses, Troy stared daggers at us as we walked across the busy parking lot.

The Silver Moon Diner had occupied the narrow glass-fronted brick building adjacent to the Sudbury Post Office since long before I was born. My father told me that the original owner, a toothpick of a man named Fred Thompson, had once made his living as a magician in a traveling circus. After the circus went belly-up somewhere north of Pittsburgh, he hopped a train to Sudbury to stay with his twin sister for a couple of weeks. An avid fly fisherman, he fell in love with the town and the river, and decided to stake his claim here. It had always been his dream to run his own eatery. After a rocky opening weekend, during which the fire department had to be called to extinguish a kitchen mishap, the diner soon became a local favorite. The wooden sign out front promised GOOD EATS CHEAP in red painted capital letters—and that humble motto proved to be a winner. Tragically, Mr. Thompson was killed in a hunting accident the year I started grade school—despite many rumors, it happened up north in Maine and not in the woods around Church Street—and my mom said nearly half the town turned out for his funeral. Nowadays, Fred's eldest son, Gary, ran the diner and still donned an apron to work the grill on most weekends. He was known across multiple county lines for his perfectly seasoned burgers and hot turkey and roast beef platters drowned in homemade gravy. None of that out-of-the-jar stuff. Over the years, Gary had initiated a number of upgrades to his father's business: silver aluminum siding and a dark green awning out front, an outdoor picnic area beneath some trees, and even a brand-new, fancy dessert cooler. I figured roughly 99 percent of Sudbury's teenagers had at one time or another taken a date to the Silver Moon Diner. Me included.

A bell jangled overhead when we pushed open the diner's heavy glass doors. I sighed in relief as the air-conditioning washed over my body. An older woman behind the counter—her name was Kitty and she'd worked the morning and afternoon shifts at the Silver Moon Diner for as long as I could remember—finished refilling a customer's coffee and looked over at us. "Have a seat wherever you like." If she recognized me, she gave no indication.

Melody thanked her and picked out a booth by the front window. I sat across from her, and Troy slid in next to me. "What's good here?" he asked, rubbing his hands together. The prospect of food in his belly had finally calmed him down.

I took out three menus from behind the miniature jukebox at the end of the table and passed them around. "From what I remember, everything."

A waitress smelling of cigarette smoke, her auburn hair stacked high in a hairnet, approached the table with a put-on smile. "Can I start you folks off with a drink?"

Melody ordered a Diet Coke with no ice. Troy and I went for the freshly squeezed lemonade we'd seen advertised on a sandwich board outside on the sidewalk.

The doorbell jingled.

A man wearing a New York Yankees baseball cap strolled in and went directly to the cash register. I recognized him immediately. Mr. Cavanaugh. A neighbor across the street from my parents' and a longtime member of my father's bowling team. I watched as Kitty rang up his carryout order. When they were finished, I looked down at my lap, hoping he wouldn't spot me on his way out the door.

"Friend of yours?" Melody asked, glancing over her shoulder.

"Something like that," I said, still hiding my face. "Friend of my parents."

Troy leaned across the table for a better look. "Should we ask if he'll sit for an interview?"

"No," I said, remembering the way Mr. Cavanaugh used to yell at us when we rode our skateboards in front of his house. "Definitely not him."

The bell jangled again. A young Black man wearing an Army uniform held open the door for a middle-aged couple. The woman nodded a polite thank-you, and then all three of them took empty stools at the counter.

"Is that five?" Melody looked over at Troy with her eyebrows scrunched. "Or six?"

He thought about it. "Five . . . four was the kid with the fishing pole."

Confused, I stared at Mel across the table and then at Troy. "What are you two talking about?"

"People of the non-white persuasion," Troy said.

"Huh? What does that mean?"

Melody smiled awkwardly and lowered her voice. "It means people that look like me and Troy . . ."

". . . and not *you*," he finished.

I glanced at the serviceman sitting at the counter—and my mouth dropped open.

Troy nudged me in the side. "Ahh, *now* you're getting it."

"You guys are . . . counting? Why would you do that?"

"It's not a big deal, Billy." Melody was practically whispering. "Just something Troy and I were talking about this morning after breakfast."

"Last night, when we drove through town on the way to the campground," Troy continued, "we saw all those people at the ice cream shop . . . some others who were walking around . . . and then those kids on skateboards in front of the high school . . ."

"Yeah . . . so what?"

He leaned closer. "They were *all* white."

MEMORIALS

I had no idea if he was right or not. I hadn't paid any attention. "Okay..."

Melody shrugged. "That's all we're saying. You grew up in a predominantly white community. I guess it surprised us."

"Might as well rename it Honkyville."

The smoky waitress returned with our drinks. I paid attention to see if she looked at Mel or Troy differently—but if she did, I couldn't tell. She jotted down our lunch order in a notepad and went away in a hurry.

No one said anything for a moment, all of us searching for the right words. It was a sensitive subject and we had to be careful. Finally, I spoke up first. "I'm really sorry if you guys feel... out of place. If anyone says or does anything to make you feel uncomfortable, I'll—"

Melody reached over and touched my arm. "It's fine, Billy. It was just an observation, that's all."

"Sudbury's a farming community," I explained. "Always has been. I guess that's part of the reason why... and I mean, I don't remember even a single instance of racism or..." I was struggling to make sense. Until two years ago, I'd lived here all my life. I'd gone to school and church here, buried my parents here—and somehow I'd never even fundamentally acknowledged that most everyone looked the same? What did that say about me?

"Hell, even your uncle's basketball picture on the wall," Troy said. "You notice what was missing? Brothers!"

He was right, of course, and sure enough, I naively hadn't even picked up on it. I was mortified. "I'm really sorry. To both of you. I—"

"Stop right now," Melody said. "You have nothing to be sorry for, silly. You had no control over the environment in which you were raised."

The bell over the door jangled. Grateful for the interruption, I took a peek.

And my stomach did a somersault.

"Now what?" Melody asked. "You look like you just saw a ghost."

And in a way, I had.

A pair of teenage girls strutted toward the counter. The dark-haired one was dressed in tight designer jeans and a black T-shirt. There was a pack of cigarettes tucked into one rolled-up sleeve. Her long, dark eyelashes were caked with blue mascara. The girl following behind her was a small-town stunner. Blonde hair. Blue eyes. Cutoff jeans showing off shapely tan legs.

"I gather you know them," Troy said. He whistled under his breath. "Whoa, they're a couple of babes."

"Shh." I put my elbow down on the table and used my hand to shield my face.

I heard footsteps approach. *Please no.*

And stop. *Uh-oh.*

"Well, well, if it isn't Billy *Anderson*," an overly sweet voice said.

Too late. Busted.

Despite the sudden overwhelming urge to flee, I calmly looked up and smiled at the blonde girl standing in front of our table. "Hey, Naomi." And then over her shoulder to her friend sitting at the counter. "What's up, Jenny?"

"Aren't you going to introduce me to your friends?" the blonde girl said, her eyes lingering on Melody.

I stared at her dumbly.

"Oh, never mind. I'll do it myself." She reached out her hand to Melody. I noticed right away that she was still wearing the ring I'd given her junior year. "Hi. I'm Naomi Flynn—Billy's old girlfriend."

16

It felt like I was guest starring in one of those Friday-night sitcoms my mother used to watch.

Somewhere unseen, a studio audience was observing our every move and laughing their asses off at my predicament.

Naomi and I had moved to a booth at the opposite end of the diner in order to have some privacy. Melody and Troy remained by the window, eating their lunches and trying their best not to stare. A rubbernecking Troy was doing a particularly poor job of it. Jenny was already off in her own little world, chatting away with an older guy dressed in mechanic's overalls. His stitched-on name tag read: LENNY. The guy's left eye was bruised and swollen, most likely the aftermath of a rowdy late night spent at Barney's, Sudbury's one and only redneck bar.

"It was accurate to say 'old girlfriend,' right?" Naomi asked, stealing a french fry from my plate. "I mean, we never did actually break up." She shrugged dramatically. "You just stopped writing and calling and didn't come home for over a year. And even then, you didn't bother telling me you were back in town. I had to hear it from friends."

"I don't blame you for being pissed off."

She swiped a dismissive hand in front of her face. "Oh, I'm not pissed off. Not anymore. Hell, I'm not even sad anymore. Not much anyway. Haven't cried in over a year."

"I'm really sorry." I'd known this day would come, and now that it was here, I felt horrible. It was even worse than I'd imagined.

She cocked her head and looked at me. "After all this time . . . that's the best you can do . . . you're *sorry*."

I stared at the cheeseburger growing cold on my plate. I felt like a misbehaving child being scolded by the strictest teacher in school. And I deserved every last bit of it.

"It's not an excuse . . . at least not a very good one . . . but, Naomi, you have no idea how fucked up I was. I could hardly get out of bed most days . . . I was lost and confused and . . . I don't know, a lot of things."

"You've been lost and confused for almost two years?"

Looking up at her, I started to say something and stopped. Finally, I just nodded and mumbled under my breath, "Still am."

She must have seen the truth in my eyes or heard it in my voice because her face softened. "Can you at least tell me what you've been doing all this time?"

17

VIDEO FOOTAGE
(2:19 p.m., Saturday, May 7, 1983)

"My name's Naomi Flynn."

The girl sits at a picnic table. Her posture is rigid. There's an uneasy smile on her face, and she keeps glancing off camera, as if she's looking to someone for direction.

"I'm eighteen years old, and I've lived here in Sudbury, Pennsylvania, my whole life."

She takes a deep breath and her shoulders begin to relax. She clasps her hands together on the table in front of her.

"I grew up on the next street over from the Andersons' house. Our families were friends. I went to school with Billy Anderson from grade school up. He was a year ahead of me. At the time of the accident, we were boyfriend and girlfriend. We'd started dating my freshman year of high school."

The uneasy smile is gone.

"Billy was at my house when the accident happened. We were swimming with my little sister. He was in a goofy mood that day, and I remember laughing a lot. Later that afternoon, we changed out of our swimsuits and walked into town to get ice cream. That's when the police pulled over and told Billy what'd happened. Then they gave us a ride to the hospital."

She looks off camera again, this time for longer, like she's listening to someone.

"I really loved Mr. and Mrs. Anderson. They were

like a second family to me. Mr. Tom was always helping people around the neighborhood. He was kind of a handyman. And he always took the time to talk to me. Not just a polite 'Hey, how're you doing?' but really talk. He'd ask how school was going or if I had any funny new lifeguarding stories. Or he'd ask if I'd seen any good movies lately. He loved movies. Especially the scary ones."

She pauses to catch her breath.

"Mrs. Lori was really sweet. Billy's an only child, and I think she'd always wanted to have a daughter too. You know, someone to do girl stuff with. We used to look at magazines together. Talk about movie stars and fashion and all the latest gossip from Hollywood. Sometimes, I'd help her in the garden and she'd help me with my geometry homework. Every once in a while, we'd even go shopping together. I loved the way she dressed. Retro but with a ton of style. It reminded me of old photos of Jackie Kennedy. She was so pretty and put together."

Melody's voice floats in from off-screen—although not quite loud enough to hear what she is saying.

"The first time I went to the accident site was with my parents. Billy and his Aunt Helen were busy making arrangements for the funeral. My mom and dad took flowers. I had one of my stuffed animals and a card I'd made. There were three or four cars parked mostly in the road when we got there. A bunch of others driving by. Lookie-loos, my father called them. He said there was liable to be another accident if folks weren't careful, so we parked all the way down by the bridge and walked back. Someone had put up a cross, and there were a bunch of flowers and balloons and some candles burning. Shortly after we got there, one of my girlfriends from school showed up with her brother and father. And Mrs. Thompkins, our math teacher, pulled up as we were leaving."

Naomi begins coughing into her hand. A moment later, Troy reaches into frame with a bottle of water. She takes a long drink and continues.

"The next time I went there was with Billy, the night after the funeral. God, it felt like half the town was there. Even the local news. The cops had a section of the road blocked off. Everyone was holding candles and people started singing church hymns. Mr. and Mrs. Anderson were super-active in the community, so they had a ton of friends. We saw lots of familiar faces. Strangers too . . ."

18

"That was really hard."

Naomi had made it through the entire interview without getting emotional, but now that we were finished, there were tears swimming in her eyes. We were standing behind the van, just out of view of my nosy traveling companions, who were impatiently waiting to leave. The plan was to gas up on our way out of town, and then head west over the bridge into hill country.

"I haven't talked about them like that in a long time," she said. "Or *you*, for that matter."

Unsure of what to say, I glanced over her shoulder across the parking lot. Jenny was sitting on a bench in the shade, smoking a cigarette and watching us. A short distance behind her, several young boys darted from tree to tree, pelting each other with acorns. Their bare knees were covered in scabs and grass stains.

"What a day... I don't see or hear from you for a year and a half, and then just like that, there you are." She sighed. "And all because Jenny wanted a stupid iced tea."

"Are you sorry we ran into each other?"

Jesus, why would I ask her that?

"I'm not sure yet. It depends." She hesitated before going on. "Are you coming back after you finish your documentary or will it be another year or two?"

"I'll be back. I told Aunt Helen I want to meet her new boyfriend."

"Sheriff Peters," she said, smiling. "They make a cute couple, but I wouldn't exactly call him 'new.' They've been dating for months." She made a face. "Oh, that's right, you probably wouldn't know that."

I didn't say anything. I knew I had it coming.

"I went to your school once to find you."

"What?!" I said, unable to hide my surprise. "When?"

"Freshman year. Right after Christmas break. I got your class schedule from Aunt Helen. Jenny and I blew off school, and she drove us in her brother's car."

"I can't believe Aunt Helen gave you my—"

"Don't blame her. I practically got down on my knees and begged. I was Little Miss Pathetic back then."

"But... I never saw you. Did you actually make it to campus?"

"You didn't see me because I saw you first... and you were busy." A hint of embarrassment in her eyes now. "Class was just letting out, and we were waiting outside at the bottom of the stairs. I remember it had just started snowing. The doors opened and you walked out... with a girl. You were both smiling. She had long, pretty hair and was wearing one of those expensive cardigan sweaters and a headband like a model in a magazine. She laughed at something you said, and I saw how perfect and white her teeth were. I'd never seen someone with more beautiful teeth."

"Oh my God, Naomi. I swear I have no idea who you're talking about. It had to be some random girl from one of my classes."

"I ran back to the car and pretty much cried the whole way home." She wiped her eyes with the back of her hand. "By the time we got to my house, I was so mad at you. I swore I'd never chase after you again."

"I'm sorry," I said, feeling miserable. "I had no idea."

"Would it have mattered?"

I forced myself to meet her eyes. "I honestly don't know."

"It was for the best," she said, standing a little taller. "If that hadn't happened, I probably would've spent the next year locked in my bedroom mooning over your stupid face."

Once again, words of wisdom eluded me. I stared at the ground and kicked at a rock with my shoe.

"Kimmy's going to be really sad she missed you." Naomi's little sister. Once upon a time, we'd been very close. We'd played about a million games of Uno, watched every new episode of *Scooby Doo*, and even hunted crawdads together in the local creeks.

"Tell her I'll be back." And all of a sudden, I really meant it. "Tell her we'll all go fishing."

That sassy look of hers again. "All of us?"

"If you want to."

"We'll see . . . I guess."

I gazed over her shoulder and noticed Troy's owl-like eyes in the passenger-side mirror. Not only was the bastard spying on me, but he'd stolen my seat.

"Well, I should probably get—"

Gesturing to the van. "Do you have any idea how jealous I am of you and your friends?"

"Why would you—"

"You're heading off on this grand adventure, and I'm stuck here . . . like always . . . working at Walmart for the summer."

"It's a school project. I wouldn't exactly call it a grand adventure."

"I would." Her shoulders sagged and she stuck out her lower lip.

And I melted.

My God, I'd forgotten how damn cute she was.

And then like a bolt of lightning from a clear summer sky: *There's room in the van for her. She could come with us.*

Startled, I took a step back and almost tripped over my own feet.

No, no, no. What in the hell is wrong with you, Billy Anderson? An hour and a half ago, you were ready to kiss Melody, and now you're swooning over an old girlfriend. You're either losing your damn mind or all this fresh air is turning you into a horndog.

"Is something wrong?" She was staring at me with alarm in her eyes.

"What? No. No. Nothing's wrong." I couldn't even remember what we were talking about. "I was just—"

The van horn gave a single earsplitting blast.

We both jumped. I might have even squealed a little.

Stepping out from behind the van, I glared at the passenger-side mirror. No matter how anxious Melody was to leave, there was no way she would've blown the horn like that—which left only Troy.

"I guess you better go," Naomi said, frowning.

So that's what I did—but only after giving her an awkward goodbye hug and a whispered promise to stay in touch.

Several miles down the road, I could still smell her perfume on my T-shirt.

19

Once Melody and Troy had finished interrogating me about Naomi— imagine a couple of red-beaked vultures plucking strips of pale flesh off a hunk of fresh roadkill on the side of the road, and you'll get a pretty good picture of what it was like—we settled in for a nice, long evening drive. Windows down, singing along with the likes of Bob Seger and Marvin Gaye and REO Speedwagon ("Hey, maybe *that's* what we should call the van," Troy said. "The Speed Wagon!"). I'd quickly discovered that the biggest perk of riding shotgun was having control of the music selection. With Troy stuck in the back seat for the rest of the day, there would be no more Reba McEntire and Conway Twitty. I liked to think I had fairly eclectic taste in music, but the truth of the matter was I'd rather eat broken glass than listen to Merle Haggard and the Oak Ridge Boys warble on and on about drunken bar fights and American-made women in tight blue jeans. I could tolerate a little Ricky Skaggs from time to time—especially once those kick-ass guitar licks of his kicked in—but even then, I had my limits.

An hour earlier, we'd come across a roadside memorial tucked behind a billboard advertising a mom-and-pop shop a few miles ahead that specialized in antique furniture and fishing bait. If Troy hadn't hollered and scared us half to death, we probably would've missed it.

Which, truthfully, would've been okay—because there wasn't much to it. A crude cross made out of splintered two-by-fours, maybe fourteen inches tall, surrounded by a dozen or so rain-filled wine bottles (I was starting to see a pattern developing with all the empty booze receptacles). A miniature American flag, faded and frayed, protruded from inside one of the bottles. Beside the display, a handful of painted rocks arranged in the shape of a smiley face. On the smooth surface of one of the rocks were four tiny stick figures. On another, a bunch of yellow-and-black flowers. The rest were decorated with various symbols and designs. My favorite resembled the shell of a small green turtle.

After surveying the memorial, I decided to leave the video camera in the van, and instead, I snapped about a dozen photos. It only took two or three minutes, and we were on our way again. Pretty much immediately, just a mile or so down the road, I regretted not getting out the video camera and taking the time to record some commentary. Whether because of mental exhaustion from our work earlier this afternoon or a bout of pure laziness, I'd failed to do my job properly. And that bothered me.

The person who'd died on the road by that billboard deserved better. Perhaps he'd been a veteran. The flag and wine bottles left behind by the former heroes he'd once served alongside. The arrangement of rocks painted by his daughter or granddaughter, a reminder of happier times. Now, we would never know. With that familiar feeling of shame surging through my veins, I promised myself that it would never happen again during our trip.

We'd just driven past a trio of young boys walking across a bridge, fishing poles slung over their shoulders like rifles, when Melody announced, "I think we should start a club."

Half-asleep, I mumbled, "What kind of club?"

Troy poked his head in between the seats. "Like a photography club? Or—"

"I was thinking more along the lines of a broken hearts club," Melody said. "Think about it. Billy and his parents. Me and my mom. You and your little brother. It's almost like Professor Tyree put us in the same group for a reason."

"I seriously doubt that Tyree knows anything about our personal lives," I said.

"I don't mean it in a literal sense, silly."

"You're talking about fate," Troy said.

She pointed at him in the back seat. "Slam, jam, applesauce."

Melody was always coming up with oddball sayings. They drove me crazy. "What does that even mean?"

"It means Troy's right. Fate brought us together for a reason. Don't you agree?"

"Fate brought us together to get an A on this project," I said.

"I was thinking more along the lines of helping each other heal from our losses."

"And how exactly are we supposed to do that? Sit around the campfire holding hands, singing 'Kumbaya'?"

"You can be a real turd sometimes, Billy, you know that?" She looked at me with genuine disappointment in her eyes. Not the first person to do that today.

Softening, I said, "I'm sorry, Mel. Look . . . I hear what you're saying . . . I just don't know if I believe in all of that . . . *fate* and everything."

"You want to hear something interesting that I noticed?" she asked.

"I do," Troy said.

"All three of us wear crucifixes."

Without meaning to, I reached up and felt for the silver cross underneath my T-shirt. It had belonged to my father. He'd been wearing it the day of the accident. I never took it off. "That doesn't mean anything. Lots of people wear crucifixes."

"Not for the reasons we do," she said, shaking her head. "There are over three thousand full-time students on campus. What are the odds that three people with our related backgrounds, who came from three different states and never met each other until school, end up in the same class, much less the same project group?" She looked at Troy for an answer.

"Basically, umm, one in 1.1 million," he said, after only a slight pause. "Or in other words, pretty fucking steep."

Melody smiled. "It's fate, I'm telling you."

"Maybe you're right," I said with a shrug. "And maybe you're both full of it. Flip a coin."

She flashed me a dirty look. "I'm being serious here. Don't make me call your aunt and turn in a bad report."

Before I could respond, something in the rearview mirror caught her attention. She tapped the brakes. "Question: Did either of you see a red Jeep in the parking lot back at the diner?"

"Not me," I said, leaning over and peeking at the side-view mirror. Sure enough, there was a red Jeep two cars behind us. Thanks to the glare of the sun, I couldn't see who was driving or if there were any passengers.

"I can't remember," Troy said.

"Your girlfriend doesn't drive a red Jeep, does she?" Her eyes darted back and forth between the road and the mirror.

"I have no idea," I said. "I know she and Jenny walked to the diner." I quickly added, "And she's not my girlfriend."

"Is someone following us?" Troy asked.

"No one's following us." I folded up the map and stashed it in the glove compartment. "It's probably just someone going fishing down at The Flats."

"All I know is that I'm almost positive I saw a red Jeep parked in front of the diner." She slowed down for a curve in the road. "There was one behind us both before and after Abbottsville, and then it turned off. Now it's back again."

"Well, now it's gone again," I said.

She looked up at the mirror. "Huh, where did it—"

"No one's following us," I said. "This isn't a spy movie, Mel. I think your greedy sister's got you paranoid."

"You leave my greedy sister out of this." She turned back to Troy with a furrowed brow. "And you better clean up those cookie crumbs, or I might just give her a call after I hang up with Billy's aunt."

Troy frowned and started brushing said crumbs into the palm of his hand.

Now it was my turn to flash her a look. "When did you become such a nag?"

"Ever since I started babysitting the two of you."

I stuck my tongue out at her.

20

Every few miles, I noticed Melody's eyes drifting to the rearview mirror. I'd given it some thought and decided that if anyone was responsible for her sudden outburst of paranoia, it was most likely Aunt Helen with all her talk of us being outsiders. The only surprise was that it was Melody reacting this way—instead of Troy.

Living in Sudbury, I'd grown up surrounded by stories of the Appalachian region and the strange people who inhabited it. Tales of hikers stumbling upon towns with no electricity or running water that didn't appear on any maps. Isolated villages with dialects all their own. Forested mountains and valleys so dark and deep and desolate that no man or woman had ever fully explored them.

For years, my father and I ventured west across the Albert Linden Bridge in search of wild trout in the secluded vales and hollows that Appalachian denizens had called home for centuries. My Uncle Frank—who'd grown up in those hills—refused to join us on our weekend fishing trips. I was only eight when he died and never really heard the full story, but from the bits and pieces of conversation I'd picked up on over time, I think it had something to do with a long-standing and bitter family dispute.

Initially, I'd believed what most of my friends did about the people who inhabited that area: they were poor white hillbillies living by choice in the poverty of a distant past. A barefoot, backward people with strange, sunken eyes and dirt-smudged faces, they talked funny and avoided any form of modern technology like it was the plague. Those rare instances when I saw them around town—heads hanging, no eye contact—they were usually riding around in rusted-out trucks with balding tires, the rear beds crammed with unblinking, round-eyed children dressed in filthy tatters. A lot of jokes were told at their expense. Mean ones. The most frequently repeated involved inbreeding, snake handlers, and gun-toting moonshiners. Even worse, there often seemed to be a sliver of truth buried in those jokes.

Uncle Frank had warned me on more than one occasion to never stray off the path while fishing on Appalachian land. He claimed there were homemade stills hidden in many a nook and cranny, with protective and heavily armed moonshiners roaming the woods. I remembered him showing me an article in the *Sudbury Sun* about a group of hikers who had gone missing in the mountains. A weeklong search had failed to turn up even a single clue as to their whereabouts. "Those folks poked their noses where they didn't belong," he told me over breakfast one morning. "Mark my words . . . they'll never be found."

And while many of these stereotypes may have proved accurate for a certain percentage of the population, my father had gone to great lengths to teach me about the Appalachian peoples' rich sense of tradition and culture and folklore. Mountain folks were proud and hardworking people, he insisted, and just because they'd resisted change for so many years, that didn't make them ignorant or inferior to the rest of us. They simply held close to different beliefs and customs than most outsiders. He'd even pointed out that there'd been a time long ago when the town of Sudbury had been considered a part of hill country. But then the railroad company had moved in and built the bridge and started modernizing the town, and its outside population had boomed overnight.

One of the most interesting stories he'd told me was about the Underground Railroad that ran through much of Appalachia, stretching all the way from the forests of Chattanooga, Tennessee, to a network of caves and tunnels deep in the mountains of Pennsylvania. Even now, while most settlements across the river were predominately white, nearly ten percent of the hill populace was made up of Black Appalachians whose families had lived there for generations.

Unfortunately, most of these educational conversations took place during the long drives home after busy weekends of hiking and fishing in the fresh mountain air—and as a result, more often than not, I was dozing off in the passenger seat instead of really listening to what he had to say. Sadly, I recalled few other details. Except, of course, the legend of the Bell Witch. I never forgot a word of that fascinating tale of otherworldly revenge. Much to the chagrin of my poor mother, who spent more than a few late nights during that memorable summer sitting at my bedside, soothing my seven-year-old nerves after yet another terrifying nightmare.

Regardless of what I did or did not remember, I was nearly certain of one thing: if there really was a red Jeep lurking somewhere on the road behind us, whoever was driving it was not of Appalachian heritage and, in fact, had no clue that the three of us even existed. The whole thing was in Melody's head.

"Hey, is that where we're headed?" Troy asked, pointing at a sun-faded green sign on the side of the road.

SUNNY VALLEY CAMPGROUND
15 MILES AHEAD

"Sure is," Melody said. "And just in time too. My butt hurts. I can't wait to get out of this van."

Troy leaned forward and looked at me. "There were bullet holes in that sign."

I shrugged. "Probably kids. Or bored hunters."

"Oh, great," he said, rubbing his hands together. "Bored rednecks with guns. Just what I wanted to hear."

21

A couple miles later, we saw the hitchhiker again.

"Hey, it's the same guy!" Troy said, his face pressed up against the window.

"Are you sure?" Melody glanced at the mirror, but the man was already out of sight.

"Positive. Long blond hair and he was wearing the same clothes. He was holding a sign this time, but I couldn't make out what it said."

"How about you, Billy?"

"I didn't notice until we were right up next to him. I think he must've been sitting in the shade, and when he heard us coming, he stood up real quick."

"You think he's following us?" Troy asked.

"He was ahead of us, Einstein. How could he be following us?"

"Oh yeah."

Melody giggled.

"I dreamed about him last night," Troy said.

I spun around in my seat. "You did what?"

"I was by myself, walking down the side of a road. For some reason, I was barefoot." He stared out the window, remembering. "It was late in the day, kind of like it is right now, going on dusk. Cornfields surrounded me on both sides. The rows were over my head, and I could hear crows cawing. Really loud, like something was agitating them. I looked over and there he was, directly across the road, walking in the opposite direction. Holding his thumb out, even though there were no cars. He nodded at me. I nodded back. The next time I looked, he was gone."

"Then what happened?"

"I don't remember," he said with a shrug. "I guess I woke up."

"Well, that's kinda weird."

"*You're* kinda weird."

"In the dream," Melody said, "did the hitchhiker have a really big sword?"

"Oh my God, don't even start with me about that."

Fighting back a smile. "Hey, it was an honest—"

Troy stuffed his fingers in his ears and closed his eyes. "I can't hear you! I can't hear you! I can't hear you!"

And then we all broke up laughing.

22

I was surprised to find that the Sunny Valley Campground was not located in a valley of any sort. Not even a gorge or a dell or a vale. Instead, it was perched along a meandering hillside overlooking a shallow basin of white pine, boulders, and scrub bush. There were thirty-six sites of various sizes spread out over eighteen acres, and every one of them appeared to be occupied.

When I returned from the campground store—I would soon learn that every respectable campground boasted a small general store, the shelves stocked with everything from consumable goods and camping supplies to last-minute necessities (think bug spray) and keepsakes—with a twenty-pound bag of ice in my hand and the latest issue of *Sports Illustrated* rolled up in my back pocket, Melody was standing outside the van with her back to me.

I started to call out, but stopped myself. The evening air was still and muggy, and I was smelly and dog-tired—but I was also suddenly in the mood for mischief. With Troy showering at the community bathhouse, this was the perfect opportunity to sneak up on Melody and scare her right out of her socks. Something I'd been threatening to do ever since we'd left campus. It was a silly game the three of us played, and we'd figured a week in the woods would provide ample opportunity for good old-fashioned scares. Melody liked to assume the role of surrogate den mother—and no question she was good at it—but she was also a big kid at heart. I couldn't even count how many times she'd sprung out from behind a parked car or a closed door and almost made me piss my pants. No longer feeling even a little bit weary, I abandoned the hard-dirt road for the soft grass where my footsteps wouldn't be heard. And I slowly circled around behind her.

As I crept closer, preparing to pounce while howling like a crazed banshee, I noticed that Melody appeared to be focused on something she was holding in her hand. It was small and shiny and black. At first I thought it might be a piece of camera equipment. Maybe a lens or one of those newfangled light meters—after all, my birthday was coming up in two weeks.

But after a few more steps, I got a better look at it and realized what it was.

A gun.

I froze—suddenly feeling like the ground was tilting beneath my feet.

Thank God I hadn't tried to scare her.

Most of my friends growing up were hunters. Deer. Rabbit. Squirrel. I'd always preferred fishing. I didn't know shit about guns. Rifles. Pistols. Revolvers. They were all one and the same to me: a fucking mystery.

What in the hell is Melody doing with a handgun? And why didn't she tell—

Before I could complete my thought, she turned around.

And smiled at me.

My heart skipped a beat.

Doing my best to appear normal, I readjusted the bag of ice in my hand and started walking again. "Almost dropped it," I said.

She immediately went to the rear of the van and dragged out one of the coolers. "Here, let me help," she said, coming over and using her fingers to claw open a hole in the plastic bag.

"Thanks," I mumbled.

As I dumped the chunks of ice into the cooler, I took a look around.

The gun was nowhere in sight.

23

"I think I'm starting to get the hang of it," Troy said, sitting down next to me. "That was much easier the second time around."

While I'd gathered kindling and gotten the fire going—daydreaming about my run-in with Naomi at the diner; *why did she have to smell so damn good?*—he'd finished setting up the tent and staking it into the ground. I was afraid he'd smash his thumb with the hammer or at the very least tear a hole in the tent—but he'd surprised me by doing an admirable job.

"You'll be an expert by the end of the trip."

"Just one more skill set for my résumé."

"You're too young for a résumé," Melody said, bringing over a paper plate stacked high with slices of watermelon. "You're just a baby."

I grabbed the biggest piece I could find. Took a big bite. And spit a mouthful of seeds in Troy's direction.

"Not true," he said, ignoring the shower of seeds. "I'll need a résumé if I want a good job in Baltimore this summer."

"What kind of job are you thinking?" she asked.

"I figured I'd start at the hospital where my mom works—that way we can ride the bus together. If that doesn't pan out, maybe Lexington Market or BGE. My cousin checks meters for BGE and doesn't hate it."

Suddenly, I wasn't hungry anymore.

Summer break was only weeks away, but I hadn't given it all that much thought. For me, "one day at a time" had become more than just a mantra; it was a survival technique. Melody would be sticking around, taking the final four credits she needed for graduation. The class wouldn't be finished until mid-August—and that was a good thing. It would at least give us some time. But Troy would be going home for the summer. The *entire* summer. The idea that I would no longer see his face and hear his voice every day was difficult to wrap my head around. As ridiculous as it sounded, I felt blindsided by the reality of his departure. He was going away soon, and things would never be the same again.

All of a sudden, more than anything, I needed to take a walk and be alone with my thoughts.

"You okay, Billy?"

I looked up at Melody. She was staring at me.

"Yeah . . . I'm fine," I lied. "Troy just got me thinking about exams. They'll be here before we know it." I got to my feet and walked to the cooler just beyond the firelight. "Anyone need a beer?"

"I'm good," Troy said around a mouthful of watermelon.

"Sure, I'll take one."

I wiped away the ice from a can of Coors and handed it to her.

"I'll be right back," I said, doing my best to avoid eye contact. "Gotta take a leak."

24

I stood alone in the woods, staring out at my friends by the campfire, and silently counted to ten, just like Dr. Mirarchi had taught me. When I was finished, I took a couple of deep breaths and started all over again.

One, two, three . . .

Everything will be okay, I told myself. *We'll talk on the telephone. Take turns visiting each other. And before we know it, it'll be September and the beginning of classes.*

. . . four, five, six . . .

I'll meet new friends. Reunite with old ones. Go home, maybe see Naomi. Eventually, I'll stop being afraid. And my world will open up again.

. . . seven, eight . . .

The way I'm feeling is perfectly normal.

. . . nine . . . ten.

"Everything will be okay," I repeated out loud.

I heard a branch snap—and an unrecognizable voice speak softly from the darkness.

"Did you hear that?"

No more than twenty or thirty feet away from where I was standing.

"*Hear what?*" a second, also unrecognizable, voice answered.

"*Dunno. Thought I heard something.*"

Off to my left, through a screen of trees, I could see the distant lights of a travel trailer and hear the faint strains of a radio playing. I wasn't positive, but I thought it was Jim Croce's "Time in a Bottle," a beautiful song that nonetheless made me want to throw myself off a cliff every time I heard it.

"*Whoa . . . you seeing what I'm seeing?*"

"*Son of a bitch. It's that sexy little senorita from McDonald's.*"

I could hear their footsteps now. Shuffling through the leaves and brush. Coming closer.

"*Where's the other guy that was with them?*"

"*Probably jerking off inside the tent. Who cares?*"

There was little doubt as to who they were talking about. Melody and Troy were sitting around the fire in plain view. And before we'd arrived at the campground a couple hours ago, we'd stopped at a nearby McDonald's for a bite to eat.

"*Think we should stop by and pay them a visit?*"

"*Would be the polite thing to do.*"

"*Maybe show them a little hospitality.*"

The footfalls abruptly stopped. Whoever it was doing the talking, they were now standing on the opposite side of the tree I was hiding behind. Close enough for me to reach out and touch them. One of the men burped—and I instantly smelled the stench of stale beer on his breath. I fought back the urge to gag.

"*Shit, we better not. Look at the time. We don't want to keep Lou waiting.*"

"*Fuck Lou.*"

Low, throaty laughter. "*Yeah . . . sure . . . I'd like to hear you say that to his face.*"

And then they were moving again. Twigs crunching beneath their boots. Traveling parallel to the tree line and away from our camp.

"*I'm not scared of Lou.*"

"*You should be.*"

"*Well, I'm . . .*"

As their voices faded away into the darkness, I held my ground for another minute or two. Just to be safe. Once I was certain they weren't coming back, I headed for camp to tell the others.

25

"So what do we do now?" Troy asked, his owl-like eyes scanning the woods.

"Stay alert in case they return," I said, "but I really don't think they will."

"Why not?"

"Because it sounded like they had business elsewhere tonight—with someone named Lou." I began kicking dirt onto the fire.

"If it's the same two guys I saw in the McDonald's parking lot, we don't have anything to worry about." Melody poured what was left of her beer onto the sputtering flames. "They were so scrawny a stiff breeze could've blown them away. I'm pretty sure they were homeless."

"Do you think they followed us?" Troy asked.

"They were scouring for leftovers in a trash can," Melody said. "I doubt they can afford a car."

"They didn't follow us," I reassured him. "They were taking a shortcut to see Lou, whoever the hell that is, and stumbled upon our camp by accident. It was nothing but blind luck."

"Not for us."

"Stop worrying," Melody said, giving his arm a nudge. "If they show up and try anything stupid, we've got them outnumbered."

I thought of the gun and wondered where she'd stashed it. Most likely someplace close by where she could get to it quickly if necessary. My best guess was her backpack.

"So much for getting any sleep tonight," Troy said, unzipping the tent. He gave the woods one final glance over his shoulder and then ducked inside.

26

"Hey, Billy. Can you come here for a minute?"

"Be right there." I was standing at the back of the van in my bare feet, rummaging through the grocery bags. After searching everywhere and having no luck, I was beginning to suspect that Troy had eaten all the peanut butter crackers. Either that or the little conniver was hiding them somewhere.

"You might want to hurry up."

A few minutes earlier, Melody had crawled out of her bunk dressed in shorts and a T-shirt, and announced that she was getting a ginger ale from the cooler. Did anyone one else want something? Troy hadn't answered, so we'd figured he was already out. So much for the scaredy-cat not getting any sleep tonight. Probably all this fresh air. He wasn't used to that. I'd asked Melody to grab me a Pepsi to wash down my bedtime snack—and that was the last I'd seen of her.

"Billy... *now*, please."

Sighing, I abandoned my quest for peanut butter crackers and made my way to the clearing, stubbing my toe on a rock in the dark. Cursing under my breath, I found Melody standing next to the firepit with her back to me, staring down at the flames.

"Is everything okay?"

She didn't look up. "I thought we put out the fire."

"We did." Confused, I walked to her side. "So why'd you start a new one?"

"I didn't. It was already going when I got here."

I gazed into the stone-encircled pit. There were no logs or large branches feeding the flames. Just a jumbled pile of twigs and brushwood. Another few minutes and it would burn itself down to cinders.

"We must not have put it all the way out." I shrugged. "And it sparked itself back to life." A reasonable-enough explanation, although it still didn't account for the pile of small branches currently aflame.

"You sure someone's not messing with us?" She glanced uneasily at the woods. "Those men from earlier?"

"We would've heard them. Hell, I would've *seen* them."

"You think I'm being silly?"

"Nah." Even though I did.

"You do." She gave my shoulder a bump. "You think I'm acting like Troy."

"Trust me . . . nothing about you reminds me of Troy."

She cracked a smile—but it didn't last very long. "Will you put it out, Billy? And be sure this time?"

I walked over to the cooler and dragged it by the handle to the edge of the firepit. Tipping it onto its side, I carefully cracked open the lid, letting loose an avalanche of ice cubes and water. Within seconds, the kindling was submerged. Thick gray smoke billowed into the air.

"Good enough?"

She nodded. "Thanks." And headed back to the van without her ginger ale.

I sat outside in the dark for a while, watching the tree line. Just in case.

27

Troy was snoring again—that same cadenced, not-unpleasant humming that had served as my lullaby the night before. When I'd unzipped the tent and clambered inside, he hadn't even stirred.

So far, there hadn't been any signs of a nightmare, but it was only the second night. We still had three more to go, and at this point in our journey, seventy-two hours felt like forever. I saw the dim glow of the battery-powered lantern coming from inside the van, which meant that Melody was probably up reading. It had been a long, emotional day, and a part of me was glad that I wasn't the only one still awake. The night felt a little less lonely that way.

Melody had been pretty freaked out about the mystery fire—I wasn't used to seeing her that way—but I was confident that there was a rational explanation. *There had to be, right? Campfires didn't just start all by themselves.*

It was almost midnight—and our watchers from the woods had yet to reappear. I'd meant what I'd told Troy earlier—I seriously doubted that they would. Still, I remained on high alert, listening for approaching footsteps or breaking branches. It felt like sleep would be a long time coming. There were too many thoughts and feelings bouncing around inside my head. I found it difficult to focus on any one thing for more than a minute or two at a time.

After everything that had happened tonight, I'd decided to give Melody the benefit of the doubt about the gun. Over the past several months, she'd earned my trust—and then some. If she felt the need to carry a weapon, there had to be a good reason. And if she hadn't yet told us about why she was carrying it, then there must have been a good reason for that too. When the time was right, I was certain I would get all the answers I needed. In the meantime, it would remain unspoken—and between the two of us. At least for now, I didn't feel the need to involve Troy. Especially knowing how he felt about guns of any kind. He had enough to worry about, both real and imagined.

Before we'd arrived at the campground earlier tonight, we'd grabbed dinner at a McDonald's drive-through just outside of Ludlow. That's where we'd crossed paths with Lou's friends. We'd eaten our burgers and fries on a blanket spread out on a grassy hill overlooking what appeared to be a church-league softball game in progress. By the time we'd finished, the yellow team had launched back-to-back homers to take a one-run lead going into the bottom of the fifth. After that, the game had gotten a bit chippy following a close call at the plate, during which a green base runner had barreled over the defenseless yellow catcher, jarring the ball loose. Ungodly comments soon followed from both benches, and the teams barely managed to avoid a fistfight. Despite the close contest, none of us expressed an interest in sticking around to see what happened next. We were too hot and tired for that.

Ordinarily the most frugal of the group—and with good reason—Troy had surprised us by treating for dinner. When it came time to pay, he'd pulled out a thick wad of McDonald's gift certificates, peeled off a few like a generous uncle showing off at a family Christmas party, leaned over Melody in the driver's seat, and handed them to the cashier. When she'd tried to give him back thirty-seven cents in change, he'd told her to keep it. I sat in the back seat and watched the entire exchange with my jaw hanging open. I hadn't seen a Micky D's gift certificate since a classmate had given me one in a card for my eighth birthday. When we asked Troy where he'd gotten them, he'd explained that his grandmother worked the register at a neighborhood franchise, and she brought home a pack of gift certificates every couple of weeks like clockwork.

Even now, after all this time, Troy Carpenter remained a revelation. I was going to miss him this summer. A lot.

And then there was Naomi. Ever since running into her at the diner this afternoon, I hadn't been able to get her out of my mind. Too many times to count, I'd found myself lifting my T-shirt to my nose and inhaling the sweet scent of her perfume. Melody had caught me once in the rearview mirror but thankfully remained quiet. The last thing I'd needed was her and Troy giving me a hard time.

Over the past year and a half I'd often thought about the possibility of a reunion—of course I had, usually with warring emotions of both hope and dread—but none of those imaginings had measured up to what had actually happened earlier today. The intensity of my reaction shocked me. Despite the initial awkwardness, seeing Naomi had felt *good*. She'd grown up since the last time I'd seen her. Somehow, she was still a teenager, but no longer a girl. Even her voice had changed. And yet, after all this time and everything I'd put her through, she still appeared to possess that same beautiful heart I'd once fallen in love with.

Sighing, I rolled onto my side and picked up the video camera. I'd spent the past forty minutes distracting myself by reviewing footage and jotting down time codes in my notebook. It was better than staring at the ceiling and would save us invaluable time once the film was ready for editing.

Peering through the viewfinder, I pressed the playback button.

28

**VIDEO FOOTAGE
(1:23 p.m., Saturday, May 7, 1983)**

Billy walks back and forth in front of the roadside memorial. His elongated shadow trails closely behind him.

"In the weeks after the funeral, I found myself coming here instead of visiting their grave. The man at

>   the cemetery told us it would take a couple months for their marker to be ready, so it was really just a patch of dirt with some grass seed sprinkled over it. For whatever reason, I felt closer to my parents here." He stops walking, and behind him, we see the photographs of his mother and father attached to the cross. "I almost felt like they could . . . I don't know . . . hear me when I was talking to them."
>
>   The camera goes close on his somber face.
>
>   "Standing here today, I'm not sure what I'm feeling. My mom and dad were my best friends. I miss them terribly, every day. Still, it's been a long time since I've been back here. More than eight months. There are lots of reasons for that but it's mainly—"
>
>   The image freezes—and blurs as it rewinds.
>
>   "—terribly, every day. Still, it's been a long time since I've been back here. More than eight months. There are lots of reasons for—"
>
>   The picture freezes again.
>
>   And remains that way.

29

Holding my breath, I squinted into the viewfinder.

I pulled away, rubbed my eyes, and looked again.

It was definitely there.

I wasn't imagining it.

On the left side of the screen, a little more than halfway up the frame, mostly obscured in a pool of shadows nestled deep within the trees—there was a man's face.

DAY THREE
SUNDAY | MAY 8

1

"So I was right!" Troy said, handing back the video camera. "Someone *was* watching us."

I placed the camera on the seat beside me and took another bite of my strawberry Pop-Tart. I'd been awake half the night, and I was starving. "It looks that way."

He glanced at Melody in the driver's seat. "And you called me a scaredy cat."

"I don't know, guys." She checked the mirror before slowly reversing out of our campsite. "I'm not seeing it."

"How can you not see it?" I asked. "It's right there in front of you."

"I saw . . . *something*," she said, shrugging. "But I'm pretty sure it was just a shadow. Probably caused by the portable lights."

"I wish I could believe that," Troy said from the passenger seat, "but it's clear as day to me." He shuddered dramatically. "There was a man hiding in the trees. The creepy bastard was spying on us."

"I'll take another look the next time we stop," she said. "But I still think you goofballs are imagining things."

"Like mysterious red Jeeps following us halfway across the state."

She grinned at me in the mirror. "Touché, smart-ass."

2

On the morning of April 4, 1981, seventeen-year-old Michael Meredith was driving home from a friend's house when he crashed his purple Mustang into a concrete bridge abutment on RR 19, a few miles west of Leesburg, Pennsylvania. A normally cautious driver with nary a parking ticket, he was six months younger than Troy was now. Death was inevitable—a lesson I'd learned the hard way several times over—but when it came for the young and healthy, it felt particularly sinister.

The Meredith boy was popular at school and in the community. With his sandy-blond cowlick, chubby cheeks, and one of those down-home "aw shucks" attitudes, most visitors never would have guessed that he was captain of the Leesburg High School baseball squad and on the verge of being named covaledictorian of his senior class. Penn State, Richmond, and the University of Maryland were among the long list of colleges that had offered him scholarships—but so far, he'd turned them all down. Meredith's skills on the diamond had also attracted the attention of a number of professional scouts from Major League Baseball, and he was expected to be taken in the early to middle rounds of the upcoming draft that July.

The folks around Leesburg knew all of this, and much more—for instance, how the Meredith boy plowed Old Man Gaylord's parking lot every winter, refusing even a penny in payment, or how he'd taught half the kids in town to catch a pop fly and hit a curveball—and they were only too proud to claim him as their own. At the time of the accident, there was already talk of a big party to be held at the community swimming pool to celebrate Meredith's MLB draft selection. There were even rumors going around school that his parents planned to surprise him with the Kawasaki motorcycle he was always talking about with his friends.

Michael Meredith's death had been major news around Leesburg in the spring of 1981. It still was—as we found out later that morning.

3

The memorial would have been hard to miss, even if we hadn't been paying attention.

Situated at the bottom of a steep hill and surrounded by acres of rolling farmland, the first thing we noticed were the balloons. A large bundle—bright green with the outline of a gray knight printed on them—had been tied to the guardrail where it adjoined the concrete bridge. Every time a car drove past, the balloons caught the blast of air and performed a fluttery little dance.

As we drew closer, we saw the posters that had been attached to the metal safety rail. There had to be at least a dozen of them. Colorful squares of thick construction paper covered with crayon artwork and messy handwriting. I MISS YOU, MICHAEL! I HOPE YOUR HAVING FUN IN HEAVEN. THANKS FOR TEACHING US HOW TO PLAY BASEBALL. The signs, which had been left by students from the local elementary school, appeared to be recent additions, none of them yet touched by wind or rain.

Directly behind the guardrail, standing amid a massive collection of flowers, candles, stuffed animals, and plastic pinwheels spinning lazily in the warm morning breeze, was the biggest trophy I'd ever seen. Topped with a gold figurine—at least fourteen inches tall—resembling a batter admiring what had to be a monster of a home run, the plaque attached to the base of the trophy read: LEESBURG KNIGHTS * 1981 STATE CHAMPIONS. Several baseball gloves and caps had been arranged in the grass beside the trophy. Right next to them, someone had left a pair of green-and-white cleats with the number seven printed on the side.

A short distance away, seven crosses stood vigil. They were painted bright white and spaced evenly apart. The grass around them had been neatly trimmed. A bright red ribbon was draped over the cross in the middle. The message on the ribbon—printed in white script—read: MAY GOD EMBRACE THIS BEAUTIFUL SOUL.

4

Flashing back to the day before when I'd chastised myself for not doing my job properly, I spent an extra fifteen minutes taking photographs of Michael Meredith's memorial. When I was finished using the 35mm, I snapped individual Polaroids of each of the baseball gloves. I'm not sure why—it just felt right.

Photography was like that for me. More than anything else, I followed my instincts. My father had taught me to do that when I was just a boy. *Trust yourself, Billy,* he'd tell me. *Trust your eyes, but don't forget to listen to your heart too.* When I was immersed in a particular subject, I often got very strong . . . *feelings.* You could even call them *compulsions.* Almost like listening to a little voice inside my head that was so quiet I couldn't quite hear it. Still, I knew it was there, whispering, guiding, coaxing, and I was determined to follow its lead. Most of the time, I felt shamefully incapable of seeing the entirety of an image through a camera's viewfinder. What I studied with my own two eyes often felt incomplete and uninspired, yet I somehow knew that there was *more* to the image, lurking just beneath the surface, waiting to be photographed and given life. And only when the final image was developed and unveiled on celluloid was I able to view its true form. For me, photography was the ultimate exercise of *faith*.

Faith of any kind was something I'd been sorely missing the last couple of years. Now, thanks to Dr. Mirarchi, I was back behind the camera again, trusting my heart and doing the best work I'd ever done. I only wished my father were around to see it.

I was standing by the bridge on the shoulder of the road, adjusting the legs on one of the tripods, when the trouble started.

I heard the truck before I saw it.

A loud rumble behind me, followed by the ear-piercing screech of brakes.

And then I breathed in a nasty burp of exhaust—and turned around.

The truck was an older model Chevy Square Body. Two-tone black and gray with dents and scratches running up and down the sideboard. The bearded man leaning out of the window was large and balding and smelled like Budweiser. Thick veins protruded from the loose flesh of his neck. His cheeks were pitted with decades-old acne scars and flushed a deep crimson. He immediately started shaking a meaty finger in my direction.

"Just what in the hell are you people doing?"

For a second, I was too stunned to speak.

So Melody did. "We're working on a school project, sir. We're making a—"

"I don't give a good greasy fuck what you're making, honey—you need to pack up those cameras and get the hell outta here. Right now." He noticed Troy standing by the van, and his bloodshot eyes darkened another shade. "I'd be more than happy to help you on your way."

"Now wait a minute," I said, recovering my composure. "We're not hurting any—"

"Do you know the Meredith family, son?"

"Well . . . no . . . not exactly, but—"

"That's what I thought!" the man said, spittle flying from his mouth. "Well, I *do*! I coached that boy since the time he could pick up a bat. He was like a son to me." He flapped his arm wildly out the window. "And this here is an invasion of his family's privacy. Get the fuck out of here. *Now!*"

"Let's just go, guys," Troy called out.

"That's right," the man slurred, glaring at Troy. "Listen to your little . . . friend . . . back there."

It was the way he said *friend* that pissed me off. I knew exactly what he'd wanted to say. I took a step closer to the truck.

"I don't know what your problem is, mister, but we checked in with the local police before we drove out here." The lie came so naturally, it startled me. "Not only do we have their permission to be here, but they're sending out one of their officers for us to interview." I looked up and down the road. "They should be here any time now, so if I were you, *I'd* get moving—*now*—unless you want them to find those empty beer bottles I'm hearing rattling around inside your truck."

The man stared at me as though I'd just pissed in his soup. He glanced up at his rearview mirror. Once. Twice. And then he started stuttering. "Goddamn cops have lost their minds if . . . I outta shove that camera up your skinny ass . . . who the fuck you think you're talking to . . ."

Craning my neck, I said, "Matter of fact—oh yeah, I think that's them coming."

The man's eyes flashed toward the side mirror and then slowly shifted back to me. His jaw was clenched so tight, I could see the tendons rippling in his cheeks. "You know what, boy . . . you ain't nuthin' but a little fucking smart-mouth. No surprise, though, you runnin' round with the goddamn colored people." Sneering, he spat a dark stream of tobacco that missed my shoes by inches. "I'll be seeing you all again. You can bet on it."

And with that he peeled out down the road, rear end fishtailing, leaving behind sinuous stripes of burning rubber and a stinking gray cloud of exhaust.

When I finally stopped coughing and turned around, Melody and Troy were huddled beside the van, staring at me with their mouths hanging open.

5

Still in shock, we worked quickly.

I didn't think the asshole redneck was coming back any time soon—if he was *that* drunk this early in the day, I figured he probably had other, more important things on his mind—but what the hell did I know? Other than how to convincingly lie right to someone's face, evidently.

Once the dust and exhaust had settled, I pulled Troy aside. "Are you okay?"

"It's fine. I'm used to it," he said with a defeated shrug. I didn't know what to say to that, so I just patted him on the shoulder like an idiot and walked away. Behind me, I heard him say, "Thanks, Billy."

All of a sudden, our earlier conversation from the diner came rushing back at me. *Could something horrible like this really happen in Sudbury? Is it already happening?* A few minutes later, I was setting up the video camera on a tripod and still thinking about the awful look on Troy's face when a boy poked his head out from behind the bridge abutment—no more than two or three feet away from where I was standing—and said, "Hey, man, what's up?"

I gasped and tumbled backward, nearly taking the camera along with me.

As the boy laughed, I scrambled to my feet.

"You okay?" Troy asked, eyeing the stranger with suspicion.

"I'm fine," I said. And I was. Just embarrassed as all get-out.

"Sorry 'bout that," the boy said, emerging from behind the buttress and high-stepping over the guardrail. "Didn't mean to scare you." But he didn't look sorry. He was smiling and eyeballing Melody's tan legs. The boy's teeth were the color of sweet tea. He reeked of marijuana and the sour tang of sweat. Dressed only in saggy blue jeans, flip-flops, and a baseball hat pulled low over his eyes, it was difficult to gauge his age. Up close, I was pretty sure he was at least a few years older than I'd first thought. Across his hairless, sunken chest, there was a tattoo of an angel with its wings unfurled. The zipper of his jeans was open.

"Just surprised me is all." For a split second, I wondered if the stranger standing before us might be the same person who'd been watching us from the trees at my parent's memorial. *Had he followed us here?*

"I didn't mean to," he said again.

I shuffled closer to the camera in case he was thinking about snatching it and taking off running.

"I was fishing under the bridge, and I heard some commotion." He rubbed the scraggly whiskers on his chin. "Figured I'd climb up here and . . . y'know, investigate."

"Any luck?" I asked without really meaning to. Fishing with my dad had been one of my favorite activities growing up. We used to go pretty much every weekend. I missed it.

"Not much. Couple of cat and one big ole crappie." He gestured down the grassy incline, glancing at Melody again. "Got 'em on a stringer if you folks want 'em."

"That's really nice of you," I said, "but we're good. Another half hour or so and we'll be done and on our way."

Finally noticing the camera, he let out a whistle. "Fancy movie projector you got there. Saw one just like it on Channel 8 when they did a story on Mikey's accident." He eyed the memorial.

"Mikey," I repeated. "Did you know the person who died here?"

"'Course I did." His eyes narrowed and the look on his face wasn't nearly as friendly as it had been just seconds earlier. "You mean . . . you don't?"

Uh-oh, here we go again. "Umm . . . well . . . we—"

"We'd like to learn more about him," Melody said, stepping forward and offering her hand. "I'm Melody. This is Billy and Troy."

The boy wiped the palm of his hand on his jeans, inspected it, and shook with Melody. "I'm Pondo." He looked over at me and Troy. "My real name's Paul, but no one calls me that. Not even my girl."

Two thoughts immediately wormed their way inside my brain: (1) somehow this guy had a girlfriend and I didn't, and (2) I had zero interest—even less than zero—in finding out why people called him Pondo instead of Paul.

"We all go to the same college," Melody explained, "and we're working on a project together." She smiled. "Maybe you could help us?"

6

And that's how we found ourselves forty minutes later driving into downtown Leesburg, Pee-Ayy, with a shirtless Pondo—along with his fishing pole, tackle box, and a stringer full of creek-mud-stinking fish—crammed into the back seat next to me. Melody had worked her magic once again. As I held my breath, a part of me hoped that the fish smell would linger long enough for Mel's bossy sister to catch a whiff.

"Yeah . . . that was Coach Watkinson. He's a real piece of work," Pondo said, having just listened to our recap of the roadside confrontation. Our guest picked at something in his teeth with a disgustingly dirty fingernail. "He knows baseball, but that's about it."

"The man has serious anger issues," Melody said.

"That he does. Years ago, he got in trouble for giving one of his players a black eye. The story I heard was that the kid had backtalked him on the bus. He's been on his best behavior at school ever since, although I've heard a few stories about him fighting in the parking lot at Shooters." He looked over at me. "You were pretty brave to stand up to him. That guy could've knocked you flat."

"Yes, you were," Melody said, and I couldn't help but notice the admiring tone in her voice.

"More foolish than brave," I said.

"Won't argue with that." He finally managed to wedge something out from between his teeth. I watched as he flicked it onto the floor of the van. Looking away in disgust, I heard him say, "Let me ask you something, Bill."

"What's that?" I stared past him out the window as Melody made the turn onto a bustling Main Street.

"This thing you're doing for school. This project. Got me thinkin.' I see that cross hangin' 'round your neck and I'm curious . . . do you believe in the afterlife?"

Based on his previous inquiries, I'd expected something a little less weighty. More along the lines of what kind of bait did I use for smallmouth. Or whether I had any tattoos on my butt. The question really surprised me, and when I didn't answer right away, Troy turned around and spoke up in my place.

"I do," he said. "I believe there's something—and someplace—waiting for all of us after our time on earth is done."

Pondo broke into a big brown-toothed smile. "Me too, partner!" He flapped his arms at the world beyond the window. "I believe there's a heaven and a hell, and everything else in between."

"I'm not so sure about heaven and hell . . . ," Troy said. "But I do believe there's . . . *something*."

"Something . . . like what?" Pondo asked, his scruffy face scrunched up in thought.

"I have no idea. Perhaps another dimension . . . or maybe a parallel universe that overlaps our own." Troy turned and faced forward again. "I'll let you know when I get there."

Pondo threw his head back and laughed, waggling his fingers. "Ooooh—you'll let me know when you get there! That's a good one, Todd!"

Troy raised a finger in the air. "My name isn't—"

"Okay, I'll play," Melody interrupted. "I was raised Catholic. From the time I started going to Sunday school until I was a teenager, the notion that there were literal places called heaven and hell and purgatory was crammed down my throat on a weekly basis." She shook her head. "And now . . . I'm not so sure I believe in any of it."

I glanced in the mirror at the gold crucifix hanging around her neck. "So . . . what? You think that when we die, we just get blown out like a candle? And there's nothing else?"

"I didn't say that," she said, swinging the van into an empty parking spot in front of the grocery store. "I have no idea what comes next . . . if anything. I'd *like* to know . . . I think about it sometimes . . . but I really don't have a clue. All I know is that I no longer believe there's a set of pearly gates waiting up there in the clouds with HEAVEN printed across the front of them."

"Huh . . . that's deep. But hang on, man—conversation to be continued," Pondo said, easing past me in the back seat. The sweat-slicked skin of his rib cage grazed the tip of my nose as he scooted by—and I fought the urge to vomit. With the ass of his saggy jeans dangling perilously close to my face, he slid open the side door of the van. "If I 'member right, Penny gets off at noon. I'm betting she'll be happy to talk with you folks." His zipper still down, he hopped out into the parking lot and practically skipped inside the store.

7

**VIDEO FOOTAGE
(12:45 p.m., Sunday, May 8, 1983)**

```
"I'll try, but I don't know if I can remember all
that."
   As the image sharpens, a young woman's face swims
into focus. Her fleshy cheeks are crowded with freck-
les. Her broad nose is sunburned and peeling. There
are dark circles beneath her dull and lifeless eyes.
Her light brown hair is cut short of her shoulders,
making her face appear flat and round.
   "He was my brother," she says "and I loved him. He
was eighteen months younger than me, which explains why
```

he was so spoiled." The woman is wearing light blue slacks and a wrinkled matching blouse. The plastic name tag clipped to her chest reads: Penny Meredith.

"He liked to tell people that I wore down Mom and Dad by getting into so much trouble. And that by the time he grew up, they'd given up and stopped being so strict."

Behind her, sunlight reflects off the long, slender stem of the trophy. The effect on Michael Meredith's roadside memorial is almost blinding.

The image blurs as the camera is readjusted—and then quickly regains clarity.

"He was a pretty good kid, I guess, a lot smarter than me, that's for sure, but it's not like he was perfect. Or even close. He could be a real pain in the ass too." She smiles, and it isn't a pretty sight. Instead, it's a jack-o'-lantern grin at midnight.

"He hated to lose. He always cheated when we played cards and board games. And he was lazy around the house. Never did his chores on time. And I'll tell you, he drank a lot more than people knew. Parties every weekend. On hunting and fishing trips. Sometimes even out back when we were burning leaves or trash. One time, he snuck a bottle of whiskey into his equipment bag and got all shit-faced on the bus ride home after a doubleheader. No one found out, of course . . . he was always lucky that way . . . but one of his teammates told me all about it and I believed him."

The picture blurs again as it fast-forwards.

When it stops, Penny Meredith is leaning against the railing of the bridge. We can see the upper halves of three of the crosses over her right shoulder, and directly above her head, green and gray balloons bob in and out of frame.

"I miss him. We didn't talk that much the last year he was alive. He was always so damn busy. A lot of the time when we were both home, he was tired and moody. Sometimes, he got mean." Her gaze wanders to the muddy creek below. "I guess I was pretty mean too . . . but I swear that boy got on my last nerve." She wipes her eyes with her forearm. At first, we think it's tears, but it soon becomes clear that it's just perspiration. Her fleshy face is glistening in the heat.

"We got in a big fight the night before the accident. A real blowout. He called me a fat, ugly bitch and threatened to tell Mom that I'd gone back on birth control. I told him that if he did, I'd show her the box of rubbers he had hidden beneath the floorboard in his bedroom. He hollered I was a big ole snoop and stormed out of the house and—"

The video fast-forwards again. Stops.

Penny's sitting cross-legged in the grass beside the shrine of baseball gloves, her fingers fidgeting with a dandelion she's just plucked. Head hanging down, face obscured by a curtain of greasy hair, she finally speaks—and it's as if the voice is coming from someone else.

"I wouldn't say I was jealous of him . . . fuck no . . . I just didn't idolize him like everyone else around here. That whole patron-saint-of-Leesburg horseshit." With a flick of her thumb, she pops off the head of the dandelion. "Sometimes, I used to dream that he died . . . even before the accident . . ."

8

At first, none of us said anything.

We just stood there on the shoulder of RR 19 and watched Penny Meredith and Pondo drive away in her beat-up Buick Skylark. In addition to needing four new tires, the windshield was cracked in about a dozen places, and the muffler was missing. We listened to the car's deep throated rumble long after it disappeared over the hill.

As usual, it was Troy who broke the silence. "Uhh . . . did anyone else think that was, like, mondo bizarre?"

I looked at him. "You mean the fact that she pretty much hated her little brother's guts and was willing to say as much on video?"

"Yeah . . . *that*."

Melody started walking toward the van. "Did you notice she never called him by his name? Not once."

"You know what?" I said. "I think you're right."

"I know I am." She climbed behind the wheel. "Who's ready for lunch?"

Troy raised his hand and made a beeline for the passenger seat.

Sliding open the door, I hopped into the back seat—and immediately began gagging. "Aw, hell . . . it stinks like dead fish back here!"

9

VIDEO FOOTAGE
(11:26 p.m., Sunday, May 8, 1983)

"I was backup center fielder on varsity for two years, so I got to know Mikey pretty well."

Pondo slaps a mosquito on his shoulder and shoos away a couple more before they can target his bare chest. The angel tattoo looks larger than life in the center of the screen. Probably because Pondo is being shot from the waist up to avoid his open zipper. His torso is bathed in sunlight.

"Mikey was never backup anything." He gives a shake of his head. "That kid had some serious skills. And boy, was he fast.

"You asked me before what he was like . . ." Pondo gazes off camera, drawing deep from the well of memory. "Mikey was smart as a whip. Always carrying around a book with him. And not just school books, neither. He read book books . . ." He pauses to find the word. "Uh . . . novels." He spits into the dirt. Wipes his mouth with his forearm. "Mikey could be a cocky SOB on the field, but he always backed it up." Squinting at the camera again. "Off the field, mostly what I remember is he was a good guy. Loyal. If he liked you, he had your back. And he made sure people knew it. Plenty of folks 'round here look down on me cuz my family's from the hills. Mikey wasn't like that. He didn't let anyone treat me different when he was around." Staring off again. "Let's see . . . what else? He was always willing to share his chew and bubble gum at practice and games. One of the girls who worked at the drug store used to sneak him packs of Bubble Yum for free, and he was always cool about spreading the wealth. A lot of the other fellas weren't like that . . ."

10

"I don't care how hot it is outside," I told Melody. "Don't you dare roll up that window."

She stopped in midcrank. "You're being dramatic, Billy. The smell's not that bad." The traffic light turned green, and she eased into the intersection.

"Oh yeah? Make sure you tell your sister that when she starts bitching."

"Just be glad your buddy Pondo hitched a ride with someone else," Troy said, "or he and his stinky-ass fish could be sitting right next to you again."

"Thank God for small miracles," I said.

After finishing up round two at the memorial, we'd decided to head back to Leesburg for a bite. We'd gotten stuck behind a couple of farm tractors, and the three-mile trip had taken forever.

"I got the feeling those two were once sweethearts," Melody said, finally making the turn onto Main Street. "Maybe they still are."

"Wouldn't surprise me." I gave an exaggerated shudder. "They make a hell of a couple. Penny and Pondo—two peas in a pod."

"Frankenstein's monster and his lovely bride," Troy added with a chuckle.

"Ahh, he wasn't that bad," Melody said, cruising past the grocery store where Penny Meredith worked. "He was actually kind of sweet."

Grinning, Troy started swaying back and forth in the passenger seat. "Melody and Pondo sittin' in a tree. K-I-S-S-I-N-G. First comes love, then comes marriage—"

"Don't make me pull over."

"—then comes Mel with a baby carriage."

The van veered to the shoulder and jerked to a stop.

"Out."

Troy smiled uncertainly and glanced at me in the back seat.

I gestured to the door.

And then Melody was laughing at both of us—and steering the van back onto the road.

"Nice," Troy muttered. "Real nice."

"All I'm saying," she continued, her smile fading, "is that he was very kind. He offered us his fish; he gave us an interview and went out of his way to introduce us to the victim's sister."

"A lot of good that'll do us," I said. "I'm not sure any part of her footage is usable."

"Not even 'I used to dream that he'd died'?"

"That whole afterlife conversation was . . . surprising," Troy said. "I didn't expect that from a guy who couldn't keep his zipper closed."

"You know what wasn't surprising?" Melody asked. "Everyone offered their opinion except Billy." She stared at me in the rearview mirror. "Mr. My Mind Is a Steel Vault and I Never Let Anyone In."

"That wasn't my fault," I said. "He went into the store to get Penny and that was the end of it."

"Uh-huh." Eyes back on the road now. "Whatever you say."

Troy swiveled around. "So? What's the deal, then? You a believer or not?"

It took me a moment to answer. "I guess you could say that I *want* to believe . . . but I'm not quite there yet."

"Ha!" Melody smacked her hand against the steering wheel. "A Billy Anderson response if I ever heard one."

"I'm being serious, though." I was starting to feel a headache coming on. A bad one. "I mean, I lost both of my parents at the same time. You don't think I'd like to believe that they're somewhere else right now? Peaceful and happy and sipping piña coladas by a celestial pool? Or maybe floating around on a cloud, watching over me?"

"I was only teasing," Melody said, the humor gone from her voice. "I didn't mean—"

"No, no, it's cool—you're fine," I said, putting my hands up. "The point . . . what's my point?" The thoughts were hard to articulate, especially in front of my friends. "The point . . . I am trying to make . . . is that just like you two, I have every reason to *want* to believe. Shit, man, some days, I *look* for reasons to believe. I see someone on TV say that their dead wife loved . . . I don't know, monarch butterflies . . . and ever since she's been gone, he sees monarch butterflies all around their yard. And at the park. And outside of his office building. And at the beach, where they really shouldn't be. And he's certain—absolutely *certain*—that it's his wife sending him a message from beyond."

Troy nodded. "A lot of people claim the same thing about cardinals, you know."

"Exactly," I said, pointing at him. "Some people say that they've been visited by loved ones in their sleep. Dreams too personal and vivid to be anything else. A widow swearing that she smells her late husband's cologne in times of extreme duress. A sign that he's there with her, trying to help calm her nerves. Others feel a touch... a *presence*... Sometimes they even hear a voice."

There was that Tuesday night before Christmas, when I'd thought I'd heard my mother singing. I'd long convinced myself that it was nothing more than my imagination playing tricks on me. Like Dr. Mirarchi had noted during one of our earlier sessions, my brain that day had been overstimulated. There'd been the Brit Lit exam in the morning, shopping all afternoon at the mall, and then a long, raucous dinner with the basketball team. I'd been worn out both mentally and physically—and stumbling upon *White Christmas* on television (especially my mother's favorite scene) had blindsided me emotionally.

I pushed those thoughts away, and they were immediately replaced by the memory of our first interview—Jennifer Harper saying that she often felt her late husband's presence in the room with her—and what I'd experienced firsthand at Chase's memorial. That unpleasant sensation had lasted only seconds—and then vanished. My oversized imagination again? A surge of adrenaline from initially stumbling upon the memorial? A genuine *presence*? But if that was the case, why Chase Harper—a complete and total stranger? And why had it felt so damn awful?

"All I can tell you is... we've all lost someone close to us," I finally said, rubbing my forehead with my thumb. The looming headache had arrived in full force. "I hope the two of you are right. I really do. My mind's open to the existence of an afterlife"—the lie felt natural coming out of my mouth—"but so far there's been no butterflies or cardinals for me. Maybe one day."

We drove the rest of the way to lunch in silence.

11

"You've got cheese on your chin."

I pointed across the table at Troy. "And your cheek." Still pointing. "And a little higher up . . . by your ear." No longer able to hold back my laughter. "Christ, maybe you should start wearing a bib."

Troy put down what was left of his crust and took a long drink of root beer. When he was finished, he sucked an ice cube into his mouth. "Should've let it cool off first. Now I've got pizza roof."

Leesburg, Pennsylvania, might have been located smack-dab in the middle of nowhere, USA—but I'll be damned if they didn't have themselves a first-class pizza joint. At nineteen and on my own for the past year and a half, I was pretty much an expert when it came to all things pizza. Frank's Pizzeria didn't look like much on the inside. A half-dozen tables covered in red-and-white-checkered tablecloths surrounded on three sides by twice as many cramped booths. There was a gumball dispenser by the cash register and a *Space Invaders* coin-op machine against one wall. Right next to it, the mouth of a narrow hallway marked RESTROOMS. A small television was mounted on the ceiling in one corner, playing what appeared to be a soap opera. The framed photographs on the walls featured Philadelphia and Pittsburgh sports stars. Many of them were autographed. But none of that really mattered. What *did* matter was whoever was working the kitchen—presumably a genius named Frank—knew his pizza. We'd ordered a large half-pepperoni for the three of us to share—and it was a goddamn gooey delight.

"I need to use the ladies room," Melody said, getting up from the table.

On her way by, she touched me on the shoulder. I could tell she still felt bad about pushing me for a response to Pondo's whole "meaning of life" conversation. She'd spent the past half hour being a little too nice. It made me uncomfortable.

Watching her leave, I picked at my salad and tried to decide whether I wanted another slice of pepperoni. I was already stuffed—thanks in part to the three big glasses of Coke I'd scarfed down—but we had a long day ahead of us and no idea where or when we might stop again.

Troy was obviously thinking along the same lines. "Where to next?" he asked, his mouth full of ice. It came out sounding like: *Where oo ext?*

"I say we keep heading west. Unless you and Melody have other ideas."

"Fine by me." He took another drink of his root beer. "How do you feel about the footage we've recorded so far?"

"It's pretty solid. Penny Meredith notwithstanding." I watched an older couple walk into the restaurant holding hands. "We just need a lot more of it."

"Think we made a bad decision focusing on backroads? That eating up too much time?"

"Nah, I think we're okay," I said, putting down my fork. "Besides, we'll hit the bigger roads on the way home."

Troy slid the last slice of pepperoni onto his plate. "In the meantime, we just keep grinding."

Returning from the restroom, Melody sat down and immediately lowered her eyes. "Okay, this is weird... Guys, don't look right away... Is it my imagination or are the three of us the big-time center of attention?"

Troy stared at his plate and spoke in a low voice. "I thought it was because I was the only Black person in here."

Melody faked a yawn and talked into her hand. "I thought it was because my shorts were too short."

I tried to be patient, but I couldn't take it any longer. Casually gazing over Melody's head, I surveyed the dining area. The older couple I'd watched arrive just a moment earlier were sitting at a table by the register. Both held menus in front of them, obscuring the lower halves of their faces. Above the menus, they were staring directly at our table. Next to them, a sheriff's deputy, his hat resting on the empty seat beside him, took a sip of what looked like iced tea. His slitted eyes were glued on the three of us. A few tables away, a man dressed in a wrinkled suit pretended to read a newspaper. Not far behind him, three teenage boys lounged in a corner booth. They didn't even bother disguising their interest. Underneath the brims of their baseball caps, they gazed at us with the same kind of dull-eyed fascination you often saw from visitors at a zoo as they lingered in front of yet another caged exhibit.

I picked up my fork, stabbed a chunk of lettuce, and slowly lifted it to my mouth. Until Melody had said something, I'd been lost in my own little world and hadn't noticed anything out of the ordinary. Now that I had, my skin was crawling.

"If this was a movie," I said, barely above a whisper, "right about now, one of us would insist that this was all our imagination."

Melody looked at me. "Do you think we're imagining it?"

Our waitress stopped at the counter and said something to the woman standing behind the cash register. They both grinned and glanced in our direction, then quickly looked away when they saw that we were watching.

"Hell no," I said, shaking my head. "These people look like they want to eat *us* for lunch."

"I was thinking the same thing," Troy said, wiping his mouth with a napkin. "I sure hope they don't like dark meat."

Our appetites gone, we paid the bill a few minutes later and got the hell out of there.

12

"Shit . . . we definitely weren't imagining it," Melody said, standing on the sidewalk with her hands on her hips.

Troy and I stared over her shoulder at the rear of the van.

The back right tire was flat.

All of a sudden, stopping in Leesburg felt like a big mistake.

"Why would someone do this?" Melody asked, looking around uneasily.

"Don't jump to conclusions." I bent down and began inspecting the deflated tire. "We could've picked up a nail or some broken glass."

"Mighty weird coincidence," she said.

Troy nervously shuffled his feet. "This place is starting to freak me out, guys."

From down on one knee, I surveyed the street. A couple of kids riding bikes. A lady in a pink dress stuffing a handful of letters into a mailbox. Shoppers coming and going from the stores that lined Main Street. Unlike our fellow diners, none of them appeared to be paying us the slightest bit of attention.

"Someone slashed it, didn't they?" Troy asked.

"I don't see anything." I stood and wiped my hands on my jeans. We'd only been outside for a matter of minutes, but I was already sweating up a storm. "But that doesn't mean much. I'm hardly an expert."

"My sister's going to kick my ass," Melody said and groaned.

"I saw a garage on our way into town." I pointed beyond the mailbox. "Bunch of tires stacked up out front. Maybe they can replace it on the cheap."

"Why would someone do this?" she asked again. "You think it might've been that redneck coach?"

"That's a distinct possibility," Troy said, eyes searching the street. "He did threaten us."

Shit. Troy could be paranoid, but this time I had to agree with him. "Okay, let's focus on getting out of here, then," I said. "Best case scenario: we won't have to mess with the spare and your sister won't even notice."

"How much does a new tire cost?" she asked.

I could hear the worry in her voice. I looked at Troy. He knew what I was thinking and nodded his agreement. "Split three ways . . . not that much."

Melody looked like she might burst into tears. "You guys are the best, you know that?"

"Of course we are," Troy said, draping a skinny arm around my shoulder. "We're a couple of real mensches."

"What are mensches?"

"I'll tell you later," he said, starting up the sidewalk. "Let's get the tire fixed and get the hell out of Dodge before those fucking weirdos finish eating and come looking for us."

I couldn't tell if he was kidding or not.

13

"Hello there!"

The man who climbed out of the tow truck was wearing dress slacks and boots and a starched white button-down shirt—and yet he didn't appear to be sweating. Even his hair looked unbothered by the heat. "Name's Ted Brown. I'm head mechanic and owner of the place. Anything I can do to help you folks?"

Given the man had pulled into the parking lot of Leesburg Towing & Repair and found three strangers banging on his locked front door and standing on crates peering into the windows, you wouldn't have thought the guy would be so darn friendly. But that was the other side of small-town living.

"We've had a little trouble," Melody said, walking closer to the man but stopping a safe distance away. "We were hoping someone could replace a flat tire for us."

Ted's smile faded. "I'm sorry to tell you, but the garage is closed on Sundays. I just stopped by to grab some paperwork on my way to a church meeting."

Melody's shoulders sagged. "Is there anyone else who can help us?"

He thought about it for a moment. "Bucky Sharretts could do it easy enough . . . but he's out of town this weekend visiting with his kids."

"It'll be okay, Mel." I walked up beside her. "We'll make do with the spare for now and pick up a new tire down the road."

Ted rubbed his square chin, his eyes lingering on Troy behind us. "You folks aren't from around here, are you?"

No shit, Sherlock, I thought unkindly. *What gave you that idea? Maybe the fact that Troy's the only Black person we've seen since entering town proper.*

"We're students," Melody said, her voice taking on a familiar sweet tone, "from York College. We're working on a documentary. We've got a couple of days left to go, but . . ."

Ted began rolling up the sleeves of his white dress shirt. "Where are you guys parked?"

"Really?!" Melody squealed. "You'll help us?"

He was smiling again. "Well, I can't just leave you all stranded here, now can I?"

"Thank you so much, mister!"

"Ted," he reminded her. And all of a sudden, I didn't like the way he was looking at her.

"Thank you, Ted! Thank you, thank you, *thank* you!"

And then, before I knew it, she was hugging the guy—which in my mind was the very definition of taking it too far. For all we knew, Ted was in cahoots with the pizza joint diners. In fact, I planned to keep a very close eye on him.

"Our van is parked just down the street from Frank's Pizzeria" I said, interrupting their embrace. "Mel, you need to give him the keys."

Still giddy, she fished them out of her pocket and handed them over.

"Be back in a flash." He sauntered over to the tow truck—and the three of us watched him drive away.

"What if he doesn't come back?" Troy asked once he was out of sight.

"Don't be silly," Melody replied. "Of course, he will."

But I wasn't so sure about that.

14

Fortunately, though, she was right.

"We're really sorry to make you late for your meeting," Melody said fifteen minutes later as Ted began loosening the bolts on the flat tire.

"Not a problem. This shouldn't take long."

"Well, you're very kind to help us," she said in that overly saccharine voice. "I can't tell you how much I appreciate it."

Ted stood and unbuttoned his shirt. He shrugged it off, exposing a white tank top underneath, and then tossed the balled-up dress shirt into the open window of his truck. Bending down to position the jack beneath the van, his muscular arms and shoulders were in full display. Melody stood a few feet away from him as he worked. For someone so distraught about her sister's van, she sure was smiling a lot.

"Methinks the lady is in love," Troy said quietly. We were watching from the shade underneath the awning in front of the building.

"Shut up."

"Methinks Teddy's a hunk, and I don't see a wedding ring on his finger."

"Gross. He's got to be at least forty."

He looked at me. "Methinks Billy is jealous."

"I'm not jealous, you moron." Another lie. "I'm just cranky and hot and anxious to get back on the road." Not a lie.

Once he'd finished jacking up the rear of the van, Ted slid off the flat tire and carefully examined it. After a moment, he looked up and said, "You've got a couple of drywall nails embedded in the tread."

I flashed him a thumbs-up and immediately felt like an idiot.

He picked up a screwdriver and began prying the rim off the tire. Sweating profusely, his muscles flexed and his bare skin glistened. Good Samaritan or not, I was pretty sure I hated him.

"There you go," I said to Troy. "A couple of nails . . . it *was* an accident."

"*Or* someone could have put them there on purpose. One nail, I can see. More than one is pushing it."

Over by the van, Melody giggled—and suddenly it was all I could do not to yell out, *What are you so damn happy about?!* As petty as it was, I had half a mind to make her pay for her own damn tire.

"Did you do that on the window?" Troy asked.

"Do what?"

He pointed at the van. The back window was coated in road dust. In the lower corner, someone had drawn something with their finger. From where we were sitting, it looked like a peace sign or maybe a stick figure.

"Wasn't me," I said.

"We had a penis bandit at our school my senior year."

I looked at him, certain that I'd misheard. "What kind of bandit?"

"A penis bandit," he said matter-of-factly.

"Explain."

"Everywhere the guy went, he drew penises. On dirty car windows.

Bathroom walls and mirrors. Desks and blackboards. I left my notebook open once at the library. Went to the restroom. Came back a few minutes later and the entire page of notes was covered in dicks."

"You say it's a guy. How do you know it wasn't a girl?"

"It wasn't a girl."

"How can you be sure? Did anyone ever bear witness to these penile crimes against the school system?"

"No. But come on, it wasn't a girl."

"Did they ever catch the person?"

"Nope. Not even after we came back from Easter break and found a giant penis spray-painted across the faculty parking lot."

"It was you, wasn't it? *You* were the penis bandit, and you're finally confessing after living with such crushing guilt."

Exasperated, he said, "God no. I would never."

I laughed. "I know that, Carp. I'm just yanking your chain."

Troy didn't say anything for a minute, then: "What do *you* think the deal was back there at the pizza joint?"

As Ted slid on a replacement tire, I noticed a small tattoo on his shoulder. From where I was sitting, it looked like an angel. I remembered the tattoo of an angel with its wings unfurled on Pondo's chest.

"The only thing I can think is . . ."

Across the street, a young couple walked by on the sidewalk. They appeared to be in their early twenties, fresh-faced and neatly dressed, like they'd just come from church service. The woman was wearing a floppy yellow hat. The man's face was glistening with perspiration. He was pushing a stroller. The canopy was up, shielding their baby from the sun. Both the man and woman were staring directly at us.

". . . that word got around about us filming at the Meredith memorial, and they didn't much like it."

The stroller hit a bump in the sidewalk, jolting violently in the man's grip and nearly tipping over. The couple continued on as though nothing had happened, neither mother nor father even bothering to glance down to check on the baby. *That's because the stroller's empty,* I thought, suddenly sure of it. *It's just a prop so they could get closer to us.*

"You think Coach What's-His-Name was behind it?"

"A strong possibility. Then again, could've been anyone. Aunt Helen was right. Small towns are like that. They take care of their own."

"Maybe . . . ," Troy said, completely unaware of the drama playing out across the street. "I still think it was me they were looking at. Black guy. My hair. It's happened before."

The couple disappeared around the corner. I turned and looked at Troy, feeling as though I'd just awakened from a long nap. "Your hair *is* kind of a disaster today."

He leaned over and rammed his shoulder into mine. Not too hard. "You *wish* you had this magnificent 'fro."

Normally, I would have laughed at such a ridiculous statement and given Troy hell for having the balls to make it. But not today. With a sinking feeling settling in the pit of my stomach, I got up from the crate and walked over to the van.

Now, more than ever, I wanted out of Leesburg. The sooner, the better.

15

The rest of the day was a blur.

We pulled away from Ted's garage shortly after 3 p.m.—thankfully, by then, he was once again wearing a shirt—and were met almost immediately by a thunderstorm of biblical proportions. Not one of the weather forecasts we'd heard on the radio that morning had mentioned even a passing shower, much less a storm containing such explosive power. Torrents of rain—often blowing sideways thanks to 45 mph wind gusts—forced us to find refuge in a nearby beauty salon parking lot. The sky around us lit up with brilliant forks of lightning and then went dark again. The ground beneath us trembled with echoing booms of thunder. The windshield wipers couldn't keep up with the deluge, so Melody didn't even bother keeping them on. Waiting out the storm in the corner of an empty lot, with rivers of rain pressing against the van's windows, made it feel like we were submerged in a giant aquarium. I kept waiting for a school of catfish or perch to swim by.

Trapped there for almost ninety minutes, the stench of Pondo's catch of the day mercifully fading, we passed the time by participating in a survey that Melody had discovered in a recent issue of *Cosmopolitan* she'd brought along. She read each of the two dozen questions aloud, and with blushing faces and squeals of embarrassment, we scribbled our answers on sheets of paper ripped from my notebook. When we were finished, we tallied up our points and compared them to a detailed chart printed in the back of the magazine. The results were hilarious. According to the "more than fifty sexual health experts" responsible for the survey, I was a Noncommunicative Partner, Melody was a Borderline Sexual Adventurist, and Troy was a Not-for-Long Virgin. After only three days on the road, the veil of privacy between us had been completely torn away. It was actually kind of liberating—a new level of openness had been reached in our mutual friendship.

When the rain finally slowed and we were able to get back on the road, we witnessed firsthand the surprising and devastating aftermath of the storm. Trees were down everywhere, some of them on landing on houses and barns. Streets and fields were flooded. Telephone lines lay twitching across roads and hung from tree branches like squirming electric eels. We drove past an overturned ambulance in a ditch and a lumber warehouse on fire, most likely from a lightning strike. I'd only seen tornadoes on television, but to me, it looked like one had touched down in the area. Despite our collective skepticism of a higher power, and the unsettling hostility of Leesburg (Ted and Pondo being the grudging exceptions), it did almost feel as if someone had been looking out for us. At the very least, we'd been extremely fortunate.

Navigating backroads littered with fallen tree limbs and detouring around swollen creeks and rivers that had overtaken low-lying roadways meant seriously slow going for the remainder of the afternoon. It also meant, courtesy of Troy, a nonstop playlist on the radio featuring the likes of Conway Twitty, Charley Pride, and T. G. Sheppard. If I heard one more twangy tune about lonely cowboys drinking beer and getting into fistfights in backwoods honkytonks, my head was going to explode.

Every once in a while, there would be a news report about the storm. The National Weather Service had yet to officially confirm a tornado in the area, but several residents of Leesburg claimed they'd witnessed a funnel cloud coming in from the east. A farmer in nearby Deerfield was interviewed live. In a remarkably calm voice, he described the loss of both of his barns due to "the twister," and explained that his wife had managed to recklessly snap several photos of the destruction as it occurred. At the time of the interview, they were waiting for the film to be developed.

Of course, Troy listened to all of these stories with a sense of mounting hysteria—and spent the next twenty or so miles with his head out the window, searching the dark skies for approaching tornadoes. If it weren't for Melody's calming influence, I think there were better than average odds that we'd be heading home right about now.

As for me, my mind was still preoccupied with other matters. I hadn't mentioned the staring couple pushing the baby stroller to either Troy or Melody—and didn't plan to. An hour out of Leesburg, I'd mostly convinced myself that I was being paranoid. Empty baby carriages used as props? Small-town spies and saboteurs? Better to keep such crazy thoughts to myself.

On the outskirts of a single-stoplight town called Parkton, we ran across a roadside memorial that had been built alongside a decorative wrought-iron fence bordering a cemetery. Excited, we'd immediately pulled over, only to discover that the storm had transformed the memorial into a wasteland of soggy debris, much of it scattered among the ancient grave markers. Out of respect for the deceased, we spent about twenty minutes cleaning up the best we could—leaving what we'd found in neat piles by the fence—and then we continued on our way.

And struck gold just down the road a bit.

While waiting for a three-man crew of county road workers to finish chainsawing a downed tree into small enough pieces to haul out of the way, we spotted a row of crosses on the shoulder up ahead. Two large crosses set in the ground surrounded by two smaller ones. The bottom half of each cross was hidden underwater thanks to the flooding.

After a brief discussion, I got out of the van and began taking photos. There were maybe a dozen other cars waiting for the road to be cleared, and the three of us had agreed that if anyone said anything, I'd immediately stop and beat a hasty retreat to the van. We'd already learned one hard lesson today.

As I was snapping photographs, the dark clouds above us began to break up and blow away. Slivers of sunlight peeked through, making the rain-soaked crosses—recently repainted by the looks of them—shimmer with a golden luminesce. I'd just crouched down to get a better angle when I heard a car window being rolled down behind me and snatches of a Creedence Clearwater Revival song on the radio.

Uh-oh, I thought, preparing to make a hasty exit. *Here it comes.*

"If it's not too much trouble," a pleasant voice said from over my shoulder, "may I ask what you're doing?"

I stood up and turned around.

The gray-haired woman sitting in the passenger seat of the faded-blue pickup truck looked so much like my grade school teacher Mrs. Flanders that it took me a moment to respond. Because of the resemblance—and the warm smile on the old lady's face—I liked her immediately.

"My friends and I are working on a project for school," I said, approaching the truck. "We're taking photos and shooting video of roadside memorials, and then trying to document the stories behind them."

The driver leaned forward until we could see each other. "A school project, you say?" The man was wearing a flannel shirt and a sun-blasted ball cap that looked roughly a hundred and fifty years old. He had the same round eyes and high forehead as the woman sitting next to him, and I found myself wondering if they were brother and sister.

"Yes, sir. My two friends"—I gestured behind us to the van—"and I go to York College. It's for our American Studies class."

"Well, I must say that you and your friends are pursuing a most honorable endeavor," the woman said. "I think the Carson family would be delighted that you want to share their story with the world."

I felt a tingle in my stomach—a good one, this time. "Did you know the Carsons very well?"

"Oh yes." She gave me a wistful smile. "They were my next-door neighbors for nine years . . ."

16

VIDEO FOOTAGE
(5:34 p.m., Sunday, May 8, 1983)

```
"Betty Carson was like a daughter to me," says the gray-
haired woman sitting in the passenger seat of the
faded-blue truck. Next to her, slouched behind the
steering wheel, almost as though he's hiding from the
camera, is a stoop-shouldered gentleman content on
listening.

   "Shortly after she and Bruce moved in next door,
Betty announced that she was pregnant. They were over
the moon. We all were. My husband, Louis—he passed
away a few years ago; a lifetime smoker—helped Bruce
build a crib for the nursery. The Carsons were like
that. They could've afforded any fancy crib in the
catalog, but they wanted something more personal.
Something they could hand down to their children when
the time came." She sighs loudly.

   The lighting on the video is less than stellar.
There are riffling reflections from the truck's metal
door frame, and every time the woman leans back in
her seat, the left side of her face is lost in
shadow.
```

"Katie was born the day after Halloween. They called her their little pumpkin baby." The old woman giggles into her hand. "And my goodness did she have a big head, that child. Oh, she was beautiful. I don't mean anything by it. She was absolutely perfect."

Somewhere in the background, the buzz of a chainsaw.

"Aaron came two years later. He had a serious issue with his heart. I can't remember what the doctors called it, but he wasn't able to come home from the hospital until he was almost four months old. It was a very difficult time for the family. Betty, especially."

The chainsaw goes silent.

"For being so young, Bruce Carson was very good at his job. He worked at one of the big advertising firms and was able to arrange for Aaron to get the best care money could buy. Within a year, Aaron was doing much better, running around the backyard like a jackrabbit. My husband used to tell me that I needed to prepare myself for the day when the Carsons moved away to a bigger house in a bigger neighborhood . . . but Betty swore that wasn't going to happen. Not unless they had a couple more kids, which they weren't planning on doing. Betty said that Sycamore Lane was home and—"

The woman stops in midsentence and looks around—as off-screen we hear a chorus of car engines rumble to life. "Oh dear. I think the road must be open again . . ."

17

"Well, that was a stroke of good luck," I said as we waved goodbye to the old lady and her brother. Before we'd started recording, they'd introduced themselves as Libby Kraus and Vernon Tolliver. Vern was seventy-six, older by three years. Ever since they'd lost their spouses, the two of them had been living together in Libby's house.

"She was just the sweetest thing," Melody said.

"And great on camera."

Troy rolled up his window. "About time our luck changed. Between this damn storm, and the creeps in the woods last night, the guy spying on us back in Sudbury, and what happened in town today... Man, your aunt and Professor Tyree weren't kidding. The road's a dangerous place."

"Do you regret coming?" Melody asked.

"No way," Troy replied, taking no time at all to consider his answer. "I wouldn't have missed it for anything."

I thought about what he'd told me sitting by the fire that first night. *I don't have many friends.* And my heart swelled.

"Taking the backroads is starting to pay off," Melody said. "That was a good call, Troy."

"Brains and beauty," he said. "We make a heck of a team." He glanced at me in the back seat. "And then, of course, there's Billy..."

I balled up my *Cosmopolitan* survey and threw it at him.

18

VIDEO FOOTAGE
(7:04 p.m., Thursday, May 5, 1983)

```
As the vehicle draws closer in the mostly empty
parking lot, we're able to make out more details.
    A van. Orange and black. Luggage rack attached to
the roof. Silver hubcaps on the tires. The mellow
purr of its engine reminds us of a Singer sewing ma-
chine.
```

"You've got to be kidding me." The camera operator, clearly unimpressed.

A dark-haired woman is driving the van, and as she brakes to a stop in the foreground, we notice a round silver Volkswagen emblem on the center of the hood.

The woman waves—and the camera swings around, making its way to the driver's-side door. The window's rolled down. We hear the faint strains of Fleetwood Mac playing on the van radio. But mostly it's the woman we're focused on. She's stunning.

"So what do you think?" she asks, smiling with perfectly white teeth.

"I think we paid three hundred bucks too much," the man behind the camera says.

"Oh, hush. It's perfect, and you know it."

"It looks like a child's lunch box."

"Wait until Troy sees it. I bet he loves it."

"Troy drives a moped."

At the sound of an approaching vehicle, the camera slowly pans to our right. As it does, we glimpse a cluster of brick-and-glass buildings, a grassy common area dotted with trees and wooden benches, and a narrow sign that reads "arts & literature" with an arrow underneath it pointing to the left . . .

. . . and then a bright red convertible Mustang takes over the frame.

Its rumbling engine sounding nothing at all like a sewing machine.

The man behind the wheel is wide and tall with a full beard and mustache. He's wearing sunglasses and a Philadelphia Phillies baseball cap. The top three buttons of his shirt are open.

"Professor Tyree!" The screen blurs as the camera is lowered and then quickly raised again.

"Melody . . . Billy . . . so this is your home away from home for the next week."

"It sure is." Melody's cheerful voice off-screen.

"Isn't it hideous?" Billy says as the picture begins to regain focus.

"Ahh." The professor smiles and removes his sunglasses. "To the contrary. Volkswagen Westfalias in this condition are a true work of art. I noticed it even has custom double doors in the rear."

"Told you, Billy." Melody sounds positively gleeful.

"As a matter of fact, I almost bought one myself a few years back," Tyree continues. "But alas, it wasn't to be." The camera goes close on his face as he stares wistfully off-screen.

"In that case," Billy says, "we'll trade you the van for the Mustang for a week."

Professor Tyree laughs. A boisterous sound. "And where will you fit all your gear, not to mention the third Musketeer, Mr. Carpenter?"

"Troy doesn't take up much space."

"You're terrible." And Melody joins in on the laughter.

"You'll watch out for him, though, won't you?" the professor asks, a serious look coming over his face. "He's not experienced much of the outside world."

"We'll take good care of him." The camera swings around and holds on Melody, who is now leaning out of the van window. "Won't we, Billy?"

The camera remains on Melody's smiling face for a beat or two longer than necessary—and then abruptly pans away and refocuses on Professor Tyree.

"Absolutely," Billy says off-screen, "we'll keep our eyes on him."

"I'll hold you to that."

"You still worried about us?" Billy asks.

"I always worry about my students," the professor says, no hint of humor in his voice. "Remain aware of your surroundings at all times and remember that you are guests—and I'm sure everything will turn out just fine."

"So much about the Appalachian region remains a mystery," we hear Melody say. "Can you tell us what we'll find there?"

The professor looks at her with a startling intensity. When he speaks, we can sense the awe in his voice. "If you look hard enough . . . you'll find the impossible . . ."

19

I was dozing off in the back seat when Melody and Troy began arguing.

"I'm telling you . . . ," Melody said. "It wasn't him."

"Was too."

"It was not, Troy. I saw him clear as day."

"So did I—and it was *him*."

"You're wrong. When we turned the corner, I saw—"

"Yeah, yeah, *you saw*. Just like you saw the man in the woods on the video."

"Whatever."

"It was him," Troy repeated.

I sat up and rubbed my eyes. "What are you kids fighting about?"

Troy turned around and looked at me. "Just the fact that Melody's going blind."

She sighed. "We drove past a man getting into a car on the side of the road. Troy's convinced it was that hitchhiker from yesterday."

"It was."

"The guy we passed today was much older. And he wasn't carrying a sign or a knapsack."

"He'd probably already stashed them in the back seat," Troy said. "Along with his axe. I was closer than you, and *I saw his face*. It was the same guy."

A thought occurred to me. I leaned in between the seats. "Hey . . . tell me something. Did you dream about him again last night?"

Troy stared out the window.

"You did, didn't you?"

"I . . . think so," he said. "It's hard to remember."

"The same dream?"

He shook his head. "We were in the woods this time."

"Was he chasing you?"

"No. Someone was chasing *us*."

"The three of us?"

Another shake of the head. He looked like a little boy. "Just me . . . and the hitchhiker. We were together, running away from someone else."

"Well, that's freaky," I said, sitting back again.

"Tell me about it."

"And that was it?"

"That's all I remember."

"Considering what you told us earlier, I suppose that's a good thing."

"What if . . . ?" He trailed off and didn't finish his question.

"What if what?" Melody asked.

"I don't know why I just thought this, but . . . what if the hitchhiker's the same person who was on the video, watching us from the woods?"

20

"What a weird-ass day," I said, holding a hot dog impaled on a birch twig over the flames. The skin was beginning to blister and char. Just how I liked it.

"No kidding," Melody said. "Today's vibe was way off."

"Except for old Teddy," I said with a grin, already working on my second beer.

She scowled at me. "What's that supposed to mean?"

"Not a thing. He saved our butts with that new tire."

"Hey, did we bring any mustard?" Troy asked, attempting to change the subject.

I pointed with my elbow. "In the cooler."

Troy got up, and I could hear the shuffling of ice cubes as he searched for the mustard container. A moment later, he was back, a yellow plastic bottle in one hand, an unopened can of beer in the other. "Found it!"

We'd set up camp shortly after 8 p.m., while it was still light out. Unlike the night before, we had no close neighbors. In fact, the entire campground appeared fairly empty, which was unusual for this time of year. The dinner menu was hot dogs and beans and Melody's homemade pasta salad. We also had fresh watermelon followed by another round of s'mores for dessert. And plenty of beer, of course.

"Pondo and that crazy bastard in the truck . . . I still can't believe that was just this morning," Melody said. "It feels like it happened a week ago."

"The entire day feels like that to me." I plopped the hot dog into a ketchup-slathered bun. "Those people at the restaurant, the flat tire, the storm . . ." I shook my head. "That's *two* weeks' worth of weirdness right there."

"You forgot about our watcher in the woods," Troy said.

"Which one?" I asked.

"The one in your video."

"Technically, that was yesterday afternoon."

"True, but you just told us about it this morning."

"By the way, I took another look at the footage," Melody said, "and I hate to disappoint you boys, but I still think it's just a shadow."

"Wait . . . when did you watch it again?" I was surprised to feel a territorial twinge in my gut about the video camera. Which was especially strange because as much as I wished it did, the camera didn't even belong to me.

"When you were using the bathroom at Rutter's. Remember? You were gone forever."

I did remember. The "using the bathroom" part of that little detour had taken all of three minutes. The "waiting in line to buy a bag of ice, a pack of Slim Jims, and a cherry Gatorade while a flustered cashier was having trouble issuing a refund for a pair of broken sunglasses" had taken the better part of fifteen.

"I gotta tell you . . . ," Troy said, "I wouldn't be at all disappointed if we were wrong about the guy in the video. I'd actually be relieved."

"You sure about that?" Melody asked. "I know how much you goofballs like being scared."

"Not with something like this," Troy said. "Someone spying on us is just plain creepy. Besides, Billy likes being scared a whole lot more than I do."

21

All that talk of dangerous hitchhikers and phantoms lurking in the woods must have put us in the mood for good, old-fashioned campfire tales—because that's exactly how we spent the next hour or so.

I'd recently watched a movie called *Ghost Story*, in which a group of elderly men living in a small upstate New York town meet regularly to regale each other with scary stories. I was only half-serious when I suggested we do the same, and was pleasantly surprised when the others agreed. The flickering firelight, dancing shadows, and dark woods provided the perfect backdrop.

Troy went first—doing his best to narrate his story in a deep, spooky voice.

"According to Cherry Hill legend, back in the mid-1960s, young Black children began to go missing from the neighborhood. Four girls and two boys, ranging in age from seven to nine, vanished without a trace within a three-month period of time. At first, local residents feared the disappearances were racially motivated. In 1960, whites represented sixty-five percent of Baltimore City's population. Within a handful of years, that number plummeted to just above fifty. Many white folks were under the impression that they were being pushed out of their homes. And they were angry.

MEMORIALS

There was a marked increase in violence and harassment, especially against Black-owned businesses.

"But those fears soon proved to be baseless in this particular instance.

"One hot July evening, not long after a seventh child was reported missing, Clarence Poke, retired school bus driver and longtime resident of Cherry Hill, had his family dinner interrupted by a violent knocking at the door. He opened it to find standing on his front porch a filthy and scared young boy dressed in tattered clothing. There was blood on the child's face. A broken shackle hung from his wrist. The boy was quickly ushered inside the house—and the police were summoned.

"A short time later, after the boy had been given food and water by the family and treated for his injuries by an ambulance crew, he led police detectives to his captor's home: a condemned office building a few blocks away—where police officials discovered a house of horrors. A Haitian man and woman, estimated to be in their midforties, had been squatting in the basement for a number of months. No one knew who they were or where they'd come from. Each time the strangers were questioned, they gave different names and backstories. None of those claims were ever confirmed to be true.

"On the night the man and woman were arrested—with the boy watching from the back seat of a patrol car parked at the curb out front—the police found in the basement hideaway a variety of body parts belonging to several of the missing children. These included hearts, tongues, ears, fingers, and toes, along with one fully intact brain. They were stowed away inside cheap foam coolers—the kind you can buy at your local 7-Eleven for a buck and change. Eleven small skulls were lined up next to each other on the dirt floor. One of the missing girls was chained to a nearby wall. What looked like the initials KP had been carved into her tiny chest. The coroner estimated that she had been dead for nearly two weeks.

"Seth Ramirez, a kid in my homeroom at school, claimed that his Uncle Bobby was one of the first police officers to arrive at the scene. He'd told Seth's father that the basement smelled like a slaughterhouse. Flies everywhere. Along with piles of human excrement. Even with their mouths and noses covered, a half-dozen cops lost their lunches right there at the crime scene. The detectives were furious. Uncle Bobby said the man and woman were naked and covered in dry blood when the cuffs were snapped on their wrists. There were all kinds of creepy voodoo symbols painted on the cinder block walls and a firepit had been dug into the basement's dirt floor. The cops found bones in the ashes and part of an infant's skull."

Troy went on to explain that because all the known victims were Black and the murders occurred in the predominantly Black area of Cherry Hill, the Baltimore Police Department swept the story under the rug. Not a single newspaper or television station reported the crimes. And no one from the neighborhood ever found out what happened to the man and woman following their arrests. There were even rumors that they had both escaped from their respective cells. Just *poof*—up and disappeared.

"The city tore down the building a few years later," Troy continued. "But not before it gained a reputation for being haunted. Many people claimed they'd heard children crying behind the boarded-up windows and doors. Others reported hearing muffled screams and the sound of tiny fingers scratching at the plywood barricades. My own mother refused to walk past that corner—day or night, it didn't make a lick of difference to her—and even now that the building has been replaced by a brand-new Rite Aid, she still prefers to pick up her prescriptions four blocks away.

"To this day, in darkened bedrooms with the covers pulled up to their eyes, kids in Cherry Hill are told the story of the Voodoo Killers—and to this day, most of them believe it to be true."

And with that, Troy got up and walked to the cooler for another beer. All that talking had made him thirsty. Realizing that the story was finished, Melody and I stood and gave a rousing round of applause. Before he sat down again, he responded with a fanciful bow—spilling most of his beer on his sneakers.

Once Troy finished cursing up a storm and we finished laughing, we got settled again—and Melody went next with a much shorter but equally chilling tale.

"I first heard of the legend of La Llorona—the Crying Woman—from my grandmother in Puerto Rico. There are many different versions of the story, depending on the area in which you live, but this is the one that was told to me:

"Jacinta was a beautiful woman from the town of Coamo, which was not far from where my family lived. She was well-liked by the other villagers and had by all accounts an ordinary life—until one day in a fit of rage, after seeing her husband with another woman, she drowned her two children in the river. Realizing what she'd done, and consumed by horror and regret, Jacinta waded deeper into the water and drowned herself.

"That should have been the end of the story—but it wasn't."

She paused, then said: "Many locals reported that Jacinta—her eternal soul trapped in purgatory—could be heard in the middle of the night crying for her lost children, begging for their return. It was said that when a person heard her cry from afar, that meant her ghost was somewhere nearby. But if the cry was heard close by, it meant her ghost was far away. Others claimed they'd seen a woman walking on the side of the road by the town's main bridge. She appeared ghostly in nature, shimmering in and out of existence, and once you made eye contact, it was useless to try to ignore her because she would just reappear inside your car. Most villagers believed that Jacinta's vengeful spirit was responsible for the many deadly accidents that occurred on or around the bridge.

"In small towns scattered all across Puerto Rico, these hauntings continue to this day . . . as do the mysterious accidents they allegedly herald."

Melody stopped talking and we fell into a prolonged silence—all three of us staring into the flames, thinking the same thing, I'm sure. *Is my hometown of Sudbury—more specifically, Dead Man's Road—haunted by its own version of La Llorona? Did she claim the lives of my parents?*

After getting up to grab another round of beers from the cooler—considering the day we'd had, we deserved a couple of extras—I rejoined my friends around the fire. And started talking.

"So . . . there's one story I forgot to tell you about the woods surrounding Church Street."

Troy groaned, and I grinned at him around my beer.

"I was thirteen when it happened—and at the time, it really freaked me out. So much so that I never even told my mom about it.

"My father and I started off taking pictures that morning down by the river, which was our normal routine. I snapped some shots of fishermen wading by the rocks in the mist, then did some wildlife, mostly birds and hawks. After a while, we backtracked through the narrow stretch of woods bordering the road to where we'd parked. I'd screwed up and left my extra rolls of film in the glove compartment. When we got to the car, there was a huge buck—I'm talking a full rack—watching us from the opposite side of the road. I'd never seen a deer that big, and neither had my father, so when it bolted into the woods, we hooted and hollered and chased after it, hoping to get a good clear photo with one of the handful of shots I had left.

"But we weren't doing much hooting or hollering fifteen minutes later when we still hadn't caught another glimpse of the damn thing—and we found ourselves standing in the middle of a clearing, the woods all around us feeling *wrong* somehow. That was the only word I could think of to describe what I felt that day, and when I said it out loud, my dad surprised me by nodding his head and agreeing with me. His eyes had gone cold and thin and watchful. I could tell he was unsettled, maybe even a little scared—and I didn't like it one bit.

"On the surface, the clearing didn't appear all that different than any other we'd stumbled upon during past fishing expeditions . . . but I *felt* the difference right away. Even without a canopy of trees overhead, it was darker. The air was thicker and harder to breathe. And there were no birds anywhere. Not even a single crow or blue jay scolding us from their nests. I wandered a couple steps and almost tripped over the remnants of an old stone foundation that was poking out of the underbrush. It had been nearly invisible from a few yards away. When I pointed it out to my dad, he stiffened and grabbed my arm and began pulling me away.

"At first, from the shocked look on his face and the urgency of his arm tugging, I thought I'd nearly stepped on a copperhead. Maybe even a whole damn nest of them. But when he didn't stop dragging me for another twenty or thirty yards, I soon realized he just wanted out of there. And fast.

"Eventually, we found our way back to the road—albeit a half mile or so farther south than I'd thought made any kind of sense—and walked back to the car. We didn't talk much on the drive home, didn't even bother turning on the radio, until my father swung into the Scoop and Serve parking lot and switched off the car.

"He turned to me then and said, 'I don't ever want you to go back there again, Billy. Promise me.'

"I knew where he was talking about, of course. Still, I was confused.

"'Why?' I asked.

"'Just promise me,' he said again, taking hold of my arm.

"'I promise. Don't worry—I never *want* to go back there.'

"'Good. That's good.' His chest heaved with relief. 'It's . . . a bad place.'

"'I felt that too. Do you have any idea why? What happened there?'

"'I don't know for certain . . . but I've heard . . . stories. I only put it all together when we were standing there in the middle of all that . . . quiet.'

"'Stories about what?' I asked.

"He didn't answer right away, and I think he was wrestling with what he wanted to tell me next.

"'Stories about a family who supposedly lived in those woods a long time ago. Before Sudbury became Sudbury. Before the bridge and the railroad even existed.'

"He took another deep breath and went on. 'The way I heard it, there were four of them. A husband and wife and two little girls.'

"'Who told you the story?'

"'Never mind that,' he said. 'Just shut up for a minute and listen. When I'm done, *we're* done. We're never talking about this again.'

"He had metal in his eyes, I'd swear to it. I'd never heard my father talk to anyone like that before, let alone me, so I did what he said: I shut right up and listened.

"'The family's closest neighbors, who lived several miles away, got worried because the family never showed up for a planned birthday celebration and one of their cows had been found running loose. So the neighbors—the father and son of the household—saddled up their horses and rode over one afternoon to check things out.

"'When they got there, they were puzzled by what they saw, and then as they investigated further, that puzzlement turned to something a lot worse. It was chilly, snow was on the ground, and yet the front door of their friends' home was standing wide open. They called out—and got no response. They walked into the house, muskets at the ready, turned and closed the big, heavy wooden door behind them—and there were deep scratch marks on the inside of the door. Then they saw what looked like streaks of dried blood on the doorframe and splattered on the dirt floor directly below it. Now they were worried that their friends had been victims of a wild animal attack, a bear or a mountain lion, so they called out again. No answer, so they began carefully searching the rest of the house. The fireplace was cold, the wood burned down to ashes. Four half-eaten bowls of stew sat on the kitchen table. Also cold. A large pot of the same waited on the stove. Next to the table, two chairs were overturned on the floor. One of them smashed into splinters. Not far from the chair, there was a man's boot, ripped open along the heel, along with a discarded bowl and spoon.

"'All of a sudden, the son called out for his father with fear in his voice.

"'The older man hurried over to his boy, who was standing in front of a window that looked out over the rear of the property. The man peered outside at what his son was staring at and could just make out four figures—two of them tall, the other pair much smaller. It was said they were standing upright just short of the tree line. Looking like scarecrows guarding a snowy field.

"'Father and son hurried around back, muskets once again leveled in front of them.

"'What they found there was a nightmare. Their friends had been fixed to the ground on wooden stakes—their arms and legs lashed to the rough beams with lengths of thick rope—and suspended off the ground. They'd been stripped naked, their throats sliced open. Their *eyes* were empty sockets, whether from hungry crows or whatever evil had committed this foul act. The snow beneath their dangling feet was stained red.

"'In the days that followed, rumors began to spread involving witchcraft and sorcery, devil worship. A story went around that, years earlier, the dead man and his wife had been cast out of a settlement in Maryland for trying to abduct a young boy. No idea why. Then one night, a group of masked men on horseback took matters into their own hands and set the abandoned house ablaze, burning it to the ground. Local settlers began to avoid the area. Travelers who ventured too close to the clearing reported seeing strange lights and hearing the sound of crying babies coming from the woods. The father—who along with his son had discovered the grisly display on that long-ago night—eventually grew old and frail. On his sickbed, surrounded by family, he recalled the deep scratch marks he'd discovered on the inside of the heavy wooden door—but spoke of them to no one. He desperately wanted the memory of that day to die along with him. But his wish wasn't to be . . . and his son eventually wrote of the experience.'"

My throat hurt from talking for so long. I took a sip of my beer, but it had gone tepid, so I spit it out. As I stood to grab a refill, Melody whistled and began applauding. "Holy hell, you win, Billy! That was a knockout of a story!"

Not looking nearly as pleased, Troy got to his feet and stretched. "On that fucked-up note, I'm going to bed—to cower in fear and stare at the ceiling for hours." Head hanging, he started toward the tent. "Oh yeah . . . I almost forgot . . . I hate you, Billy."

22

"I didn't make you mad before, did I?"

I looked at Melody in the dying light of the campfire. "Mad about what?"

Shortly after Troy crawled inside the tent—still grumbling as he went—we moved our lawn chairs closer to the flames. Melody slipped off her

Chuck Taylors and peeled off her socks. I was four beers deep and having a hard time not staring at her cute little toes wiggling around in the dirt. I was starting to think something was wrong with me.

"When I doubted you about the man's face in the video."

Shaking my head, I said, "Oh God, no. Absolutely not. Hell, I agree with Troy. I hope you're right and we *are* actually imagining it." I gazed at the dark woods. "But I guess we'll never really know."

"Also . . . before that . . . earlier this afternoon, when I kind of cornered you about that whole afterlife thing."

"You didn't corner me. I just didn't know what to say."

"It's a sensitive subject. Especially for the three of us."

I raised my eyebrows at her. "A sensitive subject brought up by a sensitive man who goes by the name of—"

"Pondo!" we both exclaimed in perfect unison—and then broke up laughing.

"I *still* believe it's fate that brought the three of us together," Melody said, her smile fading.

"Could be . . . ," I said. "Or it could be totally random, and Mr. Tyree flipped a coin to decide who was in our groups."

"Well, however it happened, I think it's been really good for us. Especially Troy." She glanced at the tent. "I think *you've* been good for him."

I started to respond with one of my usual wise-ass comments—but stopped myself. Part of me was worried that Troy might be awake and listening, and I didn't want to hurt his feelings. A bigger part of me knew that Melody was right. When we'd first started meeting as a group in class, we could hardly get a word out of Troy about anything other than the assignment at hand. Now we couldn't get the little guy to shut up.

"Hang on a second," I said, getting up from my chair. "I want to show you something."

Thirty seconds later, I was back with a stack of Polaroids.

"Show me, show me, show me," Melody chanted.

"Hold your horses." I sat down and shuffled through the photos.

Searching for the one I'd remembered. I finally found it near the bottom of the pile. "There you are, you sucker."

Smiling, I got to my feet and handed the Polaroid to Melody.

She held it up in front of her. "Oh . . . Billy . . . it's . . ." And then she brought it closer to her face, allowing the fire to illuminate the image. Voice thick with emotion, she said, "How did you . . . My God, look at him!"

"I haven't shown it to him yet."

She looked up at me in surprise. "Why not? He'll love it."

"I guess I wasn't sure . . . It felt like such a private moment."

Earlier this evening, after the storm, we'd pulled over at a scenic overlook. We'd all gotten out of the van to stretch our legs and take a look, and were surprised to discover that we were the only people there. I'd watched Troy climb atop a rock outcropping overlooking the mouth of a forested valley hundreds of yards below. With the storm clouds gone, we could see for miles. Far to the north and west, ringing the untamed wilderness like a horseshoe, stood a fog-shrouded stretch of the Appalachians. It felt like a glimpse of a prehistoric world. If a dinosaur had poked its head out of the treetops, I wouldn't have been totally shocked.

After a moment of silent awe, Troy had turned to me and said, "I've never seen mountains before, Billy. *Any* mountains. Will you please take a picture for me?"

While I snapped a half-dozen or so shots, he explained that his father's favorite novel was *The Last of the Mohicans*. And while he realized these weren't the same mountains from the book, he still wanted his father to see them when he got back home. Before I left Troy alone on the ridge, I glanced back over my shoulder and saw him standing there, so proudly, silhouetted by open sky, blues and pinks and purples, and a scattering of drifting clouds. The wind was soaring, and he appeared as if he were on the verge of taking flight. The sight stole my breath, and without even thinking about it, I snapped one last photo.

When I examined the Polaroid later, I realized that what I had captured was Troy Carpenter from Cherry Hills, Baltimore, not as the boy he currently was . . . but rather as the man he would one day become.

23

Ever since that first late night, while the others were sleeping, I'd taken advantage of the solitude and reviewed the day's video footage—but until this evening, I hadn't even bothered to glance at the Polaroids. There just hadn't been time. In the back of the van, tucked away in little gray canisters, there were eight rolls of 35mm film waiting to be developed. Almost three hundred photographs. It sounded like a lot, but I knew from experience that it wouldn't be nearly enough. Our last couple of days on the road were going to be very busy ones.

Once Melody had settled down about Troy's photo—including several moments of enthusiastic and uncomfortable praise for the photographer—I moved my chair another foot or so closer to the fire and began sorting through the remaining Polaroids. In the flickering orange glow of the dwindling flames, the images possessed an otherworldly quality, almost as if they'd been shot in another place and time. And that was precisely what I loved so much about Polaroids. They had an organic feel to them, an unpracticed, spur-of-the-moment energy and imagery that was hard to nail down in other mediums. Each and every photo had a slightly different look.

Most of the images I flipped through with just a cursory glance. The lighting from the fire wasn't bright enough to conduct a thorough inspection, so I found myself cataloging content instead. The leather motorcycle jacket from day one. Jennifer Harper sitting in her yard with the tire swing in the background. A bumblebee taking flight from the flowers at the base of a cross. The smiling little boy with the missing front teeth.

I took the next four Polaroids from the pile—the baseball gloves from Michael Meredith's memorial by the bridge—and spread them out on my lap. Presumably, his teammates had left the gloves there in his honor. Upon closer inspection, I noticed that there was a first baseman's mitt mixed in with three regular fielder's gloves. There was writing on each of them. Names and initials and jersey numbers—with an *RIP Mikey* thrown in for good measure. Someone had drawn on the webbing of the first baseman's mitt. A crude stick figure with eyes where the hands should be and a long, forked tail. Enclosed in a circle.

I stared at the strange drawing. In the wavering shadows of the campfire, it blurred in and out of focus. My eyes began to water. I wanted to look away, but there was something about it.

Something compelling.

And unsettling.

And familiar.

Where the hell had I seen it before?

On television? In a book? In class at school?

Perplexed, I sat back in the lawn chair and closed my eyes.

Within seconds, I was fast asleep.

24

When Melody shook me awake a short time later, the campsite was cloaked in darkness, the only source of light a mound of glowing embers at the bottom of the firepit. I was surprised to discover that I was shivering.

"What time is—"

She clamped her hand over my mouth.

"There's someone out there," she whispered. "Watching us."

Eyes darting all around us, I waited for her to remove her hand. "Where?"

"In the woods."

Staring at the tree line, it was hard to make out much of anything. Even the van, parked only ten or fifteen yards away, resembled nothing more than a big black blob set against an even bigger and blacker blob. The wall of trees might as well have been the towering parapets of an ancient castle.

"I can't see a fucking thing."

"Look directly over the firepit." I could smell the beer on her breath. Hopefully, she was just sauced and seeing things. "Now just a tad to the right..."

I squinted—and saw nothing.

I closed my eyes and opened them again.

And from within the inky darkness, three shadows began to slowly gain focus and solidify. Standing shoulder to shoulder. Each of them thicker than a man's torso and impossibly tall.

"I see *trees* ... I think."

"Keep. Looking." I could hear the frustration in her voice. "The person's still there. They haven't moved."

Holding my breath, I scanned the woods from one end to the other and then back again.

"Right where you told me to look ... I see a cluster of trees ... three of them ... standing apart from the others ... but that's all." I reached over and touched her on the arm. "You sure you're not—"

"Oh, shit," she hissed, looking all around us. "They're gone!"

I turned back and stared into the woods, letting my eyes adjust to the darkness.

Only two of the trees remained.

DAY FOUR

MONDAY | MAY 9

1

"I don't understand why you didn't wake me."

"We didn't want to alarm you," Melody said. "Especially after the other night."

The early morning sun felt warm on my face and shoulders. I didn't need Hair Metal Harry to tell me that today was going to be another scorcher. Our shoes already soaked from the dew-covered grass, we slowed as we approached the tree line.

"So, instead, you just left me there . . . all alone."

"You weren't alone," she said. "We were sitting twenty feet away from the tent."

"In which I was sleeping. All alone. Unaware of the danger."

I knew we weren't going to win this argument, but I hated seeing Troy so pissed off at us. "We thought about packing up and going to a hotel," I said, "but the more we talked about it, the sillier we felt."

"We'd both been drinking and had fallen asleep," Mel added. "When we woke up, it was late and the fire had gone out. It was dark. We know we saw *something*; we just aren't sure what it was. It could've been a deer for all we knew."

Troy crossed his arms over his chest. "Yet you were both concerned enough to stay awake and stand watch for the rest of the night."

"My adrenaline was pumping," I said. "No way was I falling back to sleep."

"Same," Melody said, pushing aside some low-hanging branches and entering the woods.

Troy cut in front of me and followed right behind her.

I couldn't figure the guy out. He really *was* a scaredy-cat. That wasn't just us teasing. So why the sudden burst of bravado? Was he simply running his mouth? Posturing? I didn't think so. He seemed genuinely upset that we hadn't woken him. And then the answer came to me: there was safety in numbers, and we'd left him all alone inside the tent.

Where someone could have snuck up on us in the dark, sliced it open, and stolen him away . . . or done something even worse. With all the horror movies I made him watch, I had no one else to blame but myself.

After glancing back at the van to get my bearings, I waded into the woods.

And couldn't find my friends anywhere.

What the hell? They were right in front of me just a few seconds ago.

Spinning in a slow circle, a jolt of panic knuckling my spine, I called out, "Hey! Where'd you guys go?"

Nothing. Dead silence and unruly forest.

I was getting ready to holler again when—

"Over here!" Melody yelled from somewhere off to my left.

Relieved, I pushed my way through a tangle of overhanging branches, crab-walked underneath a bunch more, tiptoed through a stand of thigh-deep sticker-brush (hoping against hope that there was no poison ivy or oak), and found Melody and Troy standing beside a pair of red oaks surrounded by a mound of mulchy earth. By the time I reached them, my hands were scratched and bleeding, my shirt sleeve was torn, and I was dripping with sweat.

"Where'd you go? I completely lost track of you."

"How's that even possible?" Troy said. "You were right behind us."

"It just happened, so you tell me."

His eyes narrowed behind his glasses. "I guess now you know how it feels to be left all alone."

"I told you . . . we didn't leave—"

"Guys, look!" Melody said. "I'm pretty sure these are the trees we saw last night."

Even from this reverse perspective, the oak trees resembled a pair of sentries standing shoulder to shoulder with perfect posture, guarding the woods from potential intruders. Stopping at her side, I peered through the canopy of branches and leaves to our campsite. I could've drawn a straight line from our present location to the firepit. "Seems about right." I glanced down at the ground. "Any sign of—"

"Over there," she said, pointing.

The forest floor was a messy carpet of broken twigs, tangles of vegetation and roots, and rocks of all shapes and sizes. The earth beneath my shoes crunched and squished with my every step. On the opposite side of the trees, I found a patch of bare earth. Maybe three square feet of dirt and moss. Stepping closer, I took a good look. The moss was disturbed in several places, as though a shoe had scraped against it and torn it from its moorings. There were a handful of identical scuff marks in the dirt. "Could've been a deer or maybe a—"

And then I saw it.

At the edge of the dirt.

A distinct indentation.

Inside the indentation, a delicate pattern.

The heel mark of a shoe.

I glanced up at Melody. "You were right. Someone *was* here."

"Looks that way."

All of a sudden, I needed a drink of water. My throat had gone bone-dry.

Troy bent down, studying the shoe print. "The question is: *Why*?"

"Uh, guys . . . there's something else you need to see over here." Melody had moved to the opposite side of the tree. Closer to our campsite. She was staring at something on the ground.

"What is it?" Troy asked as we walked over and took a look. All of a sudden, I needed something stronger to drink than water.

In a trampled-down area of brush at her feet, there was a dead rabbit. Its gray-furred stomach had been split wide open, its internal organs spilling out onto the ground. Flies buzzed all around it.

"Looks pretty fresh," I said.

"I think it's time we get the hell out of here," Troy said, unable to look away from the grisly display.

For once, I agreed with him.

2

"Why would someone do that to a poor rabbit?"

I glanced at Troy in the back seat. "It could've been another animal. We don't know that it was—"

"No way was that done by another animal," he said. "Not unless it was carrying around a pocketknife."

"Not true," I said. "It could've easily been a hawk. Their talons are like razor blades."

Melody turned the key.

The van's engine groaned, stuttered, and quit.

"You and Mel saw someone watching us from the woods last night. My money's on the creeper . . . not some hawk."

Melody tried again.

Same result.

We all shifted uneasily in our seats, looking at each other. No one said the obvious: *This is not good.* What if our watcher had tampered with the van during the night?

Staring at the silver key in the ignition, Melody muttered a quick prayer and gave it another turn.

This time, the van roared to life.

In the back seat, Troy clapped his hands and uttered an "Ohhh yessss." I sat back and exhaled a long breath I hadn't realized I was holding.

"Never doubted it for a second," Melody said, giving the steering wheel a reassuring pat before shifting into drive and leaving the campsite behind.

Leaning forward, I switched on the radio and turned the dial to 98 Rock. The grinding guitar licks of George Thorogood immediately assaulted my ears. Behind me, Troy made a loud gagging sound. I smiled and turned up the volume. Rolling down the window, I promised myself that today was going to be a better day. Super productive, no insane storms, and no more weird vibes. After all, it was just a dead rabbit. Probably lots of dead critters in these woods. It wasn't like someone had left it in the middle of our campsite.

"We should stop at Micky D's for breakfast," I said, raising my voice above the music. "Troy can use some of those gift certificates he got for his birthday."

I put my feet up on the dash and started to play a mean air guitar.

"I didn't get them for my birthday, jackass." Even with my eyes closed, I could hear the smile in his voice.

"Oh, that's right, your gran—"

Someone plucked me on my ear. My eyes flashed open.

"Ow!" I abandoned my invisible guitar and rubbed my earlobe. "That really hurt!"

"Remove your feet," Melody said in her sweetest voice over the music. "Or the next one will hurt even more."

Sulking, I slowly lowered them. "Sorrrry." I wet my fingers with my tongue and wiped away a small blemish from where my shoes had been resting. Once I was satisfied the dashboard was no worse for wear, I glanced up at the sun-dappled road in front of us—

And my stomach turned to ice.

I lowered the music. "Pull over," I said, my voice strained.

"What?"

A small object was sticking out from underneath the wiper blade on my side of the windshield.

"Why?"

I was surprised I hadn't noticed it earlier—but now that we were driving at a higher rate of speed, the object was fluttering in the wind. I was almost positive I knew what it was. "Stop the car."

"What's wrong?" Melody asked, slowing down.

I leaned closer to the windshield, praying I was wrong.

But I wasn't.

It was a deflated balloon.

Bright green with the outline of a gray knight printed on its side.

Just like the balloons we'd seen yesterday afternoon at Michael Meredith's roadside memorial.

3

"Should we call the police?" Troy asked, pacing up and down the narrow shoulder.

We were parked no more than fifteen feet away from a NO STOPPING sign, the van's left rear bumper protruding into the road. Two tractor trailers had already laid on their horns as they roared past us. The driver of the second truck had screamed, "CAN'T YOU FUCKIN' READ?!" and hurled an empty Pepsi can out the window, which sailed harmlessly over our heads and landed in the weeds.

Melody stared at the limp balloon in her hand. "The police? And tell them what?"

"Oh, I don't know . . . that some redneck racist motherfucker is stalking us halfway across Pennsylvania."

"We don't know that it was him," she said.

Troy spun around to face her. Voice shrill. Arms waving. "If it's not Coach 'You're Running 'Round with the Goddamn Colored People,' then who is it?!"

"That asshole doesn't seem like the kind of guy who plays mind games," I said. "If it was him, I think we'd know it by now."

"Then it's the man in the woods," Troy said. "The one from the video."

"Maybe," I said, trying to make sense of it all.

He started pacing again. "Someone's clearly following us. We know that now. Whoever it is spied on us from the woods in Sudbury. Then he followed us to Leesburg and the Meredith memorial and took a balloon with him as a souvenir. Later that afternoon, we just happened to get a couple of nails in our tire. Then, last night, you both saw someone in the woods at our campsite. This morning, we find a shoe print and a mutilated animal." He stopped walking and pointed at the balloon in Melody's hand. "And now this . . ."

"But why?" Melody said. "Why would—"

"Occam's razor. The simplest answer is the truth. And the truth is: because he wants us to stop. Whoever it is, and for whatever reason, he doesn't want us messing around with the memorials."

His voice sounded calmer now. And he was no longer pacing. He'd finally crossed over from that initial flurry of blind panic to thoughtful analysis, which was where Troy was at his best. I'd witnessed it dozens of times before back at school, usually when a deadline was looming for a class assignment.

"Let's say you're a hundred percent on the mark here, A-plus-plus and all that," I said. "If this person feels that strongly that what we're doing is wrong, why not confront us and make his case? Or leave a note demanding that we stop? Why all this passive-aggressive bullshit?"

"Maybe it's more fun this way," Melody said. "Maybe he's getting off on scaring us."

I wasn't convinced. "Seems like an awful lot of time and energy . . . and for what?"

She shrugged. "Hell, I don't know. I'm just guessing . . ."

"Hey, what if it's Pondo?" Troy said. "He's exactly the kind of freak who would do something like this. And he was with us at the Meredith memorial . . . and the green balloons."

"He went out of his way to help us," Melody said, frowning. "Why would—"

"Maybe he changed his mind. Or someone changed it for him."

"Penny?" I said.

"You never know."

"I guess it's possible."

"Whoever it is *wants* us to know that they're following us," Troy said. "Why else would he let you two see him in the woods last night? And then leave the balloon for us to find?"

"So he wants us to know," Melody said. "Why?"

"Because he's either playing mind games, like you said . . ." Troy glanced nervously up and down the road. ". . . or he's fucked in the head . . . and seriously dangerous."

4

I didn't know what to think.

On one hand, I was totally convinced that there was a man hiding in the background of the video I'd taken at my parents' memorial. For me, that was nonnegotiable. As for the mysterious figure in the woods at our campsite last night . . . on that point, I was a little less certain. Maybe a lot less. The truth was, I really had no goddamn clue at all. The footprint in the mud could have been left by another camper. It could have been there for days, even weeks. The six-pack of beer I'd drunk and the darkness of the woods definitely contributed to my lingering doubts.

Then there was the flat tire—for me, that was a coin toss. Accidental or sabotage? I was pretty sure we'd never really know for certain.

Which now left the balloon.

It was hard to argue with something staring you right in the face. The balloon hadn't gotten there by accident. And there was no mistaking where it'd come from. It perfectly matched the balloons we'd seen blowing in the wind at Michael Meredith's memorial, where we'd also met the enigmatic Pondo and Coach KKK. There was little question that someone had snuck into our camp last night and placed the airless balloon under our wiper blade. All of which led right back to the beginning—the man's face in the woods from the Sudbury video. The whole thing was maddening. And disturbing as hell.

"Hello? You gonna stop daydreaming and help load the tripods?" Melody asked.

"Yes, ma'am," I said, snapping out of it. I got up from the guardrail where I'd been sitting and headed for the pile of equipment. "Sorry about that. You caught me woolgathering."

"*Woolgathering*," she repeated with a sad smile. "My mom used to say that all the time."

I wasn't sure how to respond, so I said nothing at all. Par for the course for me these days.

We ultimately decided not to report the balloon incident to the police—just calling it that, the "balloon incident," highlighted how bizarre this whole thing was, and to be honest, there was the very real possibility that we would've been checked out to see if our pupils were dilated. Instead, we'd simply climbed into the van and got back on the road. An hour or so later, we'd sped past a memorial a few miles west of Smithtown. None of us were overly enthusiastic about stopping, but we also knew we had a commitment to the project. So, after a brief discussion, Melody pulled over and turned the van around, and we went to work.

As luck would have it, what we discovered on the side of the road only served to deepen our dark and dreary collective mood.

Six months earlier, a child had been killed here while riding his bicycle. Gabriel Ramos. The memorial was practically papered with his round little face. Gabriel playing soccer. Gabriel riding on the back of a pony. Gabriel wearing a suit and dancing at a wedding. According to the laminated newspaper articles thumbtacked to a nearby fence post, the driver of the car was high and fleeing from the police at the time of the tragic hit-and-run. He'd been captured and arrested a few miles down the road after causing a multicar accident at a busy four-way intersection.

The plan, now that we were done here, was to backtrack the two and a half miles to Smithtown and see if we could locate Gabriel's mother or father. One of the laminated articles noted they both worked at the county courthouse.

I picked up a pair of tripods from where they were leaning against the fence and made my way toward the van. An empty-handed Troy passed me going in the opposite direction. "Hey," he said, sounding excited. "I just came up with another theory."

"Tell me at lunch," I called over my shoulder. We'd never made that McDonald's pitstop, and my stomach was growling. I dumped the tripods in the back of the van, rearranged the coolers to make more space, and went to help with the rest of the gear.

I knew something was wrong as soon as I heard Troy's voice.

". . . it's okay . . . just tell me what happened."

Melody was staring at the empty road. Her body rigid. Her face pale.

"She was like this when I got here," Troy said, looking up at me with a helpless expression.

I stepped closer and gently placed my hand on her shoulder. "Mel? You okay?"

No reaction. Not even an acknowledgment that I was there.

Moving in front of her, blocking her view of the road, I tried again. "I'm onto you, Mel. Stop trying to scare us."

She began to blink, very rapidly, and her eyes appeared to slowly regain focus. "I . . . Billy? . . . I thought I saw . . . but . . . it . . ."

"Whoa, slow down. You're okay. Troy and I are right here."

She turned her head and looked at Troy. Then, she stepped around me, facing the road again. "I thought it was . . . Mateo . . . my ex . . . ," she said in a shaky voice. "A car slowed down. A blue-and-gray Charger. The man inside—"

From the road, we heard the rumble of a powerful engine fast approaching. All three of us whiplashed our heads around just in time to watch a convertible Corvette blow by. Leaves and street dust danced in the air all around us. Troy lifted a hand to his face and sneezed.

"The driver had long dark hair . . . just like Mateo's," Melody continued. "And he was wearing mirrored sunglasses. I haven't seen him in nearly a year. I knew it couldn't be him . . . but for just a few seconds, I thought . . ." She swallowed a sob. "Goddamn. I was so scared."

"It's okay." I pulled her close and let her cry. "It wasn't him, Mel. Just keep telling yourself that. It wasn't him."

After a moment, the tears began to slow.

I gave her a reassuring squeeze. Enjoying it more than I should have. "Besides, even if it *was* him, we have Troy to protect us."

Her head resting against my shoulder, she giggled.

"Oh, bite me, Billy."

And then I was giggling too.

And before we knew it, both of us were bent over on the side of the road, hands on our knees, belly laughing and unable to stop.

"I'm so sorry," Melody said, using the back of her hand to wipe her face.

"You should be. Assholes," Troy said haughtily. "I was just trying to help."

But she wasn't even talking to him. Pointing at my shoulder, she said, "I got snot all over your shirt."

Feigning that he was offended—at least, I *thought* he was faking—Troy stomped off to the van and slammed the passenger door behind him.

The laughter finally subsiding, I looked at Melody and asked, "You okay?"

She nodded and took a deep breath. "I feel stupid now."

"Nothing to feel stupid about. I'm sure it was quite a shock."

She stared down the road. "I've had scares before . . . but nothing like this."

I checked to make sure Troy was still inside the van. "He the reason you have a gun?"

There was no surprise in her eyes. "I kinda figured you'd seen it, but then when you didn't say anything, I'd hoped I was wrong." She hesitated, and I could tell she was deciding how much more she wanted to share. "Don't worry—it's licensed and I took a training class. All legit. I'm sorry I didn't tell you."

Melody had never said much about her ex-boyfriend. The handful of times I'd brought him up, she'd always seemed in a hurry to change the subject. Now I knew why.

"Was it really bad?" I asked.

She sighed. "For the first six months, he was a perfect gentleman. A dream." Closing her eyes, she continued, "And for the year after that . . . he was a perfect nightmare. Jealous. Controlling." Fresh tears ran down her cheeks. "Abusive." She opened her eyes and looked at me with an expression I'd never seen before. "I'm embarrassed and ashamed . . . that I let it go on as long as I did. And that a man I once loved was sent to prison because of my testimony. I only pray that he's still there."

For a change, the right words came to me. "It sounds like you were very brave . . . and have nothing at all to be embarrassed or ashamed about. He's the one who fucked up. Not you. I'm proud of you, Mel."

Fighting back another rush of tears, she whispered, "Thank you, Billy."

5

It felt like I was a character in a Norman Rockwell painting.

The park bench I was sitting on was located at the top of a small rise overlooking a grassy field lined with elm trees. At one end of the field, a group of children were playing a game of kickball. On the opposite end, a young mother was teaching her daughter how to fly a kite. Not far from the mom, two men stood talking, while their dogs—both loose and trailing leashes—chased each other in widening circles. Most of the benches surrounding the field were occupied. An elderly man feeding the squirrels. A couple of businessmen eating early lunches from brown paper sacks. Several people reading books or newspapers, enjoying a stint of fresh air before the day grew too hot. Right next to a group of stoop-shouldered, gray-haired men playing chess in the shade, a pair of food carts were set up on the sidewalk. One vendor was hawking ice cream and snow cones; the other was selling hot dogs and salted pretzels and sodas. There were long lines in front of both of them.

Across the street from Rockfield Park was a cluster of colorful storefronts. First National Bank. Reynold's Drugs. Delmar's Video Rentals. Pisano's Pizza. Lola's Flowers & Gifts. The sidewalk was busy with shoppers and lazy day strollers. Not a speck of litter on the ground. On the corner, the Smithtown Post Office, a squat brick building with the American flag flapping in the breeze out front. Catty-corner, on the next street over, stood the Smithtown County Courthouse, which was where I'd dropped off Melody and Troy thirty minutes earlier. Hopefully, by now, they'd had some luck tracking down Mr. or Mrs. Ramos.

The only dark stains to be found among this golden-hued portrait of Americana innocence were the MISSING PERSON posters. So far, I'd seen them displayed on storefront windows, light poles, and trees. On my way to the park, I'd crossed paths with a mail carrier working his route and asked him what had happened. He told me that a local woman—twenty-four-year-old Brianna Kellegher—had gone grocery shopping one early-April afternoon and never returned home. Her car was discovered later that evening in the store's parking lot, the back seat still loaded with bags of groceries—but there was no sign anywhere of the woman. An extensive search and investigation failed to turn up any substantial leads. Brianna had been married less than a year and was seven months pregnant at the time of her disappearance. The town was still in mourning.

Looking up from the spiral notebook in my lap, I glanced at the van, which was parked along the curb on a nearby side street. Keeping watch over the so-called Mystery Machine was my job this morning. The last thing we needed was another flat tire or nasty surprise waiting for us under the wiper blade. Enough was enough, for chrissakes.

Satisfied that there was no mischief going on, I picked up my pen and went back to sketching in my notebook. I was trying—with only moderate success—to replicate the mysterious symbol I'd photographed on the baseball glove at Michael Meredith's memorial. Something about it was still itching at my brain. I could've sworn I'd seen the symbol someplace else, but for the life of me I couldn't remember where. Or when. And it was really starting to nag at me.

Last night, unable to sleep after what Melody and I had seen in the woods, I'd reviewed the video footage to see if I had managed to capture a clearer image of the drawing than what was rendered in the Polaroid. Fortunately, without even realizing it, I'd done exactly that. And by freezing the video, I was able to make out numerous additional details.

I picked up the camera from the bench beside me and peered through the viewfinder at the symbol, then quickly looked back at my drawing. Close, but not quite there yet. The legs—if that's what they really were—needed to be longer.

"What you doing, mister?"

Startled, I looked up from my notebook. So much for being an attentive watchman.

A young boy—maybe eight or nine—stood in front of me. He had recently eaten a sno-ball. His lips were blue and there were smudges of melted marshmallow on his chin.

Smiling, I said, "I'm waiting on some friends and doing a little sketching. What are *you* doing?"

Ignoring the question, he pointed at the video camera.

"Oh, that. I was just working on some homework earlier."

"You look too old for homework."

I laughed. "I *feel* too old for homework." And then I had a thought. "Hey, you want to help me with something?"

The kid shrugged. "Sure."

I flipped to the front of the notebook and scanned the list of time codes I'd written down. Once I found the notation for the man in the woods, I hit rewind on the camera.

"I want you to look at something I recorded and tell me what you see."

"Okay."

Looking through the viewfinder, I watched the numbers in the upper right-hand corner streak past. After probably twenty seconds, I paused the tape. My mother and father's memorial appeared in sharp focus. Handing the camera to the boy and pointing at the viewfinder, I said, "Here you go. Just look through there."

"Whoa, it's heavy," he said, almost dropping it and nearly causing my heart to leap out of my throat. *Another one of your bad ideas, Billy.*

But the kid surprised me.

Using both hands, he steadied the camera, lifted it to his face, and took a good, long look. "What is it?" he asked after a short time.

"Focus on the trees in the background," I said. "Tell me what you see."

He was quiet for a while. I was almost ready to accept defeat, when he said, "There's someone in the woods."

I almost jumped off the bench. "You see him?" Trying to calm my voice.

"Just his face."

"But you definitely see someone?"

He nodded. "Who is it?"

"I'm not really sure."

He looked up at me with fear in his little eyes. "Is . . . it the boogeyman?"

And in that instant, I could clearly picture the boy's furious mother admonishing me as I fled toward the van: *That poor boy's gonna have nightmares for a month thanks to you! What in the hell were you thinking?!*

I'm sorry! I wasn't *thinking, ma'am. That's my prob—*

"Matty!"

I looked up. One of the shirtless kids playing kickball was standing at the bottom of the hill with his hands cupped around his mouth. "Stop talking to strangers, you dweeb, and get your bony ass out in right field."

The kid rolled his eyes. "That's Louis. My big brother. He's so bossy." He handed back the camera. "Gotta go, mister. Thanks for letting me look."

Before I could say goodbye, he was soaring down the hill like a human kite, face turned to the sun, arms pinwheeling at his sides. As he raced to his position in the outfield, I heard his brother say, "About time, ya douchebag." And then they were both giggling.

My heart aching from memories of summers long past, I put down the camera and returned my attention to the drawing.

Drawing . . . or symbol? Symbol . . . or drawing? I couldn't decide which description was more fitting, or if it even mattered. After a while, I decided that the circle around the stick figure made it lean more toward a symbol. Like a peace sign or a smiley face.

A few minutes later, I looked up and saw Melody and Troy cutting across the corner of the field with a short dark-skinned man at their side. The shirtless boy on the pitcher's mound pointed at Troy's hair and said something to his teammate. The teammate yelled something to Troy—and both boys doubled over, laughing.

Never breaking stride, Troy flashed them his middle finger and marched up the hill.

6

VIDEO FOOTAGE
(11:22 a.m., Monday, May 9, 1983)

Alvaro Ramos sits on a park bench at the top of a grassy hill. He's wearing tan work pants and a maroon short-sleeved button-down shirt. A patch over his heart reads: maintenance supervisor. His dark hair is buzzed short. His brown eyes are wide and nervous. There's a small scar above his left eye. It resembles a lightning bolt.

"Gabriel was a wonderful boy. Never any trouble."

He looks away from the camera—perhaps at the boys we can hear playing on the field below—as he speaks. His voice is gentle and laden with the weight of great suffering.

"He was a normal nine-year-old. Enjoyed playing soccer and baseball. He'd just started collecting baseball cards. He asked me for a raise in his allowance so he could catch up with his friends' collections. He loved riding that silly bicycle of his. He called it his 'chopper' because the front wheel was smaller than the one in the back. A few months earlier, he saw it in a thrift store and fell in love with it. He used part of his savings from his piggy bank to pay for half of it. His mother and I paid the other half."

He pauses for a moment.

"My wife blames herself because she supported his decision to buy the bike, but I tell her that's not right. It wasn't the bike that took him away from us. God works in mysterious ways that we don't always understand or agree with. That has always been His way."

Nodding at someone off-screen, the man's lips twitch into something resembling a smile. Still, it looks painful.

"You asked me what I miss the most about Gabriel . . . It's all of his questions. He was the most curious little boy. 'Papa, why do the clouds look different today? Papa, what kind of bird is that? Why are some people tall and others short? Why does Tommy get sunburned and I don't? Papa, what happens to people after they die?'"

He stops to catch his breath.

"He was learning to play the guitar. We couldn't afford to sign him up for lessons, so we checked out books and cassette tapes from the library. He was very dedicated to his studies. He wanted to start a band when he was older."

Mr. Ramos sighs—and it's as if we can hear another piece of his heart crumbling.

"His uncles used to tease him and call him Carlos Santana. They'd say that all of the girls would chase after him once he was in a band. Gabriel would just smile. His grandfather gave him a brand-new guitar for his birthday. It was the happiest I'd ever seen him . . ."

7

"Poor guy," Melody said, watching Mr. Ramos walk across the field on his way back to the courthouse. The kickball game had ended moments earlier. Most of the kids—including my new friend and his bossy big brother—had headed off in the direction of town. Probably on their way to the pizza shop or the arcade. A couple of stragglers remained, tossing around a Frisbee.

"And his poor wife," Troy added.

"Do you feel like we invaded their privacy?" They both turned and looked at me. "I mean, we asked a couple questions to get him started, but everything he shared with us . . . he did so willingly."

Melody started to say something but changed her mind.

"We didn't do anything wrong," Troy said, "if that's what you're asking." He glanced around the park. "But that doesn't mean someone else wouldn't disagree."

"Exactly," I said. "I'm trying to get a handle on why anyone would be so upset with what we're doing." I sat down on the bench and placed the video camera in my lap. "I get that we're strangers breezing into town asking sensitive questions, but we're not being rude and we're certainly not forcing anyone to talk to us. Nothing unethical."

"I think for some people, we're opening up old wounds," Melody remarked. "In many cases, wounds that have taken years to begin to heal. Even your Aunt Helen said something to that effect."

"*Sometimes it's better to leave the dead alone*," I said.

"Think of it like this," Melody said, "and I don't mean to be indelicate. But how would you feel if you drove past your parents' memorial one day and there was a camera crew set up taking video? How would *I* feel if people I didn't know were asking personal questions about my mom and the way she died? Or talking to Troy about the day he lost his brother?"

"Yeah . . . I've definitely considered that." I shook my head. "To be honest, I'm not sure how I'd feel. But I sure as hell know one thing: I wouldn't follow any of those folks around, spying on them from the woods and leaving creepy shit on their cars."

"I might," Troy said, and once again I couldn't tell if he was kidding or not.

Melody picked up the camera case from the end of the bench. "What do you say we grab something to eat and get back on the road while the day's still young?"

"Sounds like a plan," Troy said, starting for the van.

"Hang tight for a minute." I lifted the camera and peered into the viewfinder. "That bit about Gabriel's guitar was amazing, but it only works if we have the footage to go along with it. I want to make sure we got enough coverage of the actual guitar. If not, we'll have to go back."

8

VIDEO FOOTAGE
(9:48 a.m., Monday, May 9, 1983)

The camera slowly pans across a stretch of uneven ground—which we can't actually see because it's covered in plastic flowers, a variety of candles, miniature flags, and several papier-mâché donkeys—all of these items arranged at the base of a chain-link fence.

As the camera pulls back, we see a collage of photographs attached haphazardly to the fence, most of them depicting a young boy doing the things that young boys do. The camera lingers on one of the larger photos—the smiling boy jumping over a wave at a sandy beach—before panning further to the right and settling on a tangle of rosaries that've been draped over the top of a wooden cross.

After going close and holding on the rosaries for an extended beat, the camera continues on its way—revealing a number of newspaper articles affixed to the fence, a large colorful banner representing the Costa Rican national soccer team, and a little further along, what looks like a collection of handwritten letters inserted into plastic sleeves.

And finally we come to a guitar leaning against the fence. It appears to have been wrapped in some type of plastic to protect it from the elements. A long silver chain and combination lock secure it to a nearby fence post. It's a handsome instrument. Acoustic six-string. Spalted maple top. Rosewood fingerboard.

As the camera zooms and slowly tilts downward, we notice writing of some sort below the neck of the instrument. But it's too small and impossible to read underneath the layers of plastic.

And then we see a splash of black-and-white artwork directly below the bridge. No larger than a silver dollar. A logo? It's hard to tell at first. We catch only a glimpse as the camera shifts and begins to tilt upward.

The image abruptly rewinds—and freezes.

It's not a logo.

It's a symbol.

9

"Holy shit."

I lowered the camera and looked at the others. My face felt hot all over.

"Let me guess," Troy said. "We're going back to get more coverage?"

"You guys wait right here," I said, getting up from the bench. "I need to show you something." I hurried over to the heavy plastic case housing our one and only portable microphone and yanked my spiral notebook out from beneath it.

Behind me I heard Melody ask, "What's he fussing about?"

"No idea."

Before I'd even made it back to the bench, I said, "Look in the viewfinder. Tell me what you see."

Troy picked up the video camera and handed it to Melody. "Ladies first."

"Okay..." She leaned close to the eyepiece. "And what am I looking at?"

"Let Troy see when you're done."

Confused, she passed him the camera. He took a turn. "Are we supposed to know what this is?"

"Just tell me this," I said, opening the notebook. "Isn't the drawing on that guitar and this . . ." I held up the page so they could see the sketch I'd drawn a little over an hour ago. ". . . the exact same thing?"

10

"Okay, I agree. It's weird," Troy said, "which, by the way, is how I'd describe this entire fucking trip so far. But I still don't understand why it's such a big deal."

Melody sat down next to me. "What are you thinking, Billy?"

"I'm not exactly sure yet, but here's the thing . . . Even before I noticed the symbol on the guitar a few minutes ago, it was stuck inside my head." Gesturing to the notebook that Troy was now holding. "That's why I sketched it today while I was waiting for you." I glanced over my shoulder at the van. "I need to get the 35mm film developed. Ay-sap."

"What's the rush?" Troy asked.

"I think that same symbol appears on at least one of the other memorials. Maybe more than one. When I first spotted it in the Polaroid of the baseball glove, I was almost positive I'd seen it before . . . but I had no idea where or when. Now, I'm nearly certain it's the other memorials. Something subliminal."

"Have you considered that it might be some type of religious symbol?" Troy asked. "And that's why it was left in both places?"

"No . . . ," I admitted. "You know, I hadn't really thought of that."

"Hell, it might even be the logo of a local band that both Gabriel and Michael Meredith listened to. It's probably on T-shirts and bumper stickers."

"I guess it's possible. But—"

"You think it's somehow tied in to everything else that's been happening, don't you?"

"I think there's a cha—"

"Hold on. I have an idea," Melody said.

Troy and I turned and looked at her. After the bad scare she'd had by the side of the road earlier, she'd been a lot quieter than usual.

"Why don't we drop off the film . . . I saw a one-hour photo sign on the window of that drug store over there . . . and while we're waiting, pay a visit to the library and see what we can find out?"

"Beautiful *and* smart," Troy said with a grin. "We're two peas in a pod."

"Pondo and Penny."

And off we went, our laughter lightening my mood.

11

The number one unwritten rule in almost all of the many scary movies I'd watched in my lifetime was little more than an exercise in common sense: *Never split up*.

The implication being—as I'm sure Troy would be happy to tell you if he were still around—that there is safety in numbers.

So what did we do as soon as we walked in the front door of the surprisingly cavernous Smithtown Library?

We split up, of course.

But only after Troy looked around and said, "Don't ask me why, but Jesus Christ on a stick, this place gives me the creeps." And then off he went to find the restroom, groaning as he clutched his cramping stomach.

Watching him go, Melody announced, "I think I'll start in the regional-interest section." She looked at me. "Why don't you check out religion or maybe go talk to Miss Grumpy Face over there?" Gesturing to the stern-faced librarian sitting behind the counter before walking away.

After eyeballing the librarian from a safe distance—during which she never so much as lifted her head to look at me, no *May I help you?* or *Nice day, isn't it?*; hell, I never even saw her turn the page of the book in front of her, so maybe her heart had given up the goose and she'd passed away right there on the job—I decided to head for the stacks and see what I could find.

The library was shaped like an elongated T—and as luck would have it, the nonfiction section was located the farthest possible distance away from the front entrance. My footsteps echoed as I walked down the long corridor. The carpet lining the aisles of bookshelves was the color of pea soup, old and worn. Dust motes danced in the narrow beams of sunlight slanting through the windows. Where there were no windows, shadows gathered, forming deep, dark pools. I walked at a brisk pace. At one point, I thought I heard a child giggling somewhere behind me. I glanced over my shoulder, saw no one, and began walking even faster.

When I finally found what I was looking for—a nonfiction section that was nearly as expansive as Sudbury High School's entire library—it didn't take long for me to feel overwhelmed. There were way too many choices. *The Philosophy of Religion. Religion and Race in the South. A History of the World's Religions. Religion in the Constitution. A World Religion for the New Age. Spiritual Leaders Who Changed the World.* I didn't even know where to start, so I used the shotgun approach and selected several volumes.

I was sitting at a table along the wall skimming the contents page of a phone book–sized *Religion in the 20th Century* when Troy returned from the bathroom.

"Avoid the shitter at all costs," he said, settling into the chair across from me. "That hallway goes on forever. It's like walking into a goddamn haunted house." He looked at what I was doing and made a disapproving *tsk*ing sound with his lips. "That'll take hours." Picking up a book from the nearby stack I'd made, he flipped to the back. "First, make sure the book has an index. Then search for 'religious symbols.'"

"I'm nineteen years old, Troy. I go to college. I know how to use an index."

Ignoring me, he traced his finger down the page. "Here we go. Pages 112 and 113." A few seconds later, he slid the open book to the center of the table so we could both see what he'd found.

A two-page spread labeled *Popular Religious Symbols*. There were five rows of seven on each page—for a total of seventy small images.

"What would I do without you, oh brilliant one?" Nonetheless excited, I leaned over and began studying the various images. Some I recognized right away. Christianity. Judaism. Taoism. Even Buddhism (which I'd learned about from a girl in my freshman-year English Composition class). But most I'd never seen before.

At one point, I thought I'd found a match, but after consulting the sketch in my notebook, it wasn't even close.

I scanned the pages for a second and third time, and looked up at Troy. "Nah. No dice." I sat back in my chair. "So what now?"

"We try another book, I guess." Sensing my dejection, he quickly added, "And even if we don't find anything, I'm pretty sure there's a rational explanation."

"A rational explanation," I repeated. "From the guy who believes in the Loch Ness Monster."

"What's that supposed to mean?"

"Nothing. Don't be so defensive."

"I'm not being defensive. I really want to know. What do you mean?"

I thought about it for a moment. "I just find it interesting that you believe in all those far-out concepts like UFOs and Bigfoot and ghosts, but you don't think what we're dealing with is particularly . . . troubling."

"I never said that. The man in the woods, the balloon on the windshield, even the flat tire . . . that's all troubling as hell." He glanced at the book sitting open between us. "The symbol you found . . . what can I say? My gut tells me they're not related."

"Fair enough," I said, sliding another book off the pile.

"Don't be mad, Billy."

"I'm not mad."

"You promise?" He looked like a little boy again.

"I promise. I'm just tired . . . and confused."

"Yeah, well . . . welcome to my life," he said and stood up. "And on that note, I'm going to find Mel. See if she's having better luck."

I didn't want him to leave—it was too damn quiet back here, and for some reason I couldn't get that high-pitched giggling I'd heard out of my head—but I didn't dare say any of that out loud. "I'll finish looking through the rest of the pile and catch up with you as soon as I can."

"Sounds good. Photos won't be ready for . . ." He checked his wristwatch. ". . . another forty minutes, so we have plenty of time." Glancing over his shoulder as he was walked away, he added, "Make sure you return those books to the proper shelf. You don't want the Library Policeman coming after you."

"Ha ha ha." I tried to keep my voice light but didn't do a very good job of it.

Troy stopped and turned around. "You sure you're okay, Billy?"

"I'm fine," I said, waving a hand at him. "Go find Mel. I'll be there in a few."

He looked like he had more to say—but then he was walking away again, the sound of his footsteps fading. A moment later, he was gone and all was silent.

I turned back to my notebook, listening for the return of that rustling sound and a child's taunting laughter from deep within the gloom. When it didn't come, my mind immediately returned to the Library Policeman. I remembered the posters on the walls of my elementary school library— DON'T BE LATE . . . OR ELSE!—featuring a faceless shadow-man wearing a long, dark trench coat and old-fashioned fedora. Those images had terrified me at the time.

More certain than ever that something dark and mysterious and dangerous was lurking close by to all three of us, I picked up another book and opened it.

12

"This is the closest I could find."

Melody held up the book for me to see. A large drawing was centered on the right-hand page. She was right—it definitely bore a resemblance to the symbol I'd discovered on the baseball glove and guitar. To be certain, I opened my notebook and compared the two images side by side. At a glance, it appeared as though the drawing in the book was a work in progress—the arms and legs cruder and less developed, and there were no eyes in the hands—while the sketch I'd made based on the photograph was more of a finished product.

"Is it religious based?" I asked, closing the notebook. "How'd you find it?"

She turned the book around so we could see the cover.

The artwork was amateurish yet striking. A mist-enveloped mountain range underneath a full moon. In the foreground, a pair of glowing red eyes peering out from within the shadows between the trees. Amid the clouds floating in the night sky, the title: *Mysteries & Myths of the Appalachians*. At the very bottom, just below the red eyes, the author's name: *Larson Rutherford*.

"Fact or fiction?" Troy asked.

"Most likely a little of both," Melody said. "It's based on actual testimony from local Appalachians . . . but you know how that goes."

"Moonshine and tall tales," I said. Thanks to Uncle Frank, I was very familiar with that aspect of local tradition.

"Can I see it?" Troy said.

"Sure." Melody handed over the book. Troy took a seat and started reading. I could tell he was excited. Finally. And I knew why. After all, Bigfoot and the Loch Ness Monster had both started out as local legends and grown from there. This stuff was right up his alley.

"The book was published in 1974 by a small regional press," she said. "So probably not the most rigorous editorial staff. But the author's actually a retired English professor who moved back to the valley after teaching at Penn State for thirty-plus years."

"You never answered me," I said. "Is it a religious symbol?"

"You could say that," Troy said, staring up at us. He no longer looked excited. "Apparently, it's used by satanists."

13

The woman at the front desk turned out to be alive and well, and a whole lot friendlier than I'd initially imagined. When I approached the counter to request change for a dollar, she greeted me with a pleasant smile—that instantly transformed into a series of lengthy yawns, leading me to believe that she'd been catnapping when we first came in—and even counted out each of the coins as she placed them into my hand.

Without a Smithtown library card in our possession, we only had two options when it came to Larson Rutherford's *Mysteries & Myths of the Appalachians*. One of us could stuff the book down our pants and make a break for it. Or we could use the Xerox machine by the water fountain to photocopy the most pertinent sections.

With thoughts of the Library Policeman still rattling around inside my head, I couldn't volunteer quick enough to go ask the librarian for change. At a nickel a pop, my wrinkled one-dollar bill would net us twenty pages. Not a bad deal.

"We can also check used bookstores," Melody said, plugging a coin into the slot. "I'm sure someplace will have it."

The copier spit out another page onto the tray, and I added it to the pile. The paper felt pleasantly warm on my fingertips. The inky smell reminded me of middle school. "I never realized that satanism was such a widely accepted religion."

"I wouldn't exactly say *accepted*," Troy commented.

I searched for a better word. "Widespread?"

"Not sure I'd go that far either. But yeah, according to the book, in some areas—mainly rural—satanism *is* gaining a larger following."

"Why would anyone do that? I mean, it's one thing to not want to go to church anymore. But to worship the devil . . . ? Really?"

"Lots of reasons," Troy said. "Rebellion against authority. A profound sense of abandonment and/or abuse. Nihilism."

"So then the million-dollar question becomes—"

"Why was a satanic symbol left on the roadside memorials of a high school baseball star and a nine-year-old boy?"

"Hold on to that thought," Melody said, removing the book from the glass surface of the Xerox machine. "That was our last nickel."

"Time flies when you're *not* having fun," Troy said.

"I've got to use the bathroom before we leave." I handed the stack of photocopies to Melody. "I'll meet you guys out front."

As I made my way past the front desk, I wasn't the least bit surprised to see the librarian fighting to keep her eyes open as she sorted through a bin of recently returned books. Maybe she was burning the candle at both ends, or perhaps had a new boyfriend and wasn't getting enough sleep. I chuckled to myself just thinking about the second scenario.

The dead-end hallway where the men's and women's bathrooms were located was every bit as narrow, dark, and spooky as Troy had described. The UNDER CONSTRUCTION—PLEASE EXCUSE THE MESS sign failed to do it justice. There were loose wires hanging from ragged holes in the ceiling. Exposed pipes in sections of both walls. The carpet has been stripped, and the floor was uneven and sticky on the bottom of my shoes. It was a little like walking inside a long-abandoned movie theater at midnight. A glowing red NO EXIT sign at the end of the corridor provided the only illumination.

I hurried into the restroom, stopped in front of the first urinal I came to, unzipped, and did my business as quickly as possible. When I was finished, I washed and dried my hands and, as I was leaving, caught a glimpse of my reflection in the mirror above the sink. A jolt of shock reverberated throughout my body. It was like looking at an old photograph of my father.

His eyes. His jawline. Even the little bump on the bridge of his nose. *When the hell did this happen?* I thought. *And how did I not notice before today?*

Momentarily shaken, I pulled open the door and stepped back into the hallway. With the glare of the fluorescent lights spilling out of the bathroom, I could actually see where I was going. The bare floor at my feet even *looked* sticky.

And then the door swung closed behind me—and I was plunged into complete and total darkness.

My first instinct was to freeze—and that's exactly what I did. Raising my hands in front of me, I reached out and nervously probed the blackness.

If I heard giggling or my fingers so much as grazed the flesh of another human being, I was going to scream, shit my pants, and faint. Not necessarily in that order.

As my eyes struggled to adjust, I began walking.

The dim glimmer of light at the mouth of the hallway appeared impossibly far away.

A sound came from behind me.

Rustling?

Footsteps?

Breathing?

Had someone whispered my name?

I was halfway to the light.

And I was sure it was the Library Policeman lurking in the darkness—coming for me at last.

I picked up my pace. Almost jogging now.

Oh Jesus, or maybe it was the man from the woods . . .

I could see the corner of the display table in the lobby.

I could hear the *thump* of books being stacked on a cart as our sleepy librarian friend prepared them for a return to the shelves.

I was almost there.

At the front desk, just out of view, a telephone rang.

A part of me was so relieved I almost shouted, "Hello!"

The thought made me smile—all of my nervousness draining away.

That's when the hand reached out of the darkness behind me—and grasped my shoulder.

And I screamed.

14

"OHMYGOD, BILLY, I'M SO SORRY! I DIDN'T MEAN—"

For a second, my mouth wouldn't work. It opened and closed, like a dying fish gasping for oxygen, but no matter how hard I tried, no words would come out. *This is what it feels like to drown. Or have a heart attack.*

And then the world turned right side up again—and I found my voice.

"Naomi . . . ?!"

She shrank back a little.

"I . . . w-what the hell are you doing here?"

"I came to find you." She was struggling to hold back her laughter. *She thought this was funny?* "I swear I didn't mean to—" She crammed a hand over her mouth, but I could still see the widening grin behind it.

"It's not funny, goddammit!"

"Oh my goodness." A hushed voice at the end of the hallway. "Is everything okay?"

I turned around.

It was the librarian. She no longer looked sleepy.

15

"I still can't believe it," Naomi said with a giggle. "You screamed so loud."

We were standing outside on the library steps. Melody and Troy were nowhere in sight. Probably waiting at the van, wondering what was taking me so long. Naomi's friend, Jenny, leaned against the hood of her car a short distance away, paying us little attention. When we'd first emerged from the building, she'd given us a disinterested wave and immediately returned her attention to filing her nails.

"It was dark. I thought I was being attacked. You're lucky I didn't turn around and pop you in the face." I sighed, knowing how ridiculous I sounded. "Or faint."

"Why would someone attack you in the library?"

"Long story."

"I've got all day."

A car drove by on the street. I watched it stop at the four-way intersection and continue on its way. Still no sign of the van. "Why are you here, Naomi?" I still couldn't believe she was standing right in front of me. "How did you find me?"

"Well . . . I've been thinking about you since we ran into each other at the diner." The intensity in her eyes surprised me. She was dressed in a jean skirt and a tank top, the familiar scent of her perfume lingering in the air between us, and I was reminded once again of how much she'd grown up since we'd last been together. "And then, yesterday after dinner I got into a huge fight with my parents. It was . . . bad. I had to get out of there. So I called Jenny, and here we are."

"And you just *happened* to know where we were?"

"Not exactly . . ." For the first time, she appeared uneasy "We checked a bunch of campgrounds in the middle of the night but couldn't find you."

"Go on."

"Jenny spotted the van parked down the street a little while ago. We waited in case you came back, but when you didn't, we started looking around town. I only went in the library because I had to pee. I couldn't believe it was you in front of me in that hallway."

"There's something I don't get," I said, my suspicion mounting. "How'd you even know which direction we were traveling? I don't remember mentioning it back at the diner."

That uneasy look in her eyes again. "I . . . umm . . . your aunt . . ."

Of course. "I'm going to have to talk to that woman."

She lowered her eyes to the ground. "She was only trying to help."

"So what now, now that you've found me?" I asked, pretty sure I already knew the answer.

"I want to go with you," she said, the intensity returning to her gaze. "I want to help."

Before I could answer, the van pulled up to the curb.

16

"We thought we'd surprise you."

In the front seat, Troy held up a stack of envelopes containing the prints we'd ordered. He glanced at Naomi and Jenny, both of them standing beside Jenny's car. "But . . . it looks like the surprise is on us."

Still embarrassed from the spectacle I'd caused inside the library, I said, "You don't know the half of it."

"How'd they find us in the middle of nowhere?" Melody asked. "Did you call and—"

"No! I didn't *call* them." I wasn't sure why exactly, but it bothered me that Melody thought that. "Aunt Helen told them. I gave her a list of our likely stops before we left . . . but I never expected her to share it with anyone. Especially Naomi. I'm as shocked as you are that they're here."

She drummed her fingers on the steering wheel. "So now what? They want to come with us?"

"Just Naomi," I said. "Jenny is driving home this afternoon. With or without her."

More finger tapping. "And how do you feel about *that*?"

"I'm not sure," I said with a shrug. "I don't want to complicate things . . . but on the other hand—I have to admit, yeah, maybe she *could* help. She told me she took a class on Appalachian culture and—"

"And it has nothing to do with what she's wearing?" Melody was smiling now, really enjoying this.

"It has not a single thing to do with that," I said, rolling my eyes. "Besides, after how I treated her, I'm pretty sure she still wants to kill me in my sleep."

"Speaking of sleep," Troy said. "Does this mean we have to share the tent with her?"

"You can sleep in the van with me," Melody said, patting him on his leg. "We'll let the lovebirds have their privacy."

"We're *not* lovebirds!" I could feel my cheeks flushing red.

Troy puckered his lips and began making kissing sounds.

"Oh my God . . ."

Melody giggled.

"I have no intention of—"

The side door slid open.

Naomi stood outside the van with a big grin on her face and a pink knapsack slung over her shoulder. "Ready to get this show on the road?"

When no one said anything right away, she climbed over my legs into the back seat.

Troy turned around and studied us for a moment. Judging by the thoughtful expression on his face, I expected him to say something astute. Instead: "Okay . . . *now*, we look like a Benneton ad."

17

"Are you hungry?" I asked as we pulled into the gas station.

"Nah." Naomi brushed the hair out of her eyes. "I had an Egg McMuffin and some candy. Breakfast of champions."

"You sure? You want me to run inside and see if they have a vending machine?"

She smiled. "That's sweet of you, but really, I'm okay."

Why does it all of a sudden feel like I'm on a first date?

I felt Melody's eyes watching us in the rearview mirror. I could only imagine what she was thinking. While Troy got out and worked the pump, I brought Naomi up to speed on our trip thus far, including the recent stint of weird happenings. She mostly listened, only interrupting to ask to see the sketch in my notebook and to tell Melody that the van reminded her of the Mystery Machine from *Scooby Doo*. I was afraid that Melody was going to respond with a smart-ass comment, but instead she laughed and played along. I was grateful for that. I realized that by allowing Naomi to come along, I was risking messing up the overall chemistry of the group. I was determined to not let that happen.

When Naomi handed back the notebook, her fingers grazed my hand, and I felt an almost electric jolt pass through me. I still couldn't believe she was sitting right next to me. Our knees practically touching. The whole thing felt like a dream.

"Please take this for gas," Naomi said, leaning between the seats. She reached out a hand holding a ten-dollar bill.

Melody glanced at the money but didn't make a move for it. "Oh . . . you don't . . . it's not . . ."

"No, really. Please take it." Naomi scooted closer, extending her arm. "The last thing I want to be is a freeloader. I can also help out with food and campsite fees."

Melody reached over and took the wrinkled ten spot—and deposited it in the dashboard ashtray next to a couple of ones and some change. "Okay, since you put it that way. Thank you, Naomi. With the way this thing guzzles gasoline, that'll be a huge help."

Outside, the gas pump clicked off. The tank full, Troy replaced the nozzle and walked around the front of the van. As he passed the window on Naomi's side, he checked to make sure that she wasn't looking and then made the same kissy face as before. After climbing into the passenger seat—the faint scent of petrol hitchhiking along for the ride—he immediately turned around to face us.

Holding my breath, I braced myself. There was no telling what he might say or do next.

"Can we please look at the photographs now?"

"Let's do it," I said, with a sigh of relief—and more than a little excitement. Even with Naomi's tan leg hovering inches away from me, the urgency to get to the bottom of the mysterious symbol hadn't dulled even a bit. It'd only been fifteen minutes since we'd driven away from the library, and I'd already thought of the photos about a dozen times.

MEMORIALS

Spinning around in his seat, Troy grabbed the stack of envelopes from the dashboard and promptly almost dropped them. "I was thinking we'd divide and conquer." He handed several of the packets of photographs to Melody, several more to me, and kept the rest for himself. I didn't much like the idea of sharing—especially since I was the one who'd taken all the photos—but I reminded myself of that whole group-chemistry thing and kept my mouth shut.

Melody pulled away from the pumps and parked the van next to an old storage shed on the opposite side of the station. For the next several minutes, we sat there in silence and slowly flipped through piles of glossy, full-color five-by-seven prints. The first envelope I opened contained a series of shots from Day One. The waterlogged leather jacket. The collection of empty wine bottles. The little boy with the missing front teeth. Then came images from yesterday. The flooded crosses from Bruce and Betty Carson's memorial. The flat tire on the van. Finally, in the last packet . . . my parents' memorial. The apple crate covered in candles. The wooden cross. The wreath of artificial flowers, many of them now missing, stolen away by the wind. It was all there in sharp detail. I took my time, clearing my throat several times to keep it from going dry, and finally found what I was looking for in the next-to-last photograph. Tucked away in the lower corner of the oversized poster board, nearly hidden among all the handwritten messages—that odd symbol. My hands shaking, I looked up and snuck a peek at the others—if only to see if anyone else could hear my heart pounding.

Troy was sitting perfectly still, holding three or four photos, fanned out like playing cards, in his left hand. Melody lifted a photograph in front of her face, first moving it closer, and then farther away. After a moment, she returned it to the stack in her lap. When I glanced at Naomi, she just smiled.

Troy was the first to speak. "You were right, Billy." He turned and held up a photo. "The symbol was drawn on the baseball glove . . ." And then with a dramatic flourish, he whipped out a second print. "But it's also on a photo of Chase Harper."

Melody didn't even bother turning around. Nor did she hold up any photographs. "A painted rock behind the billboard. One of the posters on the fence by the cemetery. The symbol's on both of them."

When I didn't say anything right away, Melody shifted in her seat and stared at me in the rearview mirror. Troy began tapping his fingers on the armrest. Faster. Louder. Drumming to the beat inside his head. I knew the suspense was killing them—but I wasn't dragging it out for dramatic effect. My stomach felt sick. My head throbbed. I wasn't sure if I'd be able to speak the words out loud. Then finally:

"I found the symbol in one other photograph . . ." I swallowed the lump in my throat and raised the glossy print in front of my face. "At my mother and father's memorial."

18

After leaving the gas station, we drove back to Gabriel Ramos's memorial to see if we had overlooked anything else the first time around. Getting out of the van and walking to the fence where all the photographs and newspaper articles were displayed, it felt like I was moving in slow motion. My head bogged down with a myriad of troubled thoughts. None of the others said anything, but I could tell they were feeling the same way.

As we huddled in silence in front of Gabriel's guitar—a surprise birthday gift from his doting grandfather—I glanced over at Naomi. She was biting her lip and trying not to cry, an endearing idiosyncrasy I remembered all too well from our years of dating. I wondered if she was having second thoughts about tagging along on our class trip.

Returning my attention to the memorial, I felt a shiver of unease travel down my spine. Seeing the symbol in person for the first time—really *seeing* it—felt strange. Looking at it now, I had no idea how we'd missed it during our first visit. It was right there in front of us, like an ominous staring eye.

"I don't know about you guys," Melody said, "but that thing is giving me some seriously bad vibes." She turned and started walking away. "Take all the time you need, but I'm gonna wait in the van."

MEMORIALS

Troy didn't comment at all, just stood there staring, which was testimony enough that it was really bothering him. For a moment, my mind flashed back to the morning my father and I had discovered the old stone foundation in the woods off Church Street. Strangely enough, before last night, I hadn't thought of it in years.

For me, standing in front of the guitar and looking at the symbol up close felt eerily similar to that long-ago experience. The symbol was *wrong*. It didn't belong here—and every fiber of my being recognized that. But there was also a story behind it, and I was determined to find out what it was.

"This is all so sad," Naomi said, looking at the photos hanging on the chain-link fence. "If something like this happened to my sister, I don't know what I'd do."

Dropping to one knee, I reached out and traced the symbol with my finger.

"Don't touch it!" Troy said from behind me.

Whoever had drawn the symbol had done so after the guitar had been covered in plastic and chained to the fence. They'd used what appeared to be permanent black marker.

"I wonder how long it's been—"

The breath thickened in my throat, choking off my voice. My vision blurred momentarily, then cleared again. An acrid, burning scent clogged my nostrils, and then it, too, was gone just as quickly. All of these sensations identical to what I'd experienced three days earlier at Chase Harper's memorial.

I jerked my hand away and stood up.

"Are you okay?" Naomi asked.

"Yeah . . . I'm fine," I said, backing away from the guitar.

"You don't look fine," Troy said. "I thought you were going to lose your lunch for a second there."

"No, no, I'm good." But I really wasn't. For a moment there, it'd felt like I was dying.

Gesturing to the camera hanging around my neck, he asked, "What now? More pictures?"

"Just a few," I said, trying to hide the panic I was feeling. "We won't be long."

"You guys take your time." He narrowed his eyes at the guitar. "I've had enough, though. I'm going to keep Mel company in the van."

Naomi waited for Troy to walk away, and then she put her hand on my shoulder. "I have to say I'm really happy to see you back behind the camera. I'm proud of you."

At first, I didn't say anything. I remembered with unsettling clarity, shortly after the accident, Naomi begging me not to throw away the prints and photographs from my bedroom walls. I'd ripped up several of them in her face and she'd run from the house, crying. I'd been so damn angry back then.

"I missed it," I said in a shaky voice.

She gave my arm a squeeze and looked over at the symbol on the guitar. "So why would someone leave something like that at your parents' accident site? Or even here, for that matter. It doesn't make any sense."

"You're right, it doesn't."

"Are you going back to their memorial?"

"We haven't discussed it yet." I glanced at Melody and Troy talking inside the van. "But my guess is yes. Sudbury's on our way back to campus."

"I hate to think I came all the way out here just to have you take me back home again."

"I didn't mean we'd be going right away."

"I hope not."

I lifted the camera and snapped a photo of the guitar. "What did you get in a fight with your parents about anyway?"

"Jenny," she said. "They caught her smoking weed in my bedroom."

"That girl's always been trouble."

"Now you sound just like my father."

"He's not wrong." I lifted the camera again.

"Well . . . at least she never ran away from home like someone else I know."

And as much as I wanted to, I couldn't argue with that.

19

The further away we got from Gabriel Ramos's memorial, the more our collective mood improved. Naomi was a big part of that. At one point, as we were passing a drive-in movie theater showing a double feature of *Mausoleum* and *The Hunger*—both of which I'd recently read about in *Fangoria*—she casually asked Melody what her favorite movie was. When Mel answered *Grease* without even a moment's hesitation, Naomi squealed in delight and said, "Mine too!" And that's all it took—before long, they were discussing a rapid-fire succession of seemingly random topics, ranging from favorite actors and rock bands to how much they hated straightening their hair and how old they were when they first got their ears pierced.

By the time we reached Stoneridge, I'd convinced Troy to change the radio station, and all four of us were singing along with "Sister Golden Hair." We clearly had no future in the entertainment industry, but hey, at least we were smiling again.

"Anyone hungry?" Troy asked as we rounded a bend in the road and a billboard reading Mo's FAMOUS BBQ—ONE MILE greeted us on the right-hand shoulder.

"Ooo, I could go for some ribs," Melody said.

"I could definitely eat." Naomi nudged my leg. "How about you?"

With that delicious shiver cascading throughout my body, I smiled and said, "Let's do it."

Even at three thirty in the afternoon, the gravel parking lot of Mo's Famous BBQ was packed. Melody found an opening near the end of the last row in between a beat-up Gremlin and a panel van with BOGAN'S PLUMBING on the side. We piled out and sat down at the only empty table beneath a leaning aluminum awning that looked like it was just waiting for a strong wind to come along and spirit it away to the next county. The warm air was redolent with the rich scent of cooking meat and exotic spices. My stomach was already grumbling.

Set against the edge of the woods, a double-wide trailer had been converted into a kitchen/storage area. Out front, protected from the sun by a large canopy, two elderly Black men worked the largest flattop grill I'd ever seen. Both men had towels draped around their necks, their wizened faces dripping with sweat. I assumed that at least one of the hardworking men was named Mo.

Despite the full house, our waitress—a peppy young woman with dyed red hair and a tattoo of a topless mermaid on her shoulder—arrived within minutes, introduced herself as Madeline from Virginia Beach, and asked for our drink orders. When David Bowie's "Let's Dance" came on the boom box—a song we'd already heard on the radio several times that day—she boogied away from our table and made her way across the dining area, pumping her fist in the air for good measure.

"She was nice," Naomi said, unwrapping her plastic utensils from the napkin.

I poked Troy in the shoulder. "When she comes back, try not to stare at her tattoo so much."

His eyes widened. "Did you see—" He stopped in midsentence. "I mean . . . what tattoo? I didn't see any tattoo."

"Now that you mention it, I didn't either."

And then we were both laughing.

"Incorrigible children," Melody said, looking at Naomi. "The pair of them."

Naomi smiled and my heart melted a little bit. "With me along for the ride, at least they can't gang up on you now."

Melody pointed at Naomi across the table. "That's a fact, sister."

By the time Madeline from Virginia Beach returned with our sodas and iced teas, the song had ended and we were ready to order. When she was finished scribbling in her notepad, she looked up at us and asked, "You all local folks or away folks on your way to someplace else? 'Cause I know you ain't out here in the middle of nowhere looking for a good time."

When Melody told her we were college students and explained what we were doing, the waitress perked up another notch. "Oh, in that case, there's someone here you all need to talk to. Old dude knows everything there is to know about Stoneridge and this here part of the valley. I'll put in the good word for y'all as soon as I have a free minute." And she was gone again.

"Huh," Troy said. "This could be interesting."

Melody put down her iced tea. "Can I ask you a question, Naomi?"

"Of course."

"Where do your parents think you are right now?"

"Umm." She began squirming in her chair. "They . . . I told them . . ."

"You don't have to say if you don't want to. I'm just curious."

Naomi sighed and sat up to face the music. "They think I'm blowing off some steam with my friend Patty and her family at their lake house. The night of our big argument, I called them from a pay phone and told them that Jenny had dropped me off at the lake, and I'd be home in a few days." She looked at me. "If they knew I was here with you . . ." She shook her head.

"Oh boy," I muttered. I hadn't even thought of that. Her parents probably hated me.

"I just want to forget about them for a while," Naomi said, staring off at the mist-shrouded mountains. "I just want to forget about everything."

No one had anything to say to that. I think we could all relate to that sentiment.

The food came a few minutes later—and it was every bit as delicious as it smelled. The meat so perfectly seasoned and tender, it practically slid off the ribs onto our plates. The brisket melted in our mouths. The barbecue chicken a gift from the heavens. All of it swimming in Mo's secret sauce. And don't even get me started on the mac and cheese and coleslaw.

I took a good look around as I was eating. Most of the other diners appeared to be working men. Dressed in boots, dirt- or grease-streaked jeans, and sweat-stained T-shirts, they hunched over their plates with a somber intensity. After their meal, most likely the local bar awaited many of them, an endless blurry-eyed parade of bottles and shot glasses, until it was time to go home and sleep, wake up, and do it all over again. There were also a handful of older couples and a single table of laughing teenage boys dressed in dirty baseball uniforms. My mind immediately went to the unlucky Michael Meredith, and I did my best to push those thoughts away.

Glancing over my shoulder, I noticed a woman sitting alone at a table by the roped-off entrance. Clearly out of place with her short and spiky, almost-white Annie Lennox haircut, dark tailored pantsuit, and glittering diamond necklace, she appeared to be somewhere around her midforties. A pile of picked-clean bones sat on the plate in front of her. The woman was glaring at me. Not staring. Glaring. And unless I was mistaken, she wasn't focused on anyone else at our table. Just me.

Feeling uncomfortable, I quickly turned around and pretended to be interested in everyone else's conversation. A few moments later, when I'd finally gathered the courage to look again, the woman was gone. Vanished. The table cleared and ready for the next diner.

I was halfway convinced I'd imagined the whole thing until I spotted her walking across the parking lot. She got into a white BMW, opened the sunroof, and drove away—but not before glowering one last time in my direction.

What the hell was that all about? I wondered, using a wet wipe to scrub the barbecue sauce off my fingernails.

As I was finishing, the waitress returned to our table with an older gentleman at her side. With his neatly trimmed salt-and-pepper hair and tucked in pastel polo shirt, the two of them were a study in contrast.

"This is Robert Farnsworth," she said. "He's a good egg. Robert, these are my new friends I was telling you about."

"It's a pleasure to meet you," he said in a surprisingly deep voice. "Any friend of Madeline's is a friend of mine."

Before we could introduce ourselves, Madeline said, "I told Robert about the school project you're working on. He knows more about this area than anyone I've ever met."

MEMORIALS

"I'm afraid she exaggerates," he said, smiling. "I retired a few years ago, so I have plenty of time to read. I also belong to the local historical society."

"Please, have a seat," Melody said, pulling out the chair next to her.

"Are you sure? I don't want to intrude."

"Don't be silly," she said. "We'd love to talk to you. Actually, we sort of need to."

"Well, thank you." He sat down at the table. "But first I must insist that you tell me more about this documentary project of yours. From what little Madeline shared, it sounds fascinating."

"It was *your* idea," Melody said, looking at me. "Why don't you do the honors?"

So, I did.

Beginning with the original inspiration for the project, I took Robert from the proposal stage and Mr. Tyree's reluctant approval all the way through our most recent stops on the road. At the mention of my parents' accident, he pursed his lips and offered a single nod, but spared me of any unnecessary condolences. I liked him even more for that.

I made a point of not mentioning the strange symbol we'd found on the memorials or the video of the man in the woods or the balloon left on our windshield. Or any of the other weirdness, for that matter. I wanted him to like us and open up, not think we were a traveling band of crackpots.

When I was finished talking, he looked around the table and said, "Thanks so much for sharing, and for what you're doing. I cannot emphasize enough how impressed I am. With intelligent and thoughtful individuals such as yourselves, I think our future is in very good hands indeed."

For a moment, I thought Melody might burst into tears, she looked so happy. Troy sat ramrod straight in his chair, his chest puffed out. Naomi nudged my leg underneath the table and gazed at me with admiration. For the first time in a very long while, I felt a sudden surge of pride. I'd almost forgotten what it felt like.

"Okay, your turn now, Mr. Farnsworth," Melody said with an eagerness in her eyes that I recognized from back at school. "What's your favorite story about this area?"

"Well . . . I wouldn't exactly say it's my favorite, but it's most definitely the strangest . . . and I have to admit not at all pleasant. But it *does* involve a memorial of sorts, so you may find it interesting."

"Absolutely," Troy said. "We'd love to hear it."

"Splendid." Robert rested his elbows on the table, and interlaced his fingers as though he was preparing to pray. "So . . . in 1974, seventeen-year-old Rachel Filmore and eighteen-year-old Griffin Schutz . . ."

20

VIDEO FOOTAGE
(5:04 p.m., Monday, May 9, 1983)

". . . were high school sweethearts," says the man with the salt-and-pepper hair. "After graduation, Rachel started nursing school in nearby Clarkston, and Griffin took a job running a forklift at one of his father's warehouses. By the beginning of the new year, 1975, he was promoted to assistant manager. Six months later, Rachel announced that she was pregnant. At his family's annual Fourth of July picnic, Griffin got down on his knee and proposed—and Rachel said yes. A lavish wedding was planned for that November."

The man sits with his legs crossed on a wooden bench in front of a shimmering lake. His eyes are hidden behind sunglasses. With his confident speaking voice and easygoing demeanor, Robert Farnsworth could easily pass for a network anchorman or tenured college professor instead of a retired construction foreman and amateur historian.

MEMORIALS

"In early August, Griffin picked up Rachel from her parents' house and drove to the movie theater in downtown Clarkston. Afterward, they grabbed dinner and then headed to the lake to watch the sunset.

"Later that night . . . eleven o'clock comes around, and Rachel hasn't returned home yet. Her father calls Griffin's parents and asks if she's there. His mother tells him no, we don't know where they are, and so they start to worry too. At midnight, the kids are still missing, so the Schutzes call the police.

"Overnight, the police begin their search, mainly through local patrols, but it isn't until late the following morning that an accurate timeline is established—this after multiple witnesses confirm they saw both Griffin and Rachel at the movie theater and the restaurant.

"According to the waitress, they'd paid the check, left a generous tip, and left shortly after seven thirty. She also remembered Rachel saying something to Griffin as they were getting up to leave about 'skipping the walk and just enjoying the sunset.'

"Watching the sun setting from the shoreline of Lady Ann Lake was a long-standing romantic tradition among local teenagers. Multiple units were immediately dispatched to the area. But before any one of them reached the lake, an emergency call came into the station house.

"A fisherman walking to his secret spot had discovered Griffin Schutz's naked body sprawled across one of the wooded trails. He'd been stabbed more than thirty times in the arms, legs, torso, and head. His throat had been cut so deeply that he'd almost been decapitated. He was missing nearly all of his teeth. The dirt and grass around his body was soaked with so much blood that the fisherman told police he'd initially thought it was 'a piece of discarded red carpet.'

"There was no sign anywhere of Rachel Filmore—who was seven months pregnant. The police combed the woods surrounding the lake every day and night for two weeks. Divers searched the water. Helicopters circled the area and the National Guard was called in. Newspaper and television reporters came from as far north as Boston, and as far south as Charleston. Lab technicians tested the blood they found at the scene to see if any of it was a match for Rachel, but all of the results came back negative. A ten-thousand-dollar reward was offered for any information leading to an arrest. Once the police tape was removed, family and friends began leaving flowers at the scene. A cross was erected and . . ."

21

The trail was so narrow we were forced to walk single file.

Farnsworth, who'd agreed to come with us even though the lake was twenty minutes out of his way, took the lead. Melody, Troy, and Naomi followed right behind him. I brought up the rear, the 35mm camera draped over one shoulder, the Polaroid dangling from the other. Worried about lugging the heavy case over unfamiliar terrain, I'd left the video camera locked inside the van. Besides, this little excursion had little to do with the documentary. Instead, it fell squarely in the category of morbid fascination.

The ground beneath our feet was slippery from the recent rains. The forest around us smelled of pine needles and bark and sap. Off to our right, through a thick screen of trees, I saw flashes of sparkling blue water. From time to time, I heard the faraway *thrupp-thrupp-thrupp* of motorboats on the lake. But mostly we traveled in silence.

"No one knows what they were doing this far out in the woods," Farnsworth finally said. He was breathing heavily from the long hike. We all were. "In those days, before the county trucked in a couple tons of sand and built the beach, most folks watched the sunset from the hill overlooking the parking lot."

"Could Griffin have been killed somewhere else and his body brought here to the trail?" Troy asked.

"The vast amount of blood discovered at the scene pretty much confirmed that he'd been killed where he was found." He stopped walking and turned around to face the group. "It was right around here that the police found a torn scrap of cloth that matched the yellow maternity blouse Rachel had been wearing the night she disappeared." He gestured to the side of the path. "It was hanging from one of these branches."

Naomi shuddered and clutched my arm. The trail widened here—maybe four feet across—and sloped slightly downhill. The trees grew closer to the path, crowding us and blocking out the sunlight. I could no longer see or hear the lake.

"The cloth was analyzed, of course, but no blood or other usable evidence was detected. In all that time, with all those people working the case, that was the only physical piece of evidence they came up with . . . that single scrap." He started walking again.

"They never found any clues about the girl?" Melody asked. "Nothing at all?"

"Gone without a trace." He stepped over an uprooted tree that had fallen across the path and then turned and offered his hand to Melody. "For a while, there were rumors that she'd run away. Stories with no basis in fact that she'd been seen as far away as Pittsburgh and Baltimore. One of her former classmates while on a family vacation in Bethany Beach swore up and down that she saw Rachel in the grocery store." He shook his head. "But none of those sightings were ever confirmed."

I didn't notice the second trail up ahead—this one branching sharply to the left—until Farnsworth slowed and pointed it out. "Hardly anyone uses it anymore. Mainly just kids and fishermen. It's been what, nine years now, and a lot of people are still seriously spooked. Some even claim these woods are haunted."

What remained of the path was overgrown with a knee-deep tangle of grass, ferns, thorn bushes, and poison ivy. I was glad to be wearing jeans and boots today. When Robert waded into the thicket of creeping vegetation and signaled for us to stop after only a dozen or so yards, I found myself both surprised and relieved.

"Like I said, no one really comes here anymore." He pointed to our left, maybe ten or twelve feet off the side of the trail, where a cross was sticking out of the ground. Most of the white paint had peeled away or flaked off, littering the ground below like pieces of a jigsaw puzzle. "It's rather disheartening."

The forest floor surrounding the base of the cross was covered with hundreds of stones arranged in a roughly circular pattern. The largest stones had been placed along the outside. The closer to the cross one got, the smaller the stones became. Weeds sprouted from between the rocks, and some type of leafy vine had begun to wend its way up the cross. A huge bouquet of blackened flowers lay a short distance away. All around it were empty beer bottles, more than a few of them shattered into pieces.

I lifted the 35mm, made the necessary adjustments for lighting, and began snapping pictures.

"Both of the families eventually moved away," Farnsworth continued. "The Schutzes lasted three years before packing up and heading south to Charleston. As far as I know, they've never been back. Rachel's family stuck around quite a bit longer, almost seven years, as if they were holding out hope that she might one day return, and they wanted to make sure they were here to greet her."

I eased around Naomi and Troy to get a better angle of the stones on the ground—and froze in my tracks.

Near the top of the cross—carved into the wood, faded and discolored with age, but definitely still there—was the symbol from my notebook.

Heart pounding, I lowered the camera and turned to look at the others. The three of them stood shoulder to shoulder, bodies rigid, eyes locked on the cross, an expression of dread etched upon their faces. Troy elbowed me hard in the ribs.

"I see it," I whispered.

The only one who didn't look upset was Farnsworth. He'd wandered farther down the trail, staring off into the trees, lost in his own little world.

I quickly snapped another half-dozen or so photos of the cross, and once I was sure that our tour guide wasn't paying attention, I glanced back at the others and lifted a finger to my lips. *Shh*. Melody gave me a nod.

"Hey, Robert . . . do you happen to know what this is?"

He turned around, smiling. "Pardon me?"

"I was just wondering if you knew what this symbol was." I moved aside and pointed at the top of the cross.

He stepped closer, his smile fading. "Huh . . . I'm not really sure." And then he bent down for a better look. "I know I've noticed it before . . . but I always just figured it was graffiti of some sort. Local kids mucking around."

"No biggie, " I said, doing my best to appear nonchalant. "I was just curious." And then in an attempt to steer away from the subject, I asked, "What do *you* think happened to Rachel Filmore?"

He glanced over his shoulder at me—and for a terrifying moment I was certain, *absolutely* certain, that he'd read my mind about the symbol.

Something in his eyes flickered. Something not so friendly. And then it was gone, and he said, "I think that poor girl's somewhere in the lake."

22

We watched as Farnsworth drove out of the parking lot.

Melody looked at me in the rearview mirror. "Did you believe him?"

I shook my head. "Guy like him stumbles upon a mysterious symbol in the woods, it only makes sense that he'd spend day and night trying to figure out what it means. Instead, he dismissed it like it was nothing."

"You going to take him up on his offer?" Troy asked.

Before he got in his car, Farnsworth had mentioned that he had an author friend he planned to consult about the symbol. He'd scribbled his own phone number on the back of a napkin and told me I was welcome to give him a call in a day or two. Maybe he'd have some information by then.

"Why not?" I said. "Maybe his writer buddy will turn out to be Larson Rutherford. Wouldn't *that* be a helluva coincidence?"

Mel looked at me in the mirror. "Or fate."

23

By now—day four of our trip—I'd learned one indisputable truth about campgrounds. The bathroom and shower facilities could make or break your experience.

So far, we'd been lucky.

You could even say we'd been spoiled.

But that all ended this evening.

The Heavenly Waters Men's Bath & Shower House—denoted by the rusty metal sign on the side of the building—was nothing short of disgusting.

Nearly half of the dozen shower stalls were missing privacy curtains. The remaining sheets of hanging plastic were old and torn and covered in mildew. The showerheads—several of which dangled loosely from crumbling sockets in the wall—leaked nonstop dribbles of sour-smelling brown water onto the cracked and uneven concrete floor, forming puddles that were difficult to avoid thanks to a host of overhead lights that were no longer functioning. Scattered along the wall in one dark corner of the room was a litter of fast-food wrappers, a pair of ripped and shit-stained Fruit of the Looms, a waterlogged *Archie* comic book missing its cover, and a lonely flip-flop of indeterminate color.

The bathroom was separated from the showers by a dimly lit changing room. There wasn't much to it. A couple of plastic benches surrounded by three narrow rows of coin-operated lockers. They looked about as secure as a child's plaything.

Next door, in the bathroom, the buzzing of flies was maddeningly loud. Fluorescent lights continuously flickered. The stagnant air was unbearably hot and humid—and carried the stench of rotten meat. My immediate thought upon entering was that there had to be a dead person or animal hidden inside one of the stalls. With visions of an elderly camper imitating Elvis's unfortunate exit strategy, I took the time to check each and every stall . . .

And found them empty—except for what had to be an all-time campground record for mold, garbage, and unflushed human excrement. The rancid smell, however, was coming from what was left of a partially eaten cheeseburger crawling with maggots. For reasons unknown, someone had taken several bites and then abandoned the leftovers on one of the toilet seats. I didn't even want to consider the possible scenarios that may have led to that decision.

And yet . . . with all that said, and in such painstaking and gruesome detail . . . that age-old proverb held true: *When you have to go, you have to go.*

Which, unfortunately, I did—and with a near panic-inducing urgency.

Grim faced and gagging, my Snoopy T-shirt drenched in sweat, standing in front of a column of grime-stained sinks and fogged-over mirrors, I surveyed my scant choices.

Three of the toilets were out of order. Of the remaining five, two were missing doors and one contained the aforementioned maggot burger (not to mention about a million flies). That only left two. And it went without saying that neither one was equipped with a shred of toilet paper.

Luckily, I'd planned ahead and brought my own.

Gritting my teeth while holding my breath—not an easy thing to do, by the way—I layered the seat with toilet paper, dropped my jeans, and got down to business. If all went according to plan, I'd set my own personal campground record, and be up and out in just under three and a half minutes.

Every available inch of the stall door was covered in graffiti. To help pass the time, I gave it a thorough examination—and came to the immediate conclusion that SUCKA MY GREASY BALLS was my favorite missive, followed closely by BIGFOOT BLOWS. If only Troy were here to offer a rebuttal.

Without even meaning to, I found myself searching the stall for the mysterious symbol—and experiencing a wave of relief when I confirmed it wasn't there. I was about to reach for the roll of toilet paper I'd balanced on top of the empty dispenser when I noticed the hideous creature staring back at me.

Nearly lost amid the sea of misshapen boobs and penises and vaginas was a pen-and-ink illustration of a ghoul in man's clothing. Its head, slyly peeking out from beneath the upturned collar of a dark suit jacket, was shaped like a watermelon that had lain in the sun for too long. Its mouth was wrong. It yawned open like a fleshy zipper from the point of its chin to the base of its solitary eye. The thing possessed distinct upper and lower lips, but they ran vertically in a nasty sneer. An uneven row of jagged teeth protruded from the left side. A lolling tongue lingered on the right. A single neatly plucked eyebrow framed the creature's hungry gaze. Perched atop his wrinkled oval head was a snazzy dress hat—like the one Winston Churchill always wore in photographs. The black hat was tilted at a jaunty angle, daring you to touch it.

But perhaps most disturbing of all . . . centered beneath this grotesque caricature was the thing's name: MISTER PURPLE.

What the hell does—

I heard footsteps coming from the showers.

Not possible. I'm imagining it. Those damn flies are so damn loud I can't hear a damn thing.

Lifting my ass from the nest of toilet paper, I leaned forward and listened.

There it was again.

Not really footsteps, but the shuffling of shoes on concrete.

"Hello . . . ?"

My voice sounded very loud in the moisture-laden air.

"Hello . . . ? That you, Troy?"

Nothing but the incessant buzzing of flies.

I grabbed the roll of toilet paper and did what I had to do as quickly as I could. When I was finished, I flushed—the toilet actually worked—zipped up my pants, and stood perfectly still, leaning as close to the stall door as I could without actually touching it. One of the overhead lights flickered and went dark. And suddenly I was too scared to unlatch the door. Bending to a knee, grimacing as my jeans made contact with the piss-soaked floor, I peeked under the stall door. And scanned from left to right and back again.

The bathroom was deserted.

I slowly stood, the muscles in my lower back knotted with cramps.

The lights flickered.

Outside, in the campground, someone blew a car horn.

I reached for the latch with one hand, got ready to push open the door with the other.

And the floor tilted beneath my feet. I leaned against the side of the stall, shivering as the sweat on my arms and neck turned icy cold. Invisible smoke billowed into my eyes, clogged my throat. I couldn't breathe, couldn't see.

Feeling on the verge of passing out, my fingers blindly scrambled for the latch. Slamming open the stall door, I collapsed to my knees on the filthy bathroom floor. Gasping for air. Waving my arms at smoke that didn't—

And then all of a sudden it was over . . . and I could breathe again. See again.

I took a moment to compose myself and then slowly rose to my feet.

Directly in front of me, on the wall above the sink . . . carefully drawn in the thin layer of condensation covering the mirror . . . the symbol stared down at me.

24

"I swear this feels like the longest day of my life."

I plopped into one of the lawn chairs we'd set up outside the tent and kicked off my shoes. Naomi took a seat beside me. As she did, I caught a whiff of her perfume on the evening breeze. It made me a little dizzy—but in a good way.

"I'm sure it doesn't help that you didn't get any sleep last night." She gave a shiver. "Every time I think about someone hiding in the woods watching you guys . . . it gives me goose bumps."

If you'd seen what I just saw in that mirror, you'd be feeling a whole lot more than just goose bumps.

"At least we won't have that problem tonight," I said. The campsite we'd been assigned was located on the shoreline of a slow-moving creek. From where I was sitting, I could see another half-dozen sites, all of them occupied, and very few trees in between for someone to hide behind. Not an ideal scenario if a camper was looking for privacy, but after what we'd been through, it was the perfect spot to spend the night.

"Today was . . . interesting," Naomi said, stretching her arms above her head.

I tried my best not to stare. "Not what you expected, huh?"

"I honestly didn't know what to expect. I wasn't even sure you'd let me come with you." When I didn't say anything right away, she asked, "So . . . why did you?"

"I must've been in shock after that scare at the library."

"I'm serious, Billy. Why did you?"

I took a deep breath and decided to tell her the truth. "Seeing you at the diner . . . it made me happy. Only I'm not sure I realized it until we were miles down the road. Then when you showed up at the library . . . it kind of felt like a second chance . . . and I wasn't ready to drive away from you again."

The smile that appeared on her face was more beautiful than any lakeside sunset. "Are you going to be ready when it's time to drop me off?"

Now that was the question, wasn't it?

I placed my hand on her knee, the first time I'd been the one to initiate contact. My fingertips felt like they were on fire. "I don't want to think about that yet."

MEMORIALS

"Hey, lover boy! If you're done flirting over there, maybe you can give us a hand!"

We spun around in our chairs. Troy and Melody were crossing the dirt road behind our campsite, each of them lugging bags of ice they'd bought from the campground store. Troy was wearing a big shit-eating grin on his face. Naomi and I rushed over to help.

"I'm fine," Melody said, laughing, when Naomi tried to take one of the bags from her. "Troy's just being a nuisance."

"Troy a nuisance?" I said, grabbing both bags of ice from him. "Never!"

"That's right," he said. "And don't you forget it." He glanced around the campsite. "No fire tonight?"

"I was actually thinking about catching dinner in the creek and showing you how to clean and cook a fish—but I'm too damn tired. You think we need a fire?"

"I don't," Melody said. "It's hot enough out here."

Troy grunted and sat down. "At least you finished setting up the tent."

After dumping the ice into the coolers, I grabbed the video camera and my notebook from the van, and joined the others. Troy and Melody were arguing about *Gilligan's Island* and who was prettier—Ginger or Mary Ann. Troy insisted it was starlet Ginger. Mel was adamant it was girl-next-door Mary Ann. Naomi steadfastly refused to break the tie, proclaiming, "I'm Switzerland! I'm Switzerland!"

Smiling, I sat down and opened my notebook. A Polaroid photograph fell from between the pages and landed on my lap. I picked it up and stared at it. A close-up of the symbol carved into the cross at Lady Ann Lake.

"I thought we were taking a break for the rest of the night," Troy said, frowning.

Earlier, while driving away from the lake, the group's mood once again darkening, Melody had suggested that for the rest of the evening we shelve any further talk of the mysterious symbol, our stalker in the woods, and roadside memorials in general. The proposal was unanimously approved.

"We are," I said, suddenly feeling like a kid who'd been caught with his hand in the cookie jar.

"Doesn't look like it to me."

"I'm just double-checking today's footage. Won't take long."

"Then why do you need your notebook?"

"Time stamps."

"Well, I guess as long as you don't—"

A young girl emerged from the lengthening shadows bordering the creek bed. With her curly blonde hair, red-and-white polka-dot bikini, and deeply bronzed skin, she could have been an extra in a Coppertone commercial. She looked to be around Naomi's age and appeared upset. "Hello! I'm really sorry to disturb you!"

"Is everything okay?" Melody asked, standing.

"My boyfriend cut his foot." The girl pointed down the creek a ways. "We were jumping off the tire swing, and he must've stepped on some broken glass or a rock. It's bleeding pretty bad. I'm wondering if you might have a bandage?"

"Yeah, hang on," Melody said, already moving. "There's a first aid kit in the back of the van."

The girl hurried to catch up with her. "Thank you so much. I really appreciate it."

Naomi nudged my arm. "Put your eyes back in your head, mister."

Laughing, I nodded at Troy. "*He's* the one you should be talking to."

"Not my type," he said, barely able to suppress a lecherous grin.

"Oww! Slow down."

Turning around, I watched Bikini Girl's boyfriend limp into camp on the arm of another teenage boy. They were both tan, muscular, and shirtless. The boyfriend's mullet-styled hair was still dripping from the river. His left foot was splattered with mud and blood. His friend was wearing a backward Red Sox hat and a red bandanna around his neck. I wondered if Troy might be jealous. I'd have to ask him later.

"I told you dummies to wait for me!" the girlfriend said, returning with Melody and the first aid kit.

"He wouldn't listen," Hat Guy told her.

"Here, sit down," Naomi said, getting up.

The injured boyfriend eased into her chair. Melody and Bikini Girl immediately went to work on him. First, cleaning the wound with water and peroxide (Boyfriend: "Ow, that stings"; Girlfriend: "Oh, stop complaining, you big baby"), then applying a thin layer of gauze, and finally attaching a large adhesive bandage.

As they were finishing up, Hat Guy scowled and said, "So, you all a bunch of devil worshippers or what?"

As one, the four of us turned and stared at him. No one said anything right away. I think we were all in shock.

"Jesus, Charlie," the girl hissed. "Don't be an asshole. These people are helping us!"

Charlie leaned down and picked up my notebook from the chair. Held it up for the others to see. It was opened to my sketch of the symbol.

"We're working on a documentary for school." I walked over and took the notebook from him. "We've noticed this symbol in a few different places, so I wanted to make a record of it." I was suddenly glad that the Polaroid of the cross was tucked away in my pocket.

"Where'd you see it?" he asked, not bothering to hide his skepticism.

"Earlier today, we saw it at Lady Ann Lake," Troy said.

"On the cross at Griffin Schutz's memorial," Melody added.

That seemed to relax him a bit. "Okay . . . yeah . . . that makes sense."

"Do you have any idea what it means or where it came from?" Closing the notebook, I started to put it down on the chair, but then decided to hold on to it. "And what was that comment about devil worshippers all about?"

"That's who uses the symbol," Charlie said.

"You guys aren't from around here," the boyfriend said. "How'd you know about Griffin Schutz?"

Melody glanced at me and said, "Some old guy we met at a gas station told us about him. So we went out there to see for ourselves."

"Did he tell you how Schutz died?" Charlie asked.

Melody nodded. "Horrible."

"And he told you about the cult?"

When Melody shook her head, Charlie looked at me.

"No, nothing about a—"

"Wonder why he left out the best part."

"What . . . kind of cult are we talking about?" Troy asked.

"Satanic."

"Bullshit." Before I could check myself, it was already out of my mouth.

"You calling me a liar?" Charlie said, a hard edge creeping into his voice.

"No . . . I'm not." I could see the muscles in his arms tense. For the second time in as many days, I felt the buzz of potential violence in the air. "All I meant is that it sounds like just another one of those crazy local legends."

"Well, it's not," he snapped. "My aunt answers the phone at the sheriff's office in Stoneridge. She told me and my mom all about it."

"That's amazing," Melody said with an alluring tilt of her head. "Hey . . . you might be able to help us . . ."

25

VIDEO FOOTAGE
(7:37 p.m., Monday, May 9, 1983)

The young man in the Boston Red Sox cap sits in a lawn chair with the creek behind him. Squinting in the glare of the bright lights, he picks his nose. "What do you want me to say?"

Melody's voice from off-screen: "Just pretend like the camera isn't there and tell us what you know about Griffin Schutz's murder and his fiancée's disappearance. Maybe mention the stories and rumors that went around town . . ."

MEMORIALS

"It was more than just rumors."

"Okay . . . then tell us about that."

The teenager clears his throat, sits up straight, and puffs out his chest. He's shirtless, and we can see a fishhook-shaped scar on his right shoulder.

"Well, like I said before . . . my Aunt Yvonne works at the sheriff's office in Stoneridge. She hears about all the good stuff and is always gossiping with my mom. When Parker Jennings crashed his Trans Am into a telephone pole last fall after homecoming, she's the one who told us about the stolen car stereos he had in his trunk. He didn't get charged for it and it never made the news on account of Parker's dad being the mayor . . . but we all knew."

A second boy's voice scolds him from off camera: "They don't even know who Parker Jennings is, dumbass."

"I know that, peckerwood. I'm just saying . . . that's how I know things. It wasn't no rumor."

The cameraman's voice: "Please . . . go on."

"So, anyway, my aunt said it was in the police report and everything. Satanic cult activity suspected. That's exactly how she said it too."

"And you were how old when Griffin Schutz was murdered?" the man behind the camera asks.

Hat Guy thinks about it for a moment before answering. "I was ten . . . no, wait, nine."

"How old are you now?"

"Eighteen."

"And you remember all this from back then?"

He appears irritated. "Back then . . . and now. Are you kidding? People still talk about it. It's the biggest thing that ever happened around here. My aunt told me the investigation is still active, but she doesn't think anything will come of it."

"Keep going," the cameraman says. "I was just trying to clarify the timeline."

Hat Guy stares into the camera like he has no idea what that means. He turns and spits into the dirt—and resumes talking.

"At first, it was just graffiti. You know, like upside-down crosses. Pentagrams. Amityville Horror, that sort of shit. No one thought much of it. But then the police started getting calls about missing animals—cats and dogs. Even a couple of cows. Can you imagine? Who the hell steals a cow? Then, the animals started turning up dead around town. My next-door neighbor's beagle disappeared one night. The next morning, someone found it hanging on the gate to the cemetery. Its stomach was cut open and all of its insides were gone. A little later, some kids on motorcycles found what the cops called a 'ritual site' in the woods behind Layton's Hardware. A buncha cats had been strung up in trees and bled dry."

He slouches in the lawn chair and plucks something out of his belly button. After holding it up and examining it for a moment, he flicks whatever it is into the shadows.

"Anyway, my aunt overheard one of the detectives telling a cop that there were so many stab wounds on Griffin Schutz's body that it was impossible to get an accurate count and that a lot of them looked like they'd been made by different kinds of knives. They thought it might be like what happened to the animals. Like, I don't know, an initiation or some shit like that."

"Did they say anything about Griffin's fiancée, Rachel Filmore?" Melody again.

"Eh. It was really the baby they were mostly focused on."

"How so?"

"The cops were convinced that cult members kidnapped Rachel Filmore so they could cut out her baby and then use it in one of their rituals."

26

"So much for taking the night off," Troy said.

Melody grunted in agreement. "Tell me about it."

I now regretted not making a campfire. Except for a smattering of fireflies and a handful of lanterns glowing at distant sites, the world around us was lost in darkness. Even the moon was hiding behind clouds. After all that talk of mutilated animals and bloodthirsty satanists, I felt eerily exposed. Someone could be watching us from any one of a dozen nearby hiding places and there was nothing we could do about it.

Our surprise visitors had left a few minutes earlier. Once the interview was finished and the video camera put away, Troy had offered them some beers to keep them talking—but that gesture proved largely wasted. Charlie and the boyfriend had readily accepted the beers and then immediately proceeded to guzzle them down. Troy fished out two more cold ones from the bottom of the cooler—and it was the same thing all over again. Both cans drained dry in a matter of seconds. After serenading us with a succession of chunky burps—each one more disgusting than the last—the guys muttered their thanks and followed the blonde girl in the bikini into the shadows alongside the creek bank.

"Did anyone else think about the dead rabbit Mel found when he started talking about animal sacrifices?" Troy asked.

Naomi looked at me. "What dead rabbit?"

"Tell you later," I said. "It's not important."

"It could be," Troy said.

"My professor talked about animal sacrifices in our Appalachian Culture class last semester," Naomi said. "But I had no idea it was still going on."

Troy's eyes widened. "Did he mention anything about—"

I lifted a hand to cut off the inevitable barrage of questions. "Okay, wait. What do you say we save all that for tomorrow? It's getting late and we've got a long day ahead of us."

"Agreed. I don't know about the rest of you," Melody said, "but I'm ready for bed. We'll have plenty of time in the morning to figure this all out." And with that, she gave us a tired wave and disappeared inside the van.

"I'm right behind you," Troy said, pulling the passenger door closed and clambering his way into the back.

Somewhere, in the darkness on the opposite side of the creek, a night bird called out. High above us in the trees, something stirred in the branches. A shiver tickled the back of my neck.

"I'm not sure I can sleep right now," Naomi said. "Not after listening to all of that."

"You want to take a walk or something?"

She thought about it for a moment. "Maybe *something*."

I nudged open the tent flap. "We can play cards or just talk. Whatever you want to do."

"Sure," she said, with a coy smile that made me forget all about dead rabbits and what'd happened earlier in the campground bathroom. "We can just *talk*."

And then she crawled inside the tent.

27

At first, I thought she was having a seizure—then I realized it was a nightmare.

"Naomi!" I shook her harder. "Naomi! Wake up!"

She squirmed in my arms in the dark, eyelids twitching, hands flailing, teeth bared.

The interior light in the van flashed on, and Melody poked her head inside the tent. "Is everything okay?"

"She's dreaming. I can't wake her up."

Melody swung her legs out of the van and rushed to my side—and then both of us were shaking her. "Naomi! Hey!" Melody shouted. "You're having a bad dream! Hey—wake up!"

Naomi began turning her head violently from side to side. "No! Stop! STOP!"

Terrified that she was going to hurt herself, I placed my hands on the sides of her face and stopped her from thrashing.

And she opened her eyes.

When she saw us huddled above her, she broke down sobbing.

I sat in the corner of the tent, rocking her in my arms like a frightened child. Finally, she calmed down enough to start making sense—and told us about the nightmare.

She's standing on the shoreline of Lady Ann Lake. The cool water lapping at her bare ankles. It's late at night and she's alone. There's a full moon overhead in the sky. Bubbles begin to appear on the water in front of her. More and more of them. Until finally a tangle of wet hair breaks the surface, followed by dead pink eyes and pale sunken cheeks and a puckered black mouth with too many teeth. Terrified, she backs away from the water's edge and tumbles backward onto the sand, as Rachel Filmore—naked and decaying—emerges from the water, shambling toward her in the moonlight.

As Naomi scrambles to her feet, something else crawls out of the lake.

Rachel's unborn baby.

An umbilical cord floats beside it like a misshapen water moccasin. The symbol from the memorials has been carved into the center of the baby's forehead.

Rachel staggers closer, arms limp at her sides, grinning at Naomi. A ragged wound in her stomach yawns open, revealing an empty gray cavern where her internal organs—and unborn child—once lived.

Not far behind her, still joined by the mottled, fish-chewed umbilical cord, the baby clambers closer, its tiny fingers clawing for purchase in the sand. The baby slowly lifts its head and looks up at Naomi—and then opens its mouth wide, revealing rows of tiny razors for teeth. They glitter in the silver moonlight.

Turning to flee, Naomi hears herself scream—

And that's when she wakes up.

28

Melody and I remained by Naomi's side for the rest of the night while an oblivious Troy snored away in the back of the van. Eventually, Naomi drifted off to sleep again—and this time there were no more dreams.

Shortly before the sun rose, Melody stirred in the dark. Yawning, she returned to her bunk, leaving us alone in the tent. And my exhausted brain finally slowed down enough to ask the question that had been haunting me all throughout the night:

How is it possible that Naomi and I just had the exact same fucking dream?

DAY FIVE
TUESDAY | MAY 10

1

"You swear to God you're not teasing me, Billy."

I shook my head and glanced at the door to Waffle House. We'd just finished eating and were waiting in the parking lot. Melody and Troy were still inside, standing in line to use the restrooms. This was my first chance all morning to be alone with Naomi—and I knew the clock was ticking. "I swear. I wouldn't do that. I had the same dream last night. The bubbles in the water . . . Rachel's teeth . . . the symbol on the baby's forehead . . . *everything*. It was the exact same dream."

"Why didn't you tell me?"

"I think I was in shock . . . and you were so upset . . . I didn't want to make things worse."

"Did you tell the others?"

I gazed over her shoulder at the door again. "No, and I don't think I'm going to. Not yet, anyway."

"Why not?"

"I'm not really sure . . . but for now, let's just keep it to ourselves, okay?"

She looked confused. "If you say so."

I didn't blame her. I was pretty damn confused myself. I trusted Melody and Troy . . . so why didn't I want to tell them? Maybe it had something to do with the fact that I'd barely slept the past few nights. Everything around me looked and felt fuzzy around the edges. Like the rest of the world was moving in slow motion. Something very strange was going on, and the less noise there was surrounding us, the better chance I had of figuring out what the hell it was.

"Naomi gets shotgun today," Melody announced, striding toward us. So much for trying to be watchful. I hadn't even noticed them coming out of the restaurant.

"Hey, it's my turn," Troy whined, the Waffle House sailor's hat he'd been gifted by our waitress perched jauntily atop his Afro.

"Tough cookies. Naomi deserves it after last night."

Surprisingly, he offered no further rebuttal.

Melody unlocked the van, and Troy and I climbed into the back seat. Right away, he poked me in the shoulder. "You wanna play Travel Bingo?"

"No. I do not want to play Travel Bingo."

"You wanna play I Spy?"

"Nope."

"How about we try to find license plates from all fifty states?"

"Not gonna happen."

He pouted and stared out the window.

Melody started the van and steered out of the parking lot. Traffic on RR 19 was light. Ahead of us, bloated gray clouds crowded the horizon. The weather lady on the Waffle House television had called for afternoon showers. Based on what I could see, I predicted an early arrival.

Naomi looked back at me and smiled. I stuck my tongue out, and she giggled and turned around again. My read on the exchange was: *I wish I was sitting back there with you, handsome.* Of course, I could've been wrong. Either way, it was a nice gesture from Melody to insist that Naomi ride shotgun. Mel seemed to genuinely like her.

I liked her too—damn, maybe even *more* than that—and was still wrestling with the reality of what had happened last night. Not the fact that Naomi and I had experienced identical nightmares—but before all that. After we'd said good night to the others and crawled inside the tent, we'd *talked* in the dark for a while, whispering and giggling and eventually cuddling like it was three years ago and we were stretched out on my basement sofa. And then Naomi and I had kissed—for what felt like forever—before drifting off to sleep in each other's arms.

"Hey, when did you guys go to Fortunato's Pizza?"

"We didn't," I said.

She held up the menu I'd found on the van's windshield in front of Aunt Helen's house. As we'd driven away that morning, I'd stuffed it inside the map compartment on the passenger-side door and honestly forgotten all about it.

"Someone left that on the van when we were in Sudbury."

"Fortunato's was your first real job," she said.

Indeed it was. Waiting tables and washing dishes in the back. "God, I hated that place. I wanted to quit so bad, but my father wouldn't let me. I'm telling you right now—whenever I buy a house, my first big purchase is going to be a dishwasher."

"I used to go there with my friends just to see him," she told Melody, "but I was too chicken to say anything. Even just hi."

"That's so cute," Melody said with a smile as Naomi opened the menu.

"It's not like Jenny would've let you get a word in anyway," I said.

Naomi laughed. "That's probably true."

"No probably about it."

Naomi went quiet for a moment. She wasn't the only one who'd been too shy to say hello. It wasn't until months later, at Ricky Henderson's Halloween bonfire, that we'd finally actually spoken. And even then my courage had been boosted by three or four cups of vodka-spiked punch.

"Billy . . . when did you find the menu on the van?" Her voice sounded funny.

"When we were saying goodbye to Aunt Helen . . . Saturday morning."

"And you never opened it or looked inside?"

I glanced at Troy and then at Melody in the rearview mirror. "No . . . I guess not."

She held up the menu for all of us to see. This time it was unfolded.

Right next to COLD SUBS, someone had printed in all capital letters:

GO HOME. OR YOU'LL BE SORRY.

2

Anyone driving by the mile-marker-fourteen gravel pull-off on RR 19 that morning would've seen two couples, deeply engaged in conversation, standing outside a bright orange camper van. If they'd given the scene any passing thought at all, they most likely would've guessed that the four of us were stretching our legs after a lengthy stint on the road. Or perhaps waiting on additional passengers to return from relieving themselves in the nearby woods. It's extremely doubtful that any one of those passersby would've hit on the truth: that we were simply too frightened to continue driving.

"Stop telling me to calm down," Troy said, glaring at Billy. "This isn't like back at school. This is real shit, buddy."

"Maybe Troy's right," Melody said, "and it's time to call the police."

"And tell them what?" I said, knowing I sounded like a broken record.

"That someone's been following us for days. Watching, taunting, and now *threatening* us. And that we have no fucking idea what they're going to do next." The hysterical edge was back in Troy's voice. I wanted to hug the guy, but he probably would've slugged me if I tried.

"I understand all of that," I said. "But have they actually broken any laws or—"

"For fuck's sake, Billy!" he exclaimed. "I don't understand why you're being so stubborn!"

Was this really me being stubborn? Or something else?

Naomi cleared her throat. "I have a question . . . did anything weird happen *before* you arrived in Sudbury?"

"Not that I know of." I looked at the others.

"Same," Melody said.

"We're only talking about that first day, right?" Troy said. "We got to Sudbury Friday night?"

"Right," I said. "We got in late, camped at the park, woke up, and went to Aunt Helen's for breakfast. When we were done, we drove straight to my parents' memorial site."

"Not exactly," Troy said. "We drove by your old house on our way."

"Correct," I said, pointing at him.

"So . . . ," Naomi continued, "if there really was someone spying on you from the woods by your parents' memorial, how did he know you would be there?"

No one answered her.

"What exactly are you saying?" Melody asked. She'd started twirling her hair with her finger. A sign that she was anxious—I'd seen it many times before while she was studying for exams.

"I guess what I'm saying is . . . what if the guy in the woods is the reason all this is happening . . . but he wasn't even there because of you?"

"If that's the case, then why was he hiding?" Troy asked. "Why didn't he just say something?"

She shrugged. "Maybe he got scared. Maybe he heard the van coming and ran off into the trees."

"There were no other cars parked there," Troy said. "Not even at the turnoff by the bridge."

"He could've walked," Naomi replied. "Did you go in the woods at all? There could be a shortcut or a path. Maybe he even lives there. There are homeless camps down by the river."

Troy looked at me.

"I've seen old tents and trash in the woods down there," I said. "But it was always on the other side of the bridge."

"Well, times are changing," Naomi said. "It's been a while since you've lived there."

Ignoring the dig, I said, "So you think it was just a coincidence that we ran into the guy . . . and for whatever reason, he decided to follow us?"

"I'm just not sure it's some deep-seated conspiracy like Troy's making it out to be." She reached over and touched his arm. "No offense, of course."

Troy rolled his magnified eyes at her, and even in the tension of the moment, I almost laughed.

"You think he knew I caught him on video?"

"Or in a photo? I don't know—maybe. Or it could have nothing to do with that," she said. "Whoever it is, there's a good chance he heard and saw everything you guys did that day at the memorial. Something could've ticked him off, or even got him excited. And he's been following you ever since."

Melody looked at Naomi. "You've been to the memorial a number of times and you never noticed the symbol before."

She nodded. "That's right."

"I know it's kind of a long shot—but what if the guy went there that day to *draw* the symbol? He sees us taking photos, shooting video, overhears us talking about the documentary. Then, he worries that we might have captured *him* in one of those photos or on video. So he decides to follow us and, for whatever reason, discourage us from continuing."

I imagined a little cartoon light bulb turning on inside each of our heads. Troy must've too. He snapped his fingers. "*That* actually makes a lot of sense."

"Leave it to the girls to figure it out," I said.

"I wouldn't exactly say it's figured out," Melody said. "It still feels like a long shot. And hang on: If all this started with the guy in the woods . . . then why did someone leave a warning note on the van *before* we crossed paths with him?"

A damn good question. While my head was still spinning, Melody started walking back to the van.

"Hey, where are you going?" Troy asked.

"We're *all* going back to Sudbury," Melody said over her shoulder. "One way or another, it all started there. If there are any answers to this mess, that's where we'll find them."

3

I'd experienced that look and tone from Melody before. During group meetings in the library or cafeteria, Troy and I weren't always the easiest partners to keep in check. Troy was brilliant and often didn't feel the need to pay close attention. I was scatterbrained and at times a bad influence. Together, we were a handful—and Melody had, on more than one occasion, been forced to take control. Like right now.

"We can stay at your aunt's house. She said we were welcome any time." Looking at Naomi, she added, "I know that's not what you want to hear, but maybe you can lay low and stick around with us. Just because you're back in town, it doesn't mean you have to go home to your parents just yet."

Naomi nodded gratefully.

"If we see any memorials on our way, we'll stop and take a look. Grab some footage if Billy thinks it'll be usable. But either way, we'll keep moving."

She paused to see if there was any dissent among the group. When no one said anything, she continued: "When we get to Sudbury, we'll regroup. See what else we can find out about the symbol and whoever might have left the note. Billy, you can call Robert Farnsworth and see what he has to say—keeping in mind I think we should take whatever that man tells us with a grain of salt." She held me with her gaze. "It's entirely up to you how much you want to tell your aunt about all this."

"Maybe she'll have some idea who left us the warning," Troy said.

I shrugged. "I doubt it."

"Either way," Melody said. "We can't just keep doing what we're doing. Eventually, whoever's following us is going to get tired of playing games . . . and then what?"

4

It was nearly an hour before we ran across a Texaco station. While Troy paid the cashier and topped off the gas tank, I gave my aunt a call. The pay phone was attached to the wall between a wide-open garage bay door and a soda machine that was out of stock of everything except grape Fanta. Two men inside were working on a red truck up on a lift. Dressed in grease-stained overalls unzipped to his ample waist, the younger of the two mechanics put down a wrench and drifted over to the doorway to keep an eye on me. I gave him a polite nod—but he just stared right through me. Aunt Helen answered after the first ring.

"*Hello?*"

"Hey, sweet lady, it's your favorite nephew."

A pause. "*Jim Bob?*"

"That's riiight," I said in an exaggerated drawl.

She giggled. *"How's it going, Billy? Is everything okay?"*

"We're tired and smelly and hungry . . . so naturally I thought of you."

"Gee, thanks."

"Can I ask you for another favor?"

"Go right ahead."

"Would you mind some house guests for a night or two?"

"Oh my gosh, are you serious? I'd love that! When?"

"Tonight . . . if it's okay."

"It's more than okay! All three of you? Will you make it in time for dinner?"

I cleared my throat, even though I didn't have to and said, "Well . . . it's four of us, actually."

She paused for a moment. *"Naomi found you."* It wasn't a question.

"She sure did. We can talk about that later."

"Or, we could not and just say we did."

I smiled. It was good to hear her voice. "I'm not sure about dinner yet. Depends on if we drive straight through or stop. I'll call again when we get down the road some."

"Okay, I'll wait to hear from you. Drive safe, Billy. I love you."

"Love you more. See you soon."

"Looking forward to it."

I hung up the phone, checked the coin slot out of habit, and headed back to the van. As I did, I took a glance over my shoulder. Standing by the open bay door, both of the workers were now watching me.

5

"So you didn't tell her anything?"

Troy was sitting in the passenger seat again as we pulled away from the Texaco station. When I'd returned from making my call, Naomi asked him to switch places with her. Of course, he'd been more than happy to comply.

"Not yet," I said. "If I do, I'd rather it be in person. She'll worry less that way."

"She's dating a cop now, right?" Troy asked. "Maybe he can help us."

"I was thinking the same thing," Melody said.

"Naomi said he's actually the sheriff. And that's not a bad idea." I glanced at Naomi to see what she thought—but she was staring out the window and not paying any attention to our conversation. "I guess we'll just see how it goes."

Melody tapped the brake pedal and blew the horn at a squirrel in the road. It spun around in a tight circle before scampering away into the weeds. "You sound hesitant."

"I don't trust most cops as far as I can throw them," Troy said, "but this might be the exception."

"I'm not necessarily hesitant . . . I just don't know him . . . and it's a small town . . ."

Up ahead, on the shoulder, a woman walking alone stuck out her thumb. Melody saw her and slowed the van.

"Here we go again," Troy said.

"I'm not going to stop, scaredy-cat . . . but I don't want to run her over either, for God's sake."

As we drew closer, the hitchhiker turned and began walking backward, allowing us a good look at her. She appeared to be in her late twenties but may have been considerably younger. The drugs had taken a harsh toll. There were dark circles beneath her sunken eyes, and the skin on her face was mottled and sagging. She was wearing a filthy sleeveless sundress. Her bony arms were covered in scabs and bruises.

"Oh God," Naomi murmured.

Melody glanced at her in the rearview mirror. "Our professor mentioned there's a real epidemic spreading throughout this entire region. Heroin, mostly."

Naomi watched until the girl was gone. "That's so sad."

"I saw a couple of teenagers at the gas station yesterday," Melody said. "They were in even worse shape."

"Anyway," Troy said, getting right back to business, "give some thought to talking to your aunt's boyfriend, Billy. He could probably make some calls and save us a lot of time and energy. He might even know something about the symbol."

"I'll think about it." Like Troy, I wasn't exactly the biggest fan of law enforcement. Unlike Troy, who'd grown up on some of the most violent and corrupt streets in the country, I didn't really have a good reason for my disenchantment. At the end of my freshman year, I'd had a run-in with the York Police Department—but the entire thing had been my fault. I'd gotten into a fight outside one of the campus bars. I couldn't even remember what had started it. Both I and the upperclassman I was tussling with ended up being charged with drunk and disorderly. I was also cited for underage drinking. It was the most humiliating moment of my life, and one of the major reasons I'd decided to cut back on my alcohol consumption.

Eager to change the subject, I said, "There *is* something I want to tell you guys." I'd made the decision shortly after hanging up the phone with my aunt.

"What's up?" Melody said.

I glanced at Naomi to make sure she was still okay with it. She nodded.

"So . . . last night . . . before all the commotion . . . I, uh, had the same dream that Naomi had. The *exact* same dream."

Troy spun around. "No shit!"

"No shit. Every detail was the same. All of it. Only I woke up shortly before her."

"Why didn't you say something?" Melody asked. "I was right there with you."

"I didn't want to freak everyone out. It was terrifying enough as it was."

"Were the two of you talking about Rachel Filmore right before you fell asleep?"

Naomi shivered. "No. Not a word."

"And even if we had, that wouldn't explain the dreams being carbon copies of each other. I mean, we're talking *identical,* shared, right down to that fucking symbol on the baby's forehead."

"You think someone put a curse on you?" Troy asked, his face dead serious. "Or a spell of some sort? Maybe the guy in the woods is one of those Appalachian witches we were reading about?"

"Aren't witches always female?" Melody said.

"Good point. How about Appalachian warlock, then?"

"This is *exactly* why we can't call the police," I said. "We start talking about curses and witches and warlocks and they'll laugh us out of—"

A siren blared behind us.

Melody's eyes shot to the rearview mirror. "Ohhh, shit!"

The rest of us turned around and looked out the back window.

A yellow Pennsylvania State Police cruiser. Closing fast. Bar lights flashing.

"I'm barely speeding!" Melody said, glancing at the speedometer.

Troy turned around in his seat. "Relax . . . he's probably on his way to a call somewhere."

"Deep breath," I said, leaning forward and placing a hand on her shoulder. "It'll be okay."

"It's not okay! My sister's going to kill me!"

"No, she's not. You haven't done anything wrong. Just pull over, nice and easy."

Her eyes darting back and forth between the rearview mirror and the road, she switched on the turn signal and eased onto the shoulder. The state police cruiser did the same, slowing right behind us. My stomach sank. Once we came to a complete stop, Melody put the van in park. "Why's he doing this, Billy?"

The siren abruptly cut off, but the red and blue lights continued flashing. "I don't know, but we're about to find out. Just take another breath. I'm right here with you."

The trooper who exited the car was extraordinarily tall. At least six-five if not bigger. He tilted his chin toward the ground and slipped on his wide-brimmed hat with practiced ease, casting most of his broad face in shadow.

His square jaw looked larger than my fist. With a hand resting atop his leather holster, he slowly approached the van.

"Troy, quick," Melody said. "Get my driver's license and registration—they're both in the glove compartment."

Troy scrambled to find the cards and passed them over to Melody. Her window was already down when the trooper got there.

"Morning, miss," he said in a gravelly voice that perfectly suited the rest of him. "May I see your driver's license and registration, please." Bending over with his hands on his hips, he glanced at the rest of us with steely-gray eyes that never once blinked. He was older than I'd first thought. His face looked like it had been chiseled out of stone.

Hands shaking, Melody handed over the cards. "I'm sorry for whatever I've done wrong, Officer."

"Is this your van?" he asked, studying her driver's license.

For the first time, I realized how desolate this section of road was. Bordered by a boulder-strewn bluff and surrounded by miles of untamed forest and river, we were the very definition of all alone in the middle of nowhere.

I could hear my aunt's worried voice inside my head: *They're not real keen on outsiders.*

I glanced at Mel's door to make sure it was locked.

"No, sir, it's my sister's. That's her name and address on the registration form. We're just borrowing it." And then getting excited as she remembered, "We actually have a loan agreement we both signed, if you'd like to see it."

My eyes immediately went to the ashtray where I'd stashed the crumpled-up loan paperwork on day one. Hopefully, it was still there.

"That won't be necessary, miss." The officer pulled out a notepad from the back pocket of his striped uniform pants. "The reason I stopped you is because you have a broken taillight." He flipped open the notebook and scribbled something inside. "I see you're from out of town, so I'm not going to bother writing you a repair order. But you do need to get that taillight replaced as soon as possible, okay?"

"Yes, sir," Melody said. "I'm so sorry. I had no idea it was broken. I'll be sure to take care of it right away." Filled with relief, she glanced at me in the mirror. Her eyes were steady now, but her face remained deathly pale.

"You all headed out camping?" the officer asked.

"We're students from York College. Working on a documentary for our American Studies class."

The officer handed back Melody's license and registration. As he extended his arm into the open window, I noticed a small tattoo of an angel on the inside of his bulging left bicep. *What is it with all these fucking angels?* I thought.

"Well, good luck with your project." He bent over again and peered into the window with those same unblinking eyes. Only now they looked blue instead of gray. "You folks are a long way from home. Be careful. These backroads can be dangerous."

"Thank you, Officer." The color was beginning to return to Melody's face. "We sure will."

As the trooper sauntered back to his cruiser, Troy returned Melody's license and registration to the glove compartment and said, "When did we get a broken taillight?"

"Maybe at Waffle House?" she replied. "Although I probably wouldn't have noticed if I walked right past it. For all I know, it could've been days ago."

"Same," I said.

Troy shifted in his seat. "Should we get out and take a look?"

"No . . . no, I don't think so." Melody glanced at the rearview mirror. "He's just sitting there in his car, watching us."

I leaned in between the seats. "I say we take off before he finds an excuse to come back and talk to us again."

So that's what we did.

6

The temperature outside had dropped by at least ten degrees since we'd left the Waffle House parking lot earlier that morning, and the wind had picked up. The trees on the side of the road swayed lazily back and forth, and the cows in the fields we passed were stretched out on their bellies. Overhead, the clouds had melted together and deepened to a dingy slate gray. With the van windows rolled halfway down, we could hear long rumbles of thunder in the distance. A storm was on its way.

So far today, we'd backtracked on our initial route into Appalachian country—so there'd been little reason to keep an eye out for roadside memorials. Unless we'd missed something important on our way in, we figured there wouldn't be much to see on our way out. At least, not until we picked up Route 9 and started moving southeast again.

The radio played at low volume, and by some miracle, it wasn't tuned to 103.7— Pennsylvania's Home of Country Music. An obnoxiously peppy RadioShack commercial came to a merciful end—"*High-performance car stereos, $149! Cordless telephones as low as $99!*"—and the Bee Gees started getting their groove on. None of us were in the mood for singing along. Or, for that matter, discussing the mysterious symbol and what we hoped to accomplish at Aunt Helen's house when we finally got there. Mostly, we just stared out the windows at the darkening countryside and discussed our plans for when we finally got back to campus. We'd been gone for less than a week, but it felt like forever.

"First thing I'm gonna do is get a big-ass cheesesteak from Dino's," Troy said. "Extra cheese and onions. Then I'm gonna buckle down and hit the books for about forty-eight straight hours."

"Dare to dream," I said, rolling my eyes.

"Hey, go ahead and bomb your finals," Troy said. "See if I care."

Melody smiled. "I'm going to crawl in bed and enjoy fresh sheets and pillowcases and a room that doesn't smell like dirty laundry. And *then* I'll start studying."

"How about you, Billy?" Naomi asked after a moment, and it occurred to me how left out she must be feeling. The three of us would soon be heading back to our shared campus life. An existence she had clearly romanticized in her head. Naomi, on the other hand, would be returning to

MEMORIALS

her bedroom in her parents' house, community college, and a part-time shift at Walmart.

"I'm going to camp out in the photo lab twenty-four seven until I'm finished editing the footage for this documentary." I coughed into my hand, buying time to think about what I was going to say next. "You, uh, should come down and visit when you can."

Naomi's face lit up. "Oh, I would love that! You could give me a tour of all your favorite places!" She scooted closer and rested her head against my shoulder. The sweet scent of her strawberry lip gloss mixed with her perfume was intoxicating. I drank it all in. As I gazed at the road again, I couldn't help but notice in the mirror the amused look on Melody's face. The same one I'd almost kissed a couple days earlier in a moment of emotional weakness. Next to her, in the passenger seat, I heard Troy making those same kissy-face sounds from before.

And you know what? I didn't even care. Let them make fun of me. God knows, I would be doing the same thing if I were in their shoes.

With last night's bad dream feeling very far away, I snuggled closer to Naomi. In front of us, Melody began humming along with the radio. The song—"Come On Eileen" by Dexys Midnight Runners—was one of Troy's favorites. A rare exhibition of good taste. He turned up the volume and rolled down his window the rest of the way. Cool air swept into the van, caressing my face. I smelled rain in the breeze. It reminded me of being a kid with not a care in the world. Playing with my army men in the backyard as the skies opened up, Mom calling me inside . . . *before you get soaked, silly!* And then the song was over and Troy was begging Naomi to tell the story again about how she'd scared me in the library and made me scream—and before long we were all laughing.

Thunder rumbled in the distance.

Lightning stabbed the clouds and lit up the horizon.

The miles passed.

After a while, Naomi dozed.

Minutes later, Troy belched, startling her awake.

A Flock of Seagulls song came on the radio. When it finished playing, a disc jockey with a questionable British accent announced: "*Back in a jumping-jack-flash with smash hits from David Bowie and Michael Jackson—but first this Samantha James news break . . .*"

A woman's velvety-smooth voice trying too hard to sound solemn: "*Smithtown police officials report that there are no new leads in the disappearance of twenty-four-year-old Brianna Kellegher, whose abandoned car was discovered last month in the parking lot of the SuperSaver grocery store on Thadmont Avenue. At the time of her disappearance, Kellegher was seven months pregnant. If you have any information at all related to this case, Smithtown police ask that you contact them immediately at . . .*"

"When we went looking for you guys, Jenny and I saw a bunch of signs with that poor woman's face on them." Naomi stared out the window at two little girls playing hopscotch in front of a dilapidated cabin. A section of its roof was leaning to one side and covered in a faded blue tarp weighted down by cinder blocks. "She looked so young . . . and happy . . ."

I remembered sitting on a bench in the park, waiting for Melody and Troy to return with Mr. Ramos so we could interview him. Missing posters had been plastered on just about every tree and light post. My first impression of Brianna Kellegher had been a little different from Naomi's. I'd thought she'd looked young and pretty, sure, but there was also something naive about her—like she had no idea the world had teeth and liked to use them.

"We saw them too," Troy said. "All over town."

Naomi looked at him. "Do you think they'll ever find her?"

"Doubtful . . . it's been over a month." And then in a quieter voice: "Not alive, anyway."

The thought of Rachel Filmore entered my head—and I pushed it away.

Just outside of Smithtown, we rounded a bend and glimpsed ahead of us the Gabriel Ramos memorial on the shoulder of the road. Everyone grew quiet. Melody slowed the van. I leaned across Naomi's lap to peer out the window. She put a steadying hand on my chest, her thumb rubbing ever so softly, and for a moment I forgot how to breathe.

And then we were past it and speeding toward town.

Exhaling, I sat back in my seat.

"Wait! Wait, wait—turn around!" Troy shouted.

"We agreed we weren't going to stop," Melody stated matter-of-factly.

"Something's wrong," he said. "Go back. You need to go back!"

Melody eased onto the shoulder. I turned and stared out the window, but the memorial was too far away.

"What'd you see?" I asked.

"It's what I *didn't* see . . . the guitar . . . I think it's gone."

7

The four of us stood outside the van, staring at the section of fence where Gabriel Ramos's guitar had once been chained. There was no evidence it had ever existed. The fence hadn't been cut. There were no discarded links of silver chain. No destroyed lock. No tatters of plastic wrapping scattered on the ground.

The guitar was just gone.

I raised the Polaroid camera and snapped a photo.

"I feel like we've stepped into the Twilight Zone," Melody said.

Lightning split the sky above us, the shutter flash of illumination adding to the eeriness of the scene.

Thunder growled, closer now, and the first drops of rain began to fall. I tucked the camera underneath my shirt to keep it dry.

"I can't believe I didn't notice when we drove by." Turning to look at me, Melody said, "I can't believe *you* didn't notice."

I didn't want to tell her that Naomi had put her hand on my chest when I leaned across her to look out the window. Or how wonderful Naomi's hair had smelled. Or . . .

"I was distracted," I finally mumbled.

And that's when the sky opened up—and we all took off running for the van.

8

After stopping for lunch—gas station chili dogs for me and Troy, chicken salad sandwiches for the girls—we decided to make a detour to Lady Ann Lake. The idea was to check to see if the cross was still there or if it'd been altered in any way. Perhaps the missing guitar was just a bizarre coincidence. A case of random vandalism and theft. Maybe it wasn't connected to the mysterious symbol at all. But I wasn't convinced of any of that—hence, our little side trip. If I'd read the map correctly, the change of plans wouldn't delay our arrival in Sudbury by more than an hour or two. Hopefully, it would be worth it.

It was half past noon when we arrived at the lake. The rain, which had slowed to a steady drizzle for most of our drive, had begun to pick up again. Melody pulled the van as close to the edge of the woods as possible and we all got out. Troy was jumpy from the start.

"What if we get lost?" he said, staring nervously at the gloomy expanse of trees.

"Then we'll find the lake and follow the shoreline back to the parking lot," I replied.

There were several other vehicles parked nearby, all of them empty from what I could tell, and a pickup truck idling by the water's edge. A man and woman dressed in matching yellow slickers were lifting a canoe into the bed of the truck. I could hear their muffled voices but was too far away to understand what they were saying.

"It looks awfully dark in there," Troy said as we approached the mouth of the trail. "Maybe I should run back and grab a flashlight from the van?"

"No time for that," I said. "We need to hurry up and do this and get back on the road. My aunt is waiting for us."

The return trip to the lake had been my idea, so I took the lead. Naomi, Troy, and Melody followed close behind me in a staggered line. The trees surrounding Lady Ann Lake grew close together in this section of forest, providing a natural canopy that screened us from most of the rain. But it also acted as a trap of sorts—the air around us thick and cloying and cloaked with humidity. It was a lot like hiking inside a greenhouse—filled with hungry mosquitos. Before long, I was having a hard time catching my breath, and Troy's glasses began fogging up. Every few minutes, we were forced to slow down so he could wipe the thick lenses with his shirt.

"This seriously sucks," he complained after pausing to clean them for the third time. "My shirt's so sweaty, all I'm doing now is smearing them."

"Hey, look on the bright side," Melody said. "At least you're burning off those chili dogs."

Troy gave her a dirty look and kept on walking.

"It shouldn't be much longer," I said with no real confidence. I knew we were on the right trail, but without Robert Farnsworth walking point, I had no idea how far it was to Griffin Schutz's memorial site. I picked up the pace, hoping that the others wouldn't notice and complain. The trail soon began to slope downward. Mud sucked at our shoes as we made our way deeper into the woods.

"This entire trip is starting to feel cursed," Troy said, swatting at a mosquito on his neck. His fingers came away smeared with blood. He grimaced and wiped them on his shirt.

"Deep breath," Melody told him. "We'll be back in Sudbury before you know it. Eating Aunt Helen's home cooking and—"

"What if someone actually did put a curse on you?" Naomi said. It was the first time she'd spoken since we'd set off from the van. "Or what if all this is part of some old-fashioned ritual?"

"A ritual?" Troy groaned again. "What do you mean by that?"

"Well . . . I was thinking about something my professor said...but never mind . . . it's nothing really." She shrugged, and I could tell she regretted speaking up.

"No, no—don't stop now" I said. "Go on. Please."

Thunder crashed overhead, shaking the tree branches and the ground beneath our feet. All four of us jumped like frightened rabbits, which at that moment, we pretty much were.

"That class I mentioned . . . on Appalachian culture . . . ," Naomi continued, "it was all about *the old ways*. Most of what the hill people around here practice is what they call 'granny magic.' Harmless spells and potions, mainly designed to help people." Her voice dropped lower, like she was revealing a secret. "*But* . . . there's also supposed to be things of a darker nature, witchcraft and the like. Our teacher said it's still being practiced today, and probably always would be. Y'know, handed down from one generation to the next?"

"So what were you saying . . ." Troy tripped over a tree root snaking across the path and almost lost his balance. ". . . about a ritual?"

"There are all kinds of rituals," she said, shooing away a cloud of gnats from in front of her face. "We learned about those too. There are good ones and bad ones. The bad ones are called, surprise, *dark* rituals, and the hill people usually performed them to get back at their enemies."

"And how do you perform a dark ritual?" I asked.

"Lot of ways. Sometimes, they used a clump of their enemy's hair or a drop of their blood. Other times, all they needed was a piece of clothing or even a photograph."

Something in my stomach did a somersault.

Naomi went on: "There was this one lecture about how some of the rituals involved ancient spells that were recited. There were rumors that animals were sometimes sacrificed."

Troy gave me a look that even in the murkiness of the forest was easy enough to read: *What in the hell have you gotten us into?*

"Imagine telling a class that the locals across the river had rituals to do everything from killing a farmer's crops and making someone's hair fall out to giving someone insomnia and causing a person to go blind."

Melody shook her head. "Like I said . . . the Twilight Zone."

"Serious question," Troy said. "Is the idea of pissed-off witches and psychotic locals supposed to make me feel better or worse about everything that's happening?"

Melody poked him in the shoulder. "Not everything's about you, Troy."

"Sounds like a pretty fascinating class," I said.

"It beats a snoozefest like Philosophy 101, lemme tell you. All kinds of wild things around these parts, and right under Sudbury's nose."

I'd never really thought of it that way, and I was momentarily taken aback. It was as if Sudbury was like one of those walled cities of old, keeping out any threats lurking in the surrounding countryside.

"There were apparently a lot of hill people that were so isolated they had no knowledge of modern religion," Naomi said. "For centuries, they worshipped their own deities and gods. And there were these extravagant ceremonies designed to summon them."

Troy raised his voice dramatically. "*And what rough beast, its hour come round at last / Slouches towards Bethlehem to be born?*"

"What in the hell does that mean?" I asked, pushing some branches out of the way. My arms were slicked with sweat.

"It's from 'The Second Coming' by Yeats," he said. "That's a poem, by the way."

"I know who Yeats is, Mr. Know-It-All. He plays right field for the Milwaukee Brewers."

Melody giggled.

"Don't laugh," Troy said. "It only encourages—"

"Hey, there's the trail," I said, pointing up ahead.

The path had been much easier to spot than the first time we'd been here. The grass and brush trampled down by at least five recent pairs of shoes. From where I was standing, I could see where the heavy foliage resumed, thick and tangled and undisturbed. Just short of that, Griffin Schutz's memorial, still hidden from view, awaited.

I stopped and looked at the others. "You all can wait here. I'll check it out by myself."

"I'll go with you," Naomi said, taking my arm.

Troy emphatically shook his head and didn't stop until he was finished talking. "Nope. Uh-uh. We are *not* splitting up. Especially after everything Naomi just dropped on us."

"It's right there," I said. "You'll be able to see me the entire time."

"Doesn't matter. We're all going."

"Let's just get it over with," Melody said.

Maintaining the same order, we entered the path.

Walking slow. Eyes searching.

I saw it first.

The spiraling floor of stones.

The broken wine bottles.

The black flowers.

And finally, right where we'd left it, the peeling white cross.

The symbol etched into the vertical slat.

And right below it . . . a brand-new addition to the memorial.

A black-and-white photograph.

Its glossy surface spotted with raindrops.

My stomach churning, I hunched down to take a closer look:

A smiling Troy standing outside the van in his matching khaki shorts and shirt. Melody and I sitting on coolers in the background. Beers in our hands.

I recognized the campsite right away. Sunny Valley. The photo had been taken with a telescopic lens sometime during our second evening on the road.

The unknown photographer had used a ballpoint pen to scratch out Troy's eyes.

9

When we emerged from the woods—our hearts lodged firmly in our throats and drenched in perspiration from head to toe—the van was the only vehicle in the parking lot.

That bothered me for some reason. Especially after what we'd discovered at the memorial site. As I changed into dry shorts and a T-shirt, I reminded myself that this little side trip to Lady Ann Lake had been a spur-of-the-moment decision, and other than the four of us, no one else had known about it.

Unless you were followed . . . ever thought of that? the annoying little voice inside my head taunted me.

That's right—unless we'd been followed. It was hard to argue with that simple logic, no matter how much I wanted to.

While the girls changed their clothes in the privacy of the van, Troy got undressed right next to me in the parking lot. Unfailingly shy about his body ever since I'd met him—he'd once refused to remove his shirt to play on a "skins" pickup basketball team at the campus rec center—he now peeled off his wet clothes without hesitation. I noticed that he was shivering and began to worry that maybe he was in shock. That would certainly explain his nearly mute response to the discovery of the photograph on the cross. I'd expected terror and drama and maybe even some tears—at the very least an extended soliloquy of *Why me?!*—but so far, there'd been little of that. After initially letting loose with a minute or two of the foulest, filthiest, and most profane language I'd ever heard come from Troy's mouth, he'd trudged back to the parking lot in stunned silence.

Other than the cussing, the closest he'd come to losing it had occurred when I'd tried to examine the photograph up close. No way, though—he hadn't wanted anyone to get near it, much less touch it.

"Fucking thing is probably cursed," he'd hissed, "just like Naomi said." And I hadn't liked the way his eyes had looked when he'd said her name and glanced over at her.

Not wanting to further upset him, I'd kept my distance from the cross and snapped just a handful of shots before returning the camera to my shoulder. But then, just before I'd walked away, I'd seen an opportunity and taken it. After first making sure that Troy had already started up the trail and wasn't looking back at me, I'd reached out and yanked the photograph off the cross and stuffed it into my pocket.

Which was where it currently remained—tucked away in my soaking-wet jeans in the back of the van.

10

I needed to use a pay phone, so Melody stopped at a bait-and-tackle shop, a converted double-wide trailer perched on the side of a twisting road overlooking a stretch of white-water river. The blinking neon sign out front reading JIMMY THE CREEK'S FISHING SUPPLIES couldn't have looked more out of place had it been located on the surface of the moon. The phone out front was working, so I called Aunt Helen and gave her the update I'd promised earlier this afternoon. Once I'd brought her up to speed on our progress, I went inside to buy a couple of candy bars and a bag of ice for the cooler. Just inside the door, I spotted a cork bulletin board. A couple of flyers advertising fishing guides and an oversized postcard listing a lakeside cabin for rent took up most of the space. In between, a scattering of business cards for boat insurance, home computer sales, and income tax services. Tacked to the very bottom of the board was a wrinkled leaflet with a color photograph of a young girl. HAVE YOU SEEN THIS WOMAN? was printed across the top in bold letters. Beneath the photo, in smaller type: the woman's age, height, weight, and last known location. And her name, of course. ANNIE LOMAN. A part of me had expected it to be Rachel Filmore. Ms. Loman had been missing since February.

The man behind the cash register bore a remarkable resemblance to Barney Fife from *The Andy Griffith Show*. He kept his eyes on me the entire time. As I paid for the snacks and ice, I found myself wondering if he knew anything about our surprise in the woods. Who knew, maybe he was even responsible for what we'd found there. At this point, nothing would surprise me.

The decision to circle back to Lady Ann Lake would end up costing us nearly three and a half hours—which meant there was no way in hell we were reaching Sudbury in time for dinner. So much for my map-reading skills. Still, the detour had been worth it. At least, I thought so. Troy would most likely disagree.

After changing into dry clothes, Troy had climbed into the passenger seat of the van without a word, fastened his seat belt, laid his head back on the seat rest, and closed his eyes. There was no panicked "*Now* can we call the police?" or insistent "Take me back to campus right now." Nothing. That's when I'd realized how truly frightened he was. Like a child in bed with his blankets pulled up over his eyes, terrified to face the monster lurking in his closet. And who could blame him?

By the time I returned to the van and emptied the ten-pound bag of ice into one of the coolers, Troy had come back to the land of the living. He was sitting up in the passenger seat, deep in conversation with the girls. Melody's face had gone pale, causing the dark circles beneath her eyes to stand out in contrast.

"Tell him what you just told us," she said.

Troy looked up at me, and it was like he was a different person than the one I'd last laid eyes on. "Something happened to me when we were at Griffin Schutz's memorial. Even before I saw the photograph. I was standing behind all of you and . . . It felt like something crawled inside of me. Something *bad*."

"I experienced something similar at the Ramos memorial when we went back to photograph the guitar," Melody interrupted, "but I never said anything because I wasn't actually sure what'd happened. I thought maybe I'd just been having a *moment*. Like my mom used to have when she was overwhelmed with stress and work."

"Did either of you taste smoke?" I asked. "Almost like you were choking on it?"

Their mouths dropped open.

"It happened to you too!" Melody nearly shouted.

I nodded. "Twice."

Both Melody and Troy looked over at Naomi but didn't say anything. Neither did she.

"Naomi?"

She shook her head. "No . . . never."

"You haven't felt anything at all out of the ordinary?"

"Besides that awful nightmare . . . and being majorly freaked out ever since you told me what was happening . . . no. Nothing like that."

I stared at her for a moment—*Did she hesitate? Did her voice sound funny?*—and then quickly looked away. It was my turn to take charge.

"From here we go straight to Aunt Helen's house. No more stops for anything other than gas or food."

"And to pee," Melody added.

"If we make good time, we can still get there before dark."

11

Once we reached Trenton and hopped on the bypass, the miles started flying by.

Instead of endless stretches of woods and hills and farmland, the scenery now consisted of sprawling warehouses and office parks, strip malls surrounded by fast-food joints, and long stretches of faceless commercial buildings under various stages of construction. It felt like we had entered a different state altogether.

Even before we'd taken the entry ramp onto the interstate, Naomi had fallen asleep with her head in my lap. It reminded me of the day trips we used to take in my truck to Rehoboth Beach or Ocean City. On the way there, even in the chill, dark hours of predawn, she'd be bouncing around her seat with excitement. *I want to ride the Ferris wheel and the roller coaster and go to the haunted house on the boardwalk. And play the arcade and get a snow cone and oh my God, will you win me one of those big stuffed dolphins?* And then one of her favorite songs would come on the radio, and she'd turn up the volume and sing along as loud as she could, the sunrise streaming in through the windshield making her blue eyes sparkle like diamonds, her long hair tousled from the wind gusting in through the open window, and I'd watch as she'd brush it out of her eyes with pink-painted fingernails. And then once the song had finished, she'd go right back to planning our day. *After we swim and lay out in the sun all morning, let's grab lunch at Sunny's and eat on the balcony. They have the best view of the pier and the inlet. And after we're done I want to*

MEMORIALS

stop at that little jewelry store next door and buy a seashell pendant for Kimmy's birthday and . . .

The way home was always a different story. We'd be an hour or so into our four-hour drive, and she'd nestle her head against my shoulder. Her hair would smell like sunshine and salt water. Dressed in shorts and one of my old hoodies, her face blushed by the sun, she'd eventually curl up across the seat with her head in my lap and her toes pressing against the passenger door. She'd ramble for a bit, mostly about how much fun she'd had and how she couldn't wait to go back again, her voice growing more hushed with each passing mile. And then at some point the talking would cease altogether, and I'd feel the steady exhalations of her warm breath on my leg.

I'd drive the rest of the way home with the radio and my thoughts to keep me company. Every once in a while, I'd reach down and touch her arm or her shoulder, just to make sure she was real. I was a kid then and didn't know much, but I knew that I loved her. What I didn't know was that the world had teeth. And was forever hungry.

Up ahead, on the shoulder of the highway, a pair of police cars had a tractor trailer boxed in. Neither of the cruisers' lights were flashing. Melody signaled to move over into the left lane, and we were quickly past them.

I looked down at Naomi again. She had more freckles on her nose than I remembered. For some reason, I counted them. Fourteen. I reached to move the hair out of her eyes—and froze. What was going to happen when we got back to Sudbury? And when I returned to school? So much time had passed. The world had changed. We'd changed. Everything I was feeling—and it was a *lot*, there was no questioning that—was it real? Or just an instinctive emotional response to seeing her after all this time? Both, maybe?

Too many questions, and not enough answers. The story of my life. All of a sudden, I knew exactly what I wanted to talk about during my next session with Dr. Mirarchi.

Careful not to wake her—and with a hollow ache settling deep in my heart—I picked up the video camera and my notebook from the seat beside me, and went to work.

12

Two hours later, out of necessity, we abandoned the bypass in favor of yet another network of backroads. Once it skirted past Burwell, the interstate swung sharply to the south, and unless we wanted to take a major side trip to Gettysburg or Hanover before banging a U-turn back to Sudbury, we had no other choice but to take the exit ramp.

I found myself making excuses to look over my shoulder or retrieve things from the back of the van. First, it was a bag of pretzels; a little later, sodas for Naomi and me; finally, a ballpoint pen, even though I had several rattling around inside the knapsack at my feet.

But what I was really doing was checking to make sure that no one was following us.

Twice now, I'd suspected that we'd picked up a tail—listen to me, a *tail*! Who did I think I was, Thomas Magnum zipping around the streets of Hawaii in his red Ferrari?—and twice now, the vehicles in question had turned off after only a few miles. Clearly, my imagination was running in overdrive—but with everything that was happening, who the hell could blame me?

Our first order of business in Hastings was stopping for gas. While I went inside to pay, the others kept watch to make sure no strangers approached the van. Once I returned and began filling the tank with Troy standing guard at my side, the girls left to use the restroom. A couple days ago, I would have thought our behavior was overkill—but not anymore. Not after finding that awful photo.

"I've been thinking . . . ," Troy said as the numbers on the ancient gas pump made that *clickity* sound. "Whoever nailed that photo to the cross had no idea we were coming back to the lake."

"Right." I didn't tell him that I'd already thought of that.

"So almost assuredly, it wasn't left there to frighten us or act as any kind of warning."

MEMORIALS

Almost assuredly . . . who talks like that? The old Troy was definitely back. "I guess not?"

"So maybe Naomi was right . . . and someone *did* put a curse on us . . . or maybe the photo is part of some fucked-up ritual . . ."

Before I could respond, the girls were back.

"Let's get out of here. Now," Melody said, glancing at the side of the building where the restrooms were located. Leaning against the station wall was a pile of old pallets and a bicycle missing its front tire. The image of the speeding cyclist with blood all over his face flashed through my mind.

"What's wrong?" I asked. "Did something happen?"

"Not exactly . . . but this place is giving me the serious creeps."

"No lie—it felt like someone was watching us," Naomi said, "the whole time we were in there."

Melody shivered.

The pump clicked off.

I quickly hung up the nozzle while Troy screwed on the gas cap, and then we were all hurrying back inside the van. The entire operation had taken a little more than nine minutes—and we were back on the road again without further incident.

A few miles later, I picked up my notebook and announced my most recent findings.

"Okay, I rechecked the footage, and the best that I can tell . . . the symbol appears at *nine* of the memorials we stopped at. That's out of nineteen total." I flipped the page. "The nine include the bald biker and Chase Harper from Day One, Michael Meredith, the Carsons, the one from the Parkton cemetery, the painted rock memorial behind the billboard, Gabriel Ramos, Griffin Schutz . . ." I looked up at them. ". . . and my parents."

"So now we just need to find out what those nine have in common," Troy said.

"Might be a whole lot easier said than done," Melody chimed in. "For starters, we have a nine-year-old accident victim, an eighteen-year-old murder victim, a Hells Angel–type biker, a young father—"

"I know. And a middle-aged couple who went to church every Sunday and whose idea of an exciting weekend was going out to Cracker Barrel and playing Scrabble."

Melody looked at me in the mirror. "They all seem so different."

"They *are*," I said. "Mostly male. But with a wide range of ages. At least two had children. One had a pregnant fiancée."

"Who disappeared without a trace," Troy added.

"Oh no..." Melody pressed the brake pedal.

Up ahead in the distance, a man wearing a bright orange helmet and vest stood in the center of the lane, blocking traffic. A long line of cars waited behind him. We slowed to a stop and joined them.

"Probably another tree down from the storm," I said. "This much rain and wind, they'll be falling for weeks."

Five minutes passed, and no one budged.

Then... ten minutes.

I counted eleven cars in front of us. Several of the other drivers had turned off their engines to preserve fuel. Two men—one of them an older gentleman driving a Buick Skylark in much better condition than Penny Meredith's—got out of their vehicles and approached the worker on foot, presumably to ask what the problem was or how much longer we'd be stuck here. Another driver, less patient, swung into the other lane and performed a hasty three-point turn before speeding off in the opposite direction. I turned in my seat and watched him go. I could no longer see the end of the parade of cars waiting behind us.

"Can I see your notes for a second?" Troy asked.

"Sure." I handed him the notebook.

Outside, a second orange-clad worker appeared beside the man blocking the road. They spoke for a minute, and then the new arrival began walking down the center line, peering into each of the cars as he passed them. He was carrying a dark object in his hand. For a stomach-turning couple of seconds, I thought it was a gun. I opened my mouth to alert the others—and then quickly closed it as the object swam into clear view. It was a walkie-talkie. My entire body sagged in relief.

"It would be interesting to compare the dates of death," Troy said. "See if there's any kind of pattern."

"Uh-oh," Melody said, watching the worker's approach. "Guys . . . I don't like this." For the third or fourth time since we'd stopped, she made sure the van doors were locked.

"Nope," Troy said. "Me either."

The man was slight and not the least bit imposing. At least, not physically. If not for his scraggly red beard, I might have guessed he was a teenager. Twenty-one, at the oldest. He walked with a limp and his left cheek bulged with an enormous wad of chewing tobacco. Every now and then, he'd spit a dark splotch onto the asphalt at his feet. When the worker reached a yellow VW bug parked a couple of cars ahead of us, a young girl poked her head out the window and said something. The worker nodded, turned to the side and spit, and then continued on his way. As he approached the van, he looked us over with slitted, reptilian eyes—and for a moment, I felt like one of those poor dead insects pinned to a corkboard in high school biology class.

"Just keep going," Melody willed him under her breath.

Naomi gritted her teeth—and squeezed my thigh so tightly it left a mark.

Those lizard eyes of his still studying us, the man strolled past without a word.

I swung around and watched as he lifted the walkie-talkie to his mouth.

"He's telling someone about us on the radio," Melody said, staring at the side mirror.

"We don't know that. Maybe—"

And then just like that—the cars ahead of us began to move.

Stop and start at first, a few yards at a time, but soon after we began inching ahead without pause.

"Hallelujah," Melody said, letting out a deep breath.

A short distance in front of us, a state police car with its lights flashing was parked on the right shoulder. A pair of uniformed troopers leaned against the hood with their backs to us. Across from them, a group of orange hats and vests huddled in the opposite lane, their heads pressed together in conversation, none of them paying the least bit of attention to the crawling line of traffic just a few feet away.

"Ahh, man," Troy said, "now that's gross."

For no real reason, I lifted the video camera and began filming.

Not far from where the workers were standing, there was a huge dark red stain in the middle of the road. Bits of gristle and jagged splinters of bone floated in the grisly puddle, like tiny islands scattered in a crimson lagoon. Long, wavering rivulets of what must've been some kind of animal's blood drained into the weeds littering the far shoulder.

"What do you think happened?" Melody asked.

Naomi hid her eyes against my shoulder.

"Fuck a duck." Troy made a gagging sound. "I think I'm gonna puke."

To be honest, I wasn't feeling so great myself. I'd never seen that much blood before—and it was fucking with my head. After my parents died, I would often imagine what the accident scene had looked like when the paramedics first arrived. It wasn't something I wanted to do—far from it—but I found that I couldn't stop myself. Before long, I was driving out there to the shoulder of the road where it happened and searching for splotches of blood or bits of leftover debris from my parents' car. Eventually, talking to Dr. Mirarchi and starting the meds had put an end to those fits of madness. In fact, today was the first I'd thought about it in a long time.

Anxious to unsee the slaughterhouse mess—and with my stomach performing a series of cartwheels—I swung the camera around and focused on the workers.

They had stopped talking.

And every single one of them was staring directly at us.

It was like a scene out of *Race with the Devil*, one of my all-time pulpy favorites starring perennial cool-as-a-cucumber Peter Fonda. I could feel the skin on my scalp crawling with that frightening realization.

MEMORIALS

"You seeing what I'm seeing?" Melody asked, forcing herself to look straight ahead at the road.

One of the workers—an overweight woman with white splotches of sunscreen smeared all over her face—looked directly at me and grinned. Her gold front teeth glinted in the sunlight.

"Just keep going," I said. "If anyone tries to stop you, go around them and floor it."

"Okay..."

No one tried to stop us—and thirty seconds later, we were rolling along at a steady forty miles per hour. There were a lot of cars on the road ahead of us, and even more behind us, but that was all right. As long as we were moving again.

"Okay, we didn't just imagine that, right?" Melody asked.

"Hell no," Troy said. "It was like the pizza joint all over again."

"What pizza joint?" Naomi asked.

Before I could answer, Troy said, "The pizza joint from hell."

13

VIDEO FOOTAGE
(3:22 p.m., Tuesday, May 10, 1983)

```
The image is shaky at first, and then as it steadies
and begins to swim in and out of focus, we see the
back of a young blonde girl's head as she stares at
something outside the van. The camera moves past
her, pressing close to the glass of the
window.
    A group of road workers wearing orange helmets and
vests stand together talking. As the van slowly draws
closer to them, the camera tilts lower—
    —revealing a large puddle of blood on the road at
```

the workers' feet. Chunks of what appears to be flesh and bone litter the scene.

"Ahh, man, now that's gross." Close by but off-screen. Troy.

"What do you think happened?" Melody.

"Fuck a duck." And then prolonged gagging followed by: "I think I'm gonna puke."

Slowly, the camera tilts upward, leaving behind the gory roadway and focusing on the workers.

All of them are staring straight at the camera, their faces like stone . . .

"You seeing what I'm seeing?" Melody sounding like she's speaking through clenched teeth.

. . . except for a woman standing behind the main group of workers. She grins and her gold front tooth winks in the sunlight at the camera. The grin of a hungry crocodile.

Two of her coworkers step closer to the camera—and then they're no longer in frame as the van rolls slowly past them.

"Just keep going." The camera operator's voice. Low. Filled with tension. "If anyone tries to stop you, go around them and floor it."

And then the camera angle abruptly shifts—and we're looking out of a different window at the opposite side of the road where two state troopers lean against the hood of their car. One of the troopers is slight and wears glasses. He's smiling at something his partner just said. The second trooper is tall. Very tall. His chest broad, his neck thick. Because of his hat, most of his face is hidden in shadow.

> The image zooms in and freezes on those shadows—
> and the trooper's square jaw.

14

Troy passed the video camera to me.

"You're right," he said. "That's the same cop that pulled us over. Holy shit."

"This time *he's* the one that's a long way from home."

"What does it mean?" Melody asked. "Him being all the way out here."

"Maybe nothing," I said. "I have no idea how wide of an area troopers are expected to cover. Still, it's a pretty odd coincidence."

Once we hit the county line, the steady flow of traffic caused by the roadblock finally began to thin. At least half of the drivers ahead of us took the long, sweeping left onto Route 43, welcoming the 55 mph speed limit while heading due north. Another half-dozen or so turned onto various side streets in and around town, no doubt returning to their homes and businesses. The rest of us kept heading east. If there were no further delays, we would arrive at Aunt Helen's house in another four and a half hours.

"The whole thing was so strange," Naomi said. "It's like they were . . . leering at us or something."

"Now I know how animals in the zoo feel," Melody said.

"This was different." Troy turned in his seat so he could see all three of us. "The zoo thing . . . I grew up with that. White folks—sorry, present company excluded, of course—would drive through my neighborhood, very slowly, windows up, doors locked, faces pressed up against the glass, staring at us—no, more like studying us—with a kind of rapt fascination, like we were part of a newly discovered tribe inhabiting an island that didn't appear on any maps. Some of them even took pictures of us." He shook his head. "Today and that day at the restaurant were different. I felt genuine hatred beneath those fake smiles and blank stares. Not even a hint of fascination—just *distaste* and a fucked-up dose of cruel amusement."

"Wow," Naomi said, staring at him with admiration.

"Sometimes, I legit forget that you're so much smarter than me," I said.

"Isn't that a little like forgetting to put your clothes on in the morning?"

"Ha ha."

"I'm so sorry you had to experience that," Melody said. "Especially as a child."

Troy shrugged. "It comes with the territory. I go home for summer break in a couple of weeks, and like clockwork, it'll happen all over again."

No one said anything for a while, the weight of Troy's words settling over us like a suffocating storm cloud. I thought back to what he and Mel had told me at the Silver Moon Diner—about my hometown of Sudbury. He'd even joked and called it Honkyville. I was still trying to reconcile myself with the naivety I'd demonstrated, and doubted it would come any time soon.

Melody slowed the van and gestured to the side of the road. "We're not stopping, right?"

I glanced out the window—and saw what was easily the largest roadside memorial we'd encountered thus far on the trip. My heartbeat quickened.

About twelve feet off the shoulder, nestled against the side of an old aluminum farming shed, stood a single white cross, a foot or two taller than me, surrounded by an obnoxious number of wreaths (many on wire stands), blown-up photographs, posters, flowers, flags, balloons, and ceramic angels. The entire display was ringed by multiple strings of glowing multicolored Christmas bulbs, most likely powered by a portable generator hidden somewhere in the brush.

Before anyone could answer, we were rolling past it.

"Umm," I stammered, leaning forward in my seat. "We might as well—"

"God, I knew it," Melody said, and steered onto the shoulder.

Troy stared at me. "You never fucking learn, do you?"

"What? You guys can wait inside the van," I said, grabbing the camera. "I'll get two or three minutes of video and we're outta here." I slid open the side door.

Naomi touched my arm. "Billy."

"I'll be fine. Back in a flash."

I jumped out—and the stench hit me like a hammer blow. Something dead close by. Rotting in the heat.

"It smells like ass out there!" Troy shouted. "Jesus—shut the door!"

I reached for the handle, but Naomi beat me to it, pulling it closed in my face. So much for her being worried about me.

Walking toward the memorial, holding my breath, I realized how quiet it was. The only sound was the breeze sifting among the tree branches. I immediately reconsidered my earlier assumption that there was a generator hiding somewhere in the grass. Generators were noisy contraptions. A few more steps, and I discovered the source of the rancid odor. What was left of a groundhog sprawled in the dirt just off the gravel shoulder, its head smashed to a flattened pulp, its neck clearly broken. The rest of its body was swollen like a giant tick and concealed beneath an undulating blanket of bottleneck flies. I didn't want to be anywhere near here when it finally burst.

I stopped in front of the memorial. The deceased was a young woman. In the photographs people had left, she looked like a middle school teacher or maybe a day care worker. Big brown eyes, eager to help. A wide, contagious smile. Sensible haircut. Blouses and slacks from Macy's or Hecht's. Behind me, a car whizzed by on the road, and I nearly jumped out of my skin. Raising the camera, I hit record and repeated out loud what I'd promised Naomi before exiting the van: "Back in a flash."

I slowly panned from left to right and then back again. Tilting the camera toward the ground, I repeated the process, making sure I captured the entire garish display in frame. At a glance, I didn't see the mysterious symbol anywhere. To be sure, I zoomed in on each of the posters, adjusting the focus as the individual shots called for it. That way I could study the videotape later.

The stench had grown worse, and for a terrifying moment, I was certain that the disfigured groundhog had come back to life and was right behind me. I'd lower the camera and turn around—and it would be dragging itself along the side of the road, milky eyes glowering, teeth bared.

I heard another car approaching in the distance but didn't think anything of it. I was too busy filming the string of Christmas lights and picturing in my head a zombie groundhog with razor-sharp teeth and an undying hunger for human flesh.

Okay . . . now I had definitely overstayed my welcome. I hit the stop button and lowered the camera. Scanning the memorial with my naked eye, I still didn't see any sign of the mysterious symbol. I actually felt relieved.

What happened next took only a fraction of a second—yet for the remainder of my life, whenever the moment replayed itself during my nightmares, it always occurred in two distinctive acts.

Act One: *Holding my breath to avoid inhaling the cloying stench of dead groundhog, I start to turn around to return to the van—but before I can, I'm tackled by a blur of brown flesh and towering Afro.*

Act Two: *On my way to the ground, a missile on wheels hurtles past me, chipped red paint flashing in front of my eyes, close enough that I can feel the heat of its engine on my face and taste its sore exhaust on my tongue and smell its burning rubber deep in my nostrils, close enough for its yawning steel mouth to lunge and sink its teeth into my hip and shoulder, tearing away bits of tender skin and flesh.*

Epilogue: *The ground is hard, and it hurts. In addition to the wounds on my hip and shoulder, I'm almost positive I've bruised a rib or two. It's difficult to breathe, but at least I'm alive.*

Melody and Naomi swarmed us as we untangled ourselves.

"Are you okay?!"

"Did it hit you?!"

"Billy, you're bleeding!"

I groaned and sat up. "I'm okay, I'm okay . . . I'm fine." I looked around at the others. The world was still tottering. "I think."

"You're not fine, Billy." Melody leaned over and tugged at my T-shirt. "Your shoulder's bleeding!"

Beside me in the dirt, Troy pushed himself up to his knees. There was gravel in his hair. A cut above his left eye was bleeding. He looked dazed. "I got out to tell you to hurry up . . . saw the truck . . . it swerved . . . That motherfucker tried to run you down!" Sudden tears leaked from his eyes, cutting clear tracks through the grime on his cheeks.

I stared at him, dumbfounded. "You saved my life."

"He really did," Naomi said. "He got to you just in time."

I tried to get to my feet, but the ground shifted violently beneath me. At least that's what it felt like. Groaning, I sat down again. Troy pushed to his knees beside me.

"You're stubborn as hell and you never listen to anyone and you have shitty taste in movies," he said, "but I wasn't going to let anything happen to you." And then his skinny arms were wrapped around me, holding on for dear life, and he was sobbing against my shoulder—and as his chest heaved and his tears washed away my blood, I knew exactly who he was thinking of.

15

Moments of visceral pain and shock often give birth to bizarre and inappropriate thoughts. Unfortunately, I'd learned that hard truth from scads of personal experience—much of it horribly embarrassing—and while I wasn't certain if it applied to the rest of the world, I had a sneaking suspicion that it did.

There'd been a moment, while the priest was delivering his sermon during my parents' funeral, when I'd looked over and saw one of the neighborhood moms sitting next to her husband. She was crying. At some point, she pulled out a tissue and used it to wipe her eyes, and then she blew her nose into it. When she pulled the tissue away, there was a huge booger dangling out of her left nostril. Green and yellow and disgustingly moist. I remember thinking that maybe she had a cold or a virus. For the next several minutes, I heard nothing the priest said. I couldn't take my eyes off the woman's nose. The booger had begun to peek in and out of her nostril with every breath she took, a snot-inspired game of peekaboo. I was appalled. I was fascinated. I was delighted. More than anything, I wanted to see the booger shake loose from its mooring and tumble onto her lip and, in a moment of distress and panic, her accidentally swallow it. When her husband finally noticed and quickly wiped it away with his handkerchief, I felt the sudden urge to leap over the pew and punch him in the face for ruining my special moment. Ten minutes later, the booger forgotten, I stood at the lectern, reciting my parents' eulogy. After that, the rest of the day was a blur.

As I limped toward the van—after coming within inches of being turned into roadkill by the speeding red pickup (*sorry, Mr. Groundhog, no company for you today, you're on your own!*)—with Naomi and Troy each holding on to an arm, my brain betrayed me yet again, flashing back to my final high school football game.

We were trailing Belleville by a touchdown late in the fourth quarter, but our offense had possession of the ball and was driving. It was third and nine on our own nineteen-yard line. The play called for a ten-yard down and out of bounds to stop the clock. Their linebackers blitzed and our quarterback was forced to get rid of the ball early to avoid the sack. I caught it over my shoulder and immediately headed for the sideline. Spinning through one tackle, I lowered my head through another. And then just as I gained the first-down yardage, someone dove and grabbed my ankle from behind—and I felt something *pop!* I rolled around on the ground, screaming in pain. And just like that my football career was over. No final home game in front of my cheerleader girlfriend. No playoff run. No championship trophy. As my mother and father watched in tears from the bleachers, an assistant coach and our trainer—one under each arm—helped me off the field. The X-rays the next morning showed that I'd torn the ligaments in my ankle. I never put on the gear again—and to this day, my ankle still aches when it's about to snow.

No one commented on the dead groundhog as we shuffled past it. Not even when its fly-shrouded torso rippled and heaved like a black flag flapping in the breeze. Up ahead, Melody was waiting at the rear of the van, standing perfectly still with her back to us. At first, I thought it was odd, but then I figured she was probably just keeping watch in case the driver of the pickup decided to return.

But I was wrong.

When we reached her side, she turned and looked at us with blank, staring eyes. It was like she was in a daze. "I need to call my sister and make sure she's okay."

"Why?" Troy sounded exhausted and in pain. We were all at the end of our ropes. "What now?"

Melody slowly lifted her hand and pointed.

Once. Twice.

In the shade of the surrounding trees, both of the van's taillights were flashing red.

And neither one of them was broken.

"The cop lied to us . . . He saw the van's registration . . . They know where she lives."

16

We drove the next few hours mostly in silence. For the first time since the road trip had started, it felt like there was nothing left to say. Discovering that the cop was one of them and now had Melody's personal information—maybe all of ours, for that matter—was the tipping point. Throw in the photo from Griffin Schutz's memorial site and my near miss with the red pickup, and it felt like we were shell-shocked. More than anything, we just needed to hurry up and get to Aunt Helen's house and let our brains rest for the night. In the morning, we could regroup. In the meantime, we stared out the van windows and did our best to remain calm. We still had two hours until we reached Sudbury.

The interior of the van was strewn with fast-food wrappers and half-eaten packages of convenience store doughnuts. I was already working on my second pack of SweeTarts. I could feel the cavities forming inside my teeth with every passing mile. If it was true that some folks ate their way out of misery—instead of drinking their way out—we were living proof of that theory. We may have been caught right smack-dab in the middle of an inexplicable nightmare, but at least our bellies were full.

My ribs were bruised and sore to the touch, but I was pretty sure nothing was broken. My saliva was clear of blood and it didn't bother me at all to swallow. My shoulder, on the other hand, had a pretty nasty gash on it. Melody had asked if we should look for a local hospital in case I needed stitches, but I'd shut down that idea right away. There would be no more stops until Sudbury. Instead, Naomi cleaned the wound with water and napkins, and patched it up with bandages we'd picked up at the convenience store. I'd whined pretty much the entire time.

While Melody called her sister, Tamara, from the pay phone outside a truck-stop McDonald's, Troy stood in line and peeled off another wad of Mickey D's gift certificates, Naomi used the restroom, and I hung around by the van. Shortly after we'd left the memorial, Melody had become convinced that we were being followed by a gray sedan with dark windows. Standing in the parking lot, I kept my eyes peeled—but there was no sign of a sedan lurking about or the jacked-up red pickup that had almost ended my life. Just rows and rows of huge tractor trailers, their running lights glowing like the prowling nocturnal eyes of prehistoric creatures, and the occasional wandering lot lizard dressed in a miniskirt and ill-fitting high heels.

"Tamara's fine," Mel told us after we reconvened inside the van. Just hearing her sister's voice had worked wonders on her demeanor. Her eyes appeared brighter and she'd even gotten her appetite back. She accepted the unwrapped Quarter Pounder from Troy and dug in. "I didn't tell her what was going on . . . just said I wanted to check in and let her know the van was okay. Then I called Rosalita . . ."

I knew she'd also been worried about her roommate back in York. The cop had gotten a good look at Melody's driver's license. We all remembered him pausing to jot something down in his notepad. Most likely, her home address. Just the thought of him knowing where Melody lived made me sick to my stomach. I couldn't even imagine how she was feeling.

"Other than the entire apartment complex losing power last night—thanks to a passing thunderstorm—Rosie seems perfectly okay. She's even planning a celebratory dinner for us when we get back . . . but you guys have to pretend to be surprised."

"Not a peep from me," Troy said, zipping his lips, "especially if she makes her shrimp burritos."

Once we started driving, every few miles, I heard the distinctive *click-click* as Melody anxiously pressed the button on the side of her door, making sure that it was locked. No one said anything. We all understood. Whoever was playing this twisted game had just raised the stakes—and right or wrong, it felt like Melody was a whole lot more at risk than the rest of us.

The cop had lied to her face about the broken taillight. Why? To get his hands on Melody's personal information? To demonstrate that the game they were playing had even fewer rules than we'd imagined? To amuse himself and scare the living hell out of us?

I had a feeling the answer was that multiple-choice favorite—all of the above.

"If the guy really is a member of the Pennsylvania State Police," Troy said, "he should've been able to find out Tamara's details by simply running the license plate on the van."

"Is that supposed to make me feel better?" Melody snapped around a mouthful of chicken nugget.

Troy put his hands up to placate her. "All I'm saying is that I'd bet my last dollar he did exactly that before turning on his siren and pulling us over. So then what? Based on the information that his dispatcher provided, had he somehow known that the woman driving was someone other than the van's registered owner, Tamara Wise? Or did that even matter to him? Melody Wise or Tamara Wise . . . what difference does it make to these people?"

None at all, I thought, staring out the window. *The names don't fucking matter. They just want whoever stuck their noses where they didn't belong.*

They want us.

17

It was after eight and going on dark when we crossed over the Albert Linden Bridge, swung a hard right into the tunnel of trees, and stopped on the shoulder of the road across from my parents' memorial.

The four of us exited the van with stiff legs and sleepy eyes. After turning on the hazard lights, Melody left the engine running and the headlights on—a reminder that we wouldn't be staying very long.

Somewhere high above us, perched in the shadowy treetops, an owl called out. Not too far away, a second owl answered with a mournful cry of its own.

Wonderful, I thought, looking around. *Now all we need is the Headless fucking Horseman galloping down the middle of the road.*

Switching on the flashlight we'd brought along with our camping gear, I suddenly felt like Luke Skywalker wielding a light saber. The flashlight's narrow shine cut through the murky darkness like a laser beam. Only problem was . . . if a monster or a madman or a stormtrooper came charging out of the trees at us, the flashlight wouldn't do a damn thing to stop them.

It didn't take long to locate the symbol. Thanks to the photos I'd taken, we knew exactly where to look. I steadied the light on the lower right corner of the poster—or least I tried to. My hand was shaking. Seeing it up close and in person felt very different from studying it on the static surface of a glossy five-by-seven. Sandwiched between a drawing of a lopsided pink heart and a scribbled note from one of our neighbors, the symbol somehow felt alive in the fluttering flashlight beam. Almost as if it were breathing . . . and watching us.

"It's still here," Troy whispered right behind me—and I nearly screamed.

"Jesus . . . don't do that," I said, shining the light on his face.

He raised an arm in front of his eyes. "Do what?"

"Never mind."

I lowered the flashlight and redirected the beam back onto the poster.

MEMORIALS

Neither one of us said anything for a while. An owl cried out again, a little farther away this time. Behind us, next to the van, I heard Naomi yawn.

"Are you as creeped out as I am?" Troy finally said.

"Yes, I am." I wanted to say more, but I couldn't.

"And you have no idea when it might've been left here?"

I shook my head. "None at all."

"It might help if we can look at old photographs."

"That's a good idea," I said. "We'll stop by the newspaper office tomorrow."

Something rustled in the brush behind the memorial. Troy immediately scooted closer to my side, stepping on my foot in the process. "Sorry."

"Whatever that was, it was small," I said. "Probably a raccoon or a rabbit."

"Us city folks don't like the woods at night . . . especially when there's a witch running around in them."

"Warlock."

"Oh yeah. Thanks."

I laughed in spite of myself. "Then you're really not going to like this." And I tugged at his shirt for him to follow me.

"What . . . wait . . . where are we going?"

"I want to try to find where the man was hiding in the photo."

"This is so not cool."

Stepping into the trees, I let go of Troy's T-shirt and focused the flashlight on the ground in front of us. There was no discernable path, but the brush was sparse enough in spots to allow our passage.

"Wouldn't this be easier in the daylight?" Troy whispered. "And a whole lot safer?"

"Maybe . . . but we're here now. It should only take a minute." I shifted the light to the right and followed the bouncing beam. "Based on the angle of the photograph, he should've been standing right about . . . here . . ." I stopped and redirected the light toward the back of the memorial—and took two big steps to my left. "Or maybe *here*."

With a screen of chest-high thorn bushes obscuring most of our bodies from the road, and a cluster of close-growing pines creating an even deeper pool of shadows, this felt like the right place. If not, we were very close. I lowered the flashlight and shined it on the ground at our feet. It was mostly rocks and roots and pine needles. Not a chance in hell of finding a shoe print.

"Can we go now?" Troy asked.

"Almost." I raised the flashlight and began turning in a slow circle, inspecting the trees around us.

"Wait," Troy said. "Go back a second."

I pivoted to my left.

"A little higher."

I lifted the flashlight.

"*There*—what is *that*?" he whispered.

A small figure, made out of a lashed-together framework of sticks, had been propped up on the branch of an oak tree. It was no more than four or five inches high—and undeniably humanlike.

"Is it some kind of totem?" Troy asked.

"That looks like one of the symbols Melody showed us at the library," I said. "I have a photocopy back in the van."

Troy winced. "It's repulsive."

I stepped closer, reaching out my hand.

"Don't touch it!" he shouted.

I jerked my hand back like a snake had dropped down from the branch, fangs bared and ready to strike.

"Is everything okay?" Melody called out in a muffled voice from the roadside.

"Billy . . . ?" Naomi this time.

"We're fine!" I yelled. "We're coming out now!"

"Thank God," Troy said, nudging me toward the road.

"And then we're coming right back in. With the camera."

Troy groaned and followed me out of the woods.

18

"You poor kids look like you've been put through the wringer."

It was 9:15 p.m. We'd parked in the street in front of Aunt Helen's house ten minutes earlier, and were already washed up and seated at the dining room table. Despite our protests, she'd insisted on serving us a late dinner.

"We're not helpless," I told her, passing a plate of corn on the cob. "And you're not a waitress."

"I used to be a long time ago."

"Must've been a *very* long time ago."

"Watch it, mister." She handed a platter of crab cakes to Troy, who'd practically pushed me out of the way to take the seat next to her. I'd already decided that if he started flirting again, I was going to kick him in the shin under the table.

"It was before your time, silly Billy. A couple of summers during high school. Your mother worked there too."

I vaguely remembered my father talking about it at the dinner table one evening. Something about how cute my mother's uniform had been. And then he'd commented on her legs, and she'd gotten embarrassed and shushed him. I glanced across the table at Naomi. The thought of my mom and my aunt at Naomi's age was enough to make my heart ache.

"I hope you'll let us clear the table and wash the dishes," Melody said. "It's the least we can do."

"Nope. Not going to happen." Smiling, she filled her glass with iced tea. "I left clean towels in both of the upstairs bathrooms. When you're finished eating, you can head right up and draw straws to see who showers first."

"I see where Billy gets his stubborn streak," Troy said with a dreamy smile. A half hour ago, he was standing in the middle of the woods, his eyes the size of silver dollars. Now, he looked like a schoolboy with a crush on his teacher. I gazed across the table at him and began scratching the tip of my nose—with my middle finger. He pretended not to notice.

"The guest rooms are all set, and there are fresh linens on the bed." She looked at Naomi. "So, Billy mentioned you're staying with us?"

"Yes, ma'am—as long as that's okay."

"You're always welcome here, you know that." She arched her eyebrows. "But you're going to have to call your parents first thing in the morning. Let them know you're safe and back in town."

"I will," she said, lowering her eyes.

"Okay then . . . I'll leave the sleeping arrangements up to the four of you. We're all big girls and boys here. No judgment on my part."

And with that out of the way we got down to eating.

19

After dinner, I walked outside to the van carrying an empty laundry basket.

My stomach was full of home cooking, and more than ever, I just wanted to lay my head down on a pillow and go to sleep for about a day or two. A car slowly drove by, its headlights washing over my aunt's mailbox and the front of the van. The car's window was rolled down, and although I couldn't make out the driver's face, I could see the glowing red tip of the cigarette they were smoking. Without even thinking about it, I began to whistle—and then remembered the story I'd told Troy about whistling at night and immediately stopped.

As I unlocked the back doors and leaned inside the van to retrieve the wet clothes from our excursion at the lake, something stirred in the trees behind me. I spun and faced the woods across the street—and stood perfectly still, searching the murk. All of a sudden, I wished I'd brought along a flashlight. The dome bulb on the ceiling of the van was on, but its weak glow barely touched the darkness. After a moment of seeing and hearing nothing, I turned around and quickly resumed collecting our foul-smelling laundry. As I tossed each piece into the basket, cold, dirty water drained between my fingers and leaked into a puddle on the road.

Earlier, while clearing the dishes from the table, I'd struck a deal with Melody. I'd go outside and get the clothes if she'd take care of washing and drying them. It not only seemed like a fair trade, it more importantly provided me with the opportunity to grab the photograph of Troy with his eyes scratched out from the pocket of my jeans.

My 32-waist straight-leg Levi's were rolled up into a ball, soaked and dripping and remarkably heavy. There was little chance that the photo inside the pocket wasn't ruined, but that didn't really matter to me. It wasn't like we were going to turn it in as evidence to the police. For some reason, I just hadn't wanted to leave it there in the woods—like maybe removing it from the cross and disposing of it would take away its power.

I unrolled the jeans. One of the legs was turned inside out from the rush to shuck them off in the parking lot at the lake. I straightened the leg and gave the pants a good squeeze. Rainwater cascaded onto my shoes.

"Aw, shit." Dancing backward, I held the jeans out in front of me.

When the dripping slowed to a trickle, I began checking the pockets.

I couldn't remember where I had put it—only that I'd snatched the photograph in an impulsive flurry, worried that Troy might see me.

The back pockets were empty.

Front right, then . . . it had to be.

But I was wrong again.

Okay . . . then definitely front left, the pocket facing away from where Troy was walking down the trail.

It, too, was empty.

No longer tired, I carefully searched the other pieces of clothing inside the basket. With the exception of a half-eaten roll of soggy breath mints in Troy's khakis and a pair of quarters in Naomi's jean shorts, they were all empty.

Next, I looked in the rear of the van—but it wasn't there either.

Finally, I turned in a slow circle, scanning the road at my feet in case it had fallen unnoticed.

The photograph was gone.

Someone had taken it.

20

Instead of drawing straws—did people even do that anymore?—Troy and I decided to act like gentlemen and insisted that the girls shower first. From where I was sitting in the living room, I could hear the hot water rushing noisily through the pipes above my head. From the year I'd spent living here, I knew that the furnace was even louder during the wintertime. It was an old house and it spoke in a multitude of voices.

Fortunately—for me, at least—Troy's stomach was acting up. For the past twenty minutes, he'd been locked away in the downstairs bathroom with the ceiling fan going, allowing me some much needed alone time with my aunt. I'd already shown her some of the footage I'd taken, as well as a handful of photographs, including a close-up of the poster with the symbol clearly visible in the foreground. I'd wanted to see if she might notice and say something—but she'd flipped right past it without comment. I still couldn't get the photo from Griffin Schutz's memorial out of my head. *Who in the hell had taken it? And why?*

"I asked Jason to join us for breakfast tomorrow. I hope you don't mind."

"Of course not." I could tell she still felt sheepish talking about the new man in her life. I wasn't used to seeing that side of her. She was usually so open and self-assured. "You didn't tell me he was the sheriff. That's kind of a big deal."

"Not really." She gave me a funny look. "You checked up on him? You run one of those background checks like you're doing for the accident victims?"

"Not at all," I said, amused by her defensiveness. "Naomi mentioned it."

"Oh." She tucked her legs beneath her on the sofa. "So . . . I saw you two holding hands when you first came in. Does that mean what I think it means?"

The question caught me by surprise. It shouldn't have, but it did. "I'm honestly not sure what it means."

She narrowed her gaze at me. "You broke her heart once, Billy. Just maybe you shouldn't be holding hands . . . or doing other things . . . until you *are* sure."

Of course, she was absolutely, 100 percent correct—and it pissed me off.

My jaw tightened. "Why'd you send her chasing after me in the first place, then?"

"I didn't send her chasing after you. She asked if I knew where you were going. I told her I did not. She asked if I knew the route you were traveling. I told her about the note you gave me before you left."

"And what made you think that was a good idea?"

"I didn't *know* if it was a good idea or not," she said, lowering her voice. "What I did know was that she wasn't going to let go of the idea of finding you. She was going, with or without my help."

"Really?" I asked, sounding like a lovesick teenager.

"I could hear it in her voice, Billy. It was like she'd been struck by a bolt of lightning."

I let out a deep breath—and all of my anger went with it. All of a sudden, it felt like I was fourteen years old again instead of nineteen. I was shocked to realize that I was on the verge of tears. "Me and Naomi . . . I'm still getting used to the idea."

She scooted closer to me on the sofa. Rested her head on my shoulder. I wondered if she knew that my mom used to do the same thing. "Just please be careful, that's all I'm asking. Take care of that beautiful heart of yours . . . and be mindful of hers."

I swallowed about a million jumbled thoughts, cleared my throat, and said, "I promise."

In the next room, the toilet flushed. Hopefully, Troy was feeling better. Aunt Helen heard it, too, and got to her feet, yawning. "I think it's time for this old girl to turn in."

"You're not old," I said, standing. "You're awesome. Thanks again . . . for everything."

"Are you kidding? Twice in one week. This is a gift." Halfway across the room, she stopped and looked back at me. "Are you okay, Billy? You and your friends. The trip. Is everything all right?"

"Everything's fine," I said.

"You sounded kind of out of it on the phone."

"I'm just really tired. We all are." And then I felt my shoulders sag—and once again I was fighting back tears. "It's been hard . . . harder than I thought."

"You want to talk about it?"

I shook my head. "Not right now."

"In the morning?"

"Maybe."

"Well . . . I'm here if you need me." She started up the stairs. "Night, Billy. Dream good things."

God, I hoped so.

21

I watched Naomi slip on one of my old T-shirts, and all I could hear was my aunt's scolding voice rattling around inside my head: *Just maybe you shouldn't be holding hands . . . or doing other things . . . until . . .*

I still couldn't believe I was sitting in my old bedroom with Naomi Flynn.

When we were dating and my parents were still alive, it was never allowed. Not just the two of us. And especially with the door closed.

If it hadn't been for the events of the past couple days and the tantalizing smell of her freshly washed hair, I might have thought I was hallucinating.

"I'll be waiting for you when you get out of the shower," she said, crawling under the sheet.

Which was exactly what I was afraid of.

Taking no chances, I delayed my return as long as I could. I shaved twice. I shampooed my hair twice. I stood under the steady stream of water until it turned freezing cold and I could no longer stand it. After toweling off and getting dressed—shivering the entire time—I replaced the bandage on my shoulder. Then, I closed the toilet lid and sat in the quiet, contemplating the mysteries of the universe and the fate of the American League East. God, I missed baseball.

Then, and only then, did I finally unlock the bathroom door and make my way back to the bedroom. Naomi was curled up on the far side of the bed, facing the wall. She never stirred when I turned off the light and climbed in next to her.

22

I woke from a dream I couldn't remember, rubbed my eyes, and looked over at the nightstand.

Glowing red digits stared back at me: 2:14 a.m.

Rolling onto my side, I untangled my arms from the sheet and reached for Naomi in the dark. Just to make sure she was real and this whole wacky week wasn't a dream.

She wasn't there.

Her side of the bed cool to the touch.

I sat up, squinting into the shadows, and whispered her name.

"Naomi?"

No response.

Slipping out of bed, I crept toward the hallway, the floor groaning beneath my bare feet. Visitors often fawned over the house's original hardwood flooring—over 120 years old, Uncle Frank used to boast—but Aunt Helen hated it. She constantly complained that the floor was uneven and noisy. She swore that one day she was going to crash right through it and end up in the cellar with a broken back.

And yet I hadn't heard a single sound when Naomi got up and left the bedroom.

That's because you were sleeping, dummy.

Holding my hands out in front of me, I navigated the room by memory. Desk to my left by the window. Watch out for the chair. Dresser by the door. Careful, don't kick the trash can and wake the entire house.

My fingers brushed the wall and found the outer edge of the door frame. Halting at the entrance to the hallway, I tilted my head and listened. The house was dead silent.

"*Naomi?*" I whispered again.

And waited for a response.

Still nothing.

Starting to feel the first stirrings of unease, I poked my head into the hall. To my immediate left was the guest room, where Melody and Troy were sleeping in separate queen-sized beds. A little farther down, the bathroom. That was where I'd expected to find Naomi—but the light was off. If Naomi was peeing, she was doing it in the dark. Across from the bathroom was Aunt Helen's bedroom. I was pretty sure her door was closed, but I couldn't be certain. First thing tomorrow, I was driving to Kmart and buying a couple of night-lights.

Unsure of what to do next, I eased into the hallway and tiptoed to the head of the stairs. To my surprise, I saw a light coming from the living room. Dim and flickering. Wavering shadows dancing on the wall at the bottom of the stairway. *Is someone using the fireplace? In May?*

Grabbing hold of the railing, I started down.

And quickly froze with my foot dangling over the second step.

In the living room, someone was humming.

No . . . now I could hear bits and pieces of whispered words . . .

. . . not humming.

Chanting.

My spine turned to ice.

They'd found us!

And they had Naomi!

Letting go of the railing, I hurtled downstairs and skidded around the corner into the living room.

The furniture had been moved.

The antique rug rolled back against the wall behind the sofa.

Dozens of candles burned in a circle on the floor—illuminating a gigantic version of the memorial symbol, which had been carved into the wood at the center.

Sitting outside the circle, legs crossed in front of him, was the tall state trooper who'd pulled us over. His muscular bare chest was smeared with blood. As was his hateful, grinning mouth.

A naked Naomi sat directly across from him. Tan, taut flesh glistening in the firelight. In her hand, she held a curved dagger with a shiny turquoise handle. I watched her lips move as she recited the same unintelligible incantation.

A sudden rush of footsteps on the stairs behind me.

"What the fuck—!"

"Oh my God!"

Melody and Troy, hair mussed, eyes wide.

The chanting grew louder.

Holding it with both hands now, Naomi lifted the dagger above her head, angling it toward her chest.

I lunged to save her.

But my legs stopped working—and I dropped to my knees on the hardwood floor. My arms fell limp to my sides. My mouth opened and closed, but I found that I could no longer speak.

Something else had control of me now.

Naomi slowly turned her head and looked at me. Her eyes were bottomless pools of darkness. In a dreamy voice dripping with lust, she said, *"I've been waiting for you, darling."*

23

In the still darkness on the second floor of my aunt's old farmhouse, tucked away in our separate bedrooms, Melody, Troy, Naomi, and I woke up screaming at the exact same moment.

DAY SIX
WEDNESDAY | MAY 11

1

At 7:35 a.m., Aunt Helen's backyard patio was untouched by sunlight. Surrounded by the house on one side and a U-shaped column of crab apple trees on the other three sides, the gray concrete pavers remained cool throughout the most sweltering of summer mornings, providing an ideal hideaway for my aunt to drink coffee and catch up on her reading. Dressed only in shorts and a Rolling Stones T-shirt, I blew into my hands and rubbed the goose bumps on my arms as I listened to the others talk about the nightmare we'd all shared.

"Your poor aunt probably thinks we're crazy," Melody said, peering over my shoulder to make sure we were still alone. "Either that, or on some killer drugs."

"I'm pretty sure she thinks it was just *me*. She said her door was closed and didn't mention hearing anyone else." I sat down at the picnic table and tucked my bare feet underneath the bench.

"That dream last night was no 'granny magic,'" Troy said, "or whatever it was you called it before." He was looking at Naomi.

"No, it wasn't."

"I mean, that was some hard-core occult mindfuck . . . The only thing missing was a pentagram."

"I still can't believe we *all* dreamed it," Melody said. "And at the same time."

"I know a few things about shared dreams from psych class last semester," Troy said.

Melody managed a tired smile. "Of course you do."

"They're rare, as you probably guessed. As few as ten percent of the population ever experiences them."

"What causes them?" I asked.

"They're usually indicative of an emotional closeness and occur between people with shared existences and common experiences."

"The broken hearts club," Melody said.

Troy waved a finger at her. "Yes. *That*. I was thinking the exact same thing."

"What's the broken hearts club?" Naomi asked. She'd mostly been quiet since we'd awakened from the nightmare. Unlike the rest of us, who'd assumed the roles of helpless observers, she'd been an active participant in the dream. I think that was the part really bothering her.

"Something Melody brought up before you joined us," Troy said, looking at Melody to finish answering.

"I'd suggested that because we'd all lost someone important in our lives, the three of us should start our own club . . . *but* I wasn't really serious. I was mainly just pointing out that it felt like we'd been brought together for a reason." She looked at me. "Billy wasn't so keen on that idea."

"Why not?" she asked.

"It's not that I wasn't keen on the idea." A part of me was irritated that Melody and Troy had brought up the subject again, especially in front of Naomi. "I just wasn't looking at this trip as some master plan from above to help us heal from our losses."

"Billy's a little too meat-and-potatoes to believe in Peter Pan philosophies like fate," Troy said.

"Not true at all." I could feel my face growing red. "I'm squarely on the fence when it comes to fate and destiny and—"

"Bigfoot," Troy added.

I gave him a look. "Okay, I admit I'm not so sure about that one."

"Say what you want, but one day soon you'll have indisputable proof for yourself." Troy once swore that after we graduated, the two of us were hopping on a plane to the wilderness of the Pacific Northwest and participating in a Sasquatch expedition. He'd even mailed away for an information packet from one of the more popular guide outfits.

"What about the *presence* we felt at the memorials?" Melody asked. "Isn't that at least some—"

The back door swung open. My aunt, her hair still wet from the shower, poked her head outside. Her eyes moved over us with a healthy trace of suspicion.

"And what's so doggone important that you have to hide out here to discuss?"

"We're not hiding," I said, speaking too fast. "Just making plans for the day."

"Well . . ." She clearly didn't believe me. "Breakfast'll be ready in ten." She started to close the door but hesitated. "Jason had a call this morning, so unfortunately he won't be joining us."

"Everything okay?" I asked.

"Oh, sure," she said. "Some kids broke into the elementary school and spray-painted graffiti on the walls in one of the classrooms." She looked at me. "Good thing I know where you were last night . . ." And winked. ". . . or I might have to turn you in."

2

This time we refused to take no for an answer.

While Naomi and I washed and dried the dishes at the counter, Melody and Troy cleared the dining room table and wiped it clean. Aunt Helen sat at the breakfast nook in the corner of the kitchen, lecturing me on the proper way to towel-dry plates and ignoring the newspaper spread out in front of her.

"There you go, Billy . . . that's better!" she said, talking to me like I was ten years old.

I rolled my eyes and stacked the clean plate on top of the others. "Gee, thanks . . ." I stopped myself before a sarcastic *Mom* could slip out of my mouth. Back when my parents were still around, it had been a frequent retort to my aunt's good-natured nagging. After the accident, it was no longer funny.

"So . . . ," she said, recognizing what had almost just happened. "Can you share your plans for the rest of the day or are they top secret?"

"Nothing secret about them," I lied. "We have a list of names from the memorials we stopped at. Now we need to dig up as much background information as possible. Melody and Troy are going to start at the newspaper office. Naomi and I are headed to the library."

"I can come along with you, if you want."

I was pretty sure that was the last thing we wanted. "No need. Stay here and enjoy your morning off. Besides, it wouldn't be right accepting your help for a class project. Troy would probably consider it a direct violation of the honor code."

Aunt Helen laughed, but I could tell she wasn't entirely convinced I was telling the truth—or at the very least, giving her the complete story. "Well, if there's anything I can do, just let me know."

"There *is* actually one favor I need to ask."

"What's that?"

"Would it be okay if we used your phone to make a few long-distance calls? We're happy to pay whatever it—"

"Stop it. Don't be silly," she said, waving a hand at me. "You're welcome to use it as much as you'd like."

"Are you sure?"

"Of course." She looked at Naomi, who'd just turned off the faucet at the sink. "And that reminds me, young lady . . . it's time for you to call your parents."

Naomi glanced at me for support. When I didn't say anything, she mumbled under her breath, "Fine." And marched into the living room to use the phone in private.

3

"Can you hear what she's saying?" Aunt Helen got up from the table and pressed her ear against the wall.

"No, and I don't want to."

"Chicken."

"You're damn right I am. Her parents probably hate me."

"Oh, no they don't, Billy. They feel terrible about everything that happened."

Pity's even worse than hate. At least you know where you stand with folks that dislike you. I walked over to the counter and picked up my notebook from where I'd left it after breakfast. Melody and Troy had gone upstairs to get ready, leaving us alone for a few minutes. It was now or never.

"Hey, I wanted to ask you something. Have you ever seen this before?" I said, flipping to the page with the sketch of the symbol.

She took the notebook from my hand, eyes narrowing. "No . . . I don't think so." She began tracing the outer lines of the drawing with the tip of her finger, just as I'd done earlier. "What is it?"

"We're not really sure."

"Where did you see it?"

"A bunch of places. It was left at a couple of the memorials."

She looked up at me. "What do you mean, left?"

"Someone drew it."

"That's odd."

"Yeah, we thought so too. Anyway, I was just curious if—"

"Well, *that* was fun," Naomi said, barging into the kitchen. She plopped into a chair at the table.

Aunt Helen sat down across from her. "What did they say?"

"My mom wants me home right away, but I negotiated for a few more hours of freedom." She looked over at me. "I have to be back in time for . . ." Using two fingers from each hand, she made emphatic air quotes. ". . . 'dinner and a looong talk.' They probably called Father Paul to come to the house and perform an exorcism."

Aunt Helen laughed. "Naomi Flynn! You're terrible!"

"*You* are . . . for making me call them."

"I beg your pardon, young lady."

"I know, I know. Just let me pout for a little while longer."

"No time for that," I said. "If you have to be home for dinner . . ." I imitated her air quotes. ". . . 'and a looong talk,' then we need to get moving."

"Okay with me," she said, getting up from the table. "Let's go before Mom comes looking for me."

Smiling, I followed Naomi out of the kitchen—and glimpsed something unsettling from the corner of my eye:

As she rose to her feet, Aunt Helen deliberately nudged my spiral notebook underneath the newspaper, which was still spread out across the table. Then, shoving her hands into her pockets, she trailed us into the living room.

4

While Melody phoned her sister in Richmond and her roommate, Rosalita, back home in York, Troy, Naomi, and I waited outside on the front porch. Aunt Helen had excused herself a few minutes earlier and gone upstairs to take a shower. As soon as I heard the water turn on, I'd snuck back into the kitchen and retrieved my notebook from underneath the newspaper. Now, I sat in a rocking chair at the end of the porch, thinking about what I'd seen.

Why the hell would she do that? No matter how hard I tried, I couldn't come up with a single reasonable explanation. It'd happened in a flash. *Was I mistaken?* After the terror of last night's dream, had my exhausted eyes been playing tricks on me?

"You sure you want to ride bikes into town?" Troy asked. "We can drop you off at the library and swing back later to pick you up."

"It's not far," Naomi said, "and it's a beautiful day. It'll be fun. Right, Billy?"

I heard my name, but not much else. When I looked over at them, both Naomi and Troy were staring at me. "Yeah . . . sure."

Troy laughed. "*That* sounded convincing."

"Sorry. I'm dragging ass after last night."

His smile faded. "Remember the nightmare I told you about? The one where I'm being chased?"

I nodded.

"Last night was way worse. I can't get it out of my head."

Naomi turned away, watching a butterfly flutter in circles before landing on the porch railing. I could tell by the pinched look on her face that she was uncomfortable listening to us talk about the dream. I didn't blame her.

"I'm trying my best to pretend it never happened." I glanced at the door. "What's taking Melody so long?"

"Probably Rosie... she can talk."

"It feels like we're never getting out of here," Naomi said, surveying the street. I could tell she was still worried that her mother might show up.

"We can leave right now," I said, getting up from the rocking chair. "I'll touch base with Farnsworth later this afternoon." I looked over at Troy. "Tell Melody we got—"

The front door swung open.

Melody stepped out onto the porch.

"Speak of the devil," Troy remarked.

Melody's eyes flashed wide. "Don't say that!" And she swatted him on the shoulder.

5

"So everything was okay with your sister?" I asked Melody, walking my old BMX trail bike into the street.

"I think so," Melody said, although something in her tone suggested otherwise.

Troy leaned against the side of the van. For some reason, he was wearing the Waffle House hat again. "You guys blabbed forever."

"That's the thing," Melody replied. "Rosalita never picked up. I called twice and it just rang and rang. I was on the phone the entire time with Tamara... and that's not like her. She hates talking on the telephone. Always has." Melody began twirling her hair with her fingers. "She said all the right things and swore that she was fine. But..."

"But what?" I asked.

"It was like she didn't want to get off the phone with me. Almost as if she was stalling."

"Call her back later today," I said. "Make sure."

She nodded. "I think I'll do that. I'll try Rosie again, as well." She unlocked the van and opened the driver's door. "So, meet you in the park at one?"

"In front of the bandstand." I checked my watch. It was almost nine thirty. We were off to a late start.

Naomi straddled my aunt's ten-speed, flashing a glimpse of long, tan legs, and began riding in circles in the middle of the street. Troy gave me a weird little salute, straightened his Waffle House hat, and climbed into the van's passenger seat. I mounted my bike, adjusted my butt on the narrow seat, and was about to push off when Melody put her hand on my arm.

"Listen," she said in a quiet voice. "This isn't easy to say because I really like her. I think you know that by now." Melody was staring directly at Naomi as she spoke. "But please be careful. The dream we had last night . . . it feels like a warning . . . for the three of us . . . and there's something else—"

"Come on, slowpoke!" Naomi breezed by us on the bicycle. "Let's go!"

"In a minute," I said, with a wave of my hand.

But by the time I looked back at Melody, she'd gotten into the van and slammed the door.

6

In the movie version of my life—if anyone managed to stay awake past the opening credits—this would be the montage scene. The only thing missing was the music.

As Naomi and I rode our bicycles toward downtown Sudbury, it felt as though I were watching a slideshow of my youth.

Ralph Tipton, one of my father's oldest friends, was mowing the grass in his side yard, his liver-spotted arms, legs, and nose smeared with sunscreen. I gave him a wave as we sped past, and he reciprocated, even though I could tell by the confused look on his face that he didn't recognize me.

Further down the street, on the corner of Vista and Park, the driveway was empty in front of the split-level house where my old friend Todd Richardson had grown up. As far as I knew, Todd was wrapping up his spring semester at Gettysburg College, where he was on the lacrosse team. Another couple of weeks, and his metallic-blue Camaro with the glass-pack muffler would once again be parked at the curb, drawing complaints from the neighbors.

Leaving the maze of houses and streets behind us, we merged onto the long downhill straightaway of Franklin Avenue—and the world opened up.

MEMORIALS

On our left, there was Potter's Cornfield, where one memorable Halloween night we'd hid from the cops after decorating our freshman-year math teacher's car with streamers of toilet paper and gobs of shaving cream. When we were kids, we'd nicknamed the straw-stuffed scarecrow that stood guard at the center of the field "Mister Boogeyman," on account of the creepy burlap mask that concealed its pumpkin-shaped head. Through watering eyes, I spotted his dark silhouette poking out of the stalks and gave an involuntary shudder.

A little farther down, on the opposite side of the road, we passed the bottleneck entrance to Jensen's Junkyard. Located at the end of a narrow gravel drive, the gate stood open seven days a week, from 6 a.m. till 8 p.m. Jensen's was the largest privately owned dump in the county—and ever since the previous owner was arrested for selling weed and stolen car parts, the source of considerable controversy. Editorials had been written in the *Sudbury Sun*. A local women's group had picketed the entrance. There'd even been talk of possible FBI raids. As far as I knew, those raids never materialized, and the new ownership was on the straight and narrow.

Really moving now, hair whipping wildly in the wind, Naomi squealing in delight as she negotiated a sweeping bend in the road, hands high in the air like she was riding a roller coaster instead of a ten-speed bike, we blasted over the old stone bridge, startling a squirrel searching for a late breakfast. Directly below—no, already behind us now!—the swimming hole. Every town has one. Ours was about twelve feet deep—depending on the rains—and safe enough for diving or doing flips off the tire swing. Years ago, when I was in middle school, an older girl, Sue Wilson, almost drowned when she developed a bad cramp and no one noticed until it was nearly too late. Jeff Pruitt, a senior on the basketball team pulled her out and gave her CPR right there on the shoreline. I heard they're married now and living in Hanover.

The half-mile stretch of woods that came next had once upon a time served as our own private playground. Within its shadowed confines, my friends and I had built treehouses and forts. Played hide-and-seek and flashlight tag. Shot BB guns and slingshots. We'd waged imaginary wars against imaginary enemies and used packs of matches we'd swiped from cigarette machines to make fires to keep us warm in the snow. In dreams still occasionally visited, it was here that I transformed into Robin Hood roaming free in Sherwood Forest. And in the weeks that followed my parents' accident, I often found myself sneaking off to deep within these woods—to escape all the noise and confusion, the pity and the stares.

And then we were speeding past it, the trees thinning, giving way to rolling green meadows sprinkled with goldenrod, the bittersweet memories whisking away in the soon-to-be-summer breeze behind us, and suddenly downtown Sudbury was stretched out before us like a village in a fairy tale, basking in the morning sunlight, a welcoming golden glaze reflecting off store windows and car windshields, twin church spires rising high into the air, marking the horizon line, the sound of a train running fast alongside the river and an ice cream truck's jangling bell even at this dawn-lit hour, because in Sudbury it was never too early to eat ice cream—and for the first time since the day of the accident, it actually felt like home again.

7

As we rounded the final bend into town, our legs burning and eyes watering, the iron-gated cemetery that stretched from the rear parking lot of St. Ignatius to the edge of the woods beyond swam slowly into view. In the blazing morning sunlight, the polished stone grave markers appeared to be made of glass.

"Do you want to stop?!" Naomi shouted above the rush of the wind, and when I didn't answer: "I think we should!"

As I stared at the grassy hillside where my parents were buried, the tires of my bike drifted dangerously close to the crumbling dirt edge of the drainage ditch that ran alongside the road. Beneath the muddy water, cattails grew and bullfrogs croaked.

"Billy! Watch out!"

Jerking the handlebar hard to the left, I crow-hopped to the center of the gravel-lined shoulder—and then, grinning like a lunatic, lifted both of my hands into the air, as if signaling a touchdown. It was a move I had performed hundreds of times during my childhood, but the nineteen-year-old me had not even the slightest idea how I'd managed it. Heart pounding, I followed Naomi into the St. Ignatius parking lot and pulled up beside her.

"You're crazy, you know that?!" Her long blonde hair had blown free from the pink scrunchie holding it in place. She swiped a tangle of curls out of her eyes and spit the leftover strands from her mouth. With her sun-dazzled eyes and flushed red cheeks, she looked like the high school girl I'd once fallen in love with.

"I had it all the way," I said, wiping the sweat from my brow.

"Uh-huh . . . whatever you say." She stared across the lot at the cemetery. "I hope it's okay that I stopped . . . It just didn't feel right to keep going." I could tell by the sheepish look on her face that she was worried she'd overstepped her bounds.

"It's fine." I leaned over and kissed the tip of her nose. "I'm overdue for a visit."

And I was. The last time I'd been there was October. The woods bordering the cemetery had looked like they were on fire that day—trees bursting with autumn reds and yellows and oranges. Windswept leaves dancing in the breeze. The tang of woodsmoke filling the air. And yet, I still hadn't wanted to be here. I felt much closer to my mom and dad at the Church Street memorial than I did at the cemetery. Don't ask me why; it had *always* been like that. Maybe because, in some strange way, the shoulder of the road where they had died that afternoon felt like it belonged to them . . . and only them . . . while the cemetery belonged to everyone.

I'd talked about these feelings with Dr. Mirarchi, and the last time it came up, we'd conducted an interesting exercise. She'd asked me to close my eyes and picture myself standing at my parents' memorial. After about a minute, she'd said, *Okay, Billy, with your eyes still closed, tell me the first word that comes to mind that best describes how you felt.* My immediate answer: *Calm*. After a short break, we tried the exact same visualization, except this time with me imagining that I was at the cemetery. My just-as-quick answer: *Alone*.

And that right there pretty much summed it up for me. Dr. Mirarchi had a way of doing that.

There were only a handful of cars parked in front of St. Ignatius—the church itself as intimidating as ever with its rough stone walls, stained glass windows, and sky-piercing steeple—including Father Paul's boat of a white Cadillac. As Naomi and I made our way to the back of the lot, I listened for the once familiar strains of Mrs. Crabtree practicing her hymns on the organ. But the building remained silent, dozing in the morning sun.

After cruising past the small metal shed where parishioners dropped off clothes and shoes and canned goods for the poor, we stopped our bikes just short of the grass. Naomi looked at me and said, "I'll wait for you here."

"You sure?"

She straddled the ten-speed, stretching her arms above her head. It felt especially sinful to admire her legs in such close proximity to a church, so I purposely looked away.

"Yeah . . . you go ahead." She gazed at the sea of gravestones. "I come here a lot."

I didn't know how to answer that, so I said nothing and started walking. The grass in the cemetery was longer than I remembered, and my shoes made a *swish*ing sound as I wound my way between the gravestones. *Probably all those thunderstorms making it grow faster . . . the poor groundskeeper can't keep up.* I detoured around a narrow rectangle of recently turned earth. The lawn around it was trampled and faded. Someone had been buried there recently. I wondered who it was and if perhaps I might have known them.

As I walked, my eyes were drawn to the names and numbers on the headstones. Many of them dated hundreds of years apart. LUCINDA RADFORD * 1891–1947. THOMAS ARCHER * 1784–1809. RICHARD EVERGREEN * 1903–1911. CHARLES BEAUMONT * 1949–1977. Dozens of engraved angels stared back at me, tracking my progress with unblinking eyes.

Until I stopped beside a wooden bench adorned with a silver plaque bearing my parents' names. A gift from my father's former boss. Directly in

MEMORIALS

front of the bench, matching bouquets of fresh flowers rested atop my parents' gravestone. Probably Aunt Helen or Naomi had left them there. I sat down.

Thomas William Anderson   Lori Marie Anderson
1938–1980   1939–1980
In Loving Memory

"Hey, Momma. Hey, Pops . . . I'm sorry it's been so long. School's been really busy . . . and I'm trying to focus a little more on the present these days . . . and not so much on the past. That doesn't mean I don't think about you, though. Because I do. All the time." Despite the fact that I was alone in the cemetery and Naomi was standing too far away to hear, I found myself whispering. "A few months ago . . . I started seeing a counselor. You'd both really like her. She's smart and nice and sees right through my bullshit. She's helped me a lot."

My voice was beginning to waver—which meant it was time to wrap it up. "Anyway, I just wanted to say hello . . . and tell you that I really miss you. Aunt Helen and I are taking good care of each other. She's pretty amazing . . . but you already know that. Well . . . I guess that's all for now . . ."

I stood up from the bench. "Oh yeah . . . I'm back to doing photography again . . . and I've made some new friends at school. Really good people. I thought that would make you happy . . ."

I wiped my eyes with the back of my hand and turned to go.

Father Paul was standing right behind me.

"Jesus . . ." I stumbled backward. "Christ!" And then remembered where I was and who I was talking to. "Sorry, Father."

He lifted a hand. "No, no, entirely my fault. I apologize. I should have kept my distance." He grinned that cherub grin. "I just got excited . . . seeing you twice now within a week."

Glancing behind him, I noticed that the parking lot was empty. The ten-speed left abandoned in the grass. A finger of unease tickled the back of my throat. "Did you see Naomi?"

He gestured to the church. "She went inside to use the ladies' room. She told me to tell you she'll be right back."

"Oh, okay . . . thanks."

We started walking.

"All finished with your documentary?"

"I wish. We're headed to the library to do more research. And then, tomorrow, it's back to school to begin editing."

"It was nice of you to stop by and visit your mom and dad." He glanced over his shoulder. "You say hello to your uncle?"

I didn't want to lie to a priest, but the truth of it was that I hadn't even thought of stopping by Uncle Frank's grave. I was a terrible person. "Umm . . . not today . . . saving that for when we have a little more time."

He waved a meaty hand in the air. "Aww, he'd just tell you the same thing he tells me every time I wander over and pay a visit: 'Stop your damn moping and get back to living your life . . . before I crawl outta here and haunt your house.'" The priest's booming laughter echoed across the grounds. A squadron of startled birds took flight from the roof of the church.

"I ran across a box of his poker chips the other day at Aunt Helen's. I wish I'd been old enough to play with you guys . . . even just once."

"We still play! Not every week like we used to . . . but once a month or thereabouts. Son, you are hereby officially invited to the next game. Just, uh . . . don't tell your aunt."

I smiled. "It'll probably have to be this summer, but count me in."

"Of course, it's not the same without Frank." A wistful expression came over his face. "But we have a good enough time, all right. Teddy Farkins still remembers the good old days like they were last week and can tell a heck of a story. Same with Lars Beaumont, he's from across the river." The priest's eyes sparkled as he spoke. "But none of them, sorry to say, hold a candle to your uncle. That ole rascal could spin a tall tale with the best of 'em."

"Tall tale?"

He looked at me. "Oh, Billy . . . with a bunch of stubborn old skinflints like us sitting 'round the table, you didn't really think poker was our main source of entertainment, did ya?"

I honestly had no flipping idea what he was talking about—but now he had me curious. So I played along. "I . . . guess not."

"*You guess not*." That booming laughter again. "Listen, those Saturday-night card games lasted past midnight for two reasons and two reasons only. One: we ate like kings. The host each week was responsible for putting out a spread . . . and let me tell you . . ." He patted his ample belly. ". . . anything less than a veritable feast was *severely* frowned upon."

"And the second reason?" I looked up and saw Naomi strolling toward us across the parking lot.

"We swapped stories, son. Shot the breeze. Most nights, the dealing was done by eleven or so. Sometimes even earlier. We'd get tired of paying attention to the cards and just toss 'em aside and get down to talking."

"What kind of stories?"

"Oh, a little bit of everything . . . happenings around town . . . rumors making the rounds . . . the more mysterious and scandalous the better. Local myths . . . legends . . . tales from the olden days. . . ." There was no booming laugh this time, just a dry-mouthed chuckle under his breath.

"Would you be willing to do another interview for our film?" Before he could respond, I went on: "Not about the memorials . . . or my parents . . . just to add some local flavor, maybe tell a few of those interesting stories about the area." And then, scared that he was going to turn me down: "I promise it won't take long."

"What won't take long?" Naomi asked as she joined us. Her hair was once again swept back in a ponytail, her cheeks still rosy.

"I'd like to interview Father Paul again," I told her. "Later this afternoon . . . if he lets us."

Her face brightened even more. "That's a great idea."

I looked at the priest with my best puppy-dog eyes. "What do you say, Father? Do us this favor, please?"

"Tell you what," he said. "Let me invite Teddy Farkins to tag along, and you got yourself a deal."

Grinning, I stuck out my hand. "Done." And we shook on it.

8

There's a quiet efficiency to small-town mornings. Delivery trucks prowl the predawn streets like prehistoric creatures on the hunt. Groggy teenagers on bicycles toss newspapers onto stoops and driveways—and the occasional porch roof. A lonely patch of light marks the cracked sidewalk in front of the bakery. Inside, bright-eyed workers, covered in flour, are already hard at work. Just down the street, early birds and commuters, perched elbow to elbow on worn stools, down cups of black coffee and boost their cholesterol counts, while stifling a succession of yawns. A television mounted on the wall plays the morning news. No one says much—not even when the busty weathergirl takes her turn—until Old Man Potter and Chuck Tanner show up. Then, it's baseball and politics and the exorbitant price of feed—and the diner really starts to wake up.

Most of the town waits for the sun before opening its eyes. The Corner Grocery Store—how's that for a clever name?—and Freddie Cavanaugh's Gas 'n' Save. The trio of banks and the post office and schools. Drayton's Day Care and the old folks' home. Doc Tillman and both dentists—Freddy Lepp, who's been around for decades, and Jim Schall, fresh out of college in Philadelphia. The shopkeepers along Main Street show up next. Refilling their cash drawers, wiping down their windows, and flipping CLOSED signs to OPEN.

Soon enough, the sidewalks are bustling. Young mothers and children, most of them in a hurry. Strolling couples window-shopping. Joggers and fast walkers—you know the type: arms pumping, hips swiveling, human roosters in motion—weaving around the others, looking to burn calories from last night's dessert and earning the occasional dirty look from folks with no place to be.

When Naomi and I pulled up in front of the squat brick building that housed the Sudbury Library at 10:05 a.m., the town was humming with activity. Some outsiders may have thought that impossible for a small Pennsylvania town on a quiet Wednesday morning in mid-May—but they would be wrong.

We locked the bikes in the rack out front and were halfway to the door when Jenny Caldwell swung to the curb in her brother's souped-up Toyota Supra and blew the horn. Def Leppard's *Pyromania* blasted from the speakers, earning her the stink eye and a waggling finger from an old lady waiting to cross the street.

"Go ahead," Naomi said, already turning around. "I'll catch up."

I gave her a nod and kept walking—but didn't go inside. Instead, I eased behind one of the circular concrete pillars that marked the library's main entrance and stood there catching my breath.

Translation: I hid in the shadows like a rat and did my best to eavesdrop.

The only problem was, with the radio blaring I couldn't hear a damn thing.

I was about to give up when the conversation came to an abrupt halt, with Naomi spinning on her heels and storming away. Then, clear as day, I heard Jenny shout, "*SO FUCKING STUPID! I NEVER THOUGHT YOU'D FALL FOR HIS BULLSHIT ALL OVER AGAIN!*"

Before Naomi could spot me, I ducked into the library.

9

The woman at the front counter recognized me immediately.

"Hey there, Billy Anderson!" she said with a smile. "Your aunt mentioned you'd be stopping by." She put down the stack of paperwork she was holding. "Where are your friends?"

She what . . . ? Aunt Helen and her loose lips strike again. Why would she do that? I thought again of her hiding my notebook under the newspaper. *No telling what else she blabbed.*

"They're around. We split up so we could—" I heard the door swing open behind me.

"Well, there's one of them. Good morning, Naomi."

"Morning, Mrs. Brighton."

Naomi took hold of my arm, and once again, I felt that joyful jolt of electricity throughout my body. Then, just as quickly, it was gone—and I was doing my best not to pull away from her. Mrs. Brighton was staring at Naomi's hand. The longtime librarian and substitute teacher lived on the same street as Naomi. She played bridge every weekend with a group of neighborhood women, including Naomi's mom.

"Your aunt tells me you're working on a project for college." Her eyes remained glued on Naomi's hand, which was now caressing my arm. "If I can be of any help . . . just let me know."

"I sure will," I said, taking that as my cue to get out of there. "Thanks." With Naomi still hanging on to me and Aunt Helen's meddling swimming around in my head, I hurried toward the rows of narrow cabinets that housed the library's card catalog.

Behind us, Mrs. Brighton said, "It's nice to see you in Sudbury again, Billy. It's been far too long."

Without looking back, I flipped her a wave over my shoulder and continued walking to the far side of the room.

"You were kind of rude, don't you think?" Naomi said, finally letting go of me.

"Did you see the way she was looking at your hand on my arm?"

"So what?"

"So what if she tells your mother?"

"So what if she does?"

"I'm thinking that won't be good. I can't imagine she'd be thrilled to hear about . . . us."

She frowned. "You think too much."

"Everything okay with Jenny?" I asked, eager to change the subject.

"Eh. You know her. Always drama."

"Sorry."

"Don't be. I'm used to it."

"So . . . ," I said, stopping in front of the cabinet that housed indexes for books whose titles began with the letters *R* to *T*. "Your job is to look up newspaper articles on microfiche. See if you can find any information that ties together our list of victims . . ." Just running my fingers across the polished dark oak brought back a flood of bittersweet memories from my childhood. All the times my mother had driven me here, patiently waiting while I agonized over which books I wanted to check out. I felt a lump forming in the back of my throat. ". . . while I, um, see if I can find out anything else about the symbol."

She clicked the heels of her sneakers together. "Encyclopedia Brown reporting for duty."

"Wouldn't you rather be Nancy Drew?"

"Nope," she said, pirouetting and walking away. "Encyclopedia Brown is way cooler."

Smiling, I watched as she disappeared around the corner. I glanced at the front desk. Mrs. Brighton was studying her paperwork again—or at least doing a good job of pretending she was. For some reason, I didn't trust her. At all. Librarians were nosy by nature. Just look at Aunt Helen.

Turning back to the cabinet, I opened a drawer in the bottom row and began flipping through the throng of index cards. After a moment, I found the one I was looking for.

Across the top of the small cream-colored card, a single word had been typed: *SATANISM*.

10

Excerpt from *The Devil Is in the Details* by Matthew Kavanaugh (Limestone Publishing, 1980), page 114:

"Unfortunately, there still exists a widespread misinterpretation of what satanism actually involves," William Scales explained shortly after his June 1977 arrest. "The general public, thanks largely to backyard rumormongering and irresponsible journalism, continues to believe that satanism is a cesspool of evil and violence and debauchery. They hear the word, and it immediately conjures up images of crazy-eyed disciples dancing naked around a roaring fire while performing deadly rituals and human sacrifice."

William Scales and his wife, Barbara, both residents of Oak Hill, California, were arrested by local law enforcement officials after a monthlong investigation stemming from accusations that Mr. and Mrs. Scales were providing underage youth with illegal drugs and alcohol, as well as desecrating local monuments. Upon searching the suspects' residence, police discovered a cache of unregistered firearms, as well as numerous items that had been reported stolen from the garages and sheds of nearby neighbors. In addition, a wealth of printed material related to the Church of Satan was found on the premises . . .

Excerpt from *The Church of Satan: Dark Religion & Its Origins* by Peter McDermmit (Zebra Books, 1977), pp. 23–24:

The Church of Satan employs a specific set of guiding principles known as the Nine Satanic Statements. They were written by Church of Satan founder, Anton Szandor LaVey, and published in 1969 via The Satanic Bible. LaVey, a writer, occultist, musician, and actor viewed "Satan" not as a literal entity, but as a historic and literary figure symbolic of Earthly values . . .

Excerpt from *Satanism: Fact and Fiction* by Sandra R. Warren (Stonehenge Books, 1981), pp. 272–273:

In addition to the more widely publicized symbols utilized by many practitioners of satanism (inverted crosses, pentagrams, all-seeing eyes,

MEMORIALS

etc.), there exists a plethora of other, lesser-known cyphers representing a variety of obscure meanings.

Some of these symbols, pictured below, are used to denote sacred ground, extend invitations to secret ceremonies, and summon the presence of various demons. Others are used to solicit good fortune, provide protection, or even publicly communicate with other church members who wish to remain anonymous.

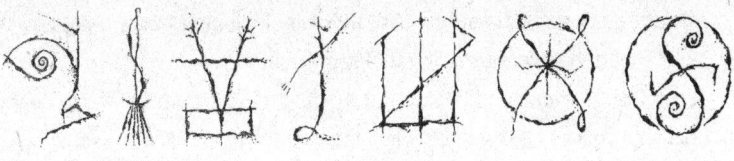

Excerpt from *The Fall of the Catholic Church* by Stephen Spinetti (Simon & Schuster Books, 1983), pp. 89–90:

"And then there's the story of seventeen-year-old Allen Jacobs from Gaithersburg, Maryland," explained Tom Nugent, a veteran reporter for the *Philadelphia Inquirer* and the author of the December 21, 1981, article entitled "Satanic Panic: An Epidemic."

"His parents first noticed a difference in their son during the summer of 1981. He began wearing dark clothing and letting his hair grow long. He painted his fingernails black and began listening to heavy metal music. When he stopped hanging around his friends from the football team and began associating with an entirely different group of teens from a nearby school, his parents sat him down and talked to him.

"Allen insisted that everything was okay. He'd simply grown apart from many of his old friends, who, according to him, were obsessed with drinking beer and smoking weed. His new friend group wasn't like that. They played card games and Dungeons & Dragons, held all-night movie marathons, and listened to music. His parents came away from the conversation convinced that Allen was telling the truth: *everything was okay.*

"But they were wrong. *Nothing* was okay.

"Allen Jacobs had fallen in with a group of eighteen-to-thirty-year-old men and women who called themselves 'The Dark Lords.' Numbering anywhere from a dozen to a dozen and a half members, the group actively worshipped the ultimate Dark Lord, Satan (whom they most often referred to as Beelzebub). The group was responsible for the violent deaths of numerous local animals, including dogs, cats, cows, and sheep that were used in ritual sacrifices.

"On the evening of September 4, 1981, days before he was to begin his final year of high school, Allen Jacobs, acting on his own, something he would later admit to local police, used a fist-sized rock he'd found in the park to knock twelve-year-old Timothy Poole unconscious. He then dragged the young boy to where his car was parked, heaved him into the back seat, and drove to one of the Dark Lords' ceremonial sites in a nearby wooded area.

"When Timothy Poole regained consciousness a short time later, he was tied with his arms behind his back to a wooden stake that had been pounded into the ground. A shirtless Allen Jacobs was standing in front of him with a knife in his hand.

"In the police report, Allen described what happened next in his own words:

As soon as he opened his eyes, I began the incantation. Just like I'd practiced. I used the knife to cut myself across the chest, and then I sliced off Timothy's T-shirt. He immediately started crying. When I drew the knife across his chest, he began flailing and screaming. He was so loud I became worried that someone might hear, so I used what was left of his shirt to gag him. When that was done, I continued with the invocation . . . first, wetting my fingers with my blood and wiping it onto his chest, and then repeating it with his blood and my own chest. Then, I bent down and began drinking a mixture of our blood from his breast. As I did, something moved high in the trees above me. I heard branches shift and break, and then a voice calling out my name. A few seconds later, I felt His warm breath on the back of my neck. I don't remember anything else after that . . .

"Allen Jacobs's father called the police and reported him missing just before midnight that same evening. Allen had skipped a family dinner at 7 p.m., and none of his friends, new or old, knew where he was. At 1:37 a.m., Allen's car was located in a parking lot alongside a popular basketball court. It was empty and there was no apparent signs of foul play. At 2:14 a.m., a patrol officer discovered Allen wandering down the middle of nearby Pinecrest Street. His chest, arms, and face were smeared with blood. He was holding a gore-streaked hunting knife, later identified as having belonged to his father. Allen was noncommunicative, his pupils were fully dilated, and he appeared to be in a deep stupor. The officer immediately suspected drugs, but later that day Allen's blood screen came back negative. At 4:02 a.m., Timothy Poole's body was discovered in the woods. He had been disemboweled and his neck had been sliced so deeply that the coroner suspected that Allen Jacobs had attempted to decapitate him. The boy's eyes were missing . . ."

11

I looked up from the book I was reading—and Naomi was standing there watching me.

"Jesus!" I said, pushing my chair away from the table. "You've got to stop sneaking up on me."

"I didn't sneak. I walked."

"Then why didn't you say something? Instead of just standing there spying on me."

Easy, Billy . . . watch your tone. I'd been thinking about what Melody had said to me earlier by the van—about last night's dream being a warning for the three of us. What she obviously hadn't had a chance to say was that she thought we needed to keep a closer eye on Naomi.

"I wasn't spying on you," she said, walking closer. "And I didn't say anything for two reasons. One: you were so into whatever it was you were reading . . . you looked adorable. You kept rubbing your eyes and doing that thing with your lip where you—"

"Yeah, yeah," I said, smiling now, but wanting more than anything for her to stop.

Lowering her voice, she said, "And two: I didn't want Mrs. Brighton to hear me."

I glanced at the front counter. The stool behind it was empty. "Why not?"

"She wouldn't leave me alone. She kept barging in with one excuse after the other. Trying to peek at what I was doing. If you ask me . . . *she's* the spy."

12

The bandstand was located at the northern end of Sudbury Park.

In all the years I'd lived there, I'd only seen it officially in use during the town's annual Fourth of July celebration. Once the parade was finished marching the four-and-a-half-block route from the parking lot in front of the high school to the intersection of Main Street and Ripley Avenue, the band waited until just before dusk to reassemble and then played a rousing concert while fireworks lit up the sky above the park. Half the town gathered on blankets and lawn chairs. Red-white-and-blue bunting hung from the bandstand's wooden railings. Members of the Rotary Club handed out miniature American flags. Fathers with beer on their breath laughed too loud, little kids with ice cream–smeared faces chased each other around with sparklers grasped in their tiny fingers, and tired mothers called out for them to be careful and stop running before someone tripped and really hurt themselves, while the older teenagers snuck away in the dark to the nearby woods to light cherry bombs and make out.

When I was twelve, I got into my first real fight—if you could even call it that—in front of the bandstand. It was a Saturday afternoon, and my friends and I were on our way home from the movie theater. None of us saw Floyd Roebuck sitting there smoking or we would have cut across the park to avoid him. By the time Craig McGinty noticed the plume of cigarette smoke wafting out of the shadows, it was too late.

Although we were all in the same grade, Floyd was two years older and an unrepentant bully. He'd once made a sixth grader eat a hunk of dog crap because the kid had stepped on his brand-new sneakers in the hallway at school. A head taller than the next-biggest kid in our class, Floyd walked around with a lopsided buzz cut (it was rumored that his mom cut his hair, but no one had the guts to ask him), a face full of acne, and a lazy left eye. His only friend was a ninth grader who went by the nickname of Stank. The two of them lived on the same street. On a daily basis during the school year, we all did our best to remain out of their orbit.

And it mostly worked—until that fateful (*see, Melody, I do believe . . .*) Saturday afternoon.

As soon as he spotted the cigarette smoke, Craig poked me in the ribs and nodded toward the bandstand, a stricken look on his usually cheerful face. I looked over and saw Floyd right away. He was slouched down with his scuffed-up boots propped up on one of the railings, glaring at us, the glowing tip of his cigarette looking like the little red battery light on the smoke detector my father had installed in our upstairs hallway.

Tommy Pierce and Glenn Altman, lagging a step behind us, were arguing about who was the better third baseman—Brooks Robinson or Mike Schmidt. It was a long-standing debate, and so far, neither one of them had been willing to budge. I turned around to shush them—and that's when Floyd finally spoke up.

"Hey, kid, lemme see that Orioles hat." He lowered his boots from the railing and slowly sat up, the cigarette still dangling from his mouth. Ash drifted to the bandstand's wood floor like dirty flakes of snow.

Tommy and Glenn startled into silence, we all kept walking. I felt Craig's fingers tug on the side of my T-shirt. I knew exactly what that gesture meant: *Don't stop. Keep going.*

"You deaf or something?" Floyd growled. "I said hand over the fuckin' hat."

I stopped and turned to face him. We were all wearing ball caps, but mine was the only one with the Baltimore Orioles bird on the front, so I was the target today. "My uncle gave it to me for my birthday," I said, voice cracking.

"So fuckin' what?" He tossed the still-burning cigarette over his shoulder into the grass. "I'm not gonna steal it. I just wanna take a look at it."

I thought about running—my right leg twitched and I almost took off—but I knew that he would catch me. Even with him wearing those heavy boots with the laces untied, I didn't have a chance. I'd seen him playing kickball during recess. He was big and stupid looking, but he was also *fast*. Probably because his legs were so damn long.

Sweating now, I shuffled forward until I was close enough to take off my hat and hand it to him. As he reached for it, I noticed his dirty fingernails and a swastika drawn in black ink across the top of his right hand.

He immediately placed the Orioles cap on his head, gripped it by the bill (offering another glimpse of those disgusting fingernails), and wiggled it around for a moment. Then he took it off and used both hands to stretch it out. I wanted to holler at him to stop or grab it and take off running—but instead I just stood there like the coward I was.

Speaking of cowards, Tommy, standing far behind me, chose that moment to make his escape. "Well, I'm gonna be late for dinner. See you guys tomorrow." By the time I turned around to look, he was already hurrying away toward town, but in the opposite direction of his house. Glenn, who hadn't muttered a single word, was right behind him. A part of me never forgave either of them. Only Craig remained standing his ground—all five-foot-two of him.

The next sixty seconds played out pretty much exactly as I'd feared.

Pissed off because my friends had abandoned me, I turned back to face Floyd Roebuck. My favorite Orioles cap was once again perched atop his head. The fucker had bent the bill in the middle like Thurman Munson from the Yankees—an act considered sacrilege to this longtime Orioles fan—and stretched out the elastic. A familiar sneer had wormed its way onto his ugly face. "You know what," he said with a tone of mock surprise, "I've changed my mind. I think I *am* gonna keep it."

Before I could say anything, Craig stepped up beside me. "It's not yours to keep. Give it back."

Floyd's eyes widened. "What did you just say to me?"

"You heard me, shitbird. The hat was a birthday gift. Give it back."

In an eyeblink, Floyd was up and out of the bandstand—and standing right in front of us. I could smell stale onions on his breath. With one hand, he took hold of Craig's T-shirt collar. I heard it rip. With the other, he reached around and seized the back of Craig's underwear, jerking him off the ground. Legs dangling, Craig howled in agony as his size 24 Fruit of the Looms sliced into his balls and knifed between his butt cheeks.

And that's when the script diverted entirely from my frightened expectations—the inevitable beatdown of me and my lone loyal friend, resulting in matching black eyes, bloody noses, and split lips—and the world flipped upside down.

Instead of crying and begging for mercy as so many others before him had done, Craig threw back his head and growled like a feral animal snared in a trap—and then reached up with the fingers of his right hand and clawed Floyd Roebuck in both of his eyes.

The big bully shrieked in surprise and let go of Craig's underwear. Craig dropped to the grass in a twisted heap. Above him, Floyd began spinning wildly, his balled-up fists pressed against his ravaged eyes. He screeched even louder—an ungodly sound—and a spray of thick yellow snot erupted from his nose.

Now on one knee, a red-faced Craig wound up and unleashed an uppercut directly into Floyd Roebuck's testicles. There was a meaty *smacking* sound—like the Italian Stallion, Rocky Balboa, battering a side of slaughterhouse beef—followed by a *whoosh* of expelled onion breath, and then all of the color drained out of Floyd's face. He bent over with his hands on his knees, squeezing his legs tightly together, a thin moan escaping from his lips.

Inspired by my friend's amazing act of courage and eager to get in on the action myself, I circled behind the wounded Floyd, got a good five-yard running start, and kicked him squarely in the ass. He flew forward, his forehead striking the ground with a loud *thunk*, and immediately curled up on his side with his knees pressed against his chest.

Craig and I stood over him, our hands balled into fists, listening to him moan. At that moment, I wished more than anything that I had a camera so I could capture proof of what we'd done. No one was going to believe us, especially that traitorous duo, Timmy and Glenn.

Leaning down, I snatched my hat from the ground. The Orioles logo was smeared with grass stains. The bright orange bill disfigured. Using both hands, I tried to bend it back into shape, but it was no use. "It's fucking ruined, you dickwad." I kicked a dirt clod at the back of his head, but missed.

". . . when . . . catch you . . . both dead…" He was wheezing now, one hand cradling his injured balls, the other clawing blindly at the grass. His eyes squeezed shut, a single tear cascaded down his cheek.

"Oh yeah, you big crybaby . . . why don't you go home and fuck your mom!" Craig hooted in his face, and I knew it was time for us to seriously get out of there.

With my arm draped around my friend's shoulder, we hustled across the field and took the shortcut to our houses. As we entered the overgrown path in the woods, I took one last look behind us. Floyd Roebuck was still on the ground, but he was sitting up now, staring down at his crotch. We went a little faster after seeing that.

Before he went inside, I thanked Craig for not running away and leaving me all alone. He grinned at me with those buck teeth of his and said, "No problem. You would've done the same for me." And he was right—I would have.

Fortunately for us, Floyd's family moved away not long after our battle by the bandstand. That's not to say we didn't live in fear for our lives until the afternoon we saw the moving van drive out of town. We most definitely did. And there were several close calls, too. Once, after a Friday matinee of *The Bad News Bears,* Craig and I took the shortcut through the alley behind Lowe's Department Store and almost walked right into Floyd and his cronies perched on a tower of old pallets. They were smoking weed and throwing rocks over the roof onto Main Street. Luckily, we saw them before they spotted us, and with the help of a fifty-yard head start, we were able to get away. Another time, after baseball practice, we were forced to walk home because Craig's bike had a flat tire. My bike was fine, but there was no way I was leaving him behind. As we strolled around the corner onto the street where Craig lived, we glimpsed Floyd ducking behind a telephone pole up ahead in the distance. Fighting panic, we immediately stopped in the middle of the road, pondering our options: *Abandon our bikes and turn around and run like the devil was chasing us . . . or make a break for the nearest house, ring the doorbell, and pray that someone answered.* In the end, it hadn't mattered. Mere seconds later, as if sent directly from the heavens above, Craig's father pulled up beside us in his pick-up truck, Johnny Cash warbling from the cheap speakers. We'd piled our bikes into the back and hopped in the front seat. When we cruised past the telephone pole, Floyd was nowhere in sight.

And then a week or so later, he was gone for good, without any further incident. I can't remember where his family ended up moving to, but I think his father got a job somewhere down south. Florida, maybe or

Alabama. It's weird how time and memory work. Before today, I honestly hadn't thought about Floyd Roebuck in years.

13

By the time Naomi showed me what she'd found in the microfiche files and we finished returning the stack of books to their appropriate shelves—being extra careful not to leave behind any clues for Busybody Brighton to find—we were running late for our one o'clock rendezvous with Melody and Troy.

Anxious to hear what they'd discovered at the newspaper office, we hurried across the street—me holding my breath as a red pickup truck rounded the corner behind us, the teenage girl in the driver's seat gunning the engine—and made our way into the park, dodging an endless parade of neon-clad bicyclists and weaving our way through a succession of slowpoke dog walkers. Abandoning the pathway, we hustled past the playground—overrun at this hour with packs of squealing toddlers—and cut across the outfield of the softball field. Once we cleared a stand of trees growing dangerously close to the left-field foul line—the white chalk almost invisible now after last night's doubleheader—I spotted Melody and Troy standing in the shade of the bandstand. And they weren't alone.

"That's Craig McGinty," Naomi said. "What's he doing here?"

Speak of the devil, indeed. "I have no idea."

"Well, try to be nice to him."

"I'm always nice."

"Mm-hmm."

Craig bounded down the bandstand stairs to greet us. "Billy fucking *Anderson!*"

I wanted to turn around and run. Instead, I muttered, "In the flesh. How ya doing, Craig?"

He started to come in for a hug, saw my outstretched hand, and lowered his arms in embarrassment. After we shook, he said hello to Naomi and then glanced over at Melody and Troy. "I was starting to think your friends were pulling my leg."

Troy grinned. "I told him you're never on time for anything."

"Craig was a big help to us," Melody said.

"You work at the newspaper?"

"Technically, I'm just an intern. I'm still full-time at Hillsdale Community." He gestured to Naomi. "We're actually in the same public-speaking class."

Just a handful of years ago, Craig McGinty had been one of my closest friends in the world. He'd stood up for me against Floyd Roebuck, and I'd let him cry on my shoulder when Kari Buehner broke up with him on prom night. I'd even asked him to serve as a pallbearer at my parents' funeral. Now? I knew practically nothing about him. Of course, I had everything to do with that, but still . . . his life had just moved on without me, despite how important we'd once been to each other. "That's great," I said, feeling like a first-class loser.

"I still can't believe you're here," he said. "Wait until the other guys find out. Tommy will be bummed he missed you. He'll be home from USC next week."

"How's he doing?" I asked. And I was shocked to discover that I was genuinely curious. Dr. Mirarchi had told me that this would happen—that a part of my brain would eventually unlock itself . . . and I'd begin to care again.

"You know Tommy. Wherever he goes, it's a party."

"I guess some things never change."

Craig didn't say anything right away—and I knew that he was thinking about my parents. Finally, he glanced at his wristwatch. "Man, I hate to cut this short, but I should probably get going. I only have thirty minutes for lunch and my boss is a real dick."

"Thanks again for your help," Melody said. "You really saved the day."

"My pleasure," he said with a shy smile that I remembered from any number of middle school dances. Melody had obviously once again worked her magic. The poor guy was smitten. "And good luck with your project. I'm sure you'll get an A."

"If we do, it'll be because of you," she said, and he actually blushed.

"If I hear back from anyone else, I'll call you at Billy's aunt's house."

"Our hero," Troy said, and I could tell that he meant it. Surprisingly, I felt a tiny sting of jealousy.

Turning to me, Craig reached out his hand, then quickly raised it—and patted me on the shoulder. Not knowing what else to do, I patted him back.

"I know you're headed back to York tomorrow, but I'd love to hang out next time you're in town. I've missed you, man."

I looked at Naomi. "I should be around a lot more this summer." Her smile banished the storm clouds and lit up the afternoon sky.

"Awesome!" he said. "I'll tell Tommy and the other guys. They'll be seriously stoked."

14

"Well . . . that was awkward," Troy said as the four of us stood and watched Craig walk away.

"Tell me about it," I said.

"What was that whole patting-on-the-shoulder business?" Melody asked. "Boys are so weird."

Naomi gave my arm a squeeze. "I thought it was cute."

Troy tilted his head back and made a gagging sound.

"Maybe give me a little warning next time you're going to show up with one of my old friends?"

"Yeah, sorry about that," Melody said. "He pretty much insisted on tagging along. He really wanted to see you."

"You said he was a big help . . . how much did you tell him?"

"Not much," Troy said. "Just that we were looking for background info on some of the folks we wanted to include in the documentary."

"He got on the phone," Melody said. "Talked to a couple reporters from other newspapers."

"And a woman at a local television station," Troy added. "He even spoke to someone at the sheriff's office. Your boy really came through for us, Billy."

Yeah . . . *my boy, who I haven't seen or talked to in years.*

I sighed, feeling shitty all over again. "So . . . what did you find out?"

15

"I'm not sure what it all amounts to," Troy said, spreading out several sheets of notepaper covered in his neat handwriting. "Maybe nothing."

We were sitting at a picnic table far enough away from the path to offer us some privacy. Several joggers wearing Walkman headphones strode past. A couple of teenagers on skateboards. A gray-haired man carrying a bag of peanuts on his way to feed the squirrels.

"We couldn't find out much of anything about the Harley-Davidson guy," he said. "There was no coverage in the paper about the accident, and nothing on the news."

"I didn't find anything on him either," Naomi said. She'd already filled in the group about what she'd discovered in the microfiche files. It hadn't taken very long. Unlike the York College library—which subscribed to a multitude of newspapers, ranging from small regional publications to the big guns like the *Philadelphia Inquirer* and the *New York Times*—my hometown library offered only the *Sudbury Sun*. And even then, it only went back six years.

"My guess is he isn't from anywhere around here," Melody said. "After the accident, someone from his family or maybe some friends made a pilgrimage to the site, set up the memorial in his honor, and haven't been back since."

I nodded. "That makes sense."

Naomi frowned. "That makes me sad."

"We had better luck with the other names on the list." Troy stared down at his notes and began to read out loud: "Chase Harper. Thirty-six years old. Home is Exeter, Pennsylvania. We already know about his wife, Jennifer, and their son. The old dude at the gas station said the Harper family was religious, but that doesn't really cover it. For a while, when he was younger, Chase Harper had designs on becoming a priest. He attended a seminary in Baltimore but left after a year. At the time of his death, he was a deacon at his church and also the treasurer. Jennifer Harper still teaches Sunday school classes there. Police report notes nothing odd about the accident. His wife mentioned Chase had been extra tired in the weeks before because he hadn't been sleeping well. It was late and he'd been on the road for hours. The thinking is he fell asleep at the wheel.

"Moving on to Michael Meredith. Seventeen years old. Leesburg. Hometown hero to all—except, as we saw, his older sister Penny. Between our old pal Pondo, psycho big sis, and a slew of newspaper articles about the accident, we already know quite a bit about Michael. Today, we learned a little bit more. He was no altar boy, but he really was a good kid. One of Michael's closest friends, name of Skip Phillips, was crippled in a hunting accident when he was fourteen. Ever since then, Michael had filled in as a kind of de facto older brother, helping Skip with his homework, driving him to school, even taking him back and forth to his PT appointments. Michael also talked the coach into letting Skip keep stats for the baseball team. Skip even got to ride the bus to away games. A local TV reporter said there were a lot of stories like that about Meredith. One of the parents went so far as to call him Leesburg's 'guardian angel.' However . . . there was . . ."

He traced his finger across the bottom of the sheet of paper until he found his place again.

"There *was* something kind of strange about Michael's accident. Your friend Craig spoke with someone at the sheriff's department—I didn't get the name, like a dumbass—but whoever it was made a call to a cop friend who works in Leesburg. That friend told him that no skid marks were found at the scene, and they figure Meredith was traveling in excess of eighty miles an hour when his car struck the bridge abutment. The car basically disintegrated and Michael's body was thrown over the bridge and into the creek below. The funeral was closed casket, as you can imagine."

MEMORIALS

Naomi groaned and inched closer to me on the picnic table bench. I didn't blame her. It was difficult to listen to such gruesome details, especially after what had happened to my parents.

"Evidently, there was some talk around school that maybe it *hadn't* really been an accident. A couple of his friends told their parents that Michael hadn't been himself in the days leading up to the crash. He'd seemed distant. Distracted. And how about that: he was always tired."

A sudden flash of color among the bushes lining the path caught my attention. A girl in a yellow shirt. There and gone in a blink. I was almost positive it had been Jenny Caldwell spying on us. I started to say something, but before I could, Troy picked up the story again.

"The girl he'd been dating told her mother that Michael had been moody. He'd failed a vocabulary quiz, almost got into a fight at practice. He'd also been spending an unusual amount of time at the school library. Whenever one of his friends tried to join him, he'd shoo them away. No one knows why. Your buddy Craig left a message with the librarian . . . a Mrs. Lowenstein . . . to see if she might have any more information."

Melody reached across the table and shuffled together the remaining sheets of paper. "Why don't you and Naomi read the rest for yourselves? It'll be quicker than listening to Troy's lecture."

Troy gave her a hurt look. "Well, *excuuuse* me."

She pointed toward the sky above the softball field. Dark thunderclouds had gathered along the horizon. A stiff breeze ruffled the treetops. Somewhere in the distance I heard the soothing tinkle of wind chimes. "No offense, Troy, but I think we're running out of time."

I took the notes from her hand, placed them in front of us so that Naomi could see, and began reading.

16

Ten minutes later, when I finally looked up, everyone was staring at me. I noticed right away that the temperature had dropped. Thunder rumbled in the distance.

"So . . . what do you think?" Troy asked.

To be honest, I wasn't entirely sure what I thought. It was a lot of information to take in all at once. While listening to Troy recite from his notes, I'd had to remind myself on more than one occasion that these were real people we were talking about. Not just characters in a book or on a TV show. They'd once been filled with hopes and dreams and plans for the future. They'd celebrated birthdays and holidays and fallen in and out of love and danced and played and sang in the rain. In a split second of time, all of that and so much more had been stolen away from them—not to mention from the loved ones they'd left behind.

Reading what he'd written in that ridiculously precise handwriting of his had been more of the same—only this time the somber story had been narrated by my own internal voice. And then I'd arrived at the section about the little boy in the Pittsburgh Pirates hat with the missing front teeth, and it really hit home. Somehow they'd discovered the boy's identity. His name was Oliver Grimes. The people who knew and loved him best called him Ollie. He was six years old when the car in which he'd been a passenger had crossed the center line and hit a logging truck head-on. His sister had been driving. She'd survived with a broken leg and twenty-seven stitches in her head. Ollie had been crushed and unrecognizable.

"Nothing too specific stands out to me," I said, clearing my throat. "But there's definitely . . . *something*."

"I thought so too," Troy said.

Naomi scrunched up her face like she used to do when she was working on her calculus homework at my parents' dining room table. "But what?"

Melody chimed in. "Gender, age, occupation, religious, political, and economic backgrounds . . . they're all so varied. Where's the link, Billy?"

I thought about it for a moment longer. "The folks on the list—whether they're children or adults or somewhere in between—they all appear to be decent people." I got up and began pacing. "People usually go out of their way to speak kindly of the dead . . . I get that . . . but that genuinely doesn't seem to be the case here. By all accounts, these seem to be exceptionally loving and kindhearted individuals . . . just really *good* people."

"That doesn't give us much to go on," Melody said.

"No, it doesn't," Troy replied. "But it *is* unusual, considering the current state of the world we live in. Odds are at least one of them should've been a first-class shit—or at the very least a few levels below that."

"The two missing girls," I said, "the ones who are on all those posters . . . I wonder if they were really good people too."

Troy pointed at me. "That's an interesting thought."

"What else?" Melody asked. I could tell she was eager to beat the rain and get back to the van.

"Several of the victims appeared to be acting strangely before the accidents occurred."

"Right," Troy said.

"Chase Harper. Michael Meredith. Oliver Grimes. Gabriel Ramos. Jessica Harmeyer. They all—"

"Jessica who?" Melody asked.

"The teacher from Parkton," I said.

She stared at me with a blank look on her face.

"The memorial on the fence by the cemetery? The one that was damaged by the storm? You guys are the ones who came up with her name."

"Oh yeah, that's right," she said. "Sorry . . . it's all starting to blur together at this point."

The first drops of rain began to splatter the picnic table. Troy rolled up his notes and shoved them into his pants pocket. Then he looked at us—and grinned. "Last one to the van kisses Ronnie Reagan's wrinkled white ass."

And he took off running.

17

"You sure?" Troy asked, still trying to catch his breath. Even with a head start, he'd finished dead last in the race to the van. As usual, he blamed his short legs. "I'd hate to see them get stolen."

By the time we'd reached the parking lot the rain was falling in steady, undulating sheets. Thanks to the whipping wind, it felt like we were being pelted from every direction. Soaked and shivering, with the heat turned on high inside the van, we cruised past the library. It wasn't quite two in the afternoon, but it already looked like dusk outside.

"I've been gone for a while," I said, "but I think bike heists are still pretty rare in Sudbury. We'll just swing back later when the rain stops and pick them up."

"I've been thinking," Melody said, turning up the windshield wipers. "Maybe we should head back to campus this afternoon. Now that we have Craig helping us, we're not really needed here. We can do the rest of the legwork from home."

Naomi squeezed my leg in the back seat. I knew what she was thinking. I wasn't ready to say goodbye either.

"You worried about Rosie?" I asked.

"A little," she said, nodding. "It's not like her to not answer the phone."

"You left her messages?"

She glanced at me in the mirror. "Well, that's the thing. Our answering machine's broken. I didn't have a chance to pick up a new one before we left."

I thought about it. "We've had thunderstorms pretty much every day this week. Maybe the electricity's out again."

"Maybe. I guess I could look up the rental office's number and call and ask."

"Let's try that," I said. "Aunt Helen will be seriously bummed if we duck out early."

Troy turned sideways in his seat so he could see everyone. "I've been thinking too." His Afro sparkled from the rain, rivulets of water running down his face. He took off his glasses and wiped the moisture from his eyes. "What if, once we're finished with the documentary, we go back and assemble new footage for a second film?"

"A second film about what?" Melody asked.

But I already knew the answer.

"The symbol. Its origins. What it represents. Why it was left at the various memorials. How we unraveled the mystery behind it all."

Melody raised her eyebrows. "And how do we do that when we don't have answers to most of those questions?"

"Not yet, but we will."

I admired his confidence—and I had to admit the idea of a second documentary *was* a little intriguing.

"Think about it," he went on. "We already have most of the footage we need. What's left is background research, and we've already started on that." He looked at me. "I'd even be willing to stick around for part of the summer to work on it."

And just like that a follow-up documentary focusing on the symbol seemed like the greatest idea in the world.

"Who would want to watch something like that?" Naomi asked.

"Lots of people, I bet . . . as long as our story has a resolution." His eyes twinkled behind his glasses. "Hell, even if it doesn't . . . look at *In Search Of* on TV . . . People eat this stuff up . . ."

18

By the time we pulled up in front of my aunt's house, the downpour had slowed to a drizzle and Troy had finally stopped talking. I'd only heard him that excited once before—when he was telling me about a paper he'd written for his physics class. I'd understood maybe a tenth of what he'd told me that day.

As soon as Melody turned off the van, Naomi flung open the side door and hopped out. "If the front door's locked, I'm screwed! I'm about to pee my pants!" And she was off and running, splashing through puddles as she made her way up the driveway.

Troy laughed and took off right behind her. "I call downstairs bathroom!"

Good luck with that, I thought, closing the van door. I only made it a couple of steps before Melody grabbed my arm and stopped me.

"Wait. I have to tell you something before we go inside. It's been bothering me all day." She glanced nervously at the front door before turning her back on the house.

"What's wrong?"

"I feel horrible saying this, Billy." She did look pretty miserable. "But I can't help it."

"It's okay. Just tell me."

"I'm not sure I trust Naomi and your aunt."

"What?" It felt like someone had doused me with ice-cold water. "Why? What happened?"

"This morning, when I was on the phone with my sister . . . your aunt was listening in on the other line."

Now it was my turn to glance at the house. "Why do you think that?"

"Shortly after I got on the phone, there was a weird click and then the tiniest bit of background static. I could hear it pretty much the entire time we were talking. Then right before we hung up, I heard the click again, and the noise disappeared. A couple seconds later, your aunt's bedroom door opened. Then she went into the bathroom and closed the door. The shower was running the whole time I was on the phone, but I know she wasn't in it."

"You heard all that from the kitchen?"

"No, I was on the phone in the living room."

I didn't know what to think. What she'd just told me was a long way from concrete proof that my aunt had done anything wrong. On the other hand, Melody was one of the most steadfast and rational people I knew. She wasn't one to make serious accusations without careful thought. "What about Naomi? You said—"

"Earlier in the morning, while you and Troy were upstairs, I walked in on your aunt and Naomi in the kitchen. They stopped talking as soon as they saw me. I'd obviously interrupted something important. But then I saw the looks on their faces, and Billy, my blood ran cold. It was like they were wearing masks and they'd slipped loose for a second . . . and I could *see* how they really felt about me. Then it was gone—and they were smiling again." She let out a deep breath. "But by then, it was too late. I'd already seen."

I wanted to tell her she was imagining things. That we were all tired and stressed, and her mind was playing tricks on her. But I couldn't. All I could think about was Aunt Helen pushing my notebook underneath the newspaper. "Will you be okay going inside?"

"I'll be fine," she said, turning around to face the house. "I just had to tell you before I went crazy. I wanted to say something earlier about a hundred times, but this is the first instance you and I have been alone for more than a few seconds."

As we started up the driveway, I searched the windows to see if anyone was watching—but all I could see were shadows.

19

No answer from Farnsworth.

I hung up the kitchen phone and walked into the living room where everyone was huddled around a stack of old photo albums. "I left a message. Hopefully, he'll call back."

"You didn't tell me you were baby Elvis when you were a kid," Troy said, looking up at me with a shit-eating grin. "Why'd you get rid of the pompadour?"

"Because I knew I couldn't compete with the Afro."

He laughed and flipped to the next page.

Upon our arrival, we'd immediately gone upstairs and changed into dry clothes. Troy, still shivering from the rain, took a long, hot shower. By the time we'd all returned to the first floor, Aunt Helen had a pot of tea going on the stove and a platter of cheese and crackers on the coffee table. She'd warned us not to ruin our appetites. Jason Peters was coming for dinner at seven thirty, and this time there would be no last-minute cancellation. She actually seemed excited for us to meet him.

"Oh my God," Melody said, pointing at a black-and-white photo of me at my tenth birthday party. "Look at that adorable cowboy outfit. He's even wearing little spurs!"

If Melody was faking her good mood—no longer trusting Naomi and my aunt, and yet sitting between the two of them on the sofa, sipping hot tea and giggling—she was doing a damn good job of it.

"Oh, this is downright tragic," Troy said, holding up a photo for me to see. "Weren't you a little old to be playing Tarzan?"

I looked at my aunt. "Thanks. Thanks a lot."

She smiled and said, "You're very welcome."

Eager to take a catnap, I plopped down in Uncle Frank's favorite reading chair by the fireplace. Using the lever on the side, I put my legs up and got comfortable. Before I could close my eyes, my gaze wandered across the room to the basketball team photo on the wall. I still couldn't figure it out. It was just a bunch of guys in crew cuts and funny shorts standing on the bleachers. What was it about that damn photograph that was bothering me so—

Before I could finish my thought, the telephone rang.

Aunt Helen started to excuse herself, but I held out my hand to stop her. "I got it. Stay here and make fun of me."

"Our pleasure," Troy said as I walked out of the room.

The telephone kept ringing.

"Yeah, yeah, hold your horses." I was hoping it was Robert Farnsworth. I had about a million questions for the guy.

As it turned out, it was.

20

"I'm glad you called," he said after we'd exchanged pleasantries. "I'm afraid I owe you and your friends an apology. I wasn't entirely truthful with you at the lake."

He sounded like a completely different person than the charming salt-and-pepper-haired gentleman we'd met at Mo's Famous BBQ. No more was he the confident, smooth-talking storyteller. In his place was a stranger who sounded exhausted and sad and maybe even a little drunk.

"How so?" I asked, even though I had a feeling I knew what he was going to say next.

"I was caught by surprise when you asked about the symbol on Griffin Schutz's cross. I've taken several other groups to that section of the trail, and no one's ever mentioned it before."

"We already know there's a story behind it . . ."

A distinctive *click* came through the earpiece of the receiver, along with the barely detectable hum of background static that reminded me of when my friends and I used to run around outside with walkie-talkies, pretending we were astronauts on the moon or soldiers in the jungle.

". . . and we've discovered the symbol at a number of other memorials."

He cleared his throat. "I assume you've taken photographs and shot video of the symbol?"

"Quite a bit."

He didn't say anything right away. There was just that low frequency hum in the background.

"Mr. Farnsworth, are you—"

"You need to destroy it," he said, with an urgency in his voice that hadn't been there before. "*All* of it. The film. The prints. The video footage."

"What . . . ? Why?" I couldn't believe what I was hearing. "Why would—"

"You have no reason to believe me after I lied to you before, but I'm telling you the truth now. Get rid of everything. Cancel your project. Go back to school and tell your professor you'll do something else."

"Why? What does it mean?!" I nearly shouted. "The symbol . . . where did it come from?!"

It was as if he hadn't heard me. "If you insist on going forward with your documentary, then erase all evidence of that symbol. Don't even let it appear in the background."

"Can't you just tell me what's going on?" Practically begging now. "Is it a cult? Are they satanists?"

A long drawn-out breath, at the end of which I almost expected to hear a dial tone.

"Billy . . . call it whatever you want . . . ," he said. "Witchcraft . . . sorcery . . . black magic. Whatever it is . . . it's as old as time itself. Do you realize that the mountains in this part of the world have been here for billions of years? *Billions*. Those mountains . . . they're like a primordial god in and of themselves."

"What does that have to do with the symbol?"

"Everything." He sighed. "You and your friends have stumbled onto something very bad. The people behind it are dangerous. And they *believe* in what they're doing. You need to stay far away from them. Destroy all documentation and get the hell out of there as soon as you can."

"What are they doing? Why are they leaving the symbol at—?"

"They're using the memorials as *gateways*." His voice booming as he surged past the point of no return. "They're using the *energy* . . . the grief . . . to . . ." He trailed off without finishing.

"To do what?" I pleaded. When he didn't answer me, I continued. "We went back to the lake yesterday."

"Why in the hell would you go back there?"

"We had a nightmare," I said. "About Rachel Filmore . . . and her baby."

"What do mean *we*? You've all been having dreams?!"

I nodded even though I knew he couldn't see me. "When we went back, there was a photograph on the cross . . . taken at one of our campsites . . . My friend's eyes had been scratched out."

"Oh no." His voice dropped to a whisper. "Oh Christ, no. Shit. *Shit*."

"Mr. Farnsworth . . . ?"

"It's too late. It's too late for all of you now. You've been marked."

"Marked? Marked by what?"

"I'm sorry, Billy . . . please don't call me anymore." It sounded like he was beginning to cry. "I can't help you."

"You can't just leave us like this. We're marked *how*?"

No response.

MEMORIALS

"Mr. Farnsworth!"

Nothing.

"You said the memorials are being used as gateways?" I looked around the kitchen and lowered my voice. My mouth had gone dry. A headache was building in my temple. "Gateways for *what*?"

I thought I was too late. I thought he was gone. But I was wrong.

"*Demons*," he whispered. "Okay? *Now* do you get it? You and your friends are all going to die."

And with that, he hung up the phone.

21

I walked into the living room in a daze.

All I knew of demons came from movies like *The Exorcist* and *The Evil Dead*. They were make-believe. *I heard him wrong. He said it so softly, I must've misunderstood.*

The photo albums were still piled high on the coffee table. A mug of hot tea rested on a nearby coaster. But there was no sign of my aunt and the others.

That's because someone came into the house and took them away while you were talking, my brain taunted—but this time I didn't feel the need to sneak away and count to ten in order to regain control of it. Dr. Mirarchi would've been proud of my progress.

"Hello?" I called out. "Where are—"

"Out back," Troy answered in a muffled voice.

I made my way to the sliding screen door and stepped outside onto the patio. The rain had stopped a while ago, but the sky remained thick with shifting gray clouds. With the sudden chill in the air, it looked and felt like autumn. The heat wave had officially broken.

"Troy and Naomi couldn't stop themselves from eavesdropping," Melody said with a smile that I knew was ungenuine, "so I dragged them out here and forced them to behave."

Troy rolled his eyes and stuck out his tongue at her.

"Where'd Aunt Helen get off to?"

"She disappeared upstairs. Looking for her purse to go grocery shopping." Melody flashed me a look. "Haven't seen her since."

It made perfect sense. Troy and Naomi were obviously not the only ones who couldn't resist eavesdropping. Thinking about the *click* I'd heard over the phone line, I glanced up at my aunt's bedroom window. The curtain was closed.

"So you going to tell us or what?" Troy asked, getting up from his chair. "I couldn't understand what you were saying, but by the tone of your voice, it sounded like the conversation got a little spicy."

"You could say that . . ."

Before I could go on, Aunt Helen slid open the door and walked outside, her purse hanging from her shoulder. "Another top-secret communiqué?"

"No, ma'am," I said, borrowing Melody's fake grin. "Just enjoying the cool weather."

She looked doubtfully at the dark sky above the crab apple trees—and then turned her attention to Naomi. "You headed home soon, I hope?"

Still sulking, Naomi didn't answer. Just nodded her head.

"Well, good luck and remember what we talked about. They only know what they *see*. Tell them how you *feel*. How they *make* you feel. They just might surprise you."

"I seriously doubt that."

"You seriously need to go in there with a better attitude, young lady."

"If you say so."

"I absolutely say so." She ran her fingers over the strap of her purse, making sure it was still there. My mom used to do the same thing. "Okay, I'm on my way to the store. I won't be long." Closing the screen door, she glanced back at us, smiling. "Remember, dinner's at seven thirty and we're expecting a guest."

"Looking forward to it," I said, giving her a wave. I listened to her footsteps fade away.

And then I joined the others at the table and told them everything—well, *almost* everything—that Robert Farnsworth had said.

22

All of a sudden, it felt like there were secrets everywhere.

I still hadn't told Troy—or anyone else, for that matter—about the gun I'd seen in Melody's possession. Even with everything that had happened, it hadn't felt necessary. Melody and I were also in cahoots when it came to her recent suspicions about Aunt Helen and Naomi. As brilliant as he was, poor Troy was in the dark about all of it. I would've felt terrible about the whole thing if I weren't so convinced it was the right thing to do.

When I'd told the group about my conversation with Robert Farnsworth, Troy had spiraled into a full-fledged panic attack and nearly fainted. Melody helped him to a chair, making sure he didn't face-plant onto the patio, and poured him a glass of water. His hand shaking, he tried to take a drink, but managed to spill most of it on his T-shirt. "What the fuck does *that* mean, we've been marked?! That doesn't make any—" And then he was leaning over with his head between his knees, hyperventilating.

I ran inside and grabbed a paper bag from underneath the sink. Melody got it positioned around his mouth and held it there. "Breathe, Troy! Breathe into the bag . . . nice and easy . . ."

It took a while, but he finally recovered enough to finish his water and resume asking questions. Albeit in a much calmer tone of voice.

Melody and Naomi hadn't reacted much better. The mere mention of demons—even after I'd gone out of my way to cast considerable doubt on whether I'd heard correctly—had thrown them over the edge.

"This is nothing to mess around with," Melody said, beads of sweat dotting her forehead, despite the cooled-down temperature. "I mean it, Billy. The occult is serious business where I come from." She made the sign of the cross and then lifted her crucifix and kissed it.

Troy closed his eyes and wrung his hands together. "Jesus . . . I can't believe this is happening."

All of which made me glad I'd decided not to breathe a word about Farnsworth's directive to destroy the film and video evidence we'd taken of the symbol.

I'd tried to convince myself that I'd done it so they wouldn't freak out even more than they already had. But deep down I knew the ugly truth: I'd withheld Farnsworth's warning out of a sense of pure greed and entitlement. After all . . . *I* was the one who'd shot the film and video. Therefore, it was *mine* to do with as I pleased. *Mine mine mine*, I thought, picturing that gluttonous Daffy Duck from the Saturday morning cartoon. *Minnne minnne minnne.*

And then there was Aunt Helen, the only real family I had left in this world. The woman who had almost single-handedly saved my life over the Christmas break. Who had stayed at my side and nursed me back to some semblance of health and then found Dr. Mirarchi to help me do the rest. I owed her so much more than doubt and suspicion—yet I couldn't stop thinking about the oh-so-quiet *click* both Melody and I had heard on the telephone line and the stealthy manner in which she'd hidden my notebook.

And now—while Melody kept Naomi and Troy occupied downstairs—here I was sneaking around my aunt's bedroom while she was out spending her hard-earned money in preparation for tonight's dinner. Snooping around had been Melody's idea, but I hadn't objected. In fact, I'd agreed without even a moment's hesitation. Just one more secret to keep. But then again I wasn't the only one . . . so I figured, *Fuck it, do what you gotta do.*

I was all but positive that Aunt Helen had listened in on my phone call with Farnsworth. Which meant she'd heard all about the symbol and portals and demons. She knew we were in real danger—and yet she'd opened the back door to announce that she was headed out grocery shopping with nary a hint of concern on her face. Why? Jesus, what was she hiding?! I was more determined than ever to find out.

Although I had no idea what I was looking for, I'd already given the home library and the small back room she called her office a cursory search. Nothing out of the ordinary there.

So far, her bedroom had been more of the same. The only real surprises came when I stumbled upon a plain white envelope stuffed with twenty-dollar bills at the bottom of her sock drawer and several silky, barely-there pieces of bright red lingerie in her underwear drawer.

I'd just about given up when I noticed the shoeboxes at the bottom of her closet.

On the one hand, it looked like a lot of work—the woman sure had a lot of shoes. On the other, if it was a good enough hiding place for me, maybe the same could be said for my favorite aunt.

There were three horizontal rows of boxes—nearly a dozen across—stacked neatly on top of each other. *Why the hell does anyone need thirty pairs of shoes?* Knowing that time was running short, I knelt down and made quick work of it. Boots. Sneakers. Clogs. Slippers. Heels. Flats. Sandals. A few pairs of footwear that defied description and for which I had no name. All I knew was that they looked uncomfortable. *And Melody says that guys are weird.*

Until there were only four boxes left at the end of the bottom row.

Box one: A pair of steel-toed work boots. Brand-new. Size seven.

Box two: White high heels. Fancy. Not a speck of dirt or wear. Most likely never worn.

Box three: A surprise. An antique silver pistol. All cleaned up and polished. Probably my Uncle Frank's.

I opened the lid on the final box.

At first, because of the shadows, I thought it was empty.

I picked it up—and a curved dagger with a turquoise handle slid into view with a *thunk*.

The same dagger Naomi had been holding in our collective nightmare.

I reached into the box to touch it.

To make sure it was real.

The telephone rang on the dresser behind me—and I nearly fainted from the shock.

23

By the time I carefully got everything back where it belonged and rejoined the others downstairs, Melody was saying goodbye to whoever it was on the phone. From the looks on Troy's and Naomi's faces, I couldn't tell if the call had brought good news or bad.

"Hold on," she said when I walked into the living room. "Don't hang up yet. Billy just got here." She covered the receiver with her hand. "It's Craig and you're not going to believe what he dug up." Speaking into the phone again, Melody said, "Do me a favor and tell Billy everything you just told me. Don't leave anything out . . ."

24

We were barely out of the neighborhood when Melody started in on Naomi again.

"Just be honest . . . why didn't you tell us?"

"I *am* being honest." Naomi was on the verge of tears. "I didn't know. Today's the first I've ever heard of it."

We were on our way to drop her off at home and then head across town to St. Ignatius to interview Father Paul. After that, if there was enough time before dinner, it was a straight shot north to Church Street. If Melody didn't get pulled over first for reckless driving.

"The police find a *satanic ritual site* in the woods by the memorial . . . and *you* of all people didn't know about it?! Come on, that's bullshit and you know it!"

"Why would I lie to you?"

"I don't know. *You* tell me."

Troy turned around and gave me a look. He was obviously as uncomfortable as I was with Melody's harsh line of questioning. Always the peacemaker, he spoke up. "It was almost two years ago, Mel. Craig didn't hear a whisper about it, either, until this afternoon. The cops buried the story."

Without warning, Melody pulled over to the side of the road and stopped the van. She spun around in her seat and glared at us. She looked like she hadn't slept in days. "And for two years neither one of you heard a peep about it? A rumor? A drunken backyard story? Nothing?"

Naomi shook her head.

I was beginning to lose my patience. "I've been gone, Mel. I haven't heard shit about *anything*."

"All those crazy stories going around about Dead Man's Road, and not a word gets out about a fucking altar in the woods."

I shrugged. "I guess some small towns keep their secrets."

"How did Craig find out?" Troy asked.

"He wouldn't say." Melody turned around in her seat, facing forward again. "I pushed him for a name, but he claimed he couldn't tell me."

"Rule number one," Troy replied. "Never reveal your source."

"That's what Craig said . . ." She steered the van back onto the road. "Some bullshit about journalistic integrity."

But it was more than that, and Melody knew it. Craig had sounded scared on the phone—like he'd regretted ever talking to us.

25

"I'm telling the truth, Billy. I don't know why she doesn't believe me."

We were standing by the van in front of Naomi's house. She was supposed to be home by five, and it was eight minutes past. Any second now, I expected her mother and father to storm outside and start yelling at us. Hugging her tight, I breathed in the strawberry scent of her shampoo. Her fingers caressed the back of my neck and played with the curls in my hair. I felt a subtle stirring in my jeans. And once again it felt like I was living in a dream world.

A grown-up Naomi Flynn in my arms . . . a ceremonial dagger hidden inside my aunt's closet . . . secret altars in the middle of the woods . . .

I didn't know what to think anymore. At the beginning of this trip, I had felt like a stranger roaming around my hometown. Now, it was starting to feel the other way around. Sudbury *had* changed, after all.

"She's just upset," I said. "And worried about her roommate. You know she's not like this."

"That's what makes it even worse. She's been so nice to me . . . up until now."

I gently placed my hands on her face. "That's because it's not about you. It's about *her*. Once she calms down and comes to her senses, I'm sure she'll apologize." I leaned in and kissed her on the forehead.

"I don't know, Billy. She's really pissed."

I glanced over her shoulder at the house and reached into my pocket. "Before you go, I want to show you something." I pulled out the cassette tape I'd taken from the shoebox at the bottom of my closet and handed it to her. The label along the top read: *BILLY & NAOMI'S MIXTAPE.*

Her eyes widened. "Oh my God! Billy! I can't believe—" She turned it over in her hand, examining both sides of the cassette as if she wasn't sure it was real.

After dating for nearly six months back in high school, we'd finally said *I love you* to each other for the first time while riding the Ferris wheel at the Fourth of July carnival. Early the next morning, too excited to sleep, she'd left the mixtape and a homemade card in my parents' mailbox. Using her father's cassette recorder, she'd taped more than a dozen of her favorite love songs off various albums. Andy Gibb. Carly Simon. Billy Joel. And a host of others. The recording quality was pretty abysmal, but that hadn't mattered at all. The rest of that summer, we must've listened to that tape from start to finish hundreds of times. It was a miracle it hadn't fallen apart. That was almost five years ago now.

"You kept it all this time!" The smile on her face was radiant. "Can I take it inside and listen . . . please?!"

"If you promise to give it back when you're finished."

I didn't have the heart to admit that, shortly before leaving for college, I'd tossed the tape into the trash. I'd already gotten rid of the photographs from my bedroom walls and stored my cameras in boxes. All those things were reminders of that other life I'd once lived, and I wanted nothing more to do with them.

But then something unexpected happened. That night, I dreamed of Naomi. The two of us wading side by side in the Susquehanna, fishing poles in our hands, a transistor radio perched on a nearby boulder. She was wearing the orange floppy hat she'd gotten for free at an Orioles game and cut-off jean shorts and a bright red bikini top. The sun was shining and we were happy. She set the hook on a big one and started reeling it in—and that's when I woke up.

The next morning, I pulled the cassette out of the trash can, scraped a wad of chewing gum off the plastic casing, and stashed the tape in a shoebox at the bottom of my closet. I no longer wanted it gone . . . but I also didn't want to see it every time I came home. It was a decent compromise, all things considered.

And then as more time passed, I simply forgot all about it.

Until the other morning . . . while standing in my old bedroom, a warm breeze blowing through the open window, listening to Melody and Troy and Aunt Helen laughing in the backyard. I'd felt truly alive in that moment. Excited to hit the open road with my friends. Unafraid and eager to make my mark on the world.

And as I headed for the hallway to go downstairs and join the others, I suddenly remembered the mixtape at the bottom of my closet—and a whispering voice inside my head urged me to stop and take it with me. Almost as if in my excitement for what was yet to come, I wanted something good from my past to hold on to. A kind of charm if nothing else. It wasn't until now—with Naomi's beaming face in front of me—that I recognized the voice that had spoken to me that day: It was Doctor Mirarchi.

"I'm going to make a copy," Naomi said, practically squealing with joy. "That way we both have one to listen to."

"That sounds like a plan," I said, glimpsing a flicker of movement in one of the upstairs windows. "Now go inside and try to behave . . . so your parents will let you see me later tonight."

She glared at the house. "They better."

And then she hugged me one last time—so hard it made my heart ache. I watched her jog across the lawn, ponytail bouncing, and it occurred to me that she no longer looked quite so grown up. When she opened the door and glanced back at me, I heard the squawk of her mother's voice coming from somewhere inside. She didn't sound happy. Naomi rolled her eyes and took a deep breath. I blew her a kiss for luck. She caught it.

And was gone.

26

"I'm sorry, Billy . . . she's a sweet girl . . . but I *know* she's holding back on us." Melody waited for the car in front of us to turn and then accelerated through the intersection. "The question is *why*."

It had only been a few minutes since we'd dropped off Naomi, and I was already tired of talking about it. Fortunately, Melody's mood had improved as soon as it was just the three of us again. Her anger was winding down. "I'll talk to her . . . see if there's anything she's not telling us . . . That's all I can do."

"Guys, I'm still stuck on this whole demon thing," Troy said, his fingers drumming a nervous staccato on the armrest. "I feel like a ritual site in the woods all but fucking confirms that it's true."

"I really think we should head home tonight," Melody said. "Better safe than sorry."

"We have dinner," I reminded her. "Aunt Helen's making such a big deal out of it. Plus I want to ask this Jason guy some questions."

She frowned. "Fine. Then we can leave right after."

"I'd be up for that," Troy replied.

We rounded the sweeping bend—at only five miles per hour above the speed limit, Melody no longer driving like she was competing in the Grand Prix—and turned into the St. Ignatius parking lot.

"I gotta tell you," Troy said with a sigh, "I am not in the mood to do this interview. I wish we could cancel."

"Too late." I spotted the portly priest standing next to another man outside the rectory. "Besides, after what Father Paul told me earlier today . . . I have a plan."

27

VIDEO FOOTAGE
(5:37 p.m., Wednesday, May 11, 1983)

```
The two men sit side by side in faded yellow plastic
chairs. Behind them, what looks like about a hundred
```

more of the same ugly chairs, folded up and leaning against the wall in neat stacks. Off to the side, an unplugged bingo board on wheels, the unlit rows of letters and numbers lost in the shadows.

The larger of the two men is a priest, his clerical collar impossibly white in the glare of the portable lights. His chubby cheeks are rosy red. He needs a shave. The second man is at least ten years older. He's dressed in baggy jeans and a light blue chambray shirt. His unruly gray hair and John Lennon eyeglasses lend him the appearance of a mad scientist.

Both men are fidgeting in their seats. The mad scientist keeps poking the priest in the leg and leaning over to whisper in his ear. Each time he does this, the priest shoos him away with a grumble and a less-than-charitable look on his otherwise cheerful face.

The lights dim a notch.

"Okay . . . that's better," Troy says from off-screen. "Whenever you're ready, Billy."

Both men immediately sit ramrod straight—and go totally still. With their shiny skin and wide eyes, they look like wax figures in a museum.

"Just try to relax," Billy says with an off-screen chuckle. "Pretend the camera isn't there and you're sitting around the poker table shooting the breeze."

"We allowed to cuss?" the older man asks.

The priest looks at his friend as if he's lost his mind. "We're in a church, Teddy."

"This part ain't no church," he says, looking around. "It's a bingo hall. Besides, the boy said to pretend we're playing poker."

"I knew it was a bad idea to invite you."

"Wouldn'ta hurt my feelings none if you didn't. I'm missing meatloaf night at the diner."

Billy speaks up again. "Father Paul . . . before we get started, I was hoping you'd take a look at something."

Melody appears in frame. She approaches the men, stops, and turns around to hold up a spiral notebook—so that the camera can zoom in on the strange symbol that's been drawn there.

The camera holds tight for a moment, and then as it slowly pulls back again, the woman rotates the notebook so the two men can see the sketch. They study it in silence for a moment. Some of the color noticeably draining away from the priest's cheeks. Teddy readjusts his eyeglasses. His hand appears to be trembling.

"We found this on a number of the memorials we came across," Billy continues. "We were able to trace its origins back to some type of local cult. I was wondering if you knew anything about it . . . for our background research."

Melody begins to turn away with the notebook—but Father Paul reaches out and gently takes it from her hand. She hesitates, shrugs at the camera and slowly backs out of frame.

"Have you shown this to your aunt?" the priest asks.

"She told me she'd never seen it before."

Something flickers in his eyes. "This cult, son . . . what do you know about them?"

"Just that they're from the hill country and supposedly they use this symbol in certain rituals."

MEMORIALS

Teddy reaches over and adjusts the notebook in the priest's hand so he can take a better look at it. "You mind if I ask where ya got your information from?" All of the mischief has gone out of his voice.

"All over the place . . . the library, there was a local historian, a kid whose mother works for the police department. That's the problem, though. No one's been able to tell us the complete story. It's all in parts, like this big puzzle, and we're only missing a few pieces . . . but of course, they're the most important pieces."

The priest turns to his friend and holds up the notebook to shield their faces from the camera's watchful eye, and whispering can be heard. A moment later, the notebook is lowered. "Okay . . . what exactly do you want to know, Billy?"

"The symbol . . . what does it mean?"

A deep breath. "It represents something . . . and if what it represents has a name, I don't know what it is. It's obviously not a subject I talk about regularly from the pulpit, you realize." He pauses, then continues: "Okay, here goes: Some people around these parts believe it's a god as old as the earth itself. Others claim it's something far worse." He shrugs. "And of course, most folks think it's just a legend . . . yet another sordid chapter in the never-ending saga of Appalachian folklore."

"But it's not . . . is it, Father?"

"No, it most definitely is not." He turns to Teddy. "You want to tell it or me?"

His friend waves him away. "All you, Padre. This ain't what I signed up for."

The priest sighs and lowers the notebook to his lap, making a point to turn it around so that the drawing is facing down. "I actually heard a lot of this story from your Uncle Frank . . . but there were others too . . . filling in some of the gaps over time."

The camera pans slowly to the left, losing sight of the older man, and goes close on the priest's face.

"Back in the 1800s, the Pennsylvania Railroad Company got involved in the coal industry. Their already established routes stretched as far north as the Great Lakes and well past Chicago to the west. They would eventually deliver Pennsylvania coal to nearly a dozen states. And the vast majority of it came from the Appalachian Mountains.

"Almost all of the coal from this region came from underground mines. The Appalachian hill people were hard workers. And not just the men either. Those mines were full of women and children of all ages. To the fancy suits at the Pennsylvania Railroad Company, they were a convenient source of cheap labor—even cheaper than the Chinese immigrants that had laid thousands of miles of track during the previous decade. The men in charge of the mines worked the hill people to the bone. Long hours, few safety precautions, and even fewer regulations governing the treacherous work they did. Scores of deaths resulted from cave-ins and illness, underground fires, and just plain exhaustion. Still others became lost in the never-ending maze of tunnels and were never seen again. But none of that mattered to the men in charge. In their greed, they pushed blindly ahead—and the mines went deeper and deeper into the earth. This went on for decades."

MEMORIALS

He clears his throat—and the camera slowly pulls back. Teddy returns to frame. His eyes behind his glasses are dark slits, and there's a slump to his shoulders that wasn't there before. Father Paul turns to him.

"When was it that the mines began to run dry? Do you remember?"

"'Course I do." The old man crosses his skinny arms over his chest. "It was right around the time that the Japs started planning their sneak attack on Pearl Harbor. And it happened all at once."

The priest gives a nod, encouraging his friend to go on.

"What else is there to tell?" he says with a shrug. "The mines went dry and those backstabbing bastards from the railroad cut and ran away."

Father Paul grimaces at the camera. "He's not wrong, though. Once the coal ran out—without even a proper thank-you or a goodbye tip of their big city hats—the mining companies packed up and skedaddled. Bustling villages that had provided housing and entertainment for supervisory crew members became ghost towns overnight. And the locals were left to fend for themselves. Convinced that there was still coal to be found—and with few other options at their disposal—many of the hill people returned to the abandoned mines, determined to scrape out of rock and dirt whatever meager living they could manage.

"And so the blasted fools went even deeper," Teddy says, taking off his glasses and balancing them on his leg. He rubs his eyes with a fist. "Picture it . . . Entire families diggin' side by side. In the dark and the cold. The earth shiftin' and groanin' and crumblin' all around them. Just like before, a bunch of 'em died and were injured as a result of cave-ins and accidents. Plenty of others got separated and became lost in the tunnels—and were eventually given up for dead. That should be the end of this story . . ." He looks at Father Paul, and it's clear what he is thinking: How far are you going to take this?

The priest answers by picking up where the older man left off. "But then something miraculous happened."

"Miraculous, my hairy ass." Teddy grunts and glances off camera, as though he's planning his escape.

"The missing began to return . . . after days or weeks or even months—with little or no memory of what they'd eaten or drank to survive—they began to reappear from the mines."

"And they were different . . ." Teddy adds in almost a whisper. "The ones that came back . . . they'd changed."

Father Paul waits for his friend to continue and when he doesn't, the priest carries on. "In some cases, it was subtle. A boy who had previously been unable to swim could now glide through the river's swift current like a fish. A man who wore glasses to see the stars at night no longer needed them. A woman suffering from arthritis in her hands could now take in work as a seamstress.

"But in other cases, the changes were more drastic. Eyes and hair had changed color. Birthmarks and scars had vanished or appeared where none had existed before. Feet had grown or shrunk. A few came back taller and stronger, as if something in the darkness had empowered them. Others spoke a language no one else could understand. One young man told stories of a subterranean waterfall and forest. Another claimed there were fur-covered animals living beneath the earth, species that defied description. A woman who had celebrated her thirty-ninth birthday the week before she'd disappeared returned from the mines after nineteen days as the ten-year-old girl she'd once been. She was naked when she walked out of the mine, her body as scrubbed clean as if she'd just stepped out of a bathtub. The young girl had no memory of what had transpired in the dark—and even less of the bewildered husband and twin sixteen-year-old boys waiting for her at home."

A muffled voice from off-screen followed by the sound of someone shushing them.

"I heard most of that last part from a couple of my brothers of the cloth . . . usually, I admit, after a snifter or two of fine brandy . . . but there are other stories too . . ."

"What kind of stories?" Billy asks.

"Horrible ones," Teddy says in a voice that is ice-cold. "A thirteen-year-old virgin stumbles outta the mines seven months pregnant, covered in strange bite marks. Five weeks later, she gives birth to a baby boy. The child's blind and has a full set of teeth. Sharp ones. On his back, between his shoulder blades, there's a birthmark in the shape of a crow. A little later, in the depths of night, the girl swaddles the child in a blanket and steals away to the mine. Where they still remain today.

"Another time, a man comes back after going missing for almost a month. He's pale, emaciated, able to communicate in only grunts and gestures. When he's given food and drink, his body immediately rejects it. Soon after, he disappears from the home in which he's been given care. Weeks later, under the light of a full moon, a local farmer discovers the man in one of his fields. He's killed one of the farmer's cows. He's naked, on his knees, devouring the dead animal's raw flesh and drinking its blood. The farmer shoots him in the chest with a buckshot at close range . . . and yet the man, once a respected schoolteacher, turns and flees into the nearby woods as if he's been stung by nothing more formidable than a bumblebee. A month passes, and children begin disappearing from the village."

"I don't understand. Why didn't they just close up the mine? If so many people were—"

Father Paul leans toward the camera. "A few of the townspeople tried, but most—"

". . . of the others chose just the opposite." Teddy smiles—it resembles the grin of a ghoul. "Before long, they began making pilgrimages into the mine. Thousands of feet beneath the ground, surrounded by dripping darkness, they prayed and fasted and chanted. Sacrifices were offered. Dark covenants made. And that figure you drew in your notebook witnessed it all."

"Wait a minute . . . they thought that thing was responsible for what was happening?"

Father Paul nods. "The figure had been carved into

the rock walls. All throughout the deepest sections of the mine. No one knew how it had gotten there."

"So they worshipped it? And even now . . . these people . . ."

"One generation after the next."

A silent pause, and then Billy speaks up again:

"Why are they leaving it at the memorial sites?"

"I have no idea. As far as I know, the memorials are something new."

"Is the mine still open?"

The priest shakes his head. "A few years after all this happened, crews from the Pennsylvania Railroad Company returned to the mountain and closed up the mines for good. They used something like fifteen hundred pounds of explosives to collapse various sections of tunnel and seal the numerous entrances. Some folks claim there was an armed standoff at one of the mines. Locals, armed with rifles, attempted to stop the crews from setting off the dynamite. The law intervened, and the crisis was averted."

"Do you know where the mine's located?"

"I do not." With a stern expression, he stares directly into the camera. "And don't you even think about going to look for it. It's sealed up tight, and all grown over. Besides, I don't think the folks who live around there would take kindly to visitors."

"I was . . . just curious is all."

"Just curious, huh." He coughs into his hand. It goes on for a bit. "I think it's time for a break, Billy."

"Of course. And thanks, Father. I owe you big-time."

"One of your aunt's breakfast feasts will suffice." He stares into the camera. "Speaking of your aunt, it would probably be wise if you didn't mention we had this conversation."

The picture goes dark.

28

"So, umm . . . wow . . . that was *something*," Melody said.

"That's one word for it." Troy lifted the portable lights into the back of the van. "That whole fucking story was dreadful. Talk about a nightmare."

I snapped the camera case shut and slid it off to the side next to my knapsack. "If you're still thinking about doing that second documentary on the symbol, you'll need to interview Father Paul again. Maybe get one of those other priests he was talking about to join him."

"I don't know," Melody said. "His buddy finally opened up, but he sure didn't seem too excited to talk to us today."

"That's because he was scared." Troy slammed the door to the van and looked at me. "Do we really need to go look for the clearing, Billy? Haven't we done enough already?"

"Craig McGinty's a good guy," I said, "but I'm not ready to take his word for it that this place actually exists. For all we know, his source could be full of shit. If we can find the clearing and see this altar with our own eyes, then we'll *know*."

"Or maybe you're hoping it's *not* there," Melody said, a thoughtful expression on her face, "so your girlfriend's off the hook."

Surprised and annoyed in equal measure, I walked away and climbed into the van, thinking: *Or maybe you're just jealous. How about that?*

29

**VIDEO FOOTAGE
(6:27 p.m., Wednesday, May 11, 1983)**

"Dammit, Troy. Watch where you're going. You almost—"
"—don't know why you're—"

"—told you, I wanted to test the—"

"—should've done that out by the road."

"Since when are you—"

"For God's sake, you two sound like a couple of—"

A jumble of overlapping voices over a mostly black screen. All we can see are shifting dark blobs and swirling shadows. Like floating in the middle of the ocean at night.

Until a pair of flashlight beams slice into the darkness. Bouncing wildly over the ground, briefly illuminating tangled clumps of brush and branches and leaves and the rough bark of tree trunks.

"All I'm asking for is a little room to operate." Behind the camera, Billy's breathing is hard and fast. He sounds irritated.

As one of the beams of light steadies, focusing on the ground in front of them, we glimpse jutting rocks and boulders. Thick, gnarled roots. And more and more tree trunks. We are walking amid a sea of trees.

Troy's nervous voice. Off-screen, but close by. "I just thought of something really bad."

"Of course you did." Melody this time.

"No, I'm serious." The rustle of branches scraping against arms and legs. Twigs snapping underfoot. "What if us coming out here like this . . . in the middle of freaking nowhere . . ." A deep breath. "What if it's a trap?"

The screen goes dark—and remains that way.

30

For the third time since we'd left the van, I checked the video camera to make sure it was loaded properly. We'd been walking for almost twenty minutes. Our shoes and socks were soaked. Melody and I had flashlights.

The twin beams probing the woods ahead of us like miniature spotlights. Troy stuck close enough to keep a sweaty hand on one of our shoulders at all times. There was no birdsong. No scrambling of tiny paws in tree branches. Only the graceless din of our passing.

The digital clock on the van's dashboard had read 6:19 p.m. when we parked in the grass by the tree line—leaving little more than an hour until our dinner at Aunt Helen's—but it may as well have been the middle of the night. Dead Man's Road and the surrounding woods were cloaked in darkness. On our way there, in the glare of the headlights, we'd watched in mute fascination as luminescent fingers of river mist crept over the steep embankment, swirled across the road in front of us, and disappeared into the trees. The whole thing had taken maybe twenty seconds. I'd lived in Sudbury almost my entire life and had never seen anything like it. As Melody continued driving, an awestruck Troy poked his head in between the seats and asked, *"Did you guys just see that?"* When we nodded, he started babbling with excitement: *"For a minute I thought . . . and I wasn't even scared . . . it was like an army of restless spirits on the prowl . . . and then they just vanished . . . into another world . . ."*

A few minutes later, when Melody pulled over and turned off the van's engine, it was as if we'd been transported to that other world. A world of shifting shadows and impossible silences where darkness reigned. I imagined the trees creeping ever closer to the van, unseen branches spiraling down to probe the air around us like the curious inhabitants of a faraway planet sniffing out uninvited visitors. As we readied for our hike in the woods, not a single car drove past. No creatures—large or small or in between, not even an insect—stirred. Other than the gentle burble of running water from a nearby drainage runoff, there was nary a sound to be heard. *This is a dead place,* I'd thought as I removed the camera from its case. *A graveyard.* As we entered the trees, I glanced farther down the road, realizing that just out of view, huddled in the darkness, my parents' memorial awaited its next visitor.

31

Troy wiped his hand on the back of my shirt and quickly returned it to my shoulder. When he spoke, he was so close I could smell the spearmint gum he was chewing. "Okay, let's say it's *not* a trap . . . and the people who've been messing with us aren't waiting in the woods to ambush us . . ."

"They're not," I said, although I had no way of knowing that for sure. I glanced behind me at Melody, and for the first time, I wondered if she'd brought along the gun. Everything was moving so damn fast, I'd forgotten to ask her back at the van.

Most likely because I was still pissed off at her. She'd crossed the line going after Naomi the way she had . . . and then had the nerve to come after *me*. That smart-ass comment about me hoping we didn't find the clearing so Naomi would be off the hook had been the final straw.

Or maybe she wasn't being a smart-ass at all. Maybe she really believed it?

Could she really be jealous of Naomi? The thought surfaced in my head without warning. As unexpected and dangerous as stumbling upon an angry copperhead curled up in the weeds. Melody and I had only known each other for around four months, but it honestly felt like much longer. We'd spent so much time together and shared so much of our lives. Painful, private memories that were normally impossible to talk about had come easy for us. Could she have, somewhere along the line, developed deeper feelings for me? If so, she'd done a hell of a job of hiding them.

Come on, Billy . . . be real. I climbed over a fallen log that had split in two. *You know better.* Mel was like a protective older sister—and nothing more. It wasn't jealousy that was making her act this way. It was fear and paranoia. After confiding in me that she no longer trusted Aunt Helen and Naomi, and then hearing about the disturbing details of my phone call with Farnsworth, she'd clearly begun to spiral. And learning about the ritual site had been like tossing gasoline on the—

". . . not even listening to me, are you, Billy?"

I looked over at Troy. He was tapping me on the shoulder. For how long, I had no idea.

"What? Sorry . . . I thought I heard something," I lied.

He looked around uneasily, and then: "I asked if we were really going home tonight after dinner."

"If that's what the two of you want to do . . . I'm good with it."

"We do," Melody said with a firmness to her tone.

"Then it's decided."

Troy tripped over a rock and used my arm to regain his balance. "No offense, Billy, but I gotta tell ya: I'll be a happy camper if I never set foot in this damn place ever again."

Melody flashed her light on Troy's face. "Does that mean no more second documentary about all this?"

Lifting a hand to shield his eyes, he said, "That's *exactly* what it means."

"Smarter than you look after all."

Troy made a face and mimicked her. "*Smarter than you look after all.*"

Grinning despite myself, I pushed through a veil of low-hanging branches and stopped to hold them out of the way for the others. I missed Naomi and was still annoyed with Melody, but a part of me was also relieved it was just the three of us again. Like back at school. The Three Musketeers. With Naomi out of the picture, Melody's mood had continued to improve. Earlier, she'd even giggled when Troy tried jumping over a creek, landing far short of the opposite bank and sinking up to his shins in mud. After the intensity of her earlier outburst, it was good to see her smiling again. Even briefly.

Troy gave my arm a nudge. "Do you think it'll be the same place you and your father found?"

"No clue," I said.

"Does it *feel* like we're in the same area? Anything look familiar?" Troy talked a lot when he got nervous. When he got scared, he asked a lot of questions. Even during movies, he was always striving to better understand the world around him. It was like his brain didn't know how to shut off.

"Maybe," I said, flashing my light up into a tree where this time I really *had* thought I'd heard something. "And maybe not. It's hard to tell."

He sighed. "So in other words . . . it's the blind leading the blind."

Despite Troy's sarcastic tone, he wasn't that far off. I had no idea if the clearing that Craig had told us about was the same one my father and I had stumbled upon all those years ago. All we had to go on was that it was supposedly located in the same general section of woods. There were no trails here of any kind. No tree stands or bunkers. Not many locals ventured into this part of the forest anymore. Not even hunters. If they had, the clearing most likely would have been discovered long before two years ago.

Then again, maybe it had—and people just didn't talk about it.

For what it was worth, I believed Naomi when she told us that she'd never heard about the clearing before. Between my father and Uncle Frank and his poker buddies, I figured I'd borne witness to just about every tall tale this town had to offer. Yet, just as Naomi had claimed, I hadn't caught wind of even a whisper about some secret clearing in the woods, much less an altar used in dark ceremonies.

"Do you guys smell smoke?" Melody asked, looking around uneasily.

It took me a second to realize that I did. Faint, but definitely there. I stopped walking and leaned against a tree, preparing myself for that awful drowning sensation I'd first experienced at Chase Harper's memorial.

But it never came.

"I smell it," I finally answered.

"Not me," Troy said, scratching his neck and arms. "But my skin's starting to itch like a son of a bitch. I hope I didn't catch poison ivy when I fell."

"The air . . . it feels different." Melody glanced at me in the glow of the flashlight, and I realized that she was on the edge of panic. "It's all . . . *wrong* . . . Don't you feel it?" she asked, shaking me by the arm as though she were trying to wake me from a deep sleep.

"I feel *something*," I said. My skin wasn't itching like Troy's—it was *tingling*. That unnerving, standing-too-close-to-the-power-lines feeling again. I was also nauseated. Sometime in the past couple minutes, my stomach had gone sore. I belched in the darkness. "Let's keep going just a little farther. I think we're getting close."

And I was right.

A few minutes later—after pushing our way through a head-high thicket of brambles, wading across a shallow stream, and ascending a rocky knoll carpeted with wild ferns—we came to an opening in the woods.

Behind me, in the shadows, Melody gasped.

I stopped at the edge of the trees and switched off my flashlight. Without the thick canopy of overlapping branches and leaves overhead, I didn't need it.

"*You found it*," she whispered in my ear—and a shiver of pleasure, as delicious as it was unexpected, spread throughout my body.

The clearing wasn't much to look at. Maybe forty yards of open ground separated us from the opposite tree line. It could have been even less. It was difficult to tell. The dark borders of the surrounding foliage seemed to expand and contract every time I looked away—almost as though the forest were breathing. The uneven soil was peppered with rocks and weeds and tangles of sticker brush. Several fallen trees lay across the ground, what remained of their bark spotted with poison sumac and patches of moss. A scattering of old tree stumps ringed the outer edge of the clearing. Evidence that, long ago, someone had tried to protect this land from the embrace of the encroaching wilderness. I glanced up at the treetops bending in the breeze, the roiling storm clouds hovering suffocatingly close, as if somehow drawn to this ugly hole in the forest. Forks of lightning stabbed the purple-gray sky, the rumble of thunder near enough to make the ground shake, and it was as if the heavens above the clearing belonged to another world.

"Billy . . ."

This can't be what Dad and I discovered . . .

"Billy . . ."

Troy, his face slick with sweat, eyes bulging behind his glasses, pointed over my shoulder at something in the trees. "Look."

It was a stick figure made out of broken branches. Almost identical to the one we'd found in the woods by my parents' memorial. "They're everywhere," he whispered in a voice I barely recognized.

I hadn't noticed the bizarre lattice figures at first because they blended in with the trees from which they'd been hung. There had to be hundreds of them. All different sizes. Surrounding the clearing. Perhaps even *guarding* the clearing.

The smell of smoke had grown stronger—and it was easy to see why. The police may have discovered this place two years ago, but someone else had been here much more recently. A jumbled heap of burnt timber and ash marked the center of the clearing. Right beside it, a narrow stone—flat and smooth—protruded from the earth.

There it was. An altar.

Not even waist-high, but clearly functional, its ancient surface was discolored by a series of dark smudges.

I slowly lifted the camera and began shooting.

"My head feels funny," Troy announced behind me. "I don't like it here."

"Neither do I," Melody said in a faraway voice. "My stomach . . ."

Ignoring them both, I stepped into the clearing. And as I did, I felt a buzzing sensation bloom deep inside my brain. Not the least bit unpleasant, it was warm . . . inviting. Like a quietly soothing voice I couldn't quite understand.

I paused behind one of the uprooted trees and zoomed in tight on the altar—

And immediately realized what it was: the cornerstone of an old foundation.

I had been here before. This *was* the place.

Recalling that long-ago day, I immediately panned to my right, widening the frame and adjusting the focus—and there they were. Right where I remembered them.

A staggered row of smaller stones poking out of the underbrush.

Just as I'd done as a child holding my father's hand, I imagined the stones as the broken nubs of a sleeping giant's teeth. Like something out of a storybook. The memory brought with it a smile. When I reached the end of the row, I lowered the camera, mounted the fallen tree, and climbed over it.

"Billy—be careful!"

The voice had come from somewhere behind me—but I couldn't tell exactly where or who it was that had issued the warning. The buzzing in my brain had grown louder. Filled my head. Like a hive of angry bees.

As I approached the cornerstone, I began shooting again.

But only for a moment.

Now that I was closer, I could see that the cursed symbol had been etched into the stone surface of the altar—its deep grooves stained a dark brown—and along both sides of it, an offering had been left.

Feeling like a man in a dream, I lowered the camera.

The first offering was a photograph.

The three of us standing in front of the bandstand at the park.

You've been marked.

Troy and Melody were frowning in the photo—undoubtedly at something foolish I'd just said. Naomi was nowhere in sight. She must've been standing behind us, blocked entirely from view. Melody's eyes were scratched out.

The buzzing—no longer pleasant—had now spread from the basement of my brain throughout my entire body. My skull ached. I felt it pulsing through my veins. It was so loud, piercing, I expected my eardrums to shatter at any moment.

I gazed at the second object on the altar.

And the camera slipped from my fingers to the ground.

Watch the equipment, it's expensive! a small voice called out from somewhere underneath all the noise inside my head.

I reached up and covered my ears.

Squeezed my eyes closed, then opened them again.

The buzzing remained—as did the offering.

It was a tongue. Small and pink and—

Somewhere behind me, Troy whispered, *"Please help."*

And then, in that same quiet voice, something else I couldn't quite understand.

MEMORIALS

The ground shifted beneath my feet. My vision blurred.

I took my hands away from my ears . . . blinked my eyes . . .

. . . *as a naked and moaning Naomi bends over the altar in front of me, breasts smashed against the smooth stone, ass jutting high in the air, grinding herself against my crotch. I watch myself reach down and grasp my hardness in my hand—and slowly guide it inside her. She groans and arches her back, and begins swiveling her hips, around and around, faster and faster, urging me to go harder. I tease her at first, holding back, stroking slow and easy, while I reach up and trace my fingertips across the beads of sweat that have gathered along her spine. Writhing in frustration, she moans louder. "Fuck me!" she begs. "Fuck me harder!" I wait as long as I can—and then I reach up and grab a fistful of her hair and pull. And begin thrusting deeper and deeper. She throws her head back, growling like a wild animal, pounding her ass into me, finding a rhythm, faster and faster. I yank her hair again, even harder this time, and she screams in pain and ecstasy, bucking her hips in a violent orgasm. Gasping for breath, her sweat-slick body trembling, she gazes over her shoulder at me and grins . . .*

And that's when I realize my horrible mistake.

It isn't a naked Naomi leaning over the altar.

It's Melody.

That distant whisper again. A little louder this time.

"Billy . . . she needs help."

Impossibly slow, like moving underwater, I forced my legs to turn around.

"Help me."

And as I did, from the corner of my eye, I caught a shutter-flash glimpse of the clearing as it once existed . . .

A modest stone-and-timber house stands apart from the tree line. Smoke curls from the chimney. A pair of horses are tied to a fence post. Running alongside the house, a robust garden. On the opposite side of the plowed rows of dark soil, a white cross protrudes from the ground. A man kneels before it in prayer. Shoulders quaking as he sobs. Behind him, carved into a tree at the edge of the forest, is the stick-figure symbol Melody discovered at the library . . .

. . . Autumn now, the leaves gone from the trees. Two little girls play in the grass with a homemade doll made out of straw. Neither of them is smiling. Nearby, their father chops wood with an axe, pausing to wipe his brow and chase a mangy dog away from the garden. And in the background, a hulking dark figure with glowing red eyes watches them from the shadows of the forest, just like on the cover of Larson Rutherford's book . . .

. . . A hard snow is falling, the ground covered. Despite the cold, the door to the cabin stands ajar and no smoke rises from the chimney. And we soon see why. Behind the house, not far from the tree line, the man and two young girls are tied to stakes that have been pounded into the ground. Their throats have been cut. Each is wearing a bib of blood. Strangely shaped footprints in the snow trail away from the gruesome spectacle, leading deep into the woods . . .

"GODDAMMIT, BILLY! HELP!"

Then all of it was gone—the man and the girls and the snow—and it was as if I'd passed back into this world again.

"HELP ME! SHE'S BLEEDING!"

All this time, Troy hadn't been whispering—he'd been screaming at the top of his lungs.

At the edge of the clearing where I'd left them, I saw Troy kneeling on the ground beside Melody. She was sprawled on her back in the dirt, her tear-streaked face a mask of pain and confusion as she pressed both of her hands against her stomach. Her legs were spread wide and the crotch of her jeans was soaked in blood.

32

For the first time since the trip began, we broke rule number five of Tamara Wise's rental agreement.

With Melody curled up on a couple of towels in the passenger seat, I drove over the Albert Linden Bridge and stopped at the first gas station we came to. I pulled the van as close as I could to the women's bathroom, and Troy hurried inside to ask for the key.

I managed to make the two-and-a-half-mile drive using only my left hand—because Melody refused to let go of my right.

33

I hung up the pay phone and looked at Troy.

"What'd they say?"

"They're sending a patrol car right away. I told them we'd wait at the dirt pull-off by the bridge."

"You tell them about the altar . . . and what was on it?"

"I did."

"You think they believed you?"

I shrugged. "Even if they didn't, they will soon enough."

"It was like you were in a trance," Troy said. "I kept screaming your name . . . but you acted like you couldn't hear me."

"I couldn't." I hadn't told either of them about what I'd experienced while I was standing beside the altar. I doubted I ever would.

"At one point, I started to go after you . . . to drag you out of there . . . but it was like someone hit me over the head with a hammer." Even though we were miles away, Troy glanced anxiously in the direction of the woods. "A couple of steps into the clearing, I got dizzy. A few more, and I was down on my knees puking. My head felt like someone had set it on fire. After that, it was all I could do to crawl back to Melody . . .

"And she was just as bad off as I was, if not worse. She'd started bleeding by then . . . and crying and moaning . . . and saying the most awful things . . . it was like she was in a trance . . ."

"What was she saying?" I asked, afraid to hear his answer.

Troy gave me a look and lowered his voice. "Dirty . . . things. She—"

I held up my hand, not wanting to know any more. It was my fault we'd gone looking for the clearing. My fault all this had happened. They'd just wanted to go home. Glancing at the restroom door, I asked, "You think she'll be okay?"

"She's already doing better. We all are. It started as soon as we got away from that goddamn place."

From across the gas station parking lot, the horn sounded.

"There you go," Troy said. "I guess she's all cleaned up and ready to go."

I started walking toward the van. "Let's go see what the cops have to say."

He sighed. "This day just keeps getting worse."

34

By the time we crossed over the bridge again—this time with Melody behind the wheel where she belonged—and swung the van into the narrow dirt pull-off, three green-and-white sheriff's department cruisers were waiting for us in the parking lot.

For the next thirty minutes, we answered a barrage of questions. All three deputies scribbling away in their little notepads. We kept our stories as simple as possible, leaving out the unsettling reactions we'd each experienced at the clearing. This we'd agreed upon ahead of time.

When one of the deputies asked what we were doing that far out in the woods in the first place, I told him we'd been shooting pick-up footage at the memorial when we noticed a family of deer watching us. The deer scampered away and we chased after them. Before we knew it, we were lost.

Eventually, the two younger deputies returned to their cars and left to go investigate the clearing. Even in the midst of all this chaos, they made an immediate impression because of the almost comical difference in their height. The third deputy was a heavyset gentleman, friendly enough, with the thickest pair of eyebrows I'd ever seen. He stayed behind with us in the dirt pull-off.

After tagging the video camera as evidence and filling out a receipt, he began telling us about his younger brother Alex in Boston. Married with three kids and not yet forty years old, he'd been killed in a motorcycle accident on his way to work one morning.

"You should've seen it," the deputy said, leaning back against the van.

MEMORIALS

"By the morning of the funeral, Alex's memorial stretched nearly an entire city block. Had to be at least thirty or forty of those wreathes on little stands. Flowers lined up all along the curb. Stuffed animals. Candles. Ribbons on the light poles. The works."

The deputy's eyes hardened. "And then some of the shop owners began to complain. Someone vandalized the memorial overnight. Made a big mess of the street. The next day, some of Alex's friends went down there to clean up. There was an argument, turned into a fight. One of the store windows got broken. That's when the news people got involved."

He reached into his back pocket and slid out his wallet. "City officials stepped in and worked out a compromise. A much smaller memorial was allowed at the intersection where the accident occurred. Channel 5 did a big story about it. Thirty days later, a city crew came out and cleaned it all up—and it was like it had never existed."

"I'm really sorry for your loss," Melody said. Troy and I mumbled our agreement.

The deputy took out a snapshot from inside his wallet and showed it to us. Other than sharing the same five-dollar haircut and caterpillar eyebrows, the two brothers looked nothing alike.

A little while later, the deputy returned to his car and got busy on the radio. With his window down, we could hear from across the parking lot the staticky squawk of his dispatcher's voice. Not knowing what else we were supposed to do, we stood around outside the van and waited, mostly in silence. Even Troy was uncharacteristically quiet, and I found myself wondering if he was trying as hard as I was to forget all about our horrible experience in the woods. No matter how many times I attempted to trick my brain, I couldn't stop it from replaying in vivid detail a naked Melody bent over the altar, drunk with lust and gasping for breath. Standing next to her in the parking lot, I could barely manage to look her in the eyes. Several times, I'd caught her staring at the tunnel of trees, in the direction of the clearing. The only word I knew to describe the expression on her face was *haunted*.

As seven thirty approached, I walked over to the officer, explained that we had dinner plans, and asked if we were allowed to leave. He shook his head and said he preferred that we stick around for just a little bit longer.

That was our first hint that something was wrong.

Another twenty minutes passed. The three of us getting antsy now. Even with all the questions I had rattling around inside my head about Aunt Helen's disturbing behavior, I still felt terrible that we were going to be late for dinner, knowing she would be worried sick. At least, I thought she would be.

After sneaking away to pee behind some bushes, I was on my way back to the others when the two deputies pulled into the lot.

And the shit hit the fan.

35

Red-faced and sweating, their previously neat uniforms covered in burrs and streaked with mud, the deputies sprang from their cars and stormed across the dirt pull-off in my direction.

"You think this is a goddamn joke?!" the tall deputy shouted.

For a spilt second, I thought about running. That's how pissed he looked. Instead, I held out my hands in front of me. "Whoa, whoa, whoa—I have no idea what you're talking about."

"Chasing deer . . . what kind of idiots do you think we are?"

By now he'd closed the distance between us. I could see the veins bulging in his neck and spittle flying from the corners of his mouth. His partner, a full foot shorter than him, stopped at his side, clenching and unclenching his hands. He hadn't uttered a word since the initial questioning, but he looked like he wanted to strangle me.

"Listen, I don't know what you're so pissed about, but—"

"No, *you* listen," the tall deputy said, waggling a finger in my face. "I know your aunt and the sheriff are an item, but if you think that means I won't—"

"My aunt's none of your damn business."

MEMORIALS

His eyes went dark then—and if the older officer and Melody and Troy hadn't shown up at that exact moment, there's no telling what he might've done.

"Okay, Carl. Step back. Now."

Deputy Carl's shoulders sagged, and he immediately backed up. The shorter deputy stared at the ground. For the first time, I noticed the sergeant's stripes on the older man's uniform sleeve.

"Anyone raises their voice again and this conversation is over." He looked at the two deputies. "Now tell them what you found."

I could see the muscles in Deputy Carl's jaw tightening. "Nothing," he said in a strained voice. "Unless you count a bunch of empty beer bottles and condom wrappers."

"You went to the wrong place," I said.

Turning to the sergeant, he shook his head. "No, sir, we did not. It's the only clearing in those woods. You know that."

"You didn't find the photograph?" Melody asked. "Or . . . the tongue?"

"Nope. Nothing like that." The deputy's face broke out in a smirk. "Maybe a deer came along and ate them."

Troy stepped forward. "What about the stick figures in the trees?"

His grin widened. "Deer must've eaten those too."

"This is bullshit!" I snapped. "You're covering it up . . . just like you did before!"

The deputy's face went cartoon red. I wouldn't have been shocked to see smoke come pouring out of his ears next.

"Easy, son," the sergeant said.

"I'm not your son."

He looked at me like he wanted to say something else—but only nodded.

"So what happens now?" Melody asked, an edge to her voice.

The short deputy stepped forward. "I think we should run 'em and test 'em, Sarge. I don't smell no alcohol, but they've gotta be on something. They're either lying or they're hallucinating."

The older officer ignored him and flipped open his notebook. "The three of you mentioned that you smelled smoke..."

"We found no evidence of a fire," Deputy Carl said. "The only thing we noticed—"

"Wait a minute!" I nearly shouted. "I shot the whole thing!" I couldn't believe I hadn't thought of it until now. Practically hopping with excitement, I swung around and pointed at the green-and-white cruiser parked across from the van. "You have the tape! You can go watch it right now!"

"I already did," the sergeant said—and I could tell by the look on his face that more bad news was coming. "There's nothing on it."

36

"Can they put you in jail for filing a false police report?" Troy asked.

"No one's going to jail," I said. "We didn't do anything wrong."

"Tell *them* that."

On the opposite side of the lot, the sergeant leaned against his cruiser, a cigarette dangling from his mouth. The two deputies stood in front of him, arguing their case. There was quite a bit of foot stomping and arm waving. At one point, the short detective demonstrated what appeared to be him jumping over a creek. Or maybe a fallen log. And then he pointed out a rip in his uniform pants. Every once in a while, Deputy Carl would glance over his shoulder and glare at us. I figured it was just a matter of time before they came to a decision.

"It's a misdemeanor," Melody said. "A girl from my high school once accused someone of stealing jewelry from her gym locker. The police came and filled out a report, and then the very next day the girl admitted that she'd lied. Her parents ended up paying a fine. That was it."

"I don't want to pay any fine," Troy said. "Don't want my folks to either."

"Your folks will be okay." I gave him a pat on the shoulder. "As long as the sheriff's office accepts McDonald's gift certificates."

"Asshole. That's not funny."

"You're right," I said. "It's not. I'm sorry."

He cracked a smile. "Maybe a little bit."

I smiled back. "Maybe."

"Imbeciles," Melody said, shaking her head. "I'm surrounded by imbeciles."

It was an old schtick among the three of us—Troy and I misbehaving like ill-mannered adolescents until Melody was forced to step in and scold us—and even in the middle of all this madness, it brought with it a measure of comfort and normalcy.

But this time it didn't last.

A car swung into the dirt pull-off. A plain dark blue sedan with a huge antenna on the back. The driver pulled up to where the three men were standing, and they spoke for a moment through an open window. Then the car abruptly cut across the lot and parked in front of the van, blocking us in.

Uh-oh. This isn't good.

The man who climbed out of the unmarked cruiser was tall and rangy. He was dressed in jeans and a white button-down shirt with the sleeves rolled up past his elbows. There was a badge clipped to his belt, but I didn't see a holster or a gun. Leaving the engine running and the driver's-side door open, he sauntered to the front of the car. The glare of the headlights hit his face—and it was as if the Marlboro Man had stepped out of a magazine advertisement. Chiseled cheekbones, bushy mustache, eyes the dazzling blue of a mountain lake. The only thing missing was his horse.

"Heard you folks had a bit of trouble today."

He stopped in front of me and stuck out his hand.

"I'm Jason Peters. You must be Billy."

37

"Well, this is going to make for awkward dinner conversation."

Sheriff Peters chuckled. "Don't worry. We never talk shop at the supper table. It's one of your aunt's rules." He gave a wave as the last of the three cruisers turned left onto Church Street and headed back to town. The deputy behind the wheel tapped his horn in response.

"I appreciate you calling and letting her know we'd be late. I knew she'd be worried."

"Just be ready for about a hundred and one questions when you get to the house. Do me a favor, though?"

"What's that?"

"First thing tomorrow morning, I'm coming back out here to take a look for myself."

That was a surprise. "You want me to come with you?"

He shook his head. "It's better if I go alone."

"Does this mean you believe we're telling the truth?"

"Let's just say that I don't *not* believe you."

"So you think they went to the wrong place. I told them—"

He held up a hand. "I didn't say that. Those deputies are good men. And they know these woods."

"Then why . . ." I thought about it for a moment. "You're doing this because of Aunt Helen, aren't you? She asked you to."

"Yes and no."

"What does that mean?"

"Your aunt talks about you." He gave me a look. "All the time. You're pretty much her favorite subject."

"Oh, great," I said, rolling my eyes. I didn't even want to think about those conversations.

"And from everything I've heard, you don't seem like the type of person to call in a false report."

"I'm not." I glanced at Melody and Troy waiting in the van. "*We're* not."

"So that right there's the 'yes' part. I'm willing to extend you the benefit of the doubt because of your aunt."

"And the 'no'?"

"Helen . . . your aunt . . . she didn't ask me to do anything," he said. "In fact, all she knows about today is that the three of you lost your way in the woods and stumbled upon some kind of ritual site."

"She doesn't know about . . . what we found there?"

"And I'd prefer if it stays that way until after I take a look for myself. That's where the favor comes in."

"You want us to keep our mouths shut?"

"Regarding certain specifics . . . until I say otherwise . . . yes."

"If you don't mind me asking, why?"

He took a deep breath. "She worries. Too much. If I show up at the house twenty minutes late, you can see it all over her face. Not just stress, but *fear*. She's waiting for that next phone call with bad news. She's waiting for a knock on her door. If she thinks there's some kind of, what, a cult running around town, it's only going to make things worse."

It was out of my mouth before I realized it. "Do you love her?"

His eyes went wide—and then he threw his head back and laughed. It was the kind of laughter that came from the heart instead of the belly. It reminded me of my Uncle Frank sitting in his rocking chair on the front porch—and I couldn't help but wonder if Aunt Helen felt the same way.

"Boy, you don't beat around the bush, do you?"

"It was an honest question."

"Yes, it was." He looked at me. "I do. I love Helen very much. I haven't said it out loud yet . . . at least not to her . . . but it's coming . . . I'm just waiting on the right moment."

"Well then," I said, smiling. "I guess now I have two secrets to keep."

38

As we walked across the lot to his car, I recognized the song playing on the van's radio: "Don't Stand So Close to Me" by the Police. Which could only mean one of two things: (1) the radio gods had a wicked sense of humor, or (2) Troy was up to his old tricks. The moment I saw the look on his face, I knew I had my answer.

After meeting the sheriff and going on and on about how much they adored my Aunt Helen—Mel doing a particularly impressive job considering her misgivings—Melody and Troy had immediately retreated to the van. Initially, I was irritated that they'd abandoned me so quickly. The last thing I wanted was to be alone with my aunt's boyfriend. Fortunately, to my surprise, he'd turned out to be a stand-up guy. We'd even made plans to go fishing together over the summer.

"Do me another favor," the sheriff said, "and go straight to your aunt's house? No detours along the way."

"Consider it done."

"I do have one question for you," he said, settling into the driver's seat of his unmarked sedan.

"What's that?" There was a subtle change in the tone of his voice that I didn't like. For the first time since we'd met, it felt like I was talking to a cop.

"What were you guys *really* doing out there in those woods?" He was smiling when he said it—but all of a sudden, I found myself wondering what was hiding behind that grin.

"Like I told your men . . . we were chasing deer."

He pulled the door closed and looked up at me.

"That's a long way to go for some deer."

"It was a whole family of them." I put on my best smile. "It was pretty cool at the time."

39

"I knew that deer story wouldn't hold up," Troy said from the back seat.

"I panicked and said the first thing that came to mind." It was starting to rain again. I rolled up the window and pressed the button to lock the door. "Those deputies came at us with so many questions, I could barely keep up."

"It's not your fault," he said. "We should've figured out a better excuse ahead of time."

Melody switched on the van's high beams, which cut through the

MEMORIALS

gloom of Church Street. Ever since hearing Father Paul's story, I'd found myself thinking of the tunnel of trees as the cavernous opening to a bottomless mine shaft. It was just about as dark and desolate. All three of us turned and stared as we slowly drove past my parents' memorial. No one said anything, but I'm pretty sure we all felt it: a sense of impending doom hanging thick in the air around us.

"I'm just glad he doesn't expect us to go with him tomorrow," Troy said.

Melody looked at me. "I'm never going back there."

"None of us are."

"The sheriff's a lot younger than your aunt," Troy said. "Are they serious?"

"I think so . . ." I remembered my promise. "But time will tell."

"So you liked him?"

"I liked him a lot . . . right up until the end when he asked me what we were doing in the woods." I thought about how the question had made me feel. "Then I couldn't help but wonder if everything else before that had been an act."

"You think he was playing Good Cop?"

"I hope not . . . but it's possible. Especially after what Craig told us about the cops covering up the clearing all this time."

Troy leaned in between the seats, his voice excited. "Did you hear what that deputy said when you accused him of going to the wrong place?"

"No . . . what?"

"He told his sergeant: *It's the only clearing in those woods. You know that.*"

And there it was. *Holy shit*. "If his men knew about it, it only makes sense that the sheriff would know too."

"That's what I was—"

I looked up in time to see the van drift across the center line. Steadily gaining speed. "Mel . . ." And then, all at once, we were swerving. "Mel!" The woods on the opposite side of the road rushing toward us. Filling up the windshield.

"MELODY! WATCH OUT!"

She yanked the steering wheel hard to the right—and for a split second the van tottered on two wheels. *We're going to roll!* my terrified brain cried out, and even with the world seemingly moving in slow motion, there wasn't nearly enough time to count to ten. A heartbeat later—with a teeth-rattling *thud* as the airborne tires slammed back to earth—we were riding upright again, a wide-eyed Melody pumping the brake pedal and squeezing the wheel and guiding the van to the gentlest of stops.

No one said anything at first.

The only sound: the rhythmic *whish-whoosh* of the wiper blades.

And then we were all talking at once.

"What the—!"

"I thought we were—"

"My heart is—"

"Mel, are you okay?!" Troy stammered.

"No," she said. "It . . . it was like watching myself in a dream . . . I turned the wheel on *purpose*. I gave it gas. I knew it was wrong, but I did it anyway . . ."

I thought of my father and his 1979 Subaru hatchback. The man who changed the oil and wiper blades every fifteen thousand miles. The man who logged his gas mileage in a notebook he kept in the glove compartment and had not even a single speeding ticket on his record. The man police claimed was driving at more than twice the legal speed limit when he crashed into the trees . . .

"If you hadn't screamed, Billy . . ." She lifted the crucifix to her lips and kissed it. The blood had drained from her face. She looked like a corpse. "I know your aunt expects us for dinner . . . but that's not going to happen . . . at least not for me . . . I'm going home . . . I'm getting the hell out of this crazy place . . ."

"Just take a deep breath," I said, slipping on my seat belt. "Maybe you should pull into the grass and—"

She ignored me and started driving again. Slowly. With both hands squeezing the steering wheel so tightly that her knuckles were white. "I'm bleeding again . . . and my period's not due for two more weeks . . . Billy, you know that camera better than anyone . . . There's no way that video was blank ... which means either some serious shit is going on ... or one of those cops erased it ..."

As I listened to her ramble, I glanced at the side mirror—and what I saw there made my stomach churn. The section of woods in which we'd nearly just crashed was the exact same spot we'd parked at earlier this afternoon when we'd gone looking for the clearing.

Almost as if that horrible place in the woods had wanted us back.

40

"I have to tell you about something I saw in the clearing."

Troy looked at me. "You mean besides hell on earth?"

"Besides that," I nodded.

"Are you sure we want to know?" Melody asked, and in that moment, I was almost positive she'd experienced the same X-rated vision that I had.

"I think it might be important."

She sighed. "Then I guess you better go ahead."

"Right before I woke up ... and heard Troy screaming ... I saw something." I felt Melody tense in the driver's seat. "For just a few seconds ... it was like I was peering through a window into the past ... that's the only way I can describe it. I saw the cabin. Smoke coming from the chimney. I saw the man who lived there and his two little girls. And something with red eyes watching them from the woods. Just like the cover of that library book Melody found."

We turned onto the street where my aunt lived.

"And then I blinked ... and there was snow on the ground and they were all dead ... their throats cut, eyes missing, bodies tied up to stakes... just like my father described."

"Jesus," Troy whispered.

"The only difference was there was no mother. I think my dad had it wrong about the neighbors finding all four of them in the clearing. I'm pretty sure the mother died earlier ... and it was just the three of them."

"The Three Musketeers," Melody said under her breath.

"I know what Father Paul said about the mines . . . and I believe him . . . but I think whatever this is . . . whatever's happening . . . I think it all started in that godforsaken clearing."

41

Aunt Helen was waiting on the front porch when we pulled up to the curb. *Here we go,* I thought, walking up the driveway. *Now it's my turn to earn an Academy Award.*

While I did my best to explain what had happened—sticking with the deer story and leaving out the part about the photograph and the tongue—Melody and Troy went upstairs to pack. Once they came back down, we would switch roles. They'd keep Aunt Helen occupied while I gathered my clothes and stuffed them into my knapsack. When I was finished, we'd say a quick goodbye and stop at a pay phone so I could call Naomi, and then we'd get the hell out of Dodge and make a beeline back to campus. At least that was the plan we'd come up with on the drive over here.

To my surprise, Aunt Helen didn't put up much of a fight.

"Don't worry about it," she said as we walked into the kitchen. "I already told Jason we'd have to postpone dinner." She handed me a glass of iced tea. "Tonight just wasn't meant to be . . . The chicken was overcooked and it got so late and . . ." She put a hand on my shoulder. "Are you sure you're okay, Billy?"

I nodded. "Just tired and a little freaked out—and ready to be home again."

I thought she might bristle at the mention of home being someplace other than Sudbury—but she didn't say a word about it.

"And you're sure you don't want to wait until morning?"

"Melody's worried about her roommate," I said.

"Okay, then you'll call first thing to let me know you got in okay?"

"Yes, ma'am."

When she started fidgeting with the buttons on her shirt, I guessed what was coming next. "So . . . what did you think of Jason?"

"I liked him. He seems like a good guy."

"He is," she said, really doing a number on those buttons. "You don't think he's . . . too young?"

I shook my head. "Who cares, as long as he makes you happy." I rinsed my empty glass and left it in the sink. When I turned around, she was sitting at the kitchen table, deep in thought.

"Did you know about the clearing . . . ?" I watched her face for a reaction. "The altar in the woods?"

There was no change in her expression—and no hesitation at all. "No . . . I didn't." She crossed her arms over her chest. "Just the thought of it gives me the willies."

"All those years . . . and Uncle Frank never mentioned anything about it?"

"Surprisingly, no." A hint of a wistful smile on her lips. "And thank God for small favors."

If she's a liar, she's a damn good one.

And then I remembered the soft *click* I'd heard on the telephone line when I was talking to Robert Farnsworth and the dagger from our nightmare hidden in a shoebox at the bottom of her closet.

42

Unzipping the small pouch on the front of my knapsack, I slipped my toothbrush, toothpaste, deodorant, and disposable razor inside. I started to close it but stopped when I noticed the prescription bottle resting on the ledge by the sink. *Can't forget that,* I thought, picking up the vial of pills and making a mental note to double-check my calendar for next week's Dr. Mirarchi appointment. We had a lot to talk about.

I stared at the plastic bottle in my hand. The lid wasn't screwed on. Puzzled, I turned it until I felt it lock and then stuffed it inside my knapsack and zipped it closed.

I thought about the horrible stories I'd seen on the news about little kids dying from accidental overdoses of prescribed medicine. Usually one of the parents was responsible. While there was little danger of an unsupervised child appearing in my aunt's upstairs bathroom, it still wasn't like me to leave my meds unsecured. If nothing else, it was a matter of routine. You slid out the pill, replaced the lid, and turned it until you felt and heard that tiny *click*. Finding the bottle open just now really bothered me.

Then I thought of last night's nightmare—and it suddenly made a lot more sense. This morning had been a chaotic blur. The four of us had been a mess. Looking back, a part of me was surprised I'd even remembered to take my pill.

At least, that's what I told myself. And as I'd already proved, I could be a damn good liar, too, when the situation called for it.

After scanning the rest of the bathroom to make sure I hadn't forgotten anything, I turned off the light and stepped into the hallway. I hadn't had time to stop at the store to buy night-lights. The hall was as dark as the night sky outside my bedroom window. I slung my backpack over my shoulder, listening to the murmur of voices coming from the living room. As far as I could tell, the conversation seemed pleasant enough. I was worried about Melody. Her attitude toward my aunt had taken a hard one-eighty since she'd caught her listening in on her phone call. She didn't trust her anymore. I didn't either, not fully—and that made me sad to think about. As I started down the hallway, I patted the pockets of my jeans. Money clip in right front pocket: *check*. Backup van keys in left front pocket: *check*. Back pockets empty: *che—*

There was something in my back pocket.

Something that wasn't supposed to be there.

I stopped in the light at the head of the stairs—and slid out the object with my fingers.

It was a tiny stick figure made out of twigs.

43

Aunt Helen was outside on the porch again—waving goodbye this time.

A few minutes earlier, while hugging in the foyer and once again promising to call and let her know when we got back to campus, all I could think about was the miniature stick figure I'd found in the pocket of my jeans.

How in the hell had it gotten there? Had Aunt Helen slipped it in when we were talking in the kitchen? Or one of the cops at the parking lot by the bridge? And what did it mean? Was it a warning? A curse? Part of some ritual? All I knew was that I wasn't taking any chances. Standing in the upstairs bathroom, I'd squeezed the damn thing in my fist, over and over again, until it splintered into about a dozen tiny pieces, and then I'd flushed it all down the toilet, where it belonged. After that, I'd washed my hands for several moments, soaping and re-soaping, scrubbing away its malevolent touch.

Aunt Helen waved again and blew me a kiss—and all of a sudden, I was thinking about my parents and fighting back tears. God, I was such a fucking mess.

Growing up, whenever I left the house for a special event—the homecoming dance or a big football game or a weekend trip to the beach—my mom and dad would stand side by side on the front stoop, smiling and waving. My father would be in his slippers, my mother in her apron, and they wouldn't go back inside until my car disappeared around the corner. As I drove away, I'd watch them fade in the rearview mirror, my heart swelling in my chest, certain that they would live forever. Later, when I returned home, I'd tiptoe upstairs in the dark, careful not to wake them, listening to the gentle snores coming from their bedroom. Sixteen and filled with hope, I'd climb into my bed and fall asleep under the covers, believing that the world was exactly as it should be. Dreaming the dreams of the innocent.

"Nectar of the gods . . ." Sitting in the back seat of the van, shirt covered in crumbs, Troy smacked his lips and pulled another chocolate chip cookie out of the bag that Aunt Helen had handed him before we'd left the house. "Or in the case of your aunt . . . the *goddesses*."

Melody adjusted the rearview mirror and turned the key.

The engine remained silent.

No groan, no growl, no stutter.

She sighed and tried again.

A low *click*ing sound this time.

We looked at each other. A little anxious, but no real fear.

Not yet.

We'd been here before—and the Mystery Machine had always come through.

She turned the key a third time.

Nothing. Not even a *click*.

"Fuck. This can't be happening," she muttered under her breath.

"Pop the trunk," I said, climbing out of the van. I knew that Melody was tottering on the edge of panic—she had been ever since earlier this morning—and it wouldn't take much more to send her there.

I grabbed a flashlight and walked to the rear of the van where the engine was located, fingered the release latch, and propped open the trunk.

Scattered across the engine block, hanging from loose wires, peeking out from inside the radiator, and wedged into every available nook were dozens of lattice stick figures made out of twigs. The largest was six or seven inches tall, the smallest maybe half that size.

"Is everything okay?" Aunt Helen called out, stepping down from the porch.

I lifted a trembling hand. *Give me a second.*

I didn't know much about automobile engines—but I sure as hell knew what sabotage looked like.

The tangle of multicolored wires that lay coiled like a bird's nest among the army of bizarre stickmen hadn't merely been disconnected. They'd deliberately been cut.

44

Before I could stop her, Melody charged out of the van and met Aunt Helen halfway across the lawn. It was all I could do to keep up with her, my hand grasping her shoulder to prevent my friend from doing anything stupid.

MEMORIALS

"Do you know who did this?!" she shouted. "Did *you* do this?!"

A shocked Aunt Helen physically recoiled. "Billy—what is she talking about?"

"The van . . . ," I said. "Someone tampered with the engine."

She looked past us to the curb. "They did *what*?"

"No more playing dumb," Melody hissed. "We *know*!" And she actually lunged at the older woman, nearly pulling free from my grasp.

My aunt gaped with wild and frightened eyes. "Know what, for God's sake?!" Once again, I thought that if she was acting, she deserved a Golden Globe. Maybe even an Oscar.

"You listened in on our phone calls! You spied on us! You know goddamn well who did this!"

I felt movement at my side. It was Troy. He looked scared and confused. "I did no such—"

"Oh, come on! Tell her, Billy!" Melody said. "You heard it too!"

This was awful. No matter what, I loved my aunt. And needed her. I wanted to dig a hole in the ground and crawl into it. I wanted to run away. Instead, I just nodded.

And as I did, something in Aunt Helen's eyes dimmed. The intensity of her focus wavered and was replaced by a dull, faraway gaze. Her shoulders slumped in defeat.

"You're right . . . ," she said, looking at me. "I did . . . I . . . was worried . . . worried you kids were getting in over your heads. I didn't mention it before because I didn't want to scare you . . . I know how much this trip means . . . but two young women are missing . . . One was hitchhiking . . . and now there's a third in Colonial Heights . . . She disappeared yesterday . . ."

I felt the rage leave Melody's body all at once and loosened my grip on her arm.

I recalled the MISSING PERSON flyer on the wall of the store we'd stopped at. Other posters stapled to trees in the park. Taped to store windows and telephone poles all across town.

I even remembered the women's names.

Brianna Kellegher.
Annie Loman.

And while it wasn't a good enough excuse for doing what she'd done, at least I knew this time Aunt Helen was telling us the truth. Or in any case, part of it.

45

By the time Sheriff Peters and his deputies arrived fifteen minutes later, the three of us were in no mood for any bullshit. Especially Melody. She was raring for a fight.

"So from the time you arrived here," the sheriff said, scribbling in his notepad, "showered, packed, and got back into the van to leave . . . it was no more than an hour?"

"It was forty-five minutes," Melody said. "We already told you that."

"Okay, well . . . there's no question it's unusual," the sheriff replied. Deputy Carl stood beside him with a dull expression on his face. In the street, a second officer circled the van with a flashlight. "A vehicle is much more likely to be stolen in Sudbury than vandalized."

"That's reassuring," Melody said, not bothering to hide the edge in her voice.

"Those stick figures we were telling you about earlier . . ." Troy glared at Deputy Carl and gestured to the van. "I guess they must have followed us back here from Church Street."

With her hands on her hips, Melody strutted closer to the deputy. She looked like an angry rooster. "Maybe this time you'll do your damn job and figure out what's going on . . . instead of questioning our integrity."

Deputy Carl didn't say anything. Just gritted his teeth and looked away.

The sheriff—no doubt used to dealing with irate members of the public—calmly slipped his thumb beneath his belt and hitched up his pants. When he spoke again, he was looking directly at me. "My best guess is that this is related to that school project of yours. It's my understanding, after talking to Helen, that you experienced some pushback here and there while on the road."

"You could say that." Speaking of Aunt Helen, I glanced over my shoulder, wondering where she'd disappeared to. She'd been watching from the lawn just moments earlier. Now she was nowhere in sight.

"Anything like that happen closer to home? Here in Sudbury or just over the bridge?"

"Why do you think we called the police earlier today?" Melody snapped.

"Ma'am, I was thinking more along the lines of harassment or threats." The expression on his face remained neutral—and not for the first time, I thought: *This is a man who is good at his job.*

"Someone followed us into the park this afternoon and took our picture. Then they left that picture on an altar in the woods right next to a fucking tongue that had been ripped out of someone's mouth. If that's not a threat, Sheriff, I don't know what *is*!"

She was practically yelling, so I gestured for her to lower her voice. I'd already noticed lights coming on in nearby houses.

"I understand that, Ms. Wise. I do." The sheriff glanced at the street, where his deputy was down on one knee, shining a light at the rear bumper of the van. "Let me put it another way. Have you witnessed anyone here in Sudbury—whether on the road or in town or anywhere else—following or photographing or spying on you?"

Melody and Troy looked at me to answer for the group—and I immediately understood why. *Do we tell him about the man in the woods on the video?*

I had to be careful here. If the past couple of days had shown us anything, it was that it was nearly impossible to know who we could trust.

But in the end, it didn't matter. Before I could make up my mind, the deputy with the flashlight showed up and cut short our conversation. "Need you to take a look at something, boss."

The sheriff whispered a reply and looked back at us. "We'll have to finish this later."

And then he and Deputy Carl were following the other officer toward the van.

46

I'd expected an upset Troy to harp on the fact that neither one of us had bothered to tell him about Aunt Helen's eavesdropping—but so far he hadn't uttered a word. I think he was still in shock about the van being sabotaged and Melody's outburst. I know I was.

It also helped that Troy was fixated on the stick figures that had been left on the van's engine. "Just looking at them makes my skin crawl," he said with a shudder. "It feels like those little fuckers are watching us." I decided against telling him about the tiny stick figure I'd found in my pocket. That would be better saved for later—when Melody wasn't around.

While Sheriff Peters and his deputies used flashlights and portable light stands—not dissimilar to the lighting we'd used in the tunnel of trees—to examine the van and surrounding area, the three of us crowded in front of the bay window and watched them work. They'd arrived sans lights and sirens—at Aunt Helen's request, I'm sure—but even without them, a cluster of curious neighbors had gathered across the street. My aunt had walked over and spoken with them briefly, before returning to the driveway where she was now deep in conversation with the sheriff.

All of which gave me an idea.

"I'll be right back," I said, giving Melody a look. "Holler if it looks like they're heading inside."

"Will do."

As I climbed the stairs, I thought about what Sheriff Peters had asked when he first arrived: *Let me put it another way. Have you witnessed anyone here in Sudbury—whether on the road or in town or anywhere else—following or photographing or spying on you?*

Melody and Troy had stared at me, waiting for my answer. And in that moment, I'd known that they were thinking about the man in the woods on the video.

But now my mind went someplace else . . .

Earlier this morning, the three of us, along with Naomi, sitting at a picnic table in the park. Troy had been reading his notes when I'd noticed a flicker of movement in the bushes by the path—and then I'd thought I caught a glimpse of Jenny Caldwell watching us from behind some branches. For the next several minutes, I'd trained my eyes on the bushes but didn't see anything. For reasons unknown, I'd never mentioned that incident to anyone.

A part of me actually wanted to tell Sheriff Peters about Jenny and the man in the video. Maybe he could help us and stop what was happening. Then again, at least some of the cops around here had already shown that they couldn't be trusted. Telling him might only make matters worse. Besides, Jenny was Naomi's best friend. The last thing I wanted to do was get her into more trouble than she was already in.

Speaking of Naomi, she was a mess. She'd known that we were due back for dinner by seven thirty, and when ten o'clock rolled around and she still hadn't heard from me, she'd gotten worried and called my aunt's house. Unfortunately, at that exact moment, we were gathered outside on the porch, saying our goodbyes, and no one heard the phone ring.

Right after that, we'd discovered that the van had been tampered with.

Then Melody had gone off on Aunt Helen.

Then Aunt Helen had called Sheriff Peters.

And in the midst of all that craziness, I'd only had time to call and speak with her for a handful of minutes.

There were tears and confusion and anger—and the insistence that I call her back as soon as humanly possible with a thorough explanation. Which I hadn't been able to do just yet.

At the end of the hallway, I poked my head into my aunt's bedroom and looked around.

The lamp on the nightstand was on. Next to it, a paperback book and an alarm clock displaying 11:07 p.m. in glowing green digits.

A gray sweatshirt lay crumpled on the bed.

A pair of sneakers on the floor by the television.

The closet was closed.

I'd once lived here for almost a year, but I didn't know if this was common practice or not for my aunt. All I *did* know was that earlier this morning, the closet had been wide open. Which had made my job a whole lot easier.

The clock on the nightstand clicked over to 11:08.

It was now or never.

Cursing the creaky hardwood floors, I skirted around the dresser and the bed and stopped in front of the closet. Holding my breath, I pulled open the sliding metal doors—and the high-pitched shriek was like fingernails on a chalkboard. Either the bearings or the tracks needed several squirts of WD-40. Maybe the whole damn can.

I quickly dropped to a knee and reached for the last box in the bottom row. Carefully slid it out.

Baby blue. The image of a swan on the lid. *STAUNTON* printed on its side.

I opened it.

The box was empty.

The dagger was gone.

47

When the tow truck stopped at the curb and began backing up to the van—its red-and-white emergency lights reflecting off the nearby houses like Christmas decorations in May—Melody was up and out the door in a flash.

"Whoa, whoa, whoa," she said, hurrying down the driveway and waving her hands, "what the hell is this?"

Sheriff Peters turned to face her. "It's okay. I called them."

"It's certainly *not* okay . . . at least not without my approval. That's my sister's van."

"And it needs to be repaired so the three of you can get back on the road," he replied. "Hopefully by tomorrow afternoon."

"Hopefully . . . ?" she repeated.

"That's right. Whoever did this damaged more than just a few wires. The spark plugs are gone. That's not a big deal. If we look, we'll probably find them in a sewer drain down the street. But the coolant tank was also punctured. And you're going to need a new water pump."

MEMORIALS

"Oh my God," she said. "How much is all that going to cost?"

The sheriff looked at Aunt Helen, who was standing in the grass by the road. "Not a thing if it's up to her."

"What? I don't understand," Melody said, glancing back and forth between the two of them.

"It's the least I can do after how I acted." Aunt Helen took a hesitant step closer. "I'm embarrassed—and I'm so sorry."

I swallowed the lump in my throat. I may not have had a clue what was happening here in Sudbury, but *this* was the Aunt Helen I knew and loved.

"Please let me pay for the repairs. Stay here tonight and—"

"I'll gladly accept your apology," Melody said, "if you'll accept mine. There's no excuse for my behavior. As for the van . . . I mean, I have no choice but to take advantage of your generosity. But I'm going to pay you back. Every cent once I start working in the fall."

I felt the remaining tension drain away from my shoulders.

"Okay, that's fine," Aunt Helen said. "It's not necessary—"

"But I can't stay here. I *won't* stay here."

Aunt Helen's eyes widened. And my heart sank.

Melody put up a hand. "It's not *you* . . . I don't mean to be rude or ungrateful." She looked around—at the tow truck, the staring neighbors, the dark houses lining both sides of the street. "I just don't feel safe here anymore. Not after what happened to the van. Excuse my French, but something really fucked up is going on around here."

DAY SEVEN | MIDNIGHT

THURSDAY | MAY 12

1

"Are you sure he's going the right way?"

"*Shut up*," I whispered. My knapsack rested on the floor in between my feet. Inside, I had a change of clothes, my notebook, and a couple of flashlights I'd taken from the van. The video camera the sheriff had returned while we were at my aunt's house—minus the mysteriously blank cassette cartridge they were holding on to as evidence—nested in its silver case on the seat beside me.

"*You know who else doesn't have handles on the inside of their car doors?*" A dramatic blink of those big eyes of his. "*Serial killers.*"

"Stop it. Enough."

"*You want a cookie?*"

"No, and you shouldn't be eating in here."

For the second time in my life, I was locked in the back seat of a police car. And this time I had company. Earlier, when Sheriff Peters had volunteered to drop us off at the hotel, I'd insisted that Melody ride shotgun. I now regretted that polite gesture. Troy—whose very presence in the sheriff's unmarked cruiser represented the culmination of at least three of his deepest fears—was a nervous wreck. He was convinced that the sheriff was either going to take us somewhere deep in the woods and summarily execute us or hand us over to a gang of backwoods rednecks who were going to force us to cage fight for our continued survival. Did I mention that Troy Carpenter was a revelation?

"*He's speeding,*" Troy whispered, peering over the sheriff's shoulder. "*I should make a citizen's arrest.*"

"*Jesus Christ. Stop. It.*" I reached over and grabbed his left nipple—and twisted.

He squealed in pain and slid to the opposite end of the seat, rubbing his chest with the palm of his hand.

"*Oh, I'm sorry,*" I said in a low, mocking voice. "*Did that hurt?*"

He answered with gritted teeth and a jaunty wave of his middle finger.

"Everything okay back there?" Sheriff Peters asked.

"Everything's fine," I said, "just reeducating the prisoner."

I expected a laugh or a chuckle or at least a smile from one of them—but none of those things happened. I guess, in retrospect, that shouldn't have surprised me.

Melody hadn't said much of anything since we'd gotten into the car. Even though the disappointment had been evident on Aunt Helen's face, she'd called ahead and reserved a room for us at the Holiday Inn with two queen beds and a cot. That act of kindness had earned her another reserved "Thank you" from Melody, along with a moderately enthusiastic hug. After that, Melody had barely uttered another word.

Neither had Sheriff Peters, for that matter. As the night dragged on, the affable Marlboro Man I'd met in the dirt pull-off by the bridge had transformed into the strong and silent type. Probably tired, I thought. More likely, sick *and* tired of babysitting his girlfriend's weird nephew and his friends.

Although I'd never admit it out loud, there *had* been a moment—right at the start of our drive, and to my credit, it'd only lasted about thirty seconds—when I'd thought that Troy might be right, and we might not live to see tomorrow's sunrise.

The sheriff had turned onto Franklin Avenue and cruised past Potter's Cornfield and Jenson's Junkyard. I stared out the window and couldn't believe that Naomi and I had traveled the same route earlier this morning on bicycles. It felt like that had been days ago.

As we passed over the old stone bridge, I noticed that we were picking up speed. Quite a bit of it. My favorite stretch of woods whipped by us in the darkness, looking nothing like the friendly playground of trees and vines and mounds of dirt I remembered from my childhood. For just a second, I could've sworn I saw a pair of glowing red eyes staring out at us from within the shadows . . .

And then we drifted across the center line, the cruiser's headlights veering to the left, illuminating a section of crumbling stone wall that looked like it belonged on the cover of a Maine road map. Flashing back just a handful of hours earlier to our close call on Church Street with Melody at the wheel, I'd nearly yelled out a warning—but before I could, the sheriff corrected the wheel, pumped the brake, and returned us to our proper lane. Then he'd yawned and turned up the radio as if none of it had ever happened. In the back seat, Troy had grabbed my arm hard enough to leave a bruise and mouthed: *He's going to kill us.*

When we arrived at the Holiday Inn at ten minutes past midnight, I was surprised to see we weren't the only late check-ins. A man and a woman with three whiny kids—the loudest of whom was complaining that he had to "go poo"—were slowly making their way across the parking lot. Dad, scarecrow thin, with a deer-in-the-headlights look on his face, was struggling to carry four suitcases, two in each hand. Mom was dressed in a long flowing pool dress and bright yellow flip-flops. She and the kids—two boys and a girl—were empty-handed, unless you counted half-eaten candy bars.

When the mom looked over and saw Sheriff Peters—the badge on his belt easy enough to spot in the glare of the streetlights—freeing me and Troy from the back seat, a scowl came over her face. She quickly corralled her children away from us, snatching up the smallest of the three and nearly suffocating the poor kid against her ample bosom. As she glowered over her shoulder, I realized that it wasn't *us* she was looking at. It was Troy. I was about to say something when her hapless husband shuffled by us, an apologetic look on his exhausted face.

"Need any help checking in?" the sheriff asked, yawning.

"I think we're good." I looked at the others, and they both nodded. "We really appreciate the ride."

"Not a problem," he said, lowering himself into the driver's seat.

Before he closed the door, I asked, "Do you still plan to go out to the clearing in the morning?"

"First thing."

"And you'll let us know what you find?"

"I'll be in touch . . ." He reached for the door handle. ". . . one way or the other." And pulled it closed.

As he drove away, I started walking toward the hotel's automatic doors. I couldn't wait to change clothes and collapse into bed.

"What does 'one way or the other' mean?" Troy asked.

"I was wondering the same—"

I heard the *slap-slap-slap* of rapid footfalls on the pavement behind me.

And spun around just in time to see Melody chasing the sheriff's unmarked sedan across the parking lot. "STOP! WAIT!" She caught up with it at the crosswalk and started banging on the roof.

Observing this spectacle, my wearied brain had but one reaction: *We're going to jail tonight.*

A slack-jawed Troy gave voice to my concerns: "That's it. She's gone insane."

But as it turned out, Melody was a lot more on the ball than the rest of us.

At the last moment, just as Sheriff Peters had been pulling away, she'd remembered that all of our camera equipment, video footage, and photographs had been transferred from the back of the van to the trunk of the sheriff's car.

2

"How come I have to sleep on the cot?" Troy asked. "Is it because I'm Black?"

"*Troy!*" Melody hurled a hairbrush across the room. He didn't even have time to duck. It missed his head by inches.

"I was just kidding," he said, giggling.

"Well, it's not funny."

"Then why are you smiling?"

She sighed and shook her head, like an embattled old schoolteacher. "Because, as usual, I let you two clowns drag me down into the gutter."

"Hey . . ." I tossed a green M&M at her. "How did I get pulled into this?"

She picked up the M&M from the blanket. Examined it and popped it in her mouth.

MEMORIALS

And then all three of us were laughing—and for the longest time, we couldn't stop.

"Oh God," she finally said, wiping tears from her eyes. "I really am going crazy."

In a way, I think we all were.

We were exhausted and starving and stranded—but at least we were together and safe. After the day we'd had, that was enough. The door to our room was locked and deadbolted. The curtains were closed. The television was playing a West Coast baseball game with the volume turned down. The bed closest to the window—the one I was lying across—was covered with bags of chips, candy bars, and soda cans purchased from a half-empty snack machine in the hotel lobby. All of our camera equipment and tapes were neatly arranged on the desk in the corner.

Melody was propped up against a stack of pillows, a blanket pulled over her chest. She'd already turned off the bedside lamp. Troy, wearing his favorite Bigfoot pajamas, sat on the end of the cot, munching a bag of pretzels. As usual, his chest was swathed in crumbs. I'd kicked my shoes off and changed into a pair of gray sweatpants and a clean T-shirt. But all of a sudden, I wasn't the least bit sleepy.

"This is so much better than camping," Troy said, gazing around the room. "It's like a slumber party."

"Just don't ask me to do your hair," Melody said.

"Is that what girls do at slumber parties?"

"Depends on the girls . . . and the party."

"I was never allowed to spend the night at my friends' houses."

"Why not?" I asked, and immediately regretted it.

"My parents were afraid we'd sneak out and get into trouble. That happened a lot where I grew up." He looked at the television screen. "One time, a kid in my class went to a birthday sleepover. It was mostly older boys. Someone dared him to try some pills they'd found in the dad's coat pocket. The kid died."

Melody crossed herself and muttered a prayer in Spanish. Not the first time I'd heard her do that.

"My whole class went to the funeral," he said. "And the dad was arrested."

"We should have a sleepover during exam week," I said, trying to lighten the mood. "Everyone can stay at my place. We'll study and order takeout and keep each other awake all night."

"I'd be up for that," Troy said.

"Me too. It sounds like fun." Melody leaned over and grabbed a bottle of Yoo-hoo from the nightstand—and surprised me by raising it in our direction. "To the Three Musketeers."

Troy grinned and lifted his grape soda. "The Three Musketeers."

Sitting up in bed, I hoisted my Pepsi and swallowed the lump that had formed in my throat. "To *us* . . . the broken hearts club."

Melody beamed, and I was reminded once again of how beautiful she was.

We all took a drink—and for the first time in days, it felt like everything was going to be okay.

A Burger King commercial replaced Dodger Stadium on the television. A bright-eyed teenage girl in pink tights and ballet slippers pirouetted across the screen. She had a ribbon in her hair, braces on her teeth, and freckles on her cheeks. The all-American girl next door. Balancing a Whopper in one hand and a bag of fries in the other, she twirled in the eye of the spotlight as an adoring audience rose to their feet.

The whole production was over-the-top ridiculous—but somehow it worked. My stomach started growling. I picked up a Hershey's bar with almonds, tore open the wrapper, and took a bite. When the baseball game resumed, I looked over at Melody. Her eyes were closed.

"Billy . . . ," Troy said in a quiet voice. "What are we going to do?"

"About what?" I asked.

"The documentary . . . those photos of us . . ." He took off his glasses and placed them on the dresser. Without them, he looked like a different person. Even younger. More vulnerable. "About . . . *everything* . . . I guess."

MEMORIALS

"I think we should save that discussion for the morning, after we've all had a good night's rest."

"I'm afraid to go to sleep. I don't want to have another nightmare."

I hadn't even thought of that. I glanced at Melody again. She appeared to be peacefully sleeping—but for how long?

"It's okay. We're safe here," I said. "We'll go home tomorrow and—"

Someone knocked on the door.

Melody bolted upright in bed, eyes wide with alarm. Troy leaped to his feet, overturning the cot. I dropped my candy bar to the carpet—and heard my father's voice scold me: *Toss that in the trash, Bill! Hotel rooms are like hospitals. Crawling with nasty germs.* I never knew when the memories would come.

As I started toward the door, I heard Troy's shocked voice: "*Whoa! Where the hell did* that *come from?*"

I glanced over my shoulder. Melody was standing in between the beds with the gun in her hand. It was pointed at the floor. Troy squinted at me from behind her.

Turning around again, I leaned close to the hotel door and pressed my eye to the peephole.

The tiny sphere of glass was old and dirty—but I immediately recognized the person standing outside.

I undid the lock and swung open the door.

3

"What are *you* doing here?" I peered up and down the hallway. "Is Naomi with you?"

Jenny Caldwell shook her head. "Someone . . ." Trying to catch her breath. ". . . left *this* . . ." She held up a piece of paper. ". . . on my bedroom window."

I took the typewritten note from her.

And read it:

Holiday Inn. Room 116. Bring them and any of their footage or pictures to the clearing. Naomi will be waiting. No cops.

4

"How do I know we can trust you?" I asked as we hurried across the parking lot.

"Do you have a choice?"

"We could call the sheriff. Let him handle it."

"And risk them doing something bad to Naomi?" Jenny shook her head in disgust. "Same ole Billy. Always thinking about himself."

Behind us, the hotel door glided open. I glanced back and saw Melody and Troy walk outside. Melody had changed into the same outfit she'd worn earlier today. Troy was struggling to pull a sweatshirt over his Afro. With Mel's help, he narrowly avoided walking into a parked car. Back in the room, I'd told them they didn't have to come—but they'd insisted. "*The note says 'bring* them,'" Melody had argued. "Them *means all three of us.*"

I stopped and looked at Jenny. "I saw you in the park today."

Her eyes widened. "I was . . . I didn't . . . Oh, wow, that's embarrassing."

"Why were you watching us?"

"I wasn't," she said, struggling to maintain eye contact. "I mean, I was . . . but it wasn't planned or anything. I took a walk to blow off some steam after my argument with Naomi . . . and I saw you all sitting there at the picnic table . . . so I stopped and tried to see what you were doing. But it was only for a minute or two, and then I got out of there."

"I need you to answer one question," I said. "And I need you to tell me the truth." We had about ten seconds before Melody and Troy caught up to us. "Did you take our picture in the park today?"

"What? No way," she said, a confused look on her face. "I don't even own a camera."

5

I believed her about the photograph.

Based on where I'd spotted her in the bushes, the angle was all wrong. Plus she was too close. The photo had been taken from longer range with a telescopic lens. Most likely from somewhere on the path at the opposite end of the baseball field.

"When you didn't call back, she got really worried and snuck out of the house." Jenny looked both ways and sped away from the hotel parking lot. It was shortly after 1 a.m., and the streets were empty.

"We were planning to stop at a pay phone on our way out of town," I said, "but we never got that far."

She made a grunting sound, which loosely translated to: *Sure, whatever you say, jackass.*

"He's telling the truth," Melody said. "He was going to call from the gas station."

I was sitting in the passenger seat of Jenny's brother's Toyota Supra. The smell of weed and dirty socks was overpowering. The paper bag the Holiday Inn desk clerk had given us to carry our snack machine goodies rested on the floorboard at my feet. Inside, all of the photographs we'd developed, along with several video cassette cartridges and more than a dozen canisters of film. Melody and Troy sat behind us, the gun resting on the seat between them.

"I heard the knock on my window and thought it was her," Jenny continued, turning onto Main Street.

I wasn't used to seeing her when she wasn't all dolled up in the latest fashion trend and wearing a couple of layers of makeup. Her usually teased-to-death dye-job was tied back in pigtails. She was wearing dark sweatpants with a hole in one knee and a Van Halen hoodie. She looked like the Jenny Caldwell I'd actually been friends with back in middle school.

"But no one was there," she said. "Just the note taped to the outside glass."

"You didn't see anyone?" I asked. "A car? Someone running away?"

She shook her head.

"How long ago was this?"

She thought about it. "I got dressed as soon as I finished reading it. Took me about five minutes to find Josh's car keys and get the note off my window. I probably should've worn gloves in case there were fingerprints. And then I guess another ten minutes or so to get to the hotel. So maybe . . . twenty-five minutes total." She braked at a yield sign even though there were no other cars in sight and merged onto Church Street. "Definitely no more than half an hour."

"Any idea what time it was when she snuck out of the house?"

"Right around midnight," Jenny said. "I remember looking at the clock and thinking her parents were gonna ground her for the rest of the summer if they found out."

At midnight, we'd been on our way to the hotel with the sheriff. By the time we got checked in and settled into our room, I'd decided it was too late to call. *I'll just wait and phone her in the morning,* I'd thought. And while all that was happening, Naomi was doing what? Walking to my aunt's house in the dark? It had to be at least a twenty-minute hike.

"If she snuck out, there's no way she took her parents' car, right?"

"Not a chance."

"Do you know if she rode her bike or walked?"

"She didn't say. She just said she couldn't wait around any longer. She was going stir-crazy."

I didn't want to say it because saying it out loud made it real—but I had no other choice. "If she'd made it to Aunt Helen's house, my aunt would have let her use the phone to call me at the hotel. No matter how late it was. That didn't happen. Which means whoever has her . . . grabbed her on the way."

"What I don't understand is . . . why didn't she just keep calling your aunt's house?" Troy asked. "That makes a lot more sense than sneaking out in the middle of the night."

"She tried," Jenny said. "A few times. She was pretty sure the ringer had been turned down."

After the day Aunt Helen had—waking up to my frantic screams, the last-minute cancellation of what was supposed to be a nice dinner, the tampering with the van and Melody's subsequent outburst, not to mention a

MEMORIALS

street full of cops and nosy neighbors in front of her house—I could easily see her turning down the ringer. Any way I looked at it, it felt like both of us had abandoned Naomi at a time when she'd needed us most.

"What if she's somehow involved?" Melody said, the first words she'd spoken since we'd left the hotel.

Jenny tapped the brake pedal. "Say again."

"What if all this is a sham? The note ... Naomi sneaking out and going missing ..."

"You're saying Naomi's in on it with whoever's doing this?" Troy asked.

"Think about it," Melody continued. "How else are they going to get us into the woods in the middle of the night—with the film and no cops?"

"Fuck you, lady," Jenny said. "Naomi's my best friend. She would never do that."

"But the two of you *together* might." Her voice was ice-cold. "I think you'd make a helluva team."

For a moment, I'd been too stunned to speak—but now the words finally came to me. "If you really feel that way, Mel, then why did you come? I told you you didn't have to. Maybe you should just wait in the car and—"

"I'm not going to let you walk into a trap." She tilted her head in Jenny's direction. "Especially with *her* leading the way."

Jenny slammed on the brakes. "Get out! Right now!"

"Gladly ... as long as Billy and Troy come with me."

"Fine!" she said, flinging open the driver's-side door. "I'll make you get out!"

"I'd love to see you try, little girl."

"Stop it! Both of you!" Glancing in the back seat, I saw what Jenny couldn't. The gun was no longer resting on the seat in between my friends. Melody had moved it onto her lap. Troy looked on the verge of tears. "We're wasting time!"

"You need to tell your bitch that," Jenny hissed. She tugged the door shut and jammed her foot on the gas pedal, the rear end of the Toyota fishtailing as we left rubber on asphalt.

My jaw aching from clenching it so tightly, I turned around to face Melody, prepared to stuff my hand over her mouth if necessary.

And she winked at me.

I couldn't believe it. The whole thing had been an act.

Once again, I felt like a man making his way through a dream.

"Listen . . . I'm sorry." She sounded like a completely different person now. "I didn't mean to upset anyone. All I was trying to say is that after everything that's happened, we have to be careful about who we trust."

"Whatever. Naomi told me what went down during your trip." Jenny still sounded pissed—her fingers tapping away at the steering wheel—but at least she was no longer yelling. "She also told me what you guys found in the woods today. There's no way she's involved in any of that crazy shit. And neither am I."

"We know that," I said.

She grunted to express her skepticism. "So then who is? And why do they want your stupid videotapes so bad?"

"It's a long story . . ." I took a deep breath and slowly let it out. "We stumbled upon something when we were on the road . . . something dangerous. Whoever's responsible is trying to stop us from snooping around and asking questions . . . and finishing our documentary."

"And where does Naomi fit in?"

"After what happened this afternoon, we had no choice but to get the police involved. These people are scared we'll show the sheriff everything we've found. So they're using Naomi to help get rid of the evidence."

"'These people' . . . who exactly are you talking about? Are they from Sudbury? Or—"

"I'm starting to think they're from *everywhere*."

"Well . . . whoever they are, they better not hurt her."

I thought about the red pickup truck that had nearly run me down. "I'll give them whatever they want to get Naomi back safely."

"I just know there's no way she would have gone with them unless . . ."

"Unless what?" Troy asked, leaning in between the seats.

"Either they physically forced her into the car." I could see the worry in her eyes as she spoke. "Or she knew the people . . . and went with them willingly."

6

As we entered the familiar tunnel of trees and the darkness around us thickened, the Toyota's headlights appeared to waver. Even with the high beams on, we were fighting a losing battle.

"They could probably hear us coming from a mile away," Melody said. "And now they can see us too. Terrific."

We'd decided to drive to the dirt pull-off, where earlier we'd met with the cops, to see if any cars were parked there. I seriously doubted that whoever was waiting for us had left their vehicles in plain sight, but to borrow Melody's cautionary mantra from earlier: *Better safe than sorry.* Troy was even prepared to jot down license plate numbers on a sheet of paper he'd torn from my notebook.

We all spotted the glow coming from the side of the road up ahead at the same time.

"What the hell is *that*?" Jenny asked.

I thought I knew—and the dreadful anticipation of what we were about to see made my stomach roil.

Jenny slowed the car to a crawl.

Troy pressed his face up against the window. "Jesus."

"*Madre de Dios*," Melody whispered.

I felt like I was going to be sick.

Dozens of burning candles lit my parents' memorial. Lining the roadside and scattered among the rocks and weeds, the tiny flames flickered and danced as we drifted by, sinister shadows cavorting in our wake. All of the candles were black.

Whoever did this . . . clearly did it to mock me . . . and the loss of my parents. This is personal. An act of sacrilege.

"Billy," Troy said from behind me, "check out the cross."

Hanging from the horizontal slat of the wooden cross was a lattice stick figure.

7

As expected, the dirt lot was empty.

"Now what?" Jenny asked.

"We go back and park on the side of the road," I said in a voice thick with saliva. "And we fucking get Naomi back."

Jenny turned the car around and pulled onto Church Street. "You'll have to show me where."

This time I kept my eyes closed as we drove past the memorial.

8

As it turned out, we didn't have to show her.

In the handful of minutes since we'd driven past, someone else had already parked there. A silver Jeep Cherokee. Tucked against the edge of the woods. Its headlights off. The driver waved as Jenny swung wide and did a U-turn.

"Oh shit . . . what's *she* doing here?" Melody asked.

Jenny turned off the car. "Did you see if Naomi was with her?"

"Wait here," I said, getting out. "I want to talk to her, alone."

9

As I approached the Jeep Cherokee with a flashlight in my hand, the driver's-side door swung open and Aunt Helen stepped out. She was dressed in jeans, a long-sleeve T-shirt, and a baseball hat. With her hair tucked in, she could've passed for a man.

"I can't say I'm surprised to see you." I shined the light inside the Jeep to make sure she was alone. "So . . . did you bring the dagger?"

"How did you . . ." Her eyes flashed wide and she slowly began backing away. "Oh my God . . ."

"What?"

"You're one of them."

MEMORIALS

"One of who?"

She pulled a wrinkled sheet of paper from her pants pocket. Carefully reached out her hand so I could take it. "*Them*."

I redirected the flashlight.

The note—no doubt composed on the same typewriter as the message left on Jenny's window—read:

> Bring the dagger to the clearing. No cops. We have Naomi.

The implication hit me square in the face. Aunt Helen—who knew me better than anyone else in the world—thought *I* belonged to a dangerous, satanic cult. *Me*. She was backing away out of fear. Of *me*.

"We're here because Jenny got a note too," I said, eager for her to know the truth. "She picked us up at the hotel. They want the footage we shot of the memorials."

The wide-eyed expression on her face softened a bit, but I noticed that she didn't come any closer. "If you didn't send the note . . . then how did you know about the dagger?"

"I snooped in your closet . . . but only because *you* gave me reason to. I saw you hide my notebook in the kitchen."

"I was trying to keep you *safe*."

"Like when you listened in on our phone calls?"

"Yes, I was—"

"Why have you been lying to me all this time?"

"To protect you!" A tear trickled down her cheek.

"Bullshit." I hated this, but I was done with all the secrets.

"Billy . . . your Uncle Frank was one of them."

It felt like someone had punched me in the stomach. The air went out of my body all at once. "What . . . what the hell are you talking about . . . ?"

"He grew *up* in those mountains. Do you understand that? It's how his family *raised* him." She wiped her eyes. "But he was finished with all that nonsense by the time we got engaged. He knew how much I hated it."

"You mean . . . at one time Uncle Frank actually worshipped . . . whatever that thing is?"

"No . . . not really. It was mostly his parents. His aunts and uncles and cousins. He just kind of went along with it until *I* came along. Then he just seemed embarrassed about the whole thing and never really wanted to talk about it. After he moved away, they tried to get him back. But he wouldn't listen. They blamed me, of course, and began threatening us. Frank always claimed that they'd cast a spell, causing us to lose our babies. And then when your parents died, I couldn't stop blaming myself. What if it was because of—"

"Stop it," I said. "It was a stupid accident." But at that moment, I was less certain of that than ever before.

"Damn his stubbornness. He should've given the dagger back when they first asked, but he refused. That just made them angrier. He never told me where it came from . . . just that it was a big deal. I hated it. I wanted to get rid of it after he died . . . but I couldn't. For better or worse, it was a part of the man I loved."

"So then why hide it?"

"When we were first married, there were a number of break-ins at the garage apartment we were renting. We assumed it was them, looking for the dagger. Eventually, the break-ins stopped and we figured they'd given up. But then, after all this time, someone got into the house last fall. They ransacked it pretty good, but I couldn't find anything missing. It dawned on me then what they were probably looking for. I reported the break-in to the police so I could file an insurance claim, and that's how I met Jason."

"Before we left the house tonight, while you were outside, I looked in the shoebox again and it was gone . . ."

"It was because of that damn dream." And now she did step closer to me. "You were lying this morning about why you'd woken up screaming. I *know* . . . because I had the same nightmare as you and your friends."

I felt my mouth drop open.

"Seeing the dagger in the dream was the final straw. I couldn't stand the thought of having it around even one minute longer . . . so I moved it into the shed. I figured I'd throw it in the river first chance I had. When I got home from shopping, you were all gone, and I started to get worried. It wasn't just the dream. That stupid symbol you showed me was back in my life, and it's nothing but trouble. Then Jason called to say you'd be late for dinner because you'd all gotten lost in the woods by Church Street, and damn him, I knew he was lying. I remembered the stories Frank had told me about that clearing in the forest." She hung her head. "Yes . . . I lied about that too. I'm sorry, Billy. It just felt like everything was coming to a head all at once. And when I saw those awful stick figures in the van—"

Behind us, a car door opened. "I hate to break up the festivities," Jenny called out, "but we really need to get our asses in gear!"

I held up my hand. "One minute."

"You've had several, Billy! Come on!"

"Your friends probably think I'm awful," Aunt Helen said.

"I never told them about the dagger." I shrugged when she looked surprised. "I just kept hoping there'd be a reasonable explanation."

Whatever walls had been holding her back finally collapsed. She rushed into my arms. "Billy, forgive me—*please*! I didn't know what else to do! When you showed me that awful drawing in your notebook, it felt like my world was collapsing all over again."

"Hey . . . it's all right," I said, hugging her.

"It's *not* all right. I'm so sorry you got mixed up in all of this."

I was pretty sure I already knew the answer, but I had to ask. "You didn't tell Jason that you were coming here?"

"I wanted to . . . I thought about it . . . but I was scared they'd find out and do something to Naomi." She started to say something else, but stopped herself.

"What? Tell me."

"I drove by his house on my way here. Just in case I started having second thoughts. His car wasn't in the driveway." She looked uncomfortable talking about this. "Sometimes he spends the night at the station . . . but he usually tells me."

"You're sure no one followed you?"

"I checked for headlights, but I didn't see any."

"And you have the dagger?"

She nodded against my shoulder. "It's in the car."

"Grab it," I said, signaling for the others. "We need to hurry."

10

"So you believe her?" Melody whispered.

It felt like we were walking through a fairy-tale haunted forest. Ghosts of moonlight spilled from the swaying treetops. A deep blanket of soggy leaves choked out the underbrush, muffling our footfalls and slowing our progress. Tendrils of ground mist swirled all around us.

"Yeah . . . I do. I had it all wrong. We all did. Turns out she's as much of a victim of these fucking nutjobs as we are." And then some . . . once you factored in her miscarriages.

Upon entering the woods, Melody and I had taken the lead with Aunt Helen and Troy following close behind us. Jenny, who'd volunteered to bring up the rear, was the only one without a flashlight—a fact that didn't seem to bother her at all. In my free hand, I carried the tied-off plastic bag containing all of our documentary footage. For now, Melody's gun remained hidden in the pocket of her windbreaker.

"What was that whole schtick about in the car?" I asked quietly.

"I don't trust that bitch." She glanced over her shoulder at Jenny. "I thought if I ticked her off, she might let something slip."

If anyone had told me a week ago that Melody Wise was capable of such an act, I would have laughed at them. But I'd definitely seen a different side to her these past couple of days. She could be a fierce adversary when she wanted to be. I glanced at my friend in admiration—

—and the firelit memory of her naked and sweat-slick body flooded my mind. *Bent over the altar, she looks back at me, gasping for air, urging me to thrust harder, and harder . . .*

I squeezed my eyes shut, pushing away the graphic images, willing away the painful erection that had formed beneath my jeans. *Jesus, where the hell did all of that come from?!*

The woods around us remained silent, refusing to answer. The only sounds I could hear were my labored breathing and the shuffle of our footfalls. But deep inside, I *knew*...it was the clearing calling out to me . . . goading me . . . as we got closer.

As the leaves gave way to rocks and dirt, we came to a steep ravine shrouded in thornbushes. Detouring to the south—with Aunt Helen's fingernails digging into the back of my shoulder the entire time—we made our way along a natural stone pathway overlooking a sheer drop to a rushing stream below. Walking single file, we tried not to look down, our flashlight beams bobbing back and forth in the darkness, illuminating a tangled network of branches and leaves some sixty feet off the ground—providing the surreal illusion that we were floating in midair.

Once the narrow trail ended, the forest floor softened and flattened out again. The trees began to crowd us, pools of shadow deepening in the narrow gaps between them. The damp air grew heavy and still. The reach of our flashlights diminished. Behind us, Jenny scolded Troy for walking too slow. He grumbled under his breath and picked up his pace.

The shine of Melody's flashlight swept across a stick figure dangling from a low-hanging branch. I felt an icy shiver caress the back of my neck. They were hideous-looking configurations. Primal and menacing. As I scooted past it, turning sideways to give the stickman as wide of a berth as possible, I was certain that it was watching me.

Initially, I'd worried that we wouldn't be able to locate the clearing at night. We'd only been there one time, during the daylight, and that entire experience—although not that long ago—possessed the hazy quality of an infrequent nightmare. But within minutes of departing the roadside, we'd begun running across the repulsive stick figures—hanging from branches or wedged tightly in between them—and I realized with growing dread that whoever was waiting at the clearing had left us a trail of breadcrumbs to follow.

"How much farther do you think?" Troy asked. We'd been walking for almost twenty minutes, and I could hear the fatigue in his voice. I could also hear the fear. No one had admitted it out loud yet—but we were all terrified. There was a strange taste in my mouth that I remembered from playground fights I'd had as a kid. And no matter how hard I tried, I couldn't stop licking my lips.

"What do you think?" Melody asked, shining her light at my chest. "Another ten minutes?"

"That sounds about right." I looked behind me at Aunt Helen. She hadn't said much since leaving the shoulder of the road. "You doing okay?"

"Don't worry about me. I'm fine."

"We'll stop and catch our breath when we get closer."

"And then what?" Troy asked.

"Then we go get Naomi."

"Cool," he said. "Glad you have it all figured out."

"What about you, Jenny? You doing—"

I stopped in midsentence.

And pointed my flashlight at the patch of woods directly behind Aunt Helen and Troy.

It was empty—Jenny was gone.

11

"I *knew* we shouldn't have trusted her."

As we made our way back down the slope, our orderly, single-file procession deteriorated into a four-person side-by-side wrecking crew. Between Melody's anger-fueled running dialogue and the trampling of every bush and fallen branch in sight, we were making a hell of a racket.

"Just wait until I get my hands on her."

"Everyone hold up for a second," I said. "And listen . . ."

We stopped walking. Melody and Troy swept the beam of their flashlights into the trees. The thick tangles of underbrush swallowed the light and spit out more darkness. This deep in the woods, this late at night, the sense of gloomy desolation was overwhelming. The forest all around us was eerily quiet and still. We started descending again.

"That bitch waited until we let our guard down, and then she snuck away to join her friends."

"I don't know," Troy said. "I'm not exactly her biggest fan either . . . but what if something bad happened to her? What if they took her?"

Melody lowered her flashlight and looked at him. "I'm pretty sure we would've heard something, Troy." From the tone of her voice, it was blatantly clear that her mind was made up.

I honestly didn't know what to think. Jenny had come across—to me, at least—as genuinely distraught and focused on getting her best friend back. I'd believed what she'd told me in the parking lot. Then again, maybe I just didn't want to think about the alternative.

"This doesn't change anything," I said. "Naomi's still MIA . . . With or without Jenny, we have to keep going."

Troy sighed. "I was afraid you were going to say that."

"I didn't mean all of us. You can always go back to the car and wait."

Aunt Helen stepped forward. "I'm going with you."

I looked at the others. "You two barely know Naomi. I wouldn't blame you one bit if—"

"No way," Melody said, making her way up the slope again. "We're the Three Musketeers, remember? We stick together."

"More like the Three Stooges," Troy said, trudging after her.

I'm not entirely sure, but I think I managed a smile.

There were no more smiles after that, though—for any of us.

12

We walked deeper into the woods. Mostly in silence. There was no denying that Jenny's disappearance had unnerved us even more than we already were. We spent just as much time peeking over our shoulders as we did watching where we were going. As a result, we got careless.

Aunt Helen slipped on a log and slid down a muddy embankment into a creek, soaking her jeans. No one laughed or offered a smart-aleck remark. Were it not for his glasses, Troy would have lost an eye—maybe both—after walking directly into a low-hanging branch. I twisted my ankle on a webwork of roots. I could already feel it swelling inside my boot. Only Melody seemed impervious to the pitfalls of the terrain, her renewed anger driving her forward with an intense focus. Before long, she assumed the lead.

After cutting across a rock-strewn ridge and narrowly avoiding a colossal patch of poison sumac, Melody spotted a flickering light up ahead in the distance. She signaled for us to stop. "Bonfire," she announced, pointing it out to the rest of us. "We're getting close."

We stood at the edge of the rise and stared at the orange glow in the trees—a solemn expression on each of our faces. I'd like to think, deep inside all of us, we hadn't really believed there would be anyone waiting for us at the clearing. I admit I'd had hopeful thoughts that Naomi would be all alone when we got there. Tied up and blindfolded, but otherwise unharmed; the note on Jenny's window just another cryptic warning, like the deflated balloon left under our wiper blade and the sabotaged engine.

Even now, those flashes of foolish optimism refused to go away. *Maybe they started a fire so she wouldn't be all alone in the dark. Or maybe they did it so we could find her more easily.*

But then I turned and saw the harrowing look on Melody's face—and I knew that I was kidding myself.

I took her arm. "Do you need to sit down?"

"I'm . . . I'm okay," she said, still staring at the glow in the trees. "Do you feel it? It's different this time. Not as strong."

I knew what she meant. The buzzing in my brain was back—but just barely. No louder than a pesky mosquito.

"That's because we're invited this time," Troy said. "It *wants* us to come."

Ignoring him, despite what his words had just done to my insides, I turned to my aunt. "Are you feeling okay?"

"My head's kind of fuzzy, but I think it's because I'm tired." She rubbed her side. "Maybe a little bit of a stomachache."

Melody and I exchanged a worried glance.

"I wish I had a more formidable weapon," Troy said, holding up his flashlight.

I stared at him in surprise.

"What? You don't think I can defend myself? Or you need a dictionary to look up what *formidable* means?"

He bent down and picked up a broken branch from the ground. It was maybe two feet long and four or five inches around. The end of the stick was splintered into jagged spikes. He hoisted it in the air like a club. "Ah. This'll do the trick."

It was at that moment the chanting started.

13

The rational part of my mind—what was left of it, anyway—couldn't believe what I was seeing.

Bathed in the glow of the flames, swathed in ground mist and surrounded by darkness, they looked as if they had sprung from the bowels of hell. There were six of them standing around the fire, dressed in long black hooded robes, their faces hidden beneath masks made entirely of sticks.

A short distance away, at the center of the clearing, Naomi was stretched out on her back atop the altar. Her ankles and wrists had been lashed to wooden pegs in the ground. A dirty rag had been stuffed into her mouth. She was completely naked and crying.

As we pushed our way through the foliage and stepped into the clearing, the chanting abruptly ceased—and the six robed figures slowly turned their heads to watch our arrival.

Aunt Helen gasped as Troy grappled for my arm, and for a fleeting moment, I feared he might turn and run. But as usual, he surprised me and held his ground.

I wanted to sprint to Naomi and cut loose her binds.

I wanted to pummel her captors and hurl them one by one into the blazing fire—but not before unmasking them and exposing their cowardly faces.

I wanted to destroy this cursed clearing and never return.

But it's very easy to imagine yourself as the hero of your own story. Meanwhile, I could do none of those things—and I knew it.

Out of the corner of my mouth, I asked, "So what do we do now?"

No one said anything for a moment, then: "I thought *you* were the one with the plan, Sundance."

I glanced at Troy in disbelief. Here we were facing off with a dangerous cult, and he was cracking wise about one of our favorite westerns. Despite being so scared that it felt like I was going to piss my pants at any moment, I couldn't help but be proud of the guy. He'd come a long way in the past few days.

"I think Jenny and some others are hiding in the trees," Melody whispered. "I saw them moving."

My brain immediately took me back to the disturbing vision I'd experienced the last time I was here in the clearing. *The cabin. The man and his daughters. The glowing red eyes staring out of the woods.* I followed Melody's uneasy gaze to the surrounding tree line, but all I could see were those awful stickmen hanging everywhere, watching us.

One of the hooded figures was at least a head or two taller than the others. *I bet it's that square-jawed dick of a state trooper who pulled us over,* I thought. When the tall man stepped forward and beckoned us closer, his arm and hand obscured by the sleeve of his robe, that disquieting feeling of being trapped inside a dream grew even stronger. Any second now, I expected to wake up in my apartment back in York, the alarm clock on my cluttered nightstand beeping away.

Growing impatient, the man signaled again for us to approach.

"Shit . . . let's get this over with," I said, Troy groaning in response.

As Melody muttered a prayer, we made our way deeper into the clearing. The ground beneath our feet was hard and riddled with weeds and stones. My swollen ankle throbbed with every step I took. As we drew closer, I felt the heat of the bonfire caress my arms and face. Heard the crackling and popping and sizzling of the flames. In the flickering shadows, the dark robes the men wore appeared to shimmer and absorb the light, almost as if the garments themselves had powers all their own.

When Naomi saw us, her eyes bulged and she immediately began struggling against the ropes. With tears streaming down her cheeks, she jerked her head violently back and forth, sobbing into the filthy rag. Rivulets of blood dribbled down the sides of the altar and pooled in the dirt. The symbol had been carved into the tender flesh of her stomach.

I stood there, frozen, my eyes and mind struggling to comprehend what I was seeing . . . until finally the rage inside me awakened.

Stepping forward, I hurled my flashlight as hard as I could at the tall man. It all happened very quickly after that.

14

The tall man feinted to the left, and the flashlight bounced harmlessly off his shoulder. It hit the ground, spun around a couple of times, and rolled into the fire.

Two of the hooded figures rushed me. One positioned himself in front of the altar, blocking my path. The other grabbed me by the arm. I shook loose and backed away.

"Let her go!" I shouted, unable to take my eyes off Naomi's torso. The cuts were just beginning to scab over. In the firelight, her blood appeared black instead of red. "She had nothing to do with this!"

"The footage first," the tall man said in a muffled voice. "And the photographs."

Up close, I could see a pair of round eyeholes in the primitive mask and a small horizontal slit for his mouth, no better than what you might find on a cheap Halloween costume. No wonder the man's words had been difficult to understand.

"Let her go." I held out the plastic bag. "And it's all yours."

He chuckled, a low gravelly sound. "I'm afraid that's not how this is going to work. We get the footage . . ." He turned and stared at Aunt Helen. ". . . *and* the dagger . . . and *then* we release the girl."

Aunt Helen reached into her jacket pocket and took out the dagger with the turquoise handle. She studied it for a moment and then tossed it to the ground at the tall man's feet.

He bent down and picked it up. "Ah . . . I knew you'd come back to me one day." Reverence in his voice, as if he were speaking to a long-lost lover.

When he looked up at us again, the gun was in Melody's hand.

She raised it and pointed it at the tall man's chest.

"You want to be very careful with that." Not even a hint of alarm in his voice. "Especially considering you're outnumbered."

The pair of robed figures standing beside the altar weren't nearly as calm. They immediately backed away, almost tripping over each other's feet. Behind those little round holes, I saw their now-frightened eyes flitting back and forth between the tall man and the gun. This was not going according to plan.

"Four of us against six of you, and we have *this* on our side . . ." Melody waved the gun. "I'll take those odds any day of the week."

The tree line rippled with movement.

The tall man cocked his head to the side. "You were saying?"

Turning in a slow circle, I watched in dread as a mob of similarly hooded figures emerged from the woods. Within seconds, they were all around us. Materializing out of the mist. Although dressed in the same black robes as the men around the bonfire, none of them wore masks. As they came closer, into the firelight, I recognized many of the faces.

The square-jawed state trooper who had pulled us over.

The whispering waitress from the pizza joint in Leesburg.

The well-dressed woman with the Annie Lennox haircut who had glared at me from her table at Mo's Famous BBQ.

The long-haired man dressed all in black who I'd seen from my bedroom window as he walked behind the little girl on the bicycle. I assumed he was the one who had left the menu with the handwritten warning on the van's windshield, but I couldn't be sure.

I even knew some of their names.

Larry Shaw from the post office.

Deputy Carl.

Jenny Caldwell.

Melody nudged me. "I told you that bitch was no good!"

They just kept coming. Unhurriedly, expressionless—as if they were ensnared in the web of a collective spell. There had to be twenty of them. Maybe more. Old men and women, their slack faces creased with wrinkles. Children, even. The red ribbon in one little girl's hair poking out from underneath her hood. As they began to encircle us, cutting off any possible escape, the four of us closed ranks with our backs to each other, forming a tight circle of defense.

Troy's eyes widened. "No fucking way! That son of a bitch!"

Robert Farnsworth shuffled by us. I barely noticed.

My old friend Craig McGinty—whose directions had initially brought us to this godforsaken clearing, the same guy who'd helped me kick the living shit out of Floyd Roebuck over a stolen Baltimore Orioles cap—had stopped beside the altar. He turned and stared at us with unblinking eyes, his lips pressed together in a tight, thin line.

Naomi saw him and began thrashing even harder against the ropes.

"Naomi . . . stop!" I was worried that she might reopen the wounds on her stomach. "Stop moving!"

Craig ignored us both and just stood there with that dreamy expression on his face.

Aunt Helen leaned over and whispered, *"Should we try to make a run for it?"*

"Run where?" the tall man in the mask answered. He gestured at the ring of trees. "There's nowhere else to go."

She'd spoken so softly, it should've been impossible for him to hear—but somehow he had. I wondered idly if he could read our thoughts.

"I've only got six rounds," Melody said, her eyes darting all around us. "I never thought I'd need any more."

"Where did they all come from?" Troy asked, jabbing the broken branch at several robed figures that had gotten too close.

"It's like they've been turned into zombies," Aunt Helen said. "They don't even—"

That's when I saw the stakes in the ground, camouflaged by the tree line on the opposite side of the fire. They looked like old railroad ties. There were three of them.

Troy was right, I thought, a tsunami of panic crashing over me. *It was a trap all along. They were never going to let us go.*

"No . . . we weren't," the tall man said, confirming my earlier suspicion of having a window to my thoughts. "It was never about your footage. We could have taken it all from you whenever we wanted." The man gazed over his shoulder at the stakes in the ground—and then back at us again. "It was always about you. The *three* of you."

"Take me instead of them," Aunt Helen said, her voice cracking with emotion. "They've done nothing to harm you."

"Oh, you'll get what's coming, dear Helen." Behind the mask, the man's dark eyes sparkled with anticipation. "Don't you worry about that. I've been waiting a long time to make you pay."

"So then stop waiting and do it." She stepped closer, head held high, taunting him. "Take me right now."

The tall man bobbed his head back and forth, as if pondering the decision, and said, "Well . . . if you insist." And then he swept his arm up from his side and buried the blade of the dagger in Aunt Helen's stomach. He pulled it out and plunged it in again. She gasped—her lips forming a perfect O—and collapsed to her knees, the flashlight tumbling from her fingers. A bubble of blood burst from her mouth, spraying her chest and dribbling down her chin.

Melody raised the gun and fired. Once. Twice. In rapid succession. Standing this close, it sounded like a truck backfiring.

The first bullet missed badly, slicing through the flames, striking a rock on the ground, and ricocheting into the trees. Several of the masked figures dove for cover. The others—the unmasked followers that had emerged from the woods—barely stirred.

The second shot was far more accurate. The .38 caliber bullet slammed into the man's hip, spinning him around and nearly dislodging his mask. Scrambling to cover his face, he switched the bloody dagger to his left hand while pressing his right against the wound. Still doubled over in pain, he turned to face us.

"I'm going to enjoy bathing in your blood," he said to Melody with an edge to his voice that hadn't been there before.

"I've got four bullets left," she said. "The first one's for *you* . . ." She waggled the gun at the tall man's chest—and then repeated the gesture to his three closest brethren. "And then *you* . . . and *you* . . . and *you*." None of them budged.

Kneeling in the dirt, I carefully pulled Aunt Helen's shirt up, and used both of my hands to apply pressure to her wounds. Blood, warm and sticky, oozed between my fingers. She groaned and started to sit up. "Don't," I said. "Just lay there and be still . . . silly lady."

She tried to speak and another blood bubble burst from her mouth. She began coughing—an ugly, wet sound—showering my arms with a fine red mist.

"Easy . . . ," I said, no longer able to hold back my tears.

"Is she going to be okay?" Troy asked, standing above me with the makeshift club in his hand. There were leaves in his Afro and his glasses hung askew—but his eyes appeared focused and steadfast. Our scaredy-cat had turned into a warrior.

"I don't know, man. We need to stop the—"

"Troy . . . help me!" With the revolver still trained on the tall man, Melody backed up to the altar and removed the rag from Naomi's mouth. Naomi's entire body spasmed as she gasped for air. Melody bent down and began trying to loosen the ropes. "They're too damn tight!"

Troy ran to her side and hammered the pointed end of the stick against the rope. The branch broke apart in his hands. He tossed it away in frustration, grabbed hold of the rope, and tried to pull the peg to which it was attached out of the ground. It wouldn't budge.

Melody steadied the gun at the tall man. "Give me the knife."

He stared at her through the round holes in his mask.

"Give me the fucking knife, now."

He tilted his head back. I was sure he was going to laugh at her, but instead he began to chant, his muffled voice growing in volume. Behind him, the other masked figures joined in.

It was the same incantation from our shared nightmare.

Melody stepped closer, her face etched with fury, both hands on the gun now.

"I'm not going to ask—"

"Watch out!" Troy yelled.

Craig charged past him and seized Melody from behind. He lifted her off the ground, pinning her arms, and began shaking her back and forth, trying to dislodge the gun. She squeezed off a shot, firing wildly into the dirt. Craig yelped in surprise but refused to let go. Writhing in his arms, desperate now, Melody threw her head back, ramming him in the face. His nose exploded. Howling in pain, he finally let go of her. She started to turn and raise the revolver, but before she could, the square-jawed state trooper swooped in and tackled her hard to the ground. The gun spun away into the weeds.

It's the chanting, I thought, leaning over to shield Aunt Helen. *It's waking them all up.*

Troy dove in the direction of the revolver. A robed figure—an older man with bad teeth and a huge birthmark on his cheek—leaped out of the shadows and stepped on his hand, the man's rattlesnake boots crushing Troy's fingers into the dirt. He screeched in agony—

—as the state trooper yanked a stunned Melody off the ground. Holding her by the arms, he shoved her in front of the tall man. She fell to a knee at his feet, remained there for a moment, catching her breath, and then slowly rose. Head hanging, she teetered on unsteady legs, all of the fight gone out of her. The trooper reached over and yanked the back of her hair, jerking her head up so that the man in the mask could see the defeat on her face. Without a word, the man stepped forward, lifted the turquois-handled dagger, and drew it across Melody's neck.

At first, I thought the motion was meant to be a threat. A gesture of arrogance and domination. But then I saw the yawning red smile open up beneath her chin—and the arterial gush of blood splash the tall man's chest.

"*Nooo! Melody!*" Scrambling to my feet, I started toward the two men—but then quickly froze, realizing I couldn't leave my aunt's side. Standing there helplessly, I watched as the sneering trooper picked up Melody's still-twitching body and dumped it face down on top of Naomi on the altar. "Two for one," he quipped, looking back at the tall man. I expected Naomi to scream and thrash and try to buck Melody off her, but she just lay there. Mouth agape. Staring out into space over Melody's shoulder. I guess she'd finally seen too much. Something in her mind had snapped, and she'd gone into shock. The gouts of blood still pumping from Melody's savaged throat painted Naomi's chest a glossy red and streamed down the sides of her rib cage, forming a growing puddle on the altar's stone surface.

"Save the other three for the ceremony," the tall man in the mask commanded, lowering the bloodstained dagger to his side.

The state trooper nodded and turned away from the altar. He glanced at Troy—who was still squirming in pain, his hand pinned to the ground by the old man's boot, his terror-stricken eyes fixed on the now-still body of his murdered friend—and then the trooper looked over at me and Aunt Helen.

Smiling, he started toward us.

Several of the unmasked followers, including a staggering Robert Farnsworth, followed closely behind him.

"We have to go," I told my aunt, sliding my arm beneath her back. "*Now.*"

She groaned in pain as I lifted her. Her face, already pale, went ashy gray. I put her down again as softly as I could. Kneeling next to her, I looked up at the trooper in his flowing black robe. He appeared at least seven feet tall. The hood over his head did little to conceal the cruel grin on his face. I searched for something I could use as a weapon—but all I could find was a rock the size of a golf ball. I hefted it in my hand and waited for the inevitable—

—as something in the bonfire moved.

At first, I thought one of the burning timbers had collapsed, sending a shower of glowing embers spiraling into the night sky. But then the fire flared even brighter and *swelled* . . . a broad, rippling, liquid motion . . .

And I saw a towering figure of flames detach itself from the inferno . . . and walk free.

It was like something out of a fever dream—or perhaps an ancient biblical prophecy—but whatever it was, I found myself witnessing it without fear.

Moving with the powerful, fluid grace of an ocean wave, the corporeal form swept across the clearing, leaving smears of blackened earth in its wake. The blazing entity—for that's what it was, I am certain of that—possessed no clear static form, but as it was silhouetted against the dark tree line, I swore I could make out faint and shifting features resembling arms and legs . . . and a pair of glowering scarlet eyes.

The buzzing inside my head erupted into a cacophonous roar, the sound of a million descending locusts intent on destruction. And then from within the hurricane discord there came snippets of broken words and sentences—deep and coarse and angry, as if spoken through a mouth filled with dirt—an ancient, eldritch language that swelled my head until it felt as though it might burst and poisoned my brain with forbidden images: *Melody naked, writhing and glistening with sweat atop the stone altar; my bloodied father trapped in the wreckage of his car, lifeless eyes staring sightlessly through a shattered windshield; my mother, a misshapen sack of broken bones and mangled flesh, sprawled on the shoulder of the road in the flickering headlights; a fire-blasted landscape stretching all the way to the horizon beneath a yellow-and-purple-black sky filled with scaly-winged abominations, long pointed horns protruding from the creatures' bulging foreheads.*

It occurred to me at that moment—as I stood there listening to that thing speak while staring into its burning red eyes—that I might be losing my mind. If so, I wasn't the only one.

MEMORIALS

No more than ten feet away from us, the state trooper stood motionless, the anger on his staring face replaced by pure, unadulterated awe. The others around him imitated his pose. Arms hanging limply at their sides, heads tilted upward, mouths gaping in collective astonishment. No one spoke or made a sound. The air around us crackled with energy but remained perfectly still. Not a twig or leaf stirred. It was as if the clearing itself were holding its breath, anticipating what would happen next.

It didn't have long to wait.

The thing that had manifested from the bonfire approached a pair of the unmasked followers—a man and a woman—as they cowered in the brush by the tree line. No particular reason why from what I could see—they just happened to be in the wrong place at the wrong time. They could have been husband and wife, or distant neighbors from the hills. They could have been strangers before tonight. It mattered nothing to the blazing abomination standing before them. Reaching out with fingers of fire, it gently brushed against the folds of their black robes. It did so tentatively at first, as if testing its power—but then liking what it found there, it surged forward with a resounding *whoosh*.

The couple burst into flames as if they'd been doused in kerosene.

The man dropped to the ground and began flopping like a fish left abandoned on a riverbank. Both of his shoes flew off his burning feet. After a moment, lying face down in the dirt, he convulsed one final time and went still. Tendrils of dark smoke rising from his body. The woman ran blindly into the shadows, arms flailing. Clawing at the hood of her robe, she spun wildly in ever-widening circles. Her hair was a burning bush, the skin on her face melting away in blackened strips. Still spinning, a flaming human tornado, she disappeared into the trees, her high-pitched screams echoing behind her.

Spurred by the couple's agony and suffering, the hellish entity raced with blinding speed across the clearing, setting ablaze everything and everyone in its path. Clumps of weeds and brush smoldered. Fallen logs burned. The ground turned black. Robert Farnsworth, a half-empty bottle of whiskey now clutched in his hand, was only a handful of steps away from the tree line when the flames engulfed him. Instead of fighting his fiery destiny, he calmly sat down in the dirt and crossed his burning legs, the skin on his face melting away into darkened clumps, dripping onto his lap. Beyond that, he never made a sound.

Flaming black robes scattered everywhere. The creature's hunger insatiable and indiscriminate. Charred corpses littered the clearing. The air turned hot and putrid with the stench of burning flesh. Sometimes, even now, I could smell it in my dreams.

"*Arghhh!*" A screaming man charged at us from across the clearing, his face a blistered mask of soot and blood, the tatters of his flaming robe fluttering in the air behind him. Stepping in front of Aunt Helen, I lifted the rock, prepared to defend myself. But that wasn't necessary. As the man rushed closer, his arms held out in front of him like a blinded Frankenstein's monster, he began to slow and stagger. Another few feet, and he was close enough to recognize—that asshole Deputy Carl, his scorched lips peeled back in a painful sneer, what was left of his teeth, black and glistening like tar—and then with a loud grunt, he collapsed in a heap at my feet.

I stepped around him as terrified onlookers fled in all directions, tripping over each other in the smoke—a life-and-death game of tag-you're-it. Others ran deep into the woods, hiding in the dark or stumbling blindly through the overgrown brush and trees until they eventually became lost.

Someone grabbed my shoulder. Ducking instinctively, I spun around, the hand holding the rock raised in front of me.

"We have to get out of here!" Troy yelled. He was bleeding from a cut on his cheek and clutching his injured hand against his side. Either the old man in the rattlesnake boots had run away with the others or he'd been reduced to a heap of blackened flesh and bone. I hoped for the latter.

"I have to get Naomi first!" I told him. "Can you help my aunt into the woods?"

"I can try," he said, and dropped to a knee beside her. "Oh God."

"I'm sorry." I leaned down and squeezed Aunt Helen's hand. "This is going to hurt, but we have no other choice."

"What is . . . that thing?" Her voice so weak I had to read her lips.

It was the man in the mask who answered her—but not out loud. I could hear his angry voice inside my head.

—one of the Outsiders Grandpa Logan spoke of! It knows nothing of order or obedience—only destruction! And now that it's here, there's no way to send it—

Confused, I scrambled to my feet and searched the swirling smoke. The last time I'd seen the man, he'd been standing by the altar with the dagger in his—

There! Beyond the still-raging bonfire, nearly to the tree line. The bloody dagger still clutched in his hand. A second masked figure stood next to him, tugging at his robe, trying to coax the man into the woods.

His voice came again. As clear as if he were standing right next to me.

All this work . . . all this time . . . and for what?! Collins, that fucking idiot! The girl's blood on the altar summoned it! Two for one?! You fucking idiot!

Rushing toward the altar, I tried to remember where Troy had been sprawled on the ground. Wherever it was, the gun was nearby. Unless someone else had gotten to it first.

Across the clearing, I heard a girl pleading. "No, please! *No!*" I glanced over my shoulder in time to see Jenny Caldwell—her hands held high over her head as if she were being arrested—erupt into flames like a human candle. She tore off her robe and flung it to the ground, but it was too late. The hungry flames crawled up her naked body. As she staggered toward the woods, sparks shot out of her ears.

—the three of them were the key! We wasted our goddamn chance—

I turned and ran faster, leaping over charred bodies that reminded me of old photographs of Hiroshima and Nagasaki. A woman sprinted past me, her open robe fluttering in the air behind her like a burning cape. A young boy, no older than thirteen, tripped and lost his glasses in the smoke, then got up and ran face-first into a tree, sprawling to the ground unconscious. A man dressed in shorts and a T-shirt, his robe nowhere in sight, strolled by as if he didn't have a care in the world. There was blood all over his face and his sneakers were on fire, the flames rapidly making their way up his legs. He smiled at me when I ran past him and tipped an imaginary hat.

I skidded to a stop in front of the altar and saw right away that Naomi was still in shock. Her head lolled to the side, drool dribbling from her slack mouth, eyes staring straight ahead.

"I'm going to take you home," I told her in between coughing fits. The smoke in the clearing was thickening. The air had gone rotten. Either Melody's body, slippery from the blood, had slid off Naomi all on its own or someone else had knocked it off amidst the chaos. She lay curled on her side in the weeds behind the altar, those stunning brown eyes gazing sightlessly at the night sky. Melody Wise, my beautiful friend whose name sounded like a song title. I wanted to pick her up and take her away from all this. I wanted to cover her face—*anything* to hide that awful gash in her throat—but there was no time.

Mel, oh my God, Mel, I'm so sorry.

—least we got the dagger back from that dirty whore—

He was talking about Aunt Helen again. The man's voice clearer in my mind than when I'd heard him speak out loud. And somehow familiar.

"I'll be right back," I said to Naomi, brushing the hair out of her face. "I promise."

—the hell out of here and start all over again. Fucking idiots, all of them! Ruined everything—

I rushed to get the dagger to cut her loose.

15

The man in the mask saw me coming—but it didn't matter.

When I'd told Melody earlier that I was never a star football player, I was telling the truth. My arm wasn't strong enough to play quarterback. My hands not quite soft enough for wide receiver. But as the sports reporter from the *Sudbury Sun* noted in my junior year All-County write-up, the two strengths I *did* possess earmarked me as a natural defender. Number one: I was fast. Number two: for a guy my size, I hit like a bulldozer.

By the time the man turned his head and spotted me—eyes widening in those little round holes in his mask—I was already airborne. He tried to raise the dagger but was too slow. My shoulder struck him like a missile in the chest, sending us both sprawling hard to the ground. Lying beneath me, the man grunted, and I got a whiff of rancid breath. A second later, I caught a knee in the thigh and grunted right back at him. Pressing a hand against my chest, he levered his much longer legs and rolled on top of me. In my peripheral vision, as I twisted back and forth trying to shake loose, I saw his masked buddy scamper off into the woods. Hopefully, he wasn't going for reinforcements.

Not that the son of a bitch needed anyone else's help.

The man wasn't just tall—he was *big*. And strong. The black robe had disguised it well. If only I'd realized it sooner, I may have gone with a stealthier approach. As if to prove my point, the man arched his back and elbowed me in the face. Twice. Once with each elbow. A starburst of pain exploded in my jaw. Warm blood filled my mouth. A sudden wetness spread between our bodies, and I wondered if I'd pissed myself. Then I remembered the tall man's wounded hip . . . and hoped what I was feeling was his blood.

I tried to yank my hand out from underneath him so I could shove my fingers into the bullet hole . . . but it was no use. He had me pinned. I craned my neck, searching for a glimpse of the dagger. *Did it drop to the ground when I hit him? Was it still in his hand?* If so, any second now, I was sure to feel the bite of its blade along my throat.

Desperate, I closed my eyes and headbutted him, once, twice—the sharp sticks on his mask gouging my cheeks and forehead—but with all of his weight pressing down on me, there wasn't enough wiggle room to generate any power behind my blows. Instead, all I managed to do was slice my face into bloody ribbons and piss him off even more.

"You stupid boy," he growled, inches from my face. "I'm so glad we killed your parents."

"Fuck you . . ." I spat on his mask. ". . . you fucking coward." And watched as thick globs of my own blood and mucus dripped off the latticework of sticks and landed on my face.

He laughed. "No thank you."

I knew that muffled voice from somewhere. I was sure of it.

"As a matter of fact, you do," he said, reading my thoughts again.

Before I could return the favor, he pressed his forearm against my neck and leaned on it with the bulk of his weight—cutting off my airway. A starry blackness swarmed my eyes. My chest began to burn and that familiar drowning sensation returned. Only this time it was for real.

Groaning with the effort, the man shifted his upper body, applying even more pressure on my throat.

And as he did, my right arm slithered free.

Moving by blind instinct—because that's all I had left—I slid my hand down his torso, stretching my fingers for the wound on his hip. But he was too damn tall, and I couldn't reach it. I made a fist and hammered at his kidney as hard as I could. He didn't even flinch.

I hit him again, this time in the ribs, and that took all the strength I had left. My arm fell limp to my side. There was nothing else I could do. Farnsworth had told the truth, it seemed: *We were all going to die.*

As the world around me began to dim, I thought about my parents . . . and Uncle Frank . . . and furry little Tucker, who'd always run away to the swamp. Did disobedient poodles go to heaven when they died? Did anyone, for that matter?

It was my mother's sweet voice that answered me:

Not yet, silly Billy. Not yet. But when it's time . . . we'll be waiting.

Tears streaming down my face, every ounce of my ravaged body and soul spent, I suddenly realized that the crushing weight on my throat was gone. The arm was still there, lodged snugly under my chin, but the pressure had relented. I could breathe again. The man's head rested against my shoulder as if he'd gone to sleep, the rough edges of his mask jabbing the exposed skin beneath my shredded T-shirt. His breath on my neck felt warm—and shallow.

With smoky air flooding my lungs, I pushed as hard as I could against

MEMORIALS

the man's chest—but I was still too weak. Black stars spiraled in my vision. Something sharp poked me in the ribs. I began coughing and couldn't stop. When I tried to lift my head again, I vomited in my mouth. Turning to the side, I spit out the sour chunks I hadn't swallowed, alarmed by how much blood was mixed with them.

Somewhere on the opposite side of the clearing, a woman screamed. A terrified, guttural cry that seemed to go on forever. And then a high, chortling laughter from within the smoke. An evil sound. Inhuman. I would hear it in the dark of my bedroom for years to come.

Reaching up, I slowly lifted the man's arm off my throat and pushed it aside. It flopped harmlessly to the ground, the sleeve of the man's robe snagging on a broken branch, exposing his muscular forearm. What I saw there made my swollen jaw drop open.

My fingers digging into the cloth of his black robe, I gripped both of the man's shoulders, took a deep breath, and shoved with a sense of renewed inspiration. And it worked. As I felt his upper body slowly begin to rise, I wiggled my hips and slid out from underneath him. With my chest no longer supporting his weight, the man flopped face-first into the dirt, arms outstretched at his sides, as if he were preparing to take flight.

My pants and shirt drenched in blood, I carefully pushed to my feet and surveyed the clearing. It looked like a war zone. Scorched earth and burning trees as far as I could see. Charred and smoldering bodies strewn everywhere. The roiling smoke so thick I couldn't even make out the altar, where I prayed Naomi was still waiting for me. Nor could I tell if Troy had managed to escape with Aunt Helen. "*Troy!*" I called out, but there was no answer. I didn't even bother yelling for Naomi. I already knew she was in no condition to respond.

Behind me, on the ground, the man in the mask moaned. His massive legs twitched. Otherwise, he lay still. I stood at a safe distance and watched him for a while, and then I slowly approached. After nudging him in the side a couple of times with the toe of my boot and eliciting another deep groan of pain, I leaned down and rolled him over. It wasn't easy.

Inches below his heart, the turquoise handle of the dagger protruded from the man's rib cage. The front of his torn robe was soaked in blood.

Remembering the sudden wetness that had spread between our bodies, it wasn't difficult to envision what had happened. The fatal blow must have occurred when I'd first taken him to the ground, the weight of our struggling bodies pressing the blade deeper into his chest... until he finally bled out.

Reaching down, already knowing who I was going to see, I slipped my fingers underneath his mask and lifted it over his head.

Professor Marcus Tyree stared back at me.

You sonofabitch, I thought, knowing he would hear me. *It was you in the basketball photo... standing next to Uncle Frank. Your hair was short... and you didn't have the beard... That's why I didn't recognize you. All that time, you two were classmates... teammates... friends...*

"I loved him," Tyree whispered, "like a brother. I tried to stop him..." He wheezed and dark viscous blood gushed from the corner of his mouth, staining his whiskers. "... but he wouldn't listen... He was... a traitor to his people... and our Creator."

"You don't even know how fucking crazy you are, do you?" I said aloud.

"And all because of that whore of his... He threw it away..."

"We trusted you!" I said. "You knew what we would find on this trip... and still you let us go!"

"I didn't have a choice." With his left eye filled with blood, he struggled to focus on me. "You were the chosen ones."

Staring at the tattoo of Bob Marley on his forearm, I stepped closer and pressed my boot against the bullet wound on his hip. "You killed Melody, you gutless son of a bitch."

From deeper within the smoke-filled clearing, that high, chortling laughter came again—only this time it was followed by that same gravelly voice I'd heard earlier inside my head.

"Ph'tanque mgl'watan squantle fu'loa wan'str..."

Tyree heard it too. He grinned up at me with red teeth, just like the guy on the bicycle from eons ago. "It'll be your turn soon enough. They'll never stop now. It'll... never be over."

And then he closed his eyes—and said no more.

AFTER

1

Aunt Helen survived. That's the first thing I want you to know. She lost a lot of blood in that clearing, and when Troy and I carried her out, she lost even more and cussed a blue streak that would've made Uncle Frank proud. But she lived.

After six days and five nights at Sudbury General, I finally brought her home. With the stitches in her stomach—forty-seven of them to be exact—she had a difficult time climbing stairs, so I set up a temporary bed in the family room. Sheriff Peters—Jason—visited daily. He cooked for the three of us and helped me wash the dishes. Sometimes, he spent the night on the sofa. From upstairs, in my bedroom, I could hear them talking and laughing. She was always in a better mood when he was around—and that was good enough reason for me. I decided right then and there that I liked him.

During that first night at the hospital, as the nurses were prepping my aunt for surgery, Sheriff Peters finally told her that he loved her. I was standing in the room when he said it, and I saw the tears in his eyes. Of course, she was unconscious at the time, so she didn't have much to say in return. But since that night, I've heard those three little words come out of his mouth about a thousand times—and she almost always says them back.

I've yet to tell my aunt that there was a time—while we were living through that nightmare in the clearing—that I was almost certain the man behind the mask was her boyfriend.

I probably never will.

2

Aunt Helen wasn't able to make the trip to Richmond for Melody's funeral service, so Troy and I went by ourselves. Initially, I'd thought the long drive would be good for us. We'd barely spoken in the eight days that had passed since that horrible night in the woods. It wasn't for a lack of trying, though. I'd called his house in Baltimore several times but kept getting the answering machine. And he never called me back. So I'd hoped the drive would give us plenty of time—and privacy—to talk about what had happened.

But it didn't turn out that way.

Every time we tried, it felt like we were discussing a movie we'd watched together or something we'd read about in a magazine. It didn't feel like it had happened to us. It didn't feel *real*.

Part of the problem was that we were both different people now. We'd changed. That easy back-and-forth no longer existed. If one of us tried to joke or tease, it now felt phony and forced. At one point, I made a wisecrack about the penis I was going to draw on the cast on his hand. But he didn't even crack a smile—and my cheeks burned with embarrassment for the next several miles. There were a lot of uncomfortable silences during that trip. Especially on the way home.

Dr. Mirarchi explained that it was normal for people to feel this way after sharing such a traumatic experience. Oftentimes, the mental strain was so unbearable that the only way they could overcome it was by disconnecting themselves emotionally—and sometimes even physically—from the person they associated with that experience. She also assured me that in many instances, this behavior was temporary. But I wasn't holding my breath for that.

Later on, during that same appointment, she talked to me about survivor's guilt.

3

Melody's sister, Tamara, refused to speak with me at the funeral.

The documentary had been my idea, so she openly blamed me for Melody's death. She didn't make a scene, but she didn't have to. I stood at the back of the church with a bunch of strangers during the service. Later, at the cemetery, I waited for Troy by the car while he paid his respects at Melody's graveside. The hardest moment came when I saw the orange van following directly behind the hearse in the procession. I hadn't seen the Mystery Machine since the night it'd been towed from my aunt's house, and it brought back a flood of memories. Both good and bad.

MEMORIALS

After the burial, while Melody's friends and relatives gathered at a local restaurant, we looked up Tamara's address in the phone book and stopped by her apartment on our way out of town. I jogged up the stairs and slid an envelope containing a letter I'd written underneath her door. While I knew that forgiveness was out of the question, I hoped that she might read it and at least understand how much her sister had meant to me. I thought she might even call me once her anger had subsided. Just in case, I scribbled my aunt's phone number at the bottom of the letter.

But I never heard from her again.

4

You've probably noticed that I haven't mentioned Naomi yet.

There's a good reason for that. I was hoping and praying that I would have better news to share by the time I sat down to write this—but unfortunately that isn't the case.

After nearly a week in Sudbury General, Naomi was transferred to a rehab center in downtown Pittsburgh. An experienced team of trauma counselors and psychologists work closely with her every day.

The wounds on her stomach are healing. The injuries to her mind will take much longer.

She still hasn't spoken a single word since that night in the woods.

I've tried to see her, but her parents aren't allowing any visitors. Especially me.

5

Once the police became involved, not to mention fire departments from six counties in central Pennsylvania, the media got a hold of the story—and overnight it became national news.

The events of that night in the clearing possessed all the ingredients for a blockbuster. A secret cult operating just beneath the surface in small-town rural America. A sacrificial ceremony held deep in the woods. Robed and hooded worshippers, many of whom were upstanding citizens living and working in the area. A raging, out-of-control fire. And twenty-two dead.

Not only did supermarket rags like the *National Enquirer* and *Star* scoop up the story and run with it, but so, too, did mainstream publications such as *Newsweek* and *Time*.

Unbeknownst to me at the time, a wave of fear had been sweeping across the country. Dubbed by the media as the "Satanic Panic," thousands of cases of satanic-related ritual abuse were pouring in to authorities from dozens of states. The stories—almost all of which had yet to be substantiated—were of course lurid and scandalous. Allegations included animal mutilation, mind control, orgies, murder, and the ceremonial summoning of demons. There were even whispers of a global satanic cult populated by the nation's wealthy and elite in which children were kidnapped to be used in human sacrifices and prostitution.

The "Satan comes to Sudbury" story, as it came to be known, fit right in with these other sensationalistic tales. By the end of that first week, camera crews from *60 Minutes*, *Good Morning America*, and *The Phil Donahue Show* were spotted around town interviewing local citizens (many of whom couldn't decide whether they should be excited about the story or ashamed).

The narrow street in front of Aunt Helen's house turned into a circus. A never-ending parade of press vehicles, photographers, kids on bikes and skateboards, and cars driven by out-of-town lookie-loos. Eventually, after several fender benders and near misses, deputies from the sheriff's department put up bright yellow sawhorses, closing down the road and prompting complaints from the media that my aunt was receiving special treatment because of her relationship with Sheriff Peters.

Every time I left the house—usually only to go grocery shopping or pick up a movie from the video store—I was hounded by reporters and photographers. They chased after me and hid behind bushes and parked cars, waiting in ambush. They shouted awful and embarrassing questions in public, and refused to take "no comment" for an answer. I knew from watching the news that Troy was experiencing similar harassment back home in Baltimore. He still hadn't bothered to return my last phone call.

MEMORIALS

After talking it over with Sheriff Peters, we decided that it might be a good idea for me to hold a press conference. Our thinking was that if the reporters were granted even limited access, they would back off and give me some breathing room. Members from over sixty media outlets attended the forty-five-minute conference on the steps of the courthouse.

I'd thought it went well—but if anything, the attention only increased in the days that followed.

6

Part of the problem was that I couldn't tell the truth—who the hell would have believed it anyway?—and therefore, the story felt incomplete.

Most of the participants were dead.

The handful of survivors were now either incarcerated or recovering from their injuries and not saying much.

Others, like Aunt Helen, simply didn't remember.

And then there was me at the swirling center of it all. The hometown kid who was no stranger to tragedy.

What the media didn't understand was that I had questions of my own—and I was even more desperate for answers than they were.

I was able to piece together most of the backstory by talking with my aunt and Father Paul. Sheriff Peters helped fill in the blanks by sharing what he'd learned from one of the cult members currently under guard at the hospital. It was strictly against department regulations, but it only made me like him even more.

Aunt Helen also loaned me a thick leather-bound journal that Uncle Frank had kept secret from his parents during his high school years. What surprised me most about the words he'd written was how alike we appeared to be. At eighteen years old, Frank, too, had been lost and unhappy, racked with guilt, and searching for a safe place to call home. And then he'd met my aunt.

As I would soon learn, the story of what led up to that tragic night in the woods was as fascinating as it was horrifying.

And despite its incredulous nature, I came to believe every word of it.

7

Richard Gallagher, my senior-year English teacher at Sudbury High School, used to talk about the "nuts and bolts" of a good story. The cogs and gears that made it work. "Get in and get out," he'd tell us. "Economy of language. Just enough to paint a picture in the reader's mind, and let *them* do some of the heavy lifting. Narrative drive. Explore some side streets if you must, but remember to always keep the story moving along and the pages turning. Voice. Find the narrator's voice, and remain true to it. Stay out of your own way and follow the story wherever it takes you. Most important of all, be honest—with yourself and your readers."

So that's what I'm going to try to do here.

Present to you the nuts and bolts of this astonishing story.

And stay the hell out of my own way.

8

Remember the morning when I was fourteen and my father and I first stumbled upon the clearing? Remember the story he told me in the car later that afternoon? About the father and son who traveled miles on horseback to their neighbor's home in the woods because they were worried about them—only to find the family lashed to wooden stakes in the snow-covered ground with their throats sliced open?

As it turns out, most everything he told me was true.

And as such, it now serves as the opening chapter of our own tale.

Because the Good Samaritan father who discovered the atrocity in the woods that snowy day was none other than Professor Marcus Tyree's great-grandfather. The young boy at his side—Tyree's own grandfather.

9

Much of what I'm about to tell you comes from the pages of Uncle Frank's journal. The words he'd written there were told to him by his best friend—Marcus Tyree. Many other stories were shared by Father Paul Hastings of the St. Ignatius Church, as well as his close friend and neighbor Teddy Farkins and longtime brother-of-the-cloth Father Lewis Carruthers of Lewiston. It's entirely up to you, dear reader, if you choose to believe.

The concerned neighbor who'd made the horrific discovery along with his son spent the rest of his life trying to forget what he'd seen in the clearing that day. He refused to talk about it to anyone and did his very best to avoid the frequent rumors and fireside chatter that swept through the nearby settlements.

His son, however, was an altogether different story. He grew to be obsessed with the incident. When others spoke of it, he listened and asked questions of his own. He had frequent dreams about the clearing and those red staring eyes that peered out from within the surrounding trees. Once he was old enough to go off on his own, he often visited the clearing, sitting alone for hours, staring at the strange stick-figure symbol that had been carved into the tree, reimagining what had happened to the man and his daughters, and dropping to his knees and praying to the god responsible.

What others didn't realize was that the boy had *felt* something on the day he and his father had discovered the bodies. Something amazing and powerful. *Contact* with the entity responsible. And ever since that day . . . a *calling* to return.

He told no one of this experience until the evening of his eighteenth birthday.

When he decided it was time to gather his congregation.

10

It wasn't until many years later—the young boy having matured into a grown man with a son of his own—while working deep in the mines, that Professor Tyree's grandfather finally understood the full picture of his destiny.

11

Marcus Tyree was born in 1924 as Marcus Barksdale. His parents, Abraham and Clarice, had lived their entire lives in Norrisville, Pennsylvania, as had generations of their ancestors before them. Marcus was an only child, unusual for families from the hills, but Clarice suffered from a variety of physical ailments that had made it impossible for her to get pregnant again.

Marcus was fourteen when both his grandfather and father vanished in the mine.

Ernie Ritz, a close family friend, saw them shortly before they disappeared, and this is what he told Clarice: "I thought it was kinda strange from the start. It was late at night and they weren't dressed proper for the underground. No coats. No helmets or headlamps. Hell—excuse my language—they weren't even wearing shoes. But they was happy enough, all right. I was laying in the grass smoking my pipe and looking up at the stars, and they shuffled right on past me. Heads close together, like they was telling secrets, giggling like a couple of schoolgirls. I sat up and watched them walk into the mine. Into total darkness. And I coulda swore I heard them singing . . ."

For weeks after, Marcus and his mother—his grandmother mercifully dead nearly ten years by then—believed that the men would return, as many others before them had. But that didn't happen.

Abraham Barksdale was a beloved figure in Norrisville. Not only a religious leader who had taken over the reins of the Church from his father, but also a model family man, and a kind and generous neighbor. Because of his devout faith and teachings, Abraham's loss was celebrated by the town instead of mourned—for his congregation was more certain than ever that he now walked at the side of the Creator, a spirited prophecy they had heard him preach on many a Sunday morning. For Abraham's followers, the symbols long ago discovered on the mine's rock walls—identical to the one used by the Church for generations—proved that Abraham and his elderly father had made their safe journey home. The mine had merely acted as a doorway for their ascension.

After Abraham's disappearance, Marcus withdrew into himself and began devoting all of his time to learning his father's teachings. He was no longer interested in hunting or fishing with his friends. Or playing ball and talking to girls. The Church became his singular obsession, and before long, the congregation recognized him as a child prodigy—and he soon took over the mantle of leadership his father so proudly once carried.

12

Marcus and my Uncle Frank were next-door neighbors—which in the hills meant they lived within seeing distance of each other—and best friends. How's that for fate? Nevertheless, they couldn't have been more different.

Marcus was quiet and studious. Frank was neither of those things. Marcus was big for his age, at least a head taller than most of his classmates. Frank was a squirt of a kid, even shorter than many of the girls. Their proximity to each other and their being the same age provided the initial foundation to their unlikely friendship. After that, it was their mutual love of trout fishing that bound them together.

That . . . and the talks they shared.

Right from the very beginning—without the self-conscious walls of adolescence that existed between most boys their age—the two of them could talk about anything and everything. The constellations in the sky. The animals in the forest. The way the river haunted their dreams and nightmares. How sometimes Marcus's father frightened him with the stories he told of what he had seen in the mines. How Frank's father drank too much and punched holes in the thin walls of their house. And girls, of course. They talked a lot about girls.

By the time they became teenagers, they were no longer just friends. That summer, they cut each other's palms with the blade of a pocketknife, pressed them together while shaking hands, and officially became blood brothers.

They continued to make an odd couple. Marcus was the smartest kid in every subject in school. Frank was the class clown and spent more time in detention than any other student in their grade. Marcus had grown to be a gentle giant. Frank remained small and scrappy, and never backed down from a fight. Marcus didn't care that his best friend's father was the town drunk and always between jobs. He never looked down on him or made fun of him and never once spread gossip to eager ears. And my Uncle Frank didn't care that his best friend's father was a religious zealot, a true blue Appalachian old schooler, perpetually angry at the rest of the world. And sometimes downright scary.

They were brothers, and nothing could tear them apart.

Or so they believed.

13

After Abraham Barksdale disappeared in the mine, everything changed.

All at once, Marcus no longer had time to go fishing or goof around with Uncle Frank. He was too busy studying his father's journals or going on pilgrimages deep into the mines or gone for days at a time on mysterious trips across the river. And when he started preaching on Sundays, Marcus became a completely different person than the one Frank had grown up with. He now spoke tirelessly of power and influence and vengeance against those that had oppressed his people. He spoke of gods and demons and an all-knowing Creator that would save them all one day soon.

And he relentlessly tried to convince my Uncle Frank to serve at his side.

But Frank wasn't at all interested in ancient spells and curses and revenge. Maybe Marcus had changed, but he hadn't. And the last thing Frank wanted to do was spend the rest of his life in Norrisville.

In the spring of his final year of high school, he met Helen Flanagan at a softball game in Leesburg, and never looked back.

14

At first, Marcus was despondent.

In no time at all, he'd lost his grandfather, father, and best friend.

He became distracted. He couldn't sleep. Couldn't eat. It affected his studies and the sermons he preached on Sunday mornings.

But as the weeks passed and he began to spend more time in the mines, his depression slowly turned to anger.

And then all-consuming rage.

Frank was not only a shitty friend—he was a traitor.

And one way or another, he was going to pay him back.

15

No one knows why Marcus changed his last name to Tyree when he went off to college.

There were rumors that the Church was under investigation by numerous law enforcement agencies and he did it to avoid attention in the outside world. Others claimed he changed it because he was instructed to do so by none other than the Creator.

All that's known for sure is that in May 1945, at the age of twenty-one, after only three and a half years of classes, Marcus graduated with honors from Penn State University.

While going home every weekend to preach to his congregation.

16

In the meantime, Frank was happy and in love.

He'd moved to Sudbury to be with Helen and accepted a job at the railroad yard. Within two years, he was named an assistant foreman. Helen waited tables at a local restaurant and attended classes at the community college. After she got her degree, she took on a job with an insurance company in the area.

Frank continued to hear from Marcus from time to time, even though it had been several years since Frank had considered him a friend. Pleading phone calls and letters—all duly ignored—followed soon after by threatening phone calls and letters. Unhinged in their zealotry.

And the cycle continued. Always the same.

I miss you, brother, and need you by my side.

Come live a life of destiny.

You're a traitor, and it's that harlot's fault.

You have no idea what's coming soon—and you will not be spared.

Give me back the dagger, and I'll leave you alone.

The dagger.

The strange ornate knife that Abraham had given to Marcus on his fourteenth birthday—and the cause of so much trouble to come. A family heirloom, hundreds of years old, it was said to have been used in only the most sacred of ceremonies. Shortly before Abraham's disappearance in the mine, Marcus had brought the dagger to Frank's house to show him. Frank had been captivated by the shiny turquoise handle and the intricate design on the blade. And then he'd promptly forgotten all about it.

Three years later, as Marcus was preparing to leave for college, he once again presented the dagger to Frank. This time, with an offer in hand. Join Marcus within the Church and be named second-in-command of the congregation, as well as guardian of the dagger.

When Marcus went home that day, he purposely left the dagger on the dresser in Frank's bedroom—believing that the blessing he'd placed upon it would work its magic and help guide his best friend back to his side.

But when he returned the next morning for an answer, Frank and the dagger were gone.

17

After graduating from Penn State, Marcus wasted little time in finding a teaching job. He began his career at a local community college and then taught night classes for three semesters at Swarthmore before finally settling in at York. By the end of the first grading term, he'd already garnered a reputation for being an entertaining lecturer and having an open-door policy to help struggling students. Before long, he was hand-selecting new disciples for the Church from an ever-rotating student body.

He was very careful who he targeted. Maybe one or two a year, if he was lucky, and only the chosen ones. Otherwise, he stuck to the official duties of his job and continued traveling home every weekend to tend to his flock.

Now, with the mines no longer available, Marcus soon found himself in search of alternate sources of inspiration and power. His own father had believed that the mine in which he'd eventually disappeared was actually a portal to the Creator's true home. The harrowing symbols they'd found carved in the rock walls had served as proof of this and provided them with the vestiges of a map. Marcus believed that his father and grandfather hadn't merely wandered off and gotten lost after drinking too much wine at dinner, as some of the blasphemers had claimed. They'd gone into the mine that night to be *found*.

Marcus was also certain that it was to this otherworldly realm that many of the other missing workers had disappeared. Most had chosen to remain there, while a handful of others had returned. Each and every one of them forever changed by the experience. Furthermore, he believed that if humans could pass freely through this secret portal, then so, too, could the gods and demons that reigned there. According to the visions he experienced, all Marcus had to do was find another way in—and a way to summon those gods and demons.

For a time, Marcus tried cemeteries, hoping that the pervasive energy of transition from one world to the next might create a similar "thinness in the veil," as he so often called it. But he eventually gave up on the idea, arriving at the conclusion that graveyard residual energy simply wasn't powerful enough.

Then he had a killer of an idea—why not just reopen the mine on his own? So, in the summer of 1958, he rented heavy equipment under several aliases, organized workers in rotating shifts—mostly in the dark, so as to avoid scrutiny from state and federal officials—and even hired an out-of-state bootleg crew to set explosives to blast through the layers of rubble. But progress proved interminably slow and too many townspeople were killed or injured—and eventually they were forced to give up.

Decades passed. The congregation slowly began to dwindle. By the mid-1970s, the Church's followers numbered fewer than eighty people. Older members remained content to practice the same spells and incantations that their ancestors had for hundreds of years before them, while younger members grew restless and searched for a new path forward.

Meanwhile, Marcus Tyree grew ever more desperate, spiraling into a growing insanity. The mines were unreachable. The sacrifices being offered were ignored. The stories he'd read in his grandfather's journal about the clearing in the woods by Church Street felt like just that—*stories*. He knew, though, that when he'd visited there as a boy, he'd felt *something*. A kind of shimmer or thinness in the air—and he had known that other worlds were close by. He was *convinced* of it.

So why, then, had all their attempts in the clearing proved fruitless? Eventually, after months of feverish prayer and meditation, Marcus finally discovered the answer: too much time had passed, and the power there had weakened. He needed to find another portal.

The idea of the roadside memorials came to Marcus in a dream. On the surface, it sounded bizarre, even absurd, but in the dark of night, it made perfect sense. After all, what better place of thinness than the actual ground on which a person had transitioned? And what better continuous under-the-radar source for such sacred ground than the scenes of fatal car accidents?

Some of those accidents—the Church still considered them sacrifices—Marcus caused, putting to work those trusted and true age-old spells and curses. A slip of potion in someone's drink at the bar. A snip of their hair after they'd drunk one too many. A shoulder bump in the crowd, seemingly accidental, and a pinprick of blood on a handkerchief.

Others occurred naturally—as they are wont to do these days—and were considered gifts from the Creator.

As the 1980s dawned and the Church experienced a moderate resurgence, Marcus began to feel the walls to the other side grow thinner and begin to crumble. Sometimes, standing there by himself at an accident site for which he'd been responsible, he was able to catch a glimpse of the Other Side. Endless white beaches bordering bright blue ocean. Waves crashing. Majestic mountains rising in the distance. Other times, a crimson sky split open by yellow-and-black forks of lightning. A rocky mountain peak crowned with odd-shaped skulls. Scorched desert sands surrounded by a towering forest, the leafy trees blocking out the clouds. Sometimes, he got so close, he could even smell it, taste it.

18

On the night that Tyree smelled the smoke and saw the blackened desert—while standing beside the memorial for a thirty-seven-year-old truck driver named Kip Turner—he dreamed of the dagger for the first time in years.

And remembered the clearing in the woods.

And knew exactly what he had to do.

19

When my sophomore-year econ instructor—and Professor Tyree's racquetball buddy—first suggested that I might be a good fit for Tyree's American Studies class, my name immediately rang a bell. Which surprised Tyree. William Anderson was hardly a distinctive moniker.

So he'd looked me up in the registration files—something he often did when curious about a prospective student for his machinations—and saw right away that I was from Sudbury.

It didn't take long to learn the rest.

Below-average student, recently off academic probation.

Off-campus resident at the Riverside Apartment Complex.

Son of the late Thomas and Lori Anderson of Larchmont Road.

Nephew of Helen Flanagan Abbott.

The harlot.

20

You were the chosen ones.

If I was the golden goose that had fallen into the professor's lap—after all, he'd been responsible for the deaths of my parents and now he had a chance at their son—then Melody Wise and Troy Carpenter must have been considered happy accidents. No pun intended.

Just as Mel had pointed out at the beginning of our trip—what were the odds? Three complete strangers from different states and disparate backgrounds. Suffering from tragic personal losses. Thrown together with a singular purpose.

Thinking back to those three stakes in the ground at the clearing, I imagine the idea had come to Tyree almost immediately. Most likely, around the time we'd submitted our project proposal about the roadside memorials. As deranged as it is to reflect on this now, I would've loved to have seen the look on his face when he first read the proposal. Any semblance of coincidence or chance tossed out the window on its ass by the time he'd finished.

It's meant to be, he had to have thought.

The three of them will not only open the door to the other side—they'll fucking break it down.

It's more than fate.

It's prophecy.

21

Sometimes, late at night, before the nightmares come, I lie in bed and wonder what might have happened if their ceremony had gone as planned.

I can see it . . .

The three of us tied to the stakes. Ground mist curling around our legs. Heads hanging. Throats cut. Blood soaking the dirt at our feet. The ancient dagger's intricate blade stained bright red. And then a loud rumble, as "the Creator" comes forth . . .

What might have arisen from the depths of the earth?

Or emerged from deep within the woods?

A stick figure resembling the drawing in my notebook? All-seeing, all-knowing, all-powerful? Or something else altogether? Something unimaginable?

What might the world look like right now in its aftermath?

While reading Tyree's thoughts that night in the clearing—a temporary and inadvertent side effect, I later learned, of an age-old spell Tyree had cast to read my own mind—I'd heard him angrily refer to the creature that emerged from the fire as "one of the Outsiders."

Intrigued, I visited the library and did some digging. The only curious mentions I ran across were related to the writings of a long-dead pulp author whose body of work I was unfamiliar with. A gloomy, odd-looking young man from Rhode Island named H. P. Lovecraft. Most of his short stories had been published in old magazines, the most famous of which was the aptly titled *Weird Tales*.

Additional research revealed that fire creatures were fairly common in numerous mythologies. There were dragons and djinn and salamanders; the phoenix and the chimera; and a handful of others with less colorful names. One of the books I pulled from the stacks even had a twelve-page section of drawings of what they called "reimaginings."

But none of them by a country mile resembled what I saw in the clearing that night.

Some nights—when sleep won't come, and the world is still and quiet—I find myself wondering if I might have simply imagined the whole thing. We were exhausted and terrified. There was mist and smoke all around us. It was difficult to see. And then there's this: I had already experienced firsthand that the clearing had a way of messing around with your mind—even when it wasn't swarming with pissed-off occultists wearing robes and hoods. So yeah, maybe it *had* been a hallucination . . . a waking nightmare brought on by shock and terror. It would only make sense, right?

But in the harsh reality of daylight, I know better.

Twenty-two lives were lost in the fire. Nearly 130 acres of woodland burned to the ground. The fire had eventually hopped the road and died at the riverbank. A heavily damaged Church Street is currently closed, as is the Albert Linden Bridge. No one from the town council will say for how long.

Maybe forever.

22

Ph'tanque mgl'watan squantle fu'loa wan'str . . .

Sometimes, even now, I hear its voice in my dreams.

Other times . . .

Last week, I stopped at a McDonald's drive-through to order an early lunch. When the peppy young girl finished taking my order, she gave me my total, and then added, "Please drive up to the next window. *Ph'tanque mgl'watan squantle fu'loa wan'str.*"

My hands shaking, I hopped the curb to get out of line and drove away without picking up my food.

A few days later, at the bank, a teller with braided red hair and too much mascara stamped the back of my check and asked how I would like my cash. I told her twenties and tens would be just fine. She counted out the bills in her hand and slid them across the counter in a neat stack. I thanked her and walked away. Behind me, I heard her say in a cheerful voice: *"Ph'tanque mgl'watan squantle fu'loa wan'str!* You have a great day, sir!"

I haven't told Dr. Mirarchi yet.

She knows about the cult in the woods, of course, and what happened that night to Melody and Naomi and Aunt Helen, and that Troy and I are no longer speaking.

What she doesn't know is anything about the Outsider.

Where it came from.

What it's capable of.

And that it's still out there.

23

Earlier this morning, while it was still dark outside, I got in my car and set off on the four-hour drive from York, Pennsylvania, to Richmond, Virginia. Along the way, I stopped twice at rest stops to grab something to eat and use the bathroom. The second time, I almost turned the car around and drove back home.

I wish Troy was with me. Getting crumbs all over the seat and complaining about the music on the radio and admonishing me to slow down and pay attention to the speed limit on the interstate. But we haven't spoken a word in seven weeks now. I finally stopped calling and leaving messages. I doubt he was even listening to them anyway. If no further contact is what he wants, then I need to respect that. Still, it makes me sad. Troy was my best friend, and I miss him.

MEMORIALS

The cemetery in which Melody is buried is located on a gently sloping hillside overlooking a large lake, its heavily wooded shoreline dotted with summer cabins. The last time I was here, nearly a month ago, the sky was dark and the wind was gusty. There were whitecaps on the surface of the murky green water, and not a single person in sight.

This time, the lake is calm and an almost translucent shade of blue. Spangles of sunlight reflect back at me, and as I make my way from the nearly empty parking lot to Melody's grave, I count at least a dozen boats out on the water.

When I reach the top of the rise and enter the shade of an L-shaped scattering of pine trees, I spot the gravestone right away. It's brand-new and hard to miss. I idly wonder what the workers did with the temporary marker, scold myself for having such inconsequential thoughts at a time like this, and place the bouquet of cut flowers I'd brought along with me at the base of the engraved stone. I drop to a knee and begin tracing the letters with my fingertips.

MELODY HELENA WISE
1960–1983
OUR LOVING ANGEL

And then I close my eyes and offer a silent prayer.

When I'm finished, I get to my feet, reach behind me with both hands, and unclasp my father's silver crucifix from around my neck.

I raise it to my lips and then gently place it on top of the granite marker.

You were right all along, Mel.

And as if to prove my point, a beautiful monarch butterfly flutters in the air in front of me and lands not far from the crucifix.

I miss you too.

After a moment, I walk to the edge of the trees and stare out at the lake.

I bet she loves it here. It's beautiful . . . just like she was.

I feel a tightness in my chest and it's difficult to breathe. My vision blurs with tears.

Inside my head, I immediately begin to count.

One... two... three...

And while I'm doing that, I think about the good things in my life.

...four... five... six...

Despite everything that's happened, there are many—including the eight-week-old puppy I recently gifted to my aunt.

...seven... eight...

She cried when she saw the little guy scamper across the front yard and scooped him up in her arms.

...nine... ten.

A deep cleansing breath of reaffirmation.

Already feeling better, I turn around to say goodbye.

And all of the strength drains out of my body.

On the back of Melody's gravestone, someone has drawn the symbol in black permanent marker.

Taped to the stone right above it: a black-and-white photograph. Troy and I dressed in suits, standing outside the church at Melody's funeral.

My eyes have been scratched out.

You've been marked, the traitorous Robert Farnsworth said to me in what feels like another lifetime.

It's not over, I think, frantically scanning the parking lot to see who's coming for me.

It's never going to be over.

SUDBURY SHERIFF'S DEPARTMENT REPORT
FILE #193447-C-34
EVIDENCE TAG #27B (video cassette tape)
DATE: May 26, 1983
REPORTING OFFICER(S): Sheriff Jason Peters;
                      Deputy Brian Wilberger

(9:01 a.m., Friday, May 6, 1983)

A young woman—long brown hair tied back in a ponytail, wearing a yellow sundress and white high-top Chuck Taylor sneakers—leans against the front of a bright orange van. She closes her eyes and tilts her head back, soaking in the sunshine.

A young man, dark-skinned and diminutive, dressed in tan khaki shorts and a matching button-down shirt, enters the frame. He stops next to the woman and checks the time on his wristwatch. A red bandanna is tied loosely around his neck. He's wearing thick-framed glasses and his hair is styled in an enormous Afro. His arms glisten with sweat.

"Can we get a move on, Billy?" he says grumpily. "We're already behind schedule."

In the reflection of the van's windshield, we see a second young man attaching a video camera to a tripod. The picture jiggles back and forth, momentarily losing focus.

"Just need to lock this in . . . ," the camera operator says in a cheerful voice.

We hear a loud click as it locks into place and stabilizes.

"There we go."

After a moment, the picture sharpens again.

The young man, dressed in jeans and a Rolling Stones T-shirt, hurries on-screen, turns to face the camera, and wiggles his way in between his two friends. The woman laughs as she is nudged to the side. The other man scowls, but there's the hint of a smile underneath it.

"Okay," the cameraman says, looping his arms around the other two. "Everyone say cheese."

The cranky one rolls his eyes. "I'm not saying cheese."

"The Three Musketeers, on three," the woman says.

The cameraman counts. "One . . . two . . . three . . ."

And all of them shout at the same time:

"THE THREE MUSKETEEEERS!"

As they do, the cameraman lifts his hand off his friend's shoulder—and flashes rabbit ears above his Afro.

The picture freezes on their happy faces.

AUTHOR'S NOTE

Memorials is by far the longest novel I have written to date—and it did not always come easily. That's not to say I didn't have a wonderful time writing it, because I did. Every day was a new adventure. Every backroad a carnival of sights and sounds . . . and shadows. But as the pages piled up on the corner of my desk, something surprising began to happen. I grew so fond of Billy, Melody, and Troy—Naomi and Helen, too, to a lesser extent—that I found myself rooting for them to have a happy ending. After all, the members of the "Broken Hearts Club" had already suffered enough, hadn't they?

But here's the tricky part: I don't outline my novels in advance. I simply grab hold of the story's shirttail and follow it wherever it takes me. Sometimes, with a smile on my face. Other times, kicking and screaming and with my hands crammed over my eyes. Finishing the final act of *Memorials* fell squarely in the latter category. No matter how much I wished the Three Musketeers were headed for that happy ending they so deserved . . . deep in my heart, I knew it wasn't in the cards for them.

Oh well, maybe the next book. Although, probably not.

Longtime Pennsylvania residents may have noticed that I played a little fast and loose with certain geographical details in the book (in other words, I made up a lot of stuff). I promise it was all in service to the story. Also, for all the 1980s photography aficionados . . . I adjusted the official release date for the JVC VHS video camera Billy uses in the book by about a year. There were two reasons for that decision: (1) an online article mentioning the JVC camera was "tested" at a number of universities months before its commercial release, thereby providing me with a loophole; and (2) I graduated from high school in 1983 and had a wealth of personal memories that I wanted to draw upon for the book. Sometimes, there's a method to the madness.

Speaking of madness, for me, writing a novel is the ultimate exercise in

AUTHOR'S NOTE

faith. Not only the kind you must have in yourself and the story you're choosing to tell, but also the unwavering belief of others. As usual, I had a lot of help writing this book, and I owe heartfelt gratitude to:

Kara and Billy and Noah, for putting up with my spending such long hours behind the keyboard, my blank stares as they repeatedly asked, "Are you even listening to me?" and everything else that truly matters in my life.

The Hanson Road Boys and all my friends and family, for always encouraging and believing in this dreamer.

Glenn Chadbourne, for giving artistic life to what I saw inside my mind.

Paul Michael Kane, for continued marketing expertise and friendship.

Hitesh Shroff, for much needed photography-related guidance.

The *Memorials* "Street Team," for their selfless hard work and enthusiasm.

The UVA lacrosse family, for getting me out of the house.

Lucy Nalen, for working so hard to spread the word.

Kristin Nelson, for making her own cross-country road trip to Bel Air, Maryland, and for being our guardian angel.

Ed Schlesinger, for believing in my stories and making them so much better, and for doing it with patience, grace, and kindness.

And, finally, my endless thanks to you, dear reader, for taking this journey alongside me. I hope you enjoyed my midnight campfire tale.

Turn the page for
a thrilling excerpt from the terrifying novel

WIDOW'S POINT:
THE COMPLETE HAUNTING

by Richard Chizmar and W. H. Chizmar

Video/audio footage #6A
(6:04 p.m., Friday, July 7, 2017)

The video switches on, and once again the man is standing in the foreground of the distant lighthouse, pointing the remote at the camera. The image is steadier this time. He slides the remote into the back pocket of his jeans and clears his throat.

"Okay, only have a few minutes, folks. Mr. Parker is in quite the hurry to get out of here. He's either playing the role of anxious lighthouse owner to the extreme and faking his discomfort, or he's genuinely unnerved and wants to be pretty much anywhere else but here on the property his family has owned for over a century now."

He leans over, his hands disappearing off-screen, and returns holding the knapsack, which he places close on the ground beside him. He stands with an erect but relaxed posture and folds his hands together in front of him.

"My name is Thomas Livingston, the author of *Shattered Dreams, Ashes to Ashes*, and eleven other bestselling nonfiction works of the supernatural. I'm here today on the windswept coast of Harper's Cove at the far northern tip of Nova Scotia, standing at the foot of the legendary Widow's Point Lighthouse.

"According to historical records, the Widow's Point Lighthouse—its name inspired by the large number of ships that crashed in the rocky shallows below—was erected in the summer and autumn of 1838 by Franklin Washburn II, proprietor of the largest fishing and gaming company here in Nova Scotia."

Livingston's face grows somber.

"There is little doubt that the Widow's Point Lighthouse led to a sharp decrease in the nautical accidents that occurred off her shoreline—but at what cost? Legend and nearly two centuries of firsthand accounts seem to reinforce the belief that the Widow's Point Lighthouse is cursed . . . or perhaps an even more apt description . . . *haunted*.

"The legend was born when three workers were killed during the lighthouse's construction, including Franklin Washburn's young nephew, who plunged to his death from the catwalk during the final week of work. The weather was clear that day, the winds offshore and light. All safety precautions were in place. The tragic accident was never properly explained.

"The dark fortunes continued when the lighthouse's first keeper, a by-all-accounts 'steadfast individual' named Ian Gallagher, went inexplicably mad during one historically violent storm and strangled his wife before taking his own life by cutting his wrists with a carving knife. Mr. Washburn claimed that Gallagher must have suffered some type of mental breakdown and took full responsibility for his hiring and the resulting tragedy.

"But many of the townspeople of Harper's Cove felt that something far more sinister—something *beyond* human control—was at work here.

"There had long been whispers—usually slurred in unguarded moments late at night in Harper's Cove pubs—about the unsettling incidents plaguing the lighthouse's construction. Few of the workers went so far as to utter scandalous words such as 'haunted' or 'cursed'—not in the very beginning—but the most commonly expressed midnight sentiment was the belief that 'something is wrong with that place.'

"And for many of those folks brave—or foolish—enough to speak their concerns out loud, the passage of time would seem to all but prove them correct.

"In the decades that followed, nearly two dozen mysterious deaths occurred within the cramped confines—and surrounding grounds—of the Widow's Point Lighthouse, including murder, suicide, unexplained accidents and disappearances, the 1933 mass slaughter of an entire family, and even rumors of devil worship and human sacrifice.

"After the gruesome events of 1933, in which the cold-blooded murderer of the Collins family left behind a letter claiming he was 'instructed' by a ghostly visitor to kill everyone on the premises, the most recent owner of the Widow's Point Lighthouse, seafood tycoon Robert James Parker—the grandfather of Mr. Ronald Parker, the camera-shy gentleman you glimpsed earlier—decided to cease operations and permanently shutter the lighthouse.

"Or so he believed...

"Because in 1985, Parker's eldest son, Lawrence—Ronald's father—entered into an agreement with the United Artists film studio in Hollywood, allowing them to film a movie both inside the lighthouse and on the surrounding grounds. The film—a gothic thriller entitled *Rosemary's Spirit*—was shot over a period of six weeks, from mid-September to November 8. Despite the lighthouse's troubled reputation, filming went off without a hitch... until the final week of production, when supporting actress Lydia Pearl hung herself from the iron guard railing that encircles the catwalk high atop the lighthouse.

"Trade publications reported that Miss Pearl was despondent following a recent breakup with her fiancé, Roger Barthelme, who was an all-star shortstop for the Los Angeles Dodgers. But locals here figured differently. They believed with great conviction that, after all those long years of silent slumber, the Widow's Point curse had reawakened to claim yet another victim.

"And when not even a year later, during the summer of 1986, two young girls went missing in the vicinity of the lighthouse, those whispers grew to an outcry.

"Regardless of the reasoning, in 1988, the lighthouse was once again shuttered tight against the elements, and for the first time a security fence was erected around the property, making it accessible only by scaling the over-one-hundred-and-fifty-foot-high cliffs that line its eastern border.

"So... in other words, no human being has been inside the Widow's Point Lighthouse in nearly thirty years..."

Livingston takes a dramatic pause, then steps closer to the camera, his face clenched and square-jawed.

"... until now. Until *today*.

"That's right—tonight, for the first time in more than three decades, someone will enter and spend the night in the dark heart of the Widow's Point Lighthouse. That someone is *me*, Thomas Livingston.

"After months of—if you'll pardon the pun—*spirited* discussion and negotiation, I have been able to secure arrangements to spend an entire weekend inside this legendary lighthouse. The ground rules are simple. Today is Friday, July 7, 2017. It is . . ."

He checks his wristwatch.

". . . 6:09 p.m. Eastern Standard Time. In a matter of minutes, Mr. Ronald Parker, current proprietor of the Widow's Point Lighthouse, will escort me through the only entrance or exit, and once I am safely inside, he will close and lock the door behind me . . ."

Livingston bends down, comes back into view holding a heavy chain and padlock.

". . . using these."

He holds the chain and padlock up to the camera for another dramatic beat, then drops them with a *clank* to the ground.

"I will be permitted to take inside only enough food and water to last me three days and three nights, as well as a sleeping bag, lantern, a flashlight, sanitary supplies, two notebooks and pens, this video camera and tripod, and several extra batteries. In addition, this . . ."

Backing up a couple of steps, Livingston reaches down into his knapsack and comes up with a small machine in his right hand.

". . . uh . . . Sony digital voice recorder, capable of recording over one thousand hours of memory with a battery life of nearly ninety-six hours without a single charge. And, yes, please consider that an official product placement for the Sony Corporation. Why not."

He laughs—and there's a fleeting glimpse of the handsome, charming character from the author photos on his books—and returns the voice recorder to his knapsack.

"I will not be allowed a cell phone or a computer of any kind. Absolutely no internet access. I will have no means to communicate, or should anything go wrong, no way to request assistance. I will be completely cut off from the outside world for three long and hopefully eventful days and nights."

An angry voice barks from somewhere off-screen, and a startled Livingston's eyes flash in that direction. He looks back at the camera, shaking his head, a bemused expression on his face.

"Okay, folks, it's time to begin my journey, or shall I say *our* journey, as I will be recording all of my innermost thoughts and observations in an effort to take you, my dear readers, along with me. The next time I appear on camera, I will be entering the legendary—some say *haunted*—Widow's Point Lighthouse. Wish me luck. I may need it."

Video/audio footage #7A
(6:12 p.m., Friday, July 7, 2017)

Livingston is carrying the video camera in his hand as he approaches the lighthouse, once again providing a shaky POV.

Mr. Parker remains off-screen, but his gravelly voice can be clearly heard: "Eight o'clock Monday morning. I'll be here not a minute later."

"That'll be perfect. Thank you."

The lighthouse door draws near. It's a massive structure, broad and weathered, constructed of heavy beams of scarred dark wood—most likely scavenged from ancient ships, according to local records. The men stop when they reach the entrance.

"And you're certain you can't be convinced otherwise? It's not too late to change your mind."

Livingston turns to him, and the camera finally gets a close-up of the reclusive Mr. Parker: an antique codger of a man patched together with wrinkles and bulging veins, his knobby head framed by the blue-gray sea behind him. "No, no. Everything will be fine, I promise."

The old man grunts in reply.

The camera swings back toward the lighthouse and is lowered, revealing a fleeting glimpse of Livingston's knapsack hanging from his shoulder and, resting on the ground at his feet, a dirty white cooler. PROPERTY OF EVANSVILLE LITTLE LEAGUE is scrawled across the lid in messy black marker. Livingston leans down and takes hold of one of the plastic handles.

"Then I wish you godspeed," Mr. Parker says in a dull tone.

The camera is lifted once again and focused on the imposing wooden door. A liver-spotted hand swims into view holding an old-fashioned, hollow-barrel brass key. It's inserted into an impossible-to-see keyhole drectly beneath an oversized, ornate doorknob and, with much effort, turned to the right.

The door opens with a loud *creak*—and the sigh of ancient air escaping.

"Whew, musty," Livingston says with a cough, and his hand reaches on-screen and pushes the door all the way open. Total darkness waits beyond the threshold.

"Aye. She's been breathing dead air for thirty years now."

Livingston pauses for a moment—perhaps it's the mention of *dead air* that momentarily slows his progress, or maybe he's just having second thoughts— before re-gripping the cooler's plastic handle and stepping inside.

At the exact moment that Livingston crosses over into the lighthouse, the video goes blank. Entirely blank—with the exception of the time code in the lower left corner of the screen, which now reads:

6:14 PM.

"I'll see you Monday morning," Livingston says.

The old man doesn't respond. Instead, with perfect clarity and a dread-inducing sense of finality, there's the sound of the heavy wooden door closing.

The key is once again turned in the lock and the chain is heard being wrestled into place. After a moment of quiet, the loud *click* of a padlock snapping shut is followed by one last tug on the chain. Another brief pause, and there's the muffled sound of a vehicle starting up and driving away.

Then, there is only silence . . .

. . . until a rustle of clothing whispers in the darkness, followed by the *thud* of the cooler being set down on the floor.

"And so it begins, ladies and gentlemen, our journey into the heart of the Widow's Point Lighthouse. I will now climb the two hundred and sixty-eight spiraling stone stairs to the living quarters, lantern in one hand, camera in the other. I will return downstairs later this evening for food and water supplies, after a period of initial exploration."

Livingston begins to narrate over the sound of his ascending footsteps: "Originally built in 1838, the Widow's Point Lighthouse is two hundred and seven feet tall, constructed of stone, mostly granite taken from a nearby quarry, and positioned some seventy-five yards from the edge of the sheer cliffs that tower above the stormy Atlantic . . . "

Video/audio footage #8A
(6:30 p.m., Friday, July 7, 2017)
Livingston's rapid breathing competes with the sound of his footsteps. The time code—located in the lower left corner—reads 6:30 PM. The rest of the screen remains dark.

"Two hundred sixty-six . . . two hundred sixty-seven . . . two hundred sixty-*eight*. And with that, we have reached the pinnacle, ladies and gents, and just in time too. Your faithful host is feeling rather . . . spent, I must admit."

A rustling sound and a heavy thud as Livingston unslings his knapsack from his shoulder and drops it to the floor.

"Well, as you can certainly see for yourselves, Mr. Parker spoke the truth when he claimed this place was in a severe state of ill repair. In fact, he may have actually managed to underestimate the pitiful condition of the Widow's Point living quarters."

Unintelligible noises and feet shuffling around. "But regardless of her haggard state, you can most definitely feel the sense of something *alive* here inside the lighthouse. The air is thick and stagnant, a thick layer of dust blanketing everything, but it's as if the stillness and silence possess a kind of substance, a holding of its breath, if you will . . . a *waiting*.

"Reporters and readers alike have asked me for years what I consider to be the most powerful haunt I have ever visited. My response prior to this day has always been the infamous Belasco House tucked deep in the rolling hills of upstate New York. It will be fascinating to see if my response remains the same after this weekend."

A deep sigh.

"I shall now rest for a moment, then venture upward to explore the service and lantern rooms, and perhaps even the catwalk if it appears sturdy enough to hold me. Once I've straightened up a bit and established proper housekeeping, I'll return to you with a further update.

"I also promise to discuss the mysterious incidents I referenced earlier—and many more—in greater and more graphic detail once I've made myself at home."

More shuffling footsteps.

"But, first, before I go . . . Lord in heaven . . . it's but a solitary window . . . Let us gaze upon this magnificent sight for a moment."

Livingston's voice takes on a tone of genuine awe. The phony theatrics gone, he now sounds as if he means every word he is saying.

"Resplendent mother ocean as far as the eye can see . . . and beyond. The vision is almost enough to render me speechless."

A chuckle. "Yeah . . . almost."

The time code disappears as the video ends.

Don't miss
WIDOW'S POINT:
THE COMPLETE HAUNTING
wherever you buy books!